THE FABULOUS FREAKS
OF MONSIEUR BEAUMONT

THE FABULOUS FREAKS OF MONSIEUR BEAUMONT

KELLI STUART

The Fabulous Freaks of Monsieur Beaumont
© Kelli Stuart 2021

Published by Fine Print Writing Press, a division of Fine Print Writing Services, LLC, Tampa, Florida

All rights reserved. No part of this book may be reproduced, stored in a retrieved system, or transmitted in any form or by any means—electronic, mechanical, photoshop, recording, or otherwise—without written permission of the author or publisher, except for brief quotations in reviews.

Distribution of digital editions of this book in any format via the Internet or any other means without the author and publisher's written permission of by license agreement is a violation of copyright law and is subject to substantial fines and penalties. Thank you for supporting the author's rights by purchasing only authorized editions.

This is a work of fiction. Any representation that resembles a person living or dead is purely coincidental. The people and events portrayed in this work are creations of the author.

Cover and interior by Roseanna White Designs
Cover images from Shutterstock

ISBN 978-0-578-88243-7

Printed in the United States of America

To anyone who has ever felt different.

ACT ONE

1887

It was the whistle that drew them all in—that piercing sound that cut through the dusty, Oklahoma air and announced a magical relief from the harsh earth that never seemed to give enough come harvest time. They knew the circus was coming thanks to the posters that had appeared on the walls of every building in town: large, colorful sheets plastering each flat surface, calling people to escape into a world of wonder for one day only. The locals knew it was coming, but when they heard the train whistle on the appointed day, suddenly the world exploded in color. The monotonous red of the dusty earth took on a new hue altogether. It was like the world itself woke up just in time for the Big Top to rise into the sky.

Johnston Landis saw the posters, and he heard the chatter, but he had no intention of going to the circus. Watching elephants dance and clowns fall all over themselves hardly appealed to a man who was known for showing no emotion.

"Didn't even cry when he buried his own wife," the others murmured when he walked by. "Don't care a thing about nobody else in this world 'cept hisself."

He heard the whispers. They floated through the air, flitting their way into his subconscious until he started to believe them. He decided they were right—he *didn't* care about nobody but hisself. Most days, anyway. Sometimes, the little girl left behind when his wife went screaming into the dark unknown wormed her way into his heart, and for a brief moment, he believed himself capable of loving again.

The whiskey usually did a good job of shutting those feelings down, though.

The morning after the circus tent leapt into the sky, appearing to materialize almost out of nowhere overnight, Landis stumbled home, breath sour and pockets empty after another night of drinking at the saloon. His dusty blonde hair hung over his eyes, dirty and dull from years of poor nutrition and simply giving up. He looked old, much older than his twenty-six years.

He pushed the small door of his little prairie home open and fell onto his knees in front of the table where he'd eaten his meals his entire life. His stomach recoiled, and he let out a loud belch, swallowing quickly before he vomited all over Mama's floor. He closed his eyes and counted to three as the room spun around him. When he opened his eyes again, he saw her shoes.

Pushing to his knees, he leaned back, head lolling as the whiskey continued to work its way through his system.

"Hey, Mama," he slurred.

"Don't 'Hey, Mama' me," Mary Landis replied, hands on her hips. Her brown hair was pulled into a tight bun, the greying strands around her face sticking out wildly as she looked over her drunk son. Her eyes narrowed, and she shook her head in disgust.

"Look at you, Johnston," she said, her voice low and full of accusation. He dropped his eyes in shame. Nobody in the world called him Johnston but his mama, and every time she said his name her obvious disappointment laced its way into his heart. "How'd ya even pay fer this turn, eh?" Mary asked. "Whose money'd you take this time?"

Landis pushed to his feet, his hands gripping the edge of the table as he tried to steady himself. Slowly he stood up, pushing his shoulders back and looking down at his mother. At his tallest, Landis stood head and shoulders over his petite mama. She crossed her arms, craning her neck up to look at the boy she raised, the boy who'd had such promise, but who, like his father, became a slave to the bottle.

"Don't you stand there just lookin' at me," Mary said. She gestured out the back door. "Git on out there and wash yerself. You smell like a pig in a pile of slop."

Landis nodded. "Yes, Mama," he mumbled. He willed his feet to start moving and dragged himself through the room to the door in the back. Just as he put his hand on the handle, a movement to his right drew his gaze. He turned his head slowly, willing his eyes to follow along and focus. The little girl sat on the floor holding a dirty rag doll. Her face was framed with bright, golden curls, her large blue eyes staring up at him eagerly.

"Papa?" A smile stretched across her face, pink lips opening wide to reveal tiny, white teeth.

"Hey, Emmaline," he muttered. He took a step toward her but stopped when he felt his mother's hand grip his wrist.

"Don't you go near that baby right now," Mary hissed. "Don't touch her until you can look at her without seein' double, ya hear?"

Landis glanced back at his daughter, her face looking from his to her grandmother's in confusion. She looked so much like her mama that it made his heart hurt. He wanted a drink.

With a nod of the head, Landis stepped out of the room and stumbled toward the shallow pond behind their house. His mother had already hung up a clean shirt and pair of pants for him over the tree branch.

"When you can stand up without swayin', come back in and eat. I'm takin' that baby to the circus today, and you're comin' along."

Landis spun around, nearly falling over. "No, I ain't, Mama," he answered, shaking his head vehemently. "I ain't goin' to no circus."

"Oh, you're goin' to the circus, boy," Mary shot back. She watched as her son pitched and swayed across the dusty earth, muttering incoherently. Swiping a hand over her weathered face, Mary let out a long sigh. She tried to pull up a happier memory, a vision from when he was a boy and still full of life and hope. But there was nothing there. Somehow all the memories were covered in the same sad cloud. Not enough food and too much alcohol had been the story of her life, from her own Pa, to her husband, and now her son. The one bright spot in it all rested on the head of her granddaughter, and as Mary turned back to the house, she took in the sight of Emmaline standing in the doorway. Her ratty doll was clutched between slender fingers. The child was extraordinarily beautiful, almost to the point of making Mary uncomfortable.

"C'mon, child," Mary murmured, reaching for Emmaline and pulling her into her arms. The little one nestled her head against her grandmother's shoulder with a contented sigh. Mary trudged into the house and set Emmaline on the table. Taking a step back, she studied her closely.

"We're gonna go somewhere new today," she said. She reached over to straighten one of the unruly curls on her granddaughter's head. "It's gonna be right fun, I do believe."

Emmaline cocked her head to the side and looked at her grandmother quizzically. "What's fun?" she asked.

Mary shook her head and let out a long sigh. "I know," she said, her voice barely a breath. "That word don't make no sense." Mary licked her finger and wiped a smudge of dirt off of Emmaline's soft, round cheek. "Beautiful child," she murmured, swallowing against a pang of fear that jolted through her. The child was too beautiful. Mary felt the stares and heard the whispers when she brought Emmaline into town. The attention the little girl received was dangerous, and Mary knew it.

She reached around the girl and grabbed a crusty loaf of bread off the table. Tearing a piece, she watched as the crumbs tumbled to the floor she'd just swept, flittering over the toes of her worn shoes. She held the bread out to Emmaline, who took it and bit greedily.

"Eat slow, now," Mary said. "There ain't no more where that came from."

Two hours later, Mary, Emmaline, and Landis walked through town toward the vibrant, white tent that jutted into the skyline like a mirage.

"I'll be," Mary breathed, shifting Emmaline to her other hip as her arms burned from the weight. Landis tried to pull his daughter from Mary's arms, but she held firm and shrugged away his reach. He swallowed his anger, glancing longingly at the saloon as they walked past. His empty pockets flapped in the morning breeze, but he knew that a card game would be going on inside the darkened doors. His next drink was only one good hand away.

"Don't you go starin' at that nasty place now, hear?" Mary murmured. "You just look on up at that tent. Somethin' is bound to happen today."

Landis sneered at his mother, frustration gnawing at his chest as he watched his daughter cling to her arm. Sweat beaded at Mary's temples as she walked under the weight of his child—the child he was rarely allowed to touch. Dropping a few steps back, Landis put some distance between himself and his mother.

Once again, as it had so often before, the memory of that final night with Mae swept across his mind's eye. It was a memory that he could not escape. His only reprieve from the horror of that moment came when the whiskey pushed him into a deep sleep, but even then, his dreams were fraught with hazy memories, her screams echoing through them like the scratchy wheeze of a pipe organ.

It had been cold the night Emmaline was born. Mae fell to laboring before her time was due, and panic swept through their little cabin.

"Johnston, git the doc," Mama had whispered, her eyes wild with worry as Mae moaned in the bedroom.

"Is she gon' be okay, Mama?" Landis asked, pulling his tattered shoes onto his feet. He'd had a few drinks that day, leaving him less steady. He'd blinked several times, willing the room to stop churning long enough for him to focus.

"There's too much blood," Mary replied, soaking the rags in a pink-tinged bowl on the table. "The baby ain't comin' like it should, and it's awful early. I need the doc fast, boy."

The panic in his mama's voice immediately stopped the swaying room, the floor no longer pitching beneath his feet. Landis had run out into the icy air, an impending snowstorm bearing down on them unseasonably early. Jumping on his horse, he rode into town as quickly as he could, screaming out Doc Thomas's name, his voice cutting through the air like a machete.

He'd pulled the doc from his bed, and the two raced back to the little cabin nestled on the banks of the pond. Lights glowed inside, illuminating the barren outdoors. On another night, the sight would have been tranquil, but on this night the sound of Mae's screams sliced through the black sky and carved clean through Landis' heart. Before his horse stopped moving, Doc Thomas slid from the saddle. He raced inside while Landis remained outside, ears and lungs burning in the cold, listening to the sounds of his wife dying on the other side of the wooden door he'd helped his father build when he was a boy.

The wails were more than he could bear. They were guttural, pleading. At one point, he thought he recognized his own name in the sound, but he couldn't be sure, and he couldn't wait any longer. He turned his horse and dug his heels into the animal's meaty flesh, pointing it toward the town saloon.

This is where the doc, weary with the heavy news he carried, found Landis hours later. When he stepped into the raucous hall, all activity stopped for a moment. The lot of people inside the saloon weren't generally known for their kindness or tolerance, but no one had the poor taste to jeer at Doc Thomas, particularly when blood was still visibly caked under his fingernails. He caught sight of Landis huddled in the corner, face flushed and eyes glassy. Landis watched the doc walk his way, footsteps heavy on the dirty floor.

"Congratulations, son," Doc Thomas said, his voice tired and thin. "You have a daughter."

For a moment, hope had soared in Landis' chest. Maybe it had all turned out for the best. Maybe he'd quelled Mae's screams, and she was home now with their daughter. Maybe…but no. The doc had seen the light spark in Landis' eyes and quickly snuffed it out, delivering the blow that would crush the young man's spirit permanently.

"She's gone," he said, his voice carrying through the oddly quiet saloon. "There was nothing I could do." He leaned down, looking Landis straight in the eye then. "But your child lives," he whispered. "Go to her."

Landis stumbled home after that, falling through the front door and tripping his way through the cabin to the bedroom that he'd shared with his wife. With a ragged breath, he pushed into the room, already stuffy and hot with grief, and he saw his Mama rocking gently in the corner, a tiny bundle clutched in her arms. Her face was lined with heartache as she looked up at her son and saw the drunken gaze that she knew too well looking back at her. He shifted his eyes to Mae, still and pale against the bed. Her long, blonde hair framed her smooth face, lips turned up slightly. She looked peaceful. It didn't match the horrible sounds that had torn from her body earlier. Landis longed to go to her, to wrap her hands in his, to kiss her mouth the way he'd done just a few hours before, when the baby had still rounded her belly and hope had been the tapestry of their future. He'd loved her since they were both kids in the schoolhouse. And he knew, in that moment, that his life could never be complete again.

"She got to see the baby before she left us," Mama had spoken softly. The child in her arms let out a small, weak cry. "She kissed the girl, and she told me she wanted to name her Emmaline. Then…" Mary's voice faltered as she glanced at her daughter-in-law, a young one she had loved as her very own. "Then she just slipped away," Mary gasped.

With a sigh at the memory, Landis kicked at the ground, his mother walking with Emmaline up ahead. Emmaline's blonde curls glowed in the early afternoon sunlight like a halo. Everywhere they went, people marveled at the beauty of his child. "Looks just like her Mama," they'd say, and the words seared hot in Landis' chest. He wished she didn't look so much like Mae. It'd make looking at her easier.

Ten minutes later, Landis, Mary, and Emmaline arrived at the entrance of the visiting circus. The tents had already been opened, and the scent of popcorn filled the air like an intoxicating invitation. Emmaline's eyes widened as she took in the colors that surrounded them. It was as though they'd stepped from a world of black and white into a colorful painting. Hues Emmaline had never before seen danced across her crystal blue eyes, and her cheeks flushed with excitement.

"Now don't go askin' for nothin' today, child, ya hear?" Mary said, the bitterness in her voice braiding its way through each word. "We ain't got no money to spend. I got only enough coins to get us through the opening in that tent."

Landis looked at his mother in annoyance. "You got only enough money to get us inside?" he asked. "This is how you plan to spend the only money we got?" His arm jerked toward the tent, and Mary raised her eyebrows.

"Don't you go talkin' to me about how to spend money, son," she hissed. "You ain't got no right to tell me what's wise and what ain't."

Landis bit his lip and looked back over his shoulder toward the saloon. He tried to formulate some excuse to get out of this afternoon at the circus. Already the strong scent of popcorn mingled with the fainter smell of dirty animals left his stomach rolling. He swallowed over his dry tongue and took a step backward.

"Mama," he began. Mary dropped Emmaline off her hip and set

her firmly on the ground. With one hand, she held her granddaughter, and with the other, she grabbed her son around the wrist.

"You will come with us today," Mary said, eyes flashing. Landis tried to pull from his mother's grasp, but her grip was a vise, and despite the fact that he knew himself to be stronger, he also knew that she would make his life hell if he didn't comply.

With a disgusted sigh, he wrenched his arm free. "Fine," he shot back. "I'll come, but when this is over I'm goin' out on my own."

Mary drew back her shoulders. "We'll see about that," she said, eyes narrowed.

Turning, the three followed the line of people in front of them to the entrance of the tent where a crowd had gathered to listen to a man bellowing from the top of a long, wooden stage. Next to the man, a scantily clad woman held a small sword in her hand. Her shoulders swayed back and forth, and a seductive smile spread across her face.

"Ladies and gentlemen! Boys and girls of all ages!" the man ballyhooed with great vigor, his arms gesturing wildly. "Come one and all and see the most spectacular, the wild, masterful, and mightiest feats of wonder this world has ever known! Step right up and get your tickets to see the show to end *all shows*!"

With a flourish, his arms swung up over his head and sparks shot from the base of the stage, causing the audience to gasp and then burst into excited applause. The woman standing next to the announcer raised her arm, the small sword in her hand gleaming in the mid-morning sunshine. Slowly and dramatically, she lowered the sword toward her open mouth.

"Well, I'll be," Mary gasped. She hugged Emmaline to her body, shielding the girl's eyes in case the women before them pierced straight through the back of her neck with that sword. The crowd held its breath as the blade slowly disappeared into her throat, and then erupted once more when she pulled it back out and thrust both arms triumphantly into the air.

"Get your tickets now, ladies and gentlemen! This is a show you don't want to miss! Come see wonders from around the globe. Magicians will astound you. Aerialists will leave you breathless, and our talented freaks will make you rethink how you view the world as a whole. Waste no time! Get your tickets now!"

The crowd pressed forward in a frenzy, sweeping Mary, Emmaline, and Landis toward the bright yellow wagon where a bald old man sat taking coins and issuing tickets with lightning speed. Within ten minutes, they had tickets in hand and approached the outside of the main tent. Emmaline stared in wonder at the giant canvas paintings that lined the walkway. Oversize portraits of the sideshow acts boasted about the marvelous circus' freaks.

MISS CLARABELLE:
THE FAT LADY OF THE STAGE: 750 POUNDS
MEET TINY:
THE WORLD'S TALLEST MAN: 10 FEET TALL
THE SINGING-DANCING DWARVES:
BIG VOICES IN SMALL BODIES
MEET THE SNAKE MAN,
BORN AND RAISED IN THE AFRICAN WILD

Of course, Emmaline could not read. She could only stare at the pictures, wide-eyed as she took in the sight of a large woman, pudgy hand clutching her chest and tears rolling down her round cheeks. Beside her, the poster portrayed a tall, lanky man standing next to a giraffe that looked up at him with wide eyes. Next to him was the poster of two tiny men, dressed in matching tuxedos, mouths open and eyes closed. They only reached to the knees of the tall man in the other poster.

Emmaline gawked at the pictures until Mary caught her staring. "Don't gape, child," Mary chided.

Slowly, the three marched forward until they reached the entrance of the tent. Inside, a boy who looked to be no older than fifteen stood holding a wooden box painted the brightest blue Emmaline had ever seen. The boy wore a red and white striped coat, the tails in the back hanging to just above his knees. His white shirt was crisp and stiff, almost as though it were made of wood itself. On his head stood a tall, black hat. Topping off his ensemble was his painted face, the white smeared across his features giving him a ghostly, statue-like appearance. He stood frozen, unmoving to the point that Emmaline didn't even believe him to be a real person. She reached a tentative finger out to touch his leg when all of a sudden, he bent at the waist into a low bow, his face coming to within inches of hers. With a yelp, she clamored back into her grandmother's arms.

Mary smiled as the boy straightened back up. "My apologies, little one," he said with a wink. "I didn't mean to frighten you."

Emmaline pulled away from the boy, clutching her doll closer to her chest as Mary gave her a reassuring squeeze.

"S'alright, child," Mary murmured in her ear. "He's just here to welcome us to the circus." Mary reached into the pocket of the apron tied around her long dress and pulled out the three tickets she had purchased for today's show using the money she had hidden away in a tin in the back of the cupboard so that her son couldn't find it. Tomorrow she would find a way to make more money. Today, she needed to escape reality.

The boy accepted the tickets from Mary's shaking hand. His eyes shifted to the man standing behind her, his ruddy appearance a dead giveaway for one given to cards and the bottle. Then he looked back at the child between them, her angelic face now looking at his with less fear and more intrigue.

He bowed once more, then stood and gestured his hand toward the tent. "Please," he said. "Enjoy the show." He reached out and tapped the end of Emmaline's nose with his gloved finger, and she giggled. Mary ducked into the dim tent, disappearing through the flaps as Landis reluctantly stepped up behind her.

"Beautiful child," the boy murmured as Landis walked past him. He turned to look back into the boy's black-rimmed eyes. With a slight nod, Landis stepped into the tent behind his mother, where they were immediately greeted by a man whose height didn't reach to Landis' waist.

"Popcorn for the little girl?" he said, thrusting a paper bag upward into Emmaline's hands. Mary quickly pushed it away before Emmaline could grab hold.

"No, thank you," she said firmly, trying not to gape at the little man. "We don't got no money for such indulgence."

Emmaline's head swiveled from left to right taking in the sights. The rows of wooden stands stacked high around the circular stage layered in hay were illuminated with the golden glow of a spotlight that came from some unseen location.

"'Tis free, madam," the little man said, bowing so low that his head nearly touched Mary's knees. "Every child that walks through those flaps receives a free bag of popcorn."

Mary reached a hesitant hand down and accepted the bag of popcorn. She raised it up to Emmaline, who looked inside with wide, disbelieving eyes. Carefully, the little girl reached into the bag and grabbed a single piece of popcorn, buttery and glistening in the golden lights above. She put it in her mouth and chewed slowly.

"Oh!" she cried and plunged her hand back into the bag. Mary laughed, a natural reaction that she had not experienced in some time—she didn't think she'd ever feel that freedom of joyful expression again. It felt good, as intoxicating as the popcorn. Landis watched them both with narrow eyes, growing more suspicious and untrusting of this experience by the minute.

The little man offered a wide smile, and his short arm swept to the side, pointing to the nearby stands.

"The show will begin soon," he said. "May I suggest you find a seat?"

Mary and Emmaline hastened to the long, wooden benches while Landis hung back for a moment, taking in the bustling motion around him. The stands were packed, filled with faces that he didn't recognize. Some were, of course, familiar, but many must have come from neighboring towns.

There was a buzz in the air, a hum that charged the tight space as voices talked excitedly. Greasy popcorn left smears on the mouths of rail-thin children whose eyes looked up at the tip of the tent above them in awestruck enchantment. Even Landis found his jaw falling open slightly upon looking up.

"Johnston!"

He lowered his eyes to see his mother waving at him, motioning toward a small section of open bench that she'd found in the middle of a packed row. Landis swallowed over a parched tongue and let out another long, dejected sigh. He glanced behind him at the door and saw the boy in the top hat standing next to a shorter man with jet-black hair and a mustache to match. The two whispered to one another, the portly man's mustache dancing to the beat of his animated words. Landis followed their gaze, his eyes landing on his daughter. Emmaline looked like an angel in the soft, golden light. Her perfect, smooth features sparkled beneath the magic of the room. Landis looked back at the tent entrance.

The man with the jet-black hair caught his eye and offered a slight bow before sweeping from the tent. He moved so quickly that it was almost as if he simply disappeared into thin air. Landis blinked twice, then shifted his gaze back to his daughter, and with a sigh he made his way to the spot his mother had saved for him.

"Ain't it excitin'?" Mary breathed as Landis fell onto the bench beside her. Her eyes danced in a way he hadn't seen in a long time. The last time he'd seen his mother so delighted was the day Mae told her she was with child. Landis opened his mouth to offer some response to his mother, but found he had nothing to say. His gaze shifted once again to Emmaline, whose entire face seemed to sparkle. The half-eaten bag of popcorn now sat still in her hands, and butter glistened on her pink lips. She felt Landis' gaze and turned her eyes to his. Her mouth turned up into a soft smile, and Landis' heart squeezed at the sight of his wife, so present inside her child.

"Pretty!" she grinned, pointing at the ring below them. Landis nodded and tried to offer a smile in return.

"Yeah, it's real nice, ain't it Emmaline?" he asked. He wanted to reach for her, to pull her onto his lap the way that should come so naturally to a father, but his arms felt wooden. Emmaline looked back at him, her head cocked slightly to the side. It was almost as though she understood his hesitation.

Just then, the tent went dark. In one swift motion, the overhead spotlight turned off and the open flaps in the tent dropped closed. Children cried out in alarm as their parents hushed them.

"Gammy?" Emmaline's quiet voice called.

"Sshh, child," Mary consoled. "I got you. This is just part of the show."

A stillness settled over the room. The air was stuffy and thick as they waited for the magic to begin. Landis sipped in shallow breaths, willing his stomach to stop rolling and wishing his head didn't hurt so badly.

A single light appeared directly over the center of the large circus ring. It shined down on the man Landis had seen earlier, the one with the jet-black hair and the mustache to match. He sat tall on a regal, black horse, his back rigid, and his vibrant red coat pulled taut over the paunch of his gut.

"Ladies and Gentlemen," he began, his voice filling every corner of the room, rich and deep like a roll of thunder. His words were rounded out in funny places, making it apparent that English wasn't his natural language. "Boys and Girls of ALL AGES!" He waited a beat, letting his voice ring out for a moment, excited tension building under the tent. The horse pranced as the man pulled back on the reins. They turned in a tight circle and the arena held its collective breath.

"Welcome to the show! Today you will see feats of wonder unlike any you have ever seen! You may have been to the circus before, but I guarantee... you haven't seen a show quite..." he paused, waiting as the audience scooted forward in their seats, captivated by the simplicity of this opening moment. "*Like this*!"

The horse reared back on its hind legs as the room exploded in light and color. High above their heads, a woman in a sparkling leotard that looked like a torch flew across the length of the tent, her hands gripping tightly to a trapeze bar. She let go and flipped above them in the expanse of air between the top of the tent and the ground, and the audience gasped as she hung momentarily suspended between heaven and earth. Then she grasped the hands of a man swinging toward her, hanging by his knees from a second trapeze bar, and the two swung together to a small platform where they hopped to their feet and rose their arms above their heads triumphantly. The audience erupted into applause.

Below them, on the ground, a group of clowns tumbled into the ring, flipping over and above one another until one of them caught his foot on another and the two fell into a heap on the sawdust floor. The audience gasped, then burst into laughter as the two men scuffled on the ground.

A puff of black smoke pulled their eyes back upward as a man in a long, black cape stood on another platform above the bleachers, his arms opened wide. With a flourish of his arm and a wink of his eye, a small white bird appeared in the palm of his hand.

"Well, I'll be..." Mary gasped next to Landis.

The man in the cape threw the bird into the air, where it immediately turned into a bouquet of pure white flowers, which rained down on the audience below him. Even Landis found himself awestruck at the magic. He pursed his lips to keep his jaw from dropping in wonder. Beside him, Emmaline squealed in delight, buttery hands smacking together as a small, blonde woman came tearing into the ring on the back of an ostrich. Her hair was pinned in elaborate curls on top of her head, and her sequined leotard hugged her curves. She lifted one arm, the other grasping the rope that was fitted around the non-plussed bird, and she flashed a wide smile as the audience cheered in glee. Landis squeezed his hands together in his lap to keep from clapping along.

From somewhere outside the tent, the sound of beating drums set a steady rhythm to each act's entrance. Next, two tigers, whose sleek, striped fur shone in the tent's lights, followed their trainer out, jumping through hoops and stunning the audience nearly to silence as they leapt up onto the man, one in the front and the other in back so that they hugged him between them. Then, with two blasts of a small whistle, the beasts slid back to the floor and the trainer offered a flourishing bow before making his exit, the tigers running after him and the audience cheering so loudly Landis thought his head might actually explode.

The acrobats came next. Flipping and tumbling into the ring, two of the four bounded across the center of the stage before stopping and turning, arms raised high and triumphant. A third acrobat ran toward them and with a sharp cry, he leapt through the air and landed on their outstretched hands. Balancing in a handstand, he waited as the fourth acrobat cried out. She looked young, maybe fourteen, her smooth skin and narrow eyes lit with the thrill of her shining moment. She tumbled across the floor, arms and legs flipping one over the other, until she reached the pyramid of people. Turning, she grasped the waist of the man on the bottom, then began to climb up his back, stepping her small foot on his shoulder.

The man in the handstand bent one of his legs and she grabbed onto it, and with a little hop, she swung up to the top of the perch, her two hands grasped on his one foot, legs held out in a straddle as the audience gasped and clapped at this tower of people performing the impossible.

The girl hopped off, and the man in the handstand fell backward, landing on his feet beside her. The four of them raised their hands high above their heads as the voice of the ringmaster boomed through the room.

"Ladies and gentleman, *The Amazing Freemans!*"

The audience clapped again, hands raw and throats sore from cheering. The lights in the Big Top went dim then, and a hush fell over the room. The once-stale air was now charged, as ripples of anticipation for what might come next flittered through the crowd. The man with the black hair stepped back into the ring. His eyes scanned the crowd until he saw Emmaline. He paused for a moment, studying the child just long enough to make Landis uncomfortable.

"And now," he said, his voice loud but sounding almost like a whisper. The crowd leaned forward in anticipation. "*It is time for the main event!*"

Sparks shot out of the ground and ladies screamed as the back of the tent opened up and four elephants lumbered into the room. Their dark, grey skin glistened in the lights, and the red, tasseled hats on their heads danced as the beasts made their way to the center of the ring. Two trainers, a man and a woman, walked behind the elephants, prodding them and barking out commands. When the animals entered the ring, they stopped in a single line, standing from tallest to shortest, swaying from side to side as the drums picked up their beat. With the crack of a whip and a loud cry, the taller trainer, a long, thin man with carrot-orange hair, stepped before the creatures and raised his arms high, then swept them back down to his side. All four elephants, in one swift motion, sat down on their haunches and raised their trunks high into the air.

The audience roared with laughter and clapped delightedly. At the sound of two quick blasts from a whistle, the elephants all raised their front, right feet straight up in the air. The female trainer stepped onto the foot of the first elephant in line and raised one arm up high. The elephant stood, holding her suspended above the ground on his leg, and the other three followed. The woman stepped delicately over each one of them until she got to the last one. She stepped in the final elephant's outstretched trunk, and the crowd cheered again as the elephant swung her high above his head.

On and on, the show went, with each act given a longer period of time in which to wow the crowd below. The trapeze swingers flew high above them, the magician further boggled their minds, the clowns made them howl with laughter, and the animals left jaws open in wonder.

By the time the show finally ended, Emmaline was exhausted, her head lolling against her grandmother's chest as she watched it all play out with glassy eyes. Landis rubbed at his temples as the ringmaster thanked them for coming and enjoying the magic of the circus.

"And now, ladies and gentleman," he boomed. "Before you leave today, I extend a most gracious and humble invitation to walk through our sideshow and see freakish shows of human abnormality. For just two pennies more, you can come see the tattooed man of Africa and marvel at the world's tallest man. And, of course, you won't want to miss the fat lady singing!" The audience laughed while Mary cringed in her seat next to Landis.

"Poor woman," she whispered.

"And so, without further ado, please let me thank you for visiting." The ringmaster bowed low as a burst of flames shot out of two small canons at his feet. When the smoke cleared, the center of the ring was empty, and the crowd sat in stunned silence.

Landis stood up next to his mother and daughter and swallowed hard, his tongue dry and scratchy. The scents of sawdust and animal dung and gun powder all mingled in the air, but somehow the smell of the popcorn seemed to overpower them all.

"Well, Mama," he said, looking at the open flap of the tent. "I guess we better git on outta here so she can go to bed." He nodded his head toward Emmaline, whose eyes had finally closed. She slept soundly, her face buried in the crook of Mary's neck.

"Well, I don't know," Mary replied. She looked toward the side of the tent where a crowd was lining up to see the sideshow. She had three more pennies nestled in her pocket and while she knew she should save them, the magic of the event had swept her right up.

"I think I'd like to see what the fuss is all about down there," she said.

Landis shook his head. "No," he answered, his chin jutting out stubbornly. "I came to the circus with you, but you never said nothin' about stayin' for no sideshow. I'm leaving."

Landis turned to go, stopping when he felt his mother's hand grasp his wrist. He glanced back at her.

"Don't you go back to that saloon," she whispered. Her eyes were wild as she stared at him, beads of sweat gathering at her temples. "Don't do it, son. Don't." Her eyes filled with tears, and Landis felt a familiar pang of sadness squeeze tight in his chest. He nodded slowly at his mama, not entirely sure he was telling the truth, but desperately wanting to honor her request. Mary's arms shook as she shifted Emmaline to her other hip.

"I want to see this sideshow," she repeated. "But you could sit here with Emmaline while she sleeps until I get back." She looked at him then, the magic of the circus having stirred inside her hope for new possibilities. Maybe she could try, just this once, to give him space alone with his daughter. Maybe this was the moment a bond would begin, and that connection would pull him out of the bottle's grip.

Lowering himself back onto the bench, Landis nodded, too tired and thirsty to argue. Mary gently laid Emmaline into his lap where the child nestled into his chest in a way that sent a shock through him. Mary stood watching them for a minute.

"She looks good there in your arms," she said. Reaching over, Mary ran her hand down Landis' cheek the way she had done when he was a little boy. Her heart was fit to bust with the love she felt for the two people sitting on that bench. She never understood how love and pain could be so closely matched, all pushed up against one another so that it was hard to figure which was which.

"I'll be back soon," Mary murmured, turning to leave. "I just wanna take a peek."

Landis let out a long sigh and rested his chin on top of Emmaline's head. She smelled fresh and clean. Mama had obviously bathed her that morning in preparation for the circus. He watched his mother's retreating figure until she disappeared through the flap of the tent that led to the adjoining sideshow, then he closed his eyes. Immediately Mae's face appeared.

Landis wondered what she would think of all this—of the circus, of their daughter, of the man that he had become. He often thought on his years with Mae, how she'd always made him want to be a better person, but even she'd had to compete with the bottle. She'd beg him to stop his drinking, and he would be determined to honor her, but then he'd hear of a card game starting up, and his mouth would get thirsty, and he'd end up apologizing to her again. If she had lived, would they even be here now? Would his thirst for the saloon be any less raging?

Mae would have liked the circus, Landis knew that without a doubt. She always had a flair for the dramatic. The lights and sounds would have been magical to his Mae. He squeezed his eyes tight, picturing her squealing with delight as the woman let go of the trapeze and flew through the air, back arched, eyes wide as she looked for the hands of her partner. Mae would have bounced up and down in her seat, her blonde hair bobbing behind her as she clapped her hands together over and over. Had Mae ever been to a circus before? Landis didn't think so, and the thought of her missing out on this experience brought on a fresh wave of grief and sadness. He shifted in his seat and opened his eyes to look for Mama. Instead, he found the ringmaster standing at the bottom of the stands looking up at him. They studied one another for a moment.

"You did not want to see the amazing freaks of our sideshow?" the man asked. The question was for Landis, but his eyes were focused on Emmaline. Landis put his arms around his daughter awkwardly and shook his head.

"She's sleepin'," he mumbled. The ringmaster nodded. He lifted his leg and stepped up, making his way slowly to Landis. He sat on the row in front of them and smiled.

"She is a very beautiful child," he said. His words were clipped and strange, the back end of each one sounding as if it had been swallowed before it could release. His accent made Landis uncomfortable.

"Thank you," Landis replied.

"She is your daughter?" the man asked. Landis nodded.

"And the woman who was with you earlier. That is whom?" The ringmaster shifted his gaze from Landis' face back to Emmaline's.

"My mother," Landis replied. "She'll be back soon, and we'll be headin' home."

The ringmaster nodded again. "I see. Of course," he said. He reached up and smoothed the shiny, black moustache that decorated his upper lip. "You know, I don't often run into children that are as beautiful as your daughter. She has a rare beauty—almost like an angel."

The man paused and studied the sleeping child again, taking in the sight of her naturally rosy cheeks, and red mouth. Her long, dark lashes fanned across her cheekbones, and the blonde curls on her head framed her perfect, round face. He wanted to reach out and run the back of his hand down her cheek but restrained himself. Observation told him that this man didn't really care for his child, but the ringmaster knew the effects of undermining a man's pride all too well. So, he kept his hands folded politely in front of him, the picture of restraint.

He looked back up at Landis and offered a crooked smile. "Forgive my poor manners," he said. "I am Monsieur Beaumont. Well, I suppose you would say 'Mr.' Beaumont."

Landis nodded his head tentatively. The way that the man pronounced "*Meester*" puzzled him.

"Johnston Landis," he mumbled.

Monsieur Beaumont reached out his hand. It hung suspended between the two of them for an awkward moment before Landis reached up and offered a limp shake.

"Mr. Landis," the ringmaster said. He dropped Landis' hand and pulled a handkerchief from his pocket, wiping his hands slowly while masking the disgust he felt at having just touched the filthy man before him. Turning, he looked down at the empty circus ring.

"Did you enjoy our show?" he asked. Though his voice was quiet, it came out strong. He was clearly a man of confidence.

Landis shrugged his shoulders. "I s'pose," he answered. "Ain't really my thing."

Monsieur Beaumont smiled. "Yes. I hear that from a lot of men like you," he said.

"What's that mean?" Landis asked. Emmaline shifted in his lap, his sharp words scratching her slumber.

"Oh, it is no insult, Mr. Landis, I assure you," Monsieur Beaumont replied. "It is merely an observation. American men are accustomed to hard work, especially in this area of your country. Your days are filled with the harsh realities of life. The circus..." he swept his hand out, drawing Landis' eyes to the empty tent. Devoid of the lights and action from earlier, the space now looked drab and dark.

"The circus is all about the impossible," Monsieur Beaumont continued. "This is the place for fantasy and wild imagination, where reality doesn't really exist. It is where you find magic."

Landis squinted his eyes and tried to recall the images from earlier. He remembered the magician and the trapeze artist, the animals and the clowns and the acrobats. But his memory of them was fading. Already the lights and the colors had bled away, leaving him with only the faintest scent of what had been. It seemed to Landis that the only memories in his life that remained true and bright and vivid were the ones that had cut through him like a knife. They were the painful memories, and they were the only ones lit up like a colored painting. Those were the memories he kept trying to drown.

Landis swallowed hard.

Monsieur Beaumont watched the conflict roll across the young man's face with great interest. Meanwhile, the child in his lap stirred and opened her eyes. She looked at the ringmaster with a puzzled stare. Monsieur Beaumont was captivated by the child, fully entranced by her beauty. She blinked a few times, then shifted to look up at her father. Her face lit up when she saw him, and Beaumont knew immediately that she was not accustomed to being shown affection by the man in whose arms she sat.

"Papa?" she spoke, her groggy voice sweet and innocent. Landis looked uncomfortably down at his daughter. He glanced back at the flap of the tent where his mother had disappeared and wished for her to come walking back out.

Monsieur Beaumont took a deep breath and let it out slowly. "Mr. Landis," he began. Landis shifted his gaze to the man before him. "Do you know how I acquire the acts for my show?"

Landis shook his head. Emmaline looked back up at the ringmaster with bright eyes. Beaumont tried not to stare back at the child.

"I find the most special people from around the world, and I bring them into our circus family. I give them clothing and food and the opportunity to travel all over the country. I have all the money I need to make sure that my people are given the best this world can offer."

Landis sighed, suddenly very, very tired. "What's this gotta do with me?" he asked.

Monsieur Beaumont nodded at Emmaline. "You've got a special little girl there," he said quietly. His voice was smooth and gentle. "She would be an excellent addition to our circus family. She is the most beautiful child I have ever seen in all my travels around the world. Such rare beauty is a gift, and I could help her use that gift."

Landis swallowed hard and shook his head slowly. "What're you saying?" he asked. He pulled Emmaline into his side a little tighter. She squirmed against his grip.

Monsieur Beaumont leaned forward, looking directly into Landis' eyes.

"I am saying that I could take her for you. I would pay you handsomely, of course. And I would make sure that she grows up with more opportunity than you could possibly imagine. She will see the world, will be well fed and cared for. She will be given more than any child could even imagine." He paused as Landis blinked slowly, trying to wrap his mind around the ringmaster's words. "And you would be free of her," Beaumont finally finished. His words were soft, almost a whisper, but they sliced right through Landis, tearing at muscle and bone until they settled deep inside in the darkest part of his soul—the part that had wished to hear those very words since the day Emmaline was born.

"What is going on here?"

Landis snapped his head up to see his mother walking up the steps, her eyes narrowed suspiciously at her son.

"Think about what I said," Monsieur Beaumont whispered so that only Landis could hear. "We leave tomorrow at day's break."

The ringmaster straightened up and turned, flashing his brightest smile. "Nothing at all madam," he said with a slight bow. "I was simply thanking your son for bringing you all to the circus today. I do hope you enjoyed our show."

Mary offered a wary smile in return. "Yes, of course," she replied. "It was wonderful." She glanced at her son. His face had drained of color, and his eyes were glassed over.

"Well, I s'pose we should be leaving now," she said. She reached down for Emmaline, pulling the little girl into her arms. Emmaline smiled at her grandmother, her lips still caked with dried butter. Mary smiled back, smoothing the loose curls away from Emmaline's face and kissing her soft cheek. She nodded at Monsieur Beaumont, who offered a small bow in return.

"C'mon," she said to her son. Landis stood up, his eyes meeting the ringmaster's. The man tipped his head, his eyes never moving from Landis' face. Slowly, Landis followed his mother down the dirty stands, and stepped out of the dark tent into the blazing Oklahoma sunshine. He squinted, letting his eyes adjust for a moment before following his mama's swinging skirt down the dusty path toward home.

Inside the tent, Monsieur Beaumont watched the three of them leave, running his fingers over his moustache. The boy in the top hat suddenly appeared by his side.

"So?" he asked. "How did it go?"

Monsieur Beaumont took in a deep breath and let it out slowly. He turned to look at his son, a handsome young man who was learning the art of business in his father's footsteps. Pierre Beaumont raised his dark eyebrows as he waited for his father to reply. He was a chiseled boy, tall and lean with smooth skin, dark eyes, and a strong jaw. He was shrewd, like his father. Perhaps even more so, for everyone who worked in Beaumont's circus knew that it wasn't really Monsieur that they needed to be wary of. No, the ringmaster himself was a demanding man, but predictable and easy to please if you were willing to meet his demands.

It was Pierre that they all feared most, for he was a boy unaccustomed to being told no.

"I believe that I planted the seed," Monsieur Beaumont said slowly. "That man doesn't love his daughter. He's afraid of her."

"But do you think he will let her go? Because, Papa, we need that child. Just imagine it! We could bill her as The Most Beautiful Girl in the World. Imagine the business that would bring in!"

"Patience, boy," Monsieur Beaumont said, cutting his eyes toward his son. "These things take time. You don't just snatch a man's child away from him, even if he doesn't love that child. A real man has his pride to consider. So, you appeal to that." Monsieur Beaumont nodded his head toward where Landis and his family had just exited. "That man will relinquish his daughter only if he feels he is doing it for her best interests."

Landis lay on his back, staring out the small window at the foot of his bed. The full moon shone brightly, casting a blueish glow on the world below. He felt a churning in his gut, and he balled his fists tightly to try and quell the shaking. The night was still. There were no whispers from the wind, no snapping of twigs to distract him from his thoughts. There was only silence, heavy and thick and pushing down so hard on him that he felt he might suffocate under the weight of it.

"*You will be free of her.*"

The man's words played in his mind like the warbled sounds coming from the out-of-tune piano at Miller's Saloon.

"*Free of her.*"

Landis turned on his side and swallowed hard. His mouth felt dry, his tongue thick. Throwing the covers off, Landis sat up and pulled on his pants. Reaching out, he yanked his shirt off the hook on the wall next to his bed and put it on quickly. He grabbed his shoes and his hat and tiptoed out of the room, past the bed where his mother and Emmaline slept. He paused, looking down at the two.

Emmaline lay nestled up against her grandmother, her hair fanned out on the pillow behind her. Her hand lay splayed open next to her head, little palm up so that the moonlight hit it just right, highlighting the lines stretching across the plump skin.

"*You know what I can't wait to see?*"

Landis shut his eyes as a memory of Mae swept over him. They had been laying in that very bed, the two of them, Mae's stomach stretched taut, as her time to deliver the baby grew closer.

"*What?*" Landis had asked, so totally enamored with the way that pregnancy had changed his wife. There had been a joy in her eyes, a glow that he'd never seen before.

"*I can't wait to see the baby's hands.*" She held up her own hand then, illuminated by the moonlight streaming through the window.

"*The hands?*" Landis asked. He reached up and engulfed her hand in his, pulling it down to his chest.

Mae smiled, nestling her head deeper into the pillow as she stared back at him. "*Yeah,*" she replied. "*I remember when my mama had her last baby, I would hold him and just stare at his little hands. They were so small, but so perfect. I just can't wait to hold this little one's hands.*"

Landis swallowed hard and stepped out of the room, crossing the kitchen in three soft steps and pulling open the front door without making a sound. He stepped into the night air. It was cooler tonight. Landis could smell the autumn weather, the pending change in temperature promising to bring some welcome relief to the dry, dusty land around him.

But for Landis there would be no relief. There was no salve for the constant pain that hovered over him wherever he went. He walked quickly, hands stuffed in his pockets, toward the center of town where he knew Miller's Saloon would still be hopping. Perhaps he couldn't escape the pain, but he knew how he could numb it.

It didn't take him long to arrive, and he quietly slipped through the swinging doors into the raucous world of Miller's.

"Sinners and heathens," his mother liked to mutter every time they passed the building, and Landis supposed she was right. He just didn't care much, since he fit in so well with this lot of folks.

"Hey Landis."

Charlie Townsend sat at the end of the bar, his dirty hand cradling a half-filled stein of beer. Landis slid into the chair next to him, his mouth immediately salivating.

"Hey Charlie," he answered. The two sat in uncomfortable silence until Abe Miller strode down the bar, stopping across from Landis.

"You got money to pay tonight?" he asked.

Landis sighed. He reached in his pocket and pulled out two dimes, dropping them on the counter in front of Miller.

"This s'posed to be a joke?" Miller asked. He shoved the coins back at Landis and pushed away from the bar.

"Abe, c'mon," Landis pleaded. "Just spot me a little, okay? I'll pay you back."

Abe shook his head. "Please stop," he said. "You got such a long tab in this place, I could wrap the whole building up in it twice. No more free drinks for you."

Landis fell back against his chair, his shoulders slumped. He looked at Charlie who stared intently into his own glass, refusing to meet Landis' pleading gaze.

"C'mon, Charlie," Landis begged. "Just spot me a little to get through tonight."

Charlie slid out of his seat and shrugged his shoulders. "Sorry, man," he said. "I ain't got that kinda money to spare." Landis watched him walk to a table in the corner of the saloon, then dropped his head. He sat still for a moment before finally pushing himself off his chair and turning toward the door.

"I'll buy you a drink."

Landis turned to meet the gaze of Monsieur Beaumont. He hadn't recognized the ringmaster without his flashy costume from earlier. Now he simply wore a dark suit, crisp, clean, and clearly expensive.

"What're you doin' here?" Landis asked. He felt a knot begin to form in the pit of his stomach. Something about this man made him uncomfortable.

"I like to come and mingle with the locals in every town I visit," Beaumont replied. "This has allowed me to make the acquaintance of many people over the years. It's good for business."

Landis nodded awkwardly in return.

"So, let me buy you that drink and we can sit and chat for a while," Monsieur Beaumont said. Something in Landis' gut told him he should run, but instead he nodded slowly and watched as Monsieur Beaumont pulled a wad of rolled-up bills from his pocket and handed several over to Abe.

"Just keep the drinks coming as needed," he commanded. Abe looked at Beaumont, then at Landis with narrowed eyes.

"You be careful," Abe said. Landis blinked in return and waited for his stein of beer. He reached across the bar and took it from Abe's outstretched hand and immediately put it to his lips, drawing in a long, deep gulp. His eyes closed, and for a moment he felt like he might have hope.

"Shall we sit?" Beaumont gestured to an empty table by the back wall, and Landis followed him. Before he sat down, his glass was nearly empty. Beaumont gestured to the bar girl to bring another.

Beaumont sat quietly for a long time, just watching the way that Landis fidgeted in his chair, then observing how quickly and desperately the pitiful man drained his drinks. Within ten minutes, Landis had emptied three beer steins. His eyes were already turning glassy, and Beaumont knew he needed to make his move quickly before the man was too far gone.

"Have you thought about my proposition anymore?" Beaumont asked as the bar girl delivered yet another glass. Landis shrugged.

"Yeah, I thought about it," he said, his words pulling together slightly. "Wouldn't work, though." He drew in another long drink

"And why is that?" Monsieur Beaumont asked. He twirled between his fingers a large, shiny coin. Landis watched it spin, mesmerized.

"Ain't no way my mama would let go of that little girl," he mumbled.

Monsieur Beaumont nodded and drew in a deep breath. He leaned back in his chair. "Of course. Of course," he said. "She would not willingly let go of her, but that's not really her call to make, now is it? I mean, you are the father. You decide your daughter's fate, not your mother. And what kind of father wouldn't want the best for his little girl?"

Landis traced his finger around the top of his mug, trying to sort out his thoughts. "Yea, well, I ain't never been much of a father to her," he slurred. "My mama's been the mama and the daddy."

Monsieur Beaumont leaned forward. "All the more reason to make this decision on your own," he said. His voice came out almost as a hiss, and Landis felt a shiver run down his spine. "This is your chance to do something good for your daughter—to give her the life you have been wishing you could give her. She will have the finest education. She will be clothed in material from around the world and fed regular meals. She will be a star, and it will all be because of you. You will have given that to her—the ultimate gift from her father."

Landis listened intently. He finished his last drink and slumped down in his chair. His stomach churned, and he knew he'd overdone it again. Monsieur Beaumont pushed his chair back and stood up.

"If you decide to make the right choice, then bring the girl to me at sunrise. I will make sure you are paid well."

With that, Monsieur Beaumont bowed slightly. He turned on his heel to leave, sweeping his way through the room dramatically. Abe Miller watched the man go, then shifted his gaze to Landis. He shook his head at sight of the forlorn man in the corner, so much like his father. Harrison Landis had been a man of dashed dreams and sorrow, and it seems he passed that right on to his boy. Abe sighed and went back to cleaning up behind the bar.

Landis pushed to his feet and stumbled outside. He gulped in deep breaths, trying to stifle the nausea that rolled over him. Finally, he leaned over and retched, spraying the front stoop of Abe's with his vomit.

"Aw, c'mon Landis. Git away from the door before you do that!" Abe hollered from inside. Landis stumbled away, his head hung in shame. He walked slowly back to his house, but instead of going inside, he made his way around back to the little pond. Sinking to his knees, he washed his face and made himself drink some water. Finally, he sat back on his heels and looked up at the moonlit sky. The dark expanse, dotted with fading stars, always made him feel small. When he was a boy, he'd stare at the sky and wonder if anything lay beyond it.

"*You think it's endless?*" he once asked Mae as the two of them lay sprawled out on a blanket by the creek bed. "*You think the black just stretches on and on forever?*"

Mae had shifted a bit, turning her head to take in as much of the night sky as she could. Her mouth had tilted up in a wistful smile. "*I don't know,*" she'd finally answered, her voice almost a song. "*But I sure do hope there's something more. Wouldn't that be just grand?*"

Now the dark just stretched out over him like a blanket meant to suffocate. It would be daybreak soon.

Landis spent the next few hours in and out of fitful sleep right there on the ground next to the pond. He'd drift off to sleep, and Beaumont's words filled his thoughts.

"*What kind of father wouldn't want what's best for his little girl?*"
"*You could be free of her.*"

When a sliver of sunlight sliced its way through the dark sky, Landis opened his eyes. He rolled to his back, groaning beneath his churning stomach and aching joints. He stared up at the sky above him, the black fading to a light grey as pink and orange ribbons of light brightened the world around him.

"What would Mae want?" he asked himself as he watched a bird glide effortlessly overhead, wings outstretched and floating through the quiet sky.

Landis pushed up until he sat slumped over, hands in his lap. He was dirty, and he smelled terrible. He slid forward until he could reach the pond and dip his hands into the cold water, washing the dirt from them and splashing his face. He could never seem to get himself clean.

Landis knew what Mae would want, but he didn't let himself say it out loud. She would want Emmaline at home with her father. She would want him to love their daughter, and to bring her up knowing who her mama had been.

But maybe she would understand if she could see what had become of him. He wasn't capable of showing that child love, he knew it.

The sound of a train whistle pierced his thoughts, and Landis made a rash decision. Pushing to his feet, he waited a moment until the ground stopped moving, then made his way into the house where his mother stood at the fireplace, stoking the flames in preparation for the day. She turned to Landis, anger flashing strong across her petite features.

"You told me you weren't goin' back there," she accused. Landis waved his hand in her direction, stepping into the bedroom and pulling Emmaline, still in a dead sleep, from her bed. She let out a whimper in protest, the little rag doll falling from her arms as she twisted her body, reaching back for her warm bed.

"Johnston Landis, you put that baby back to bed this minute!" Mary barked. "What're you thinkin' boy?"

"I ain't no boy, Mama," Landis growled. "I'm a grown man and this is my child. I decide what's best for her."

He grabbed Emmaline's dress off the hook on the wall and walked toward the door.

"What in the name of..." Mary's voice trailed off as she looked at her son in horror. "What do you think you're doin'?" she asked. She stepped toward Landis, reaching for Emmaline who blinked sleepily from her grandmother to her father.

"I'm bein' a father to her and givin' her what she needs," Landis replied. He stepped toward the door. Mary rushed around and stood in front of him.

"You ain't goin' nowhere until you tell me what's goin' on, Johnston," she said, hands planted firmly on her hips. Landis shook his head.

"It ain't your decision, Mama," he answered. "I gotta go now." He pushed his way around his mother, knocking Mary with his shoulder as he yanked open the front door.

"Johnston? Johnston!" Mary reached for Emmaline who had begun to cry softly.

"Gammy!" she said, reaching for her grandmother. Mary grasped her little hand.

"You ain't taking her nowhere," Mary cried, tugging Emmaline toward her.

Landis spun around and shoved his mother forcefully. Mary stumbled backward, tripping over her rocking chair and falling, her head hitting the corner of the table with a sickening crack. She slumped to the floor in a heap, blood streaming from a gash in the side of her head.

Emmaline sobbed in Landis' arms, her wails searing a new horror into his subconscious. He took a step toward his mother, then stopped short as another blast from the train whistle broke through Emmaline's cries. He looked out at the brightening sky, and he knew he had to make his move. There was no turning back.

"Sorry, Mama," he whispered. He rushed from their little home, Emmaline kicking and squirming in his arms.

"I wan' Gammy," she sobbed.

Landis climbed up on his horse and settled his daughter in front of him, squeezing her tightly with his free arm as he grabbed the reins and dug his feet into the horse's sides. They took off at a full canter toward the town center, where smoke from the waiting train floated up into the morning sky. Emmaline quit fighting her father, stunned by the cold morning air against her milky white skin. Her hair stood in tufts around her head, and her little arms hung limply by her side, exposed in her nightdress. Landis clutched her day dress in his fist and swallowed against the fear that pressed hard against his chest.

Within minutes, they had pulled up to the station. The platform was empty, the train ready for departure. Landis slid from his horse, pulling Emmaline into his arms. She didn't fight anymore, and the tears had dried on her cheeks. She looked at her father, confusion written in her eyes like an accusation.

"I just' gotta do this, Emmaline, ya hear?" Landis said as he walked down the platform, scanning the windows in search of the ringmaster. Toward the end of the train, he heard the roar of a tiger. Emmaline's head snapped up, following the haunting sound that echoed down the empty, wooden platform.

"Beaumont!" Landis bellowed. Emmaline's grip on his shoulder tightened as she began to cry again.

Two cars down, a man jumped out of the train car, smoke shrouding him so that Landis couldn't quite make out his features. He walked forward out of the smoky shadows and into the morning light.

"I had given up on you," Monsieur Beaumont said, his voice laced with annoyance.

"It wasn't that easy," Landis replied.

Beaumont offered a thin-lipped smile. "Well, I assume you're here because you've decided to make the right decision then?"

"You promise you'll take good care of her?" Landis asked.

"Of course, Mr. Landis," Beaumont replied. "I am a man of my word."

Landis looked at his daughter, tears wetting her cheeks as she shook in his arms. "Will I ever see her again?"

Monsieur Beaumont put his hands in the pockets of his coat and drew in a long breath. "Well, I don't really know," he replied. "I don't suppose that would be easy for you or for the child, now would it?"

Landis didn't respond. He didn't really know why he asked the question in the first place.

Pulling Emmaline from his arms, he handed her to Beaumont. Emmaline began shrieking as the strange man pinned her arms to her side. Landis stepped back, horror washing over his face. A thin woman with dark skin jumped off the train car beside them and rushed to Beaumont's side. She looked from one man to the next, her eyes narrowed.

"Take her, Beatrice," Monsieur Beaumont said, shoving Emmaline into her arms. She pulled the child close and began shushing her softly.

"Her name is Emmaline," Landis said, his voice tired and weak.

Monsieur Beaumont nodded, waving his hand at Beatrice to take the child away.

"Papa?" Emmaline cried. "Papa! Papa!" Her legs kicked and her wails seared into Landis' heart. He took an instinctive step toward her.

"I wouldn't do that," Monsieur Beaumont said quietly. He stepped between Landis and the train as Beatrice climbed the steps with the screaming, terrified child. The door slammed shut behind her, and Landis was left with nothing but a memory—a nightmare to add to the horrors of his sleepless nights.

Beaumont took a step back and bowed slightly. "It is time for me to be going, Mr. Landis," he said, his voice cool and calm.

"You said you'd pay me for her," Landis replied. His voice shook as the words tumbled off his tongue.

"Of course, I did, didn't I?" Beaumont replied. "How silly of me to forget."

He reached in his pocket and took out a roll of bills, pressing them into Landis' hand. Landis clutched the money, his heart constricting.

"She will have everything this world could offer, Mr. Landis."

With that, Monsieur Beaumont turned and stepped up onto the waiting train. Just then the final whistle blew and steam shot from the side of the train. Landis sunk to his knees as the train slowly jerked forward. Monsieur Beaumont disappeared into the belly of the moving machine as it picked up speed.

A wave of nausea rolled over Landis, and he retched right there on the platform. Opening his fist, he stared at the money Monsieur Beaumont had pressed into his hand. He counted it quickly, then looked back at the train in horror. Gaining speed, the last few cars rushed past him. Moments later, the smoke had cleared, and Landis was left alone on the empty platform, his shirt soiled, and his eyes wide.

Johnston Landis had sold his daughter for five dollars.

1896

"Pasha, do you not hear me?!"

Peter snapped his head up and focused on his mother, who stood in the doorway with hands firmly planted on her hips and brow furrowed tightly over flashing eyes. Her dark hair was pulled into a tight bun at the nape of her neck, tugging at the skin around her face so that it highlighted the fatigue that had settled on her usually gentle features.

"Sorry, Mama," he said. "I was just thinking." He pulled himself from the daydream that had run like clockwork through his mind since they'd seen the posters earlier in the week.

COME AND SEE THE SHOW TO END ALL SHOWS! Monsieur Beaumont's Fabulous Feats and Freaks! A One-Day Circus Sure to Wow and Astonish!

Peter would close his eyes and envision all the fabulous feats of fearlessness he was bound to see, and suddenly he was there, riding atop an elephant, the great beast under his spell. And the crowd around him cheered and clapped, shouting his name over and over: "Pa-*sha!* Pa-*sha!* Pa-*sha!*"

Peter pushed to his feet and glanced out the window at the street below, the hustle and bustle of New York City already pumping in the morning sunlight. Peter and his mama had lived in New York since he was a baby. For most of his young life, they'd shared a tiny apartment with his aunt and uncle, his grandparents, a cat named Box, and, for a time, another woman whose connection to the family the boy never quite figured out. She eventually left, though, and for that Peter was thankful because he never did like her much. She stared at him when she thought he wasn't looking.

Peter's mother, Nataliya, and her sister had come with their parents to the United States when he was a newborn. They traveled all the way from Russia to the land of promise. At night, when he had trouble sleeping, his mother would tell him the story of crossing the big ocean in the bowels of the ship. Her words always came out choppy, like the waves that hit the side of that boat. He begged her to tell him the story in English, longing for her to take to the language of their adopted land, but she claimed it unnecessary.

"It is good for *you* to learn English, and to adapt to it without accent," she would tell him, brow furrowed as she looked sternly down at him. "And you must continue to speak Russian with me, and French with your grandparents. You are a smart boy—the smartest I know. That must not go to waste."

Peter would nod his head in agreement, mostly because he knew that arguing with his mother was pointless. His was a family of scholars, and his mother made sure that he continued in the same ways of knowledge that had come before him.

"Your father was a smart man," his mother murmured when he sweated over the arithmetic she placed before him. "He was well known for his brains, and you will be too, my darling."

The boy wanted to believe her, but deep down he had his doubts. He had never met his father, and so he was left only to his own imagination as to who the man really was. Peter suspected his father was much less than his mother made him out to be. He got this feeling based on the pitying looks his grandparents exchanged with one another whenever his mother spoke of the man whose blood ran through his own veins. And, of course, the most telling information came from his aunt, Yulia, who when dressing him one hot Saturday afternoon while his mother was out working, shook her head and *tsked* her tongue as she tried to smooth his unruly hair.

"You shouldn't worry too much about the way you look," she whispered. "Your mother is right about the need to be smart. You will need to rely on your brains in life because your face will only hold you back like your father's face held him back." She'd clapped her hand over mouth then, as though the words had slipped accidentally from her tongue.

Peter asked about his father more after that, but his mother refused to give any information. And so, he continued his studies because deep down he believed his aunt must be right.

Truthfully, he didn't mind all the lessons. He liked that he could speak several languages, though his grasp of English caused him more and more anxiety as time passed. When they left the safety of their small flat, the boy found himself wishing that his mother would speak the language of the land surrounding them, rather than requiring him to do all the talking in public. Instead, he obeyed her requests to converse with strangers, even though it made him feel sick inside. The only time he pushed against her prodding was when they went to the market and she required him to walk to the counter and order the bread. He would beg her not to make him do it, but she insisted.

"Why shouldn't you talk to those people?" she would ask. "You live in America now where you have the right to speak boldly to people whenever you wish."

Perhaps this was true. He didn't like to argue with his mama. But even then, the boy knew he was different. He knew that he didn't look like everyone else, and America was just like Russia - if you didn't look the same, then you couldn't possibly be treated the same.

And so, several times a week, Peter would approach the countertop at the market on the corner with his heart hammering in his chest as the large woman behind the counter looked down at him with sharp eyes. Her hair was always tied back in a dirty, white kerchief, her thin lips pressed in a straight line. She had dark hair above her upper lip, and her face was pockmarked, with leathery skin sagging into a double chin. The woman behind the counter's greatest annoyance in life came from the ugly little boy who timidly asked for bread while his mother hovered in the corner.

It happened the same way every time.

"Two loaves of the black bread, please," he whispered, and a sly smile would turn her mouth upward revealing yellowed teeth.

"I'm sorry, but I can't hear you," she replied. The boy knew she heard him the first time. This was just the game she played.

"Two loaves of the black bread, please," he'd repeat, louder this time. If no one else was in the market with them, this was the point where she gave in and passed him his bread. But if there were other customers, she liked to keep the game going.

"I'm afraid that it is difficult to understand you, boy. Maybe because of the way your mouth sits off to the side like that. Or I could just be distracted by the hair that's growing down around your eyes. I need you to speak more clearly."

This was when Peter would blink hard against the tears of humiliation that gathered in the corners of his eyes—eyes that sagged downward in the outside corners and sat above a crooked nose and a mouth that wasn't even remotely close to being centered. He would ask a third time, practically shouting his request, which only drew the stares of the others in the market. Finally, she would hand him his bread with a wicked smile, and he'd turn and flee from the marketplace.

"Why do you make me do that?" he asked his mother one afternoon after a particularly humiliating run-in with the bread lady.

"Because, Pasha," she said, which was the name that only his family called him. She looked at him closely that day, and for the first time the boy realized that his mother saw him the same way everyone else did. She saw his deformed face, his unruly hair that grew in patches from the corners of his eyes to the back of his neck with large bald spots in between. She saw him for what he really was—a monster, a freak. The look in her eyes passed quickly, but it was there long enough for the boy to know the truth.

"Because I need you to be strong on the inside," his mama finally said, her voice stronger this time. "I need you to be strong so that you can face anything that comes your way."

Maybe it was the way that she had looked at him, or perhaps Peter was just tired of being scared, but a sort of determination welled up in him that day. He never again had to blink back tears when visiting the bread lady.

Of course, everything changed the year the circus came to town. That was also the year that both of his grandparents died within days of one another. His grandmother went first. One morning, she just didn't wake up. Three days later, his grandfather went to sleep for the final time.

"He died of sadness," Peter's mother and aunt said, as they covered him with a sheet and wiped their eyes.

Two months later, the posters appeared all over New York City. The circus had arrived, and just in time. Peter's mother was struggling to make ends meet. They were tired and hungry, and they needed a distraction.

The day to visit the circus had finally arrived, and Peter had spent the morning lost in his own imagination. He was the hero of the Big Top. No one jeered or screamed when they looked at his face. No. They thought him wonderful, a marvel worthy of praise. The vision was always the same, and it always ended with his mother staring at him from across the room, exasperated at his distant gaze and lack of response. Peter blinked hard, pushing the daydream out of his mind and willing his eyes to focus on his mama.

With a sigh, Nataliya shook her head, dropping her arms to her side in frustration.

"Right now, I need less thinking and more moving, *sinok*," she said, the edges of her words softening a bit as the look on her face dissolved from annoyance to mild amusement.

"Sorry," Peter apologized again. "What do you need?"

"I need you to go get dressed!" Nataliya answered. "If we are going to make it to the circus on time, we must leave soon. Hurry please!"

Peter's eyes lit up as he leapt from the chair. He stacked his books neatly in the corner of the table, then rushed to the little room he shared with his mother and his aunt to change into the clothes that had been laid out on the bed. He had one pair of good pants that were neither scuffed nor dirty. They were a bit too short, but Peter would never complain about such a thing. He knew that clothing was an extravagance over which his mother could not fret.

Closing the door, Peter began dressing as quickly as he could, though his webbed fingers always made the task of changing a little more difficult.

In the sitting room, Nataliya picked up Peter's books and looked over his work. He had been writing again, stories always working their way up and out of his fingertips when he was supposed to be solving equations. With a sigh, Nataliya looked at his paper. Usually, he wrote his stories in French or Russian, but for some reason lately he had taken to writing in English. Truthfully, she understood a great deal more of the English language than she let on, for she believed that knowledge was power, and she made herself a constant student. But she hadn't had time to master the English alphabet, so reading was out of the question. But as she glanced at his page, Nataliya marveled at the way her son's deformed hands had managed to form such beautiful letters.

"I think he doesn't want you to know what he's writing about," Yulia murmured from the corner.

"*Psh*. Don't be foolish," Nataliya replied. "He is just experimenting."

"Perhaps," Yulia replied with a shrug. She held her hands still, the yarn spilling over the side of her lap and into the basket by her feet. Winter was coming, and she wanted to make sure her nephew had a proper hat to keep him warm.

With a sigh, Nataliya dropped the paper back onto the stack and turned, crossing her arms. "I know what you think, *Yulichka*," she said, annoyance creeping its way back into her voice. "I know that you think I'm just looking...for *him*. But that's not what I am doing." Yulia cocked her head to the side and narrowed her eyes at her younger sister.

"Of course, it's what you're doing," she shot back. "Just admit it, Nataliya. You're trying to find him, and what a foolish thing to do." She bent her head back over her work, her slender fingers weaving the yarn in and out. Nataliya sighed and glanced out the window.

"So, what if I am?" she asked quietly. "What's wrong with looking?"

Yulia didn't respond for a long moment, the pregnant pause filling the space between them. "And what would you do if you found him?" Yulia asked. "With Pasha by your side, what would you do? Have you really thought about this—about how it could affect your boy?"

Nataliya clasped her hands together, then dropped them to her sides with a shrug. "A boy should know his father," she said with a shrug. "If I can make that a possibility for him, then I owe it to him to try."

"Yes, but Nataliya, Pasha doesn't *know*. He knows nothing about his father because you've never told him. You're taking him on this outing as though it is a gift to him, but you are putting both of you at some risk, wouldn't you agree? Honestly, sister, taking Pasha to the circus when he looks like he does is foolish! And you're doing this all for your own selfish gains, not for your son."

Nataliya sighed and slumped down into the chair by the table. She slowly traced her finger over the scratches and cracks in the wood as she blinked back tears. Yulia rested her hands and looked at her sister across the room.

"Do you remember the first time that you introduced me to Kolya? Back home, in St. Petersburg?"

Nataliya leaned back against the wall and let out a long sigh. "I remember," she answered.

"It was cold that day, and we were all bundled in our warmest clothes. You and I were walking home from school, and he followed us. I got frustrated and turned and told him to go away, but you shook your head and grabbed his hand."

Nataliya smiled. "I had invited him to walk with us, but he was scared of you. Everyone was a little scared of you back then."

Yulia sniffed, raising her chin proudly. "I do not know why," she answered. "I was very friendly to everyone I met."

Nataliya just smiled in return. Yulia waved her hand and continued talking.

"You told me that Kolya was a dear friend to you, and you wanted he and I to become friends as well." Yulia bent her head back down and began moving her fingers in and out, her knitting needles dancing in tandem to the rhythm of her hands.

"I remember," Nataliya said quietly. "You couldn't see his face because of the way he had pulled his hat down over his eyes and his coat up over his mouth."

Yulia nodded. "Yes. And I had also never noticed him before, despite the fact that he and I had gone to school together for years. He had been made invisible, and for good reason, sister."

Nataliya sighed and turned her face away.

"He broke your heart when he left, Nataliya," she said quietly. "And he left with one purpose in mind—to protect you and Pasha." Yulia paused, leaning forward so that her eyes bored into her younger sister's. "Your responsibility now is to protect your son—not to find his father. You need to teach Pasha to make himself invisible, like Kolya did." Yulia's voice was quiet but firm. "You do not need to look for him. It is a fool's mission. You must protect Pasha." Nataliya pushed to her feet, shaking her head back and forth, her eyes flashing. Yulia held up one hand and gave her sister a stern look.

"Your son is not like everyone else, Nataliya. You know this. He is a smart boy, yes. Perhaps the smartest boy I've ever met—even smarter than his father was. But, my dear, he is more terrifying to look at with each passing year. And you know how those deformities turned out for Kolya—how they drove him to make the choice he made. You must help Pasha learn to hide, and you can't do that if you parade him out in public for everyone to see just because you have some foolish notion of finding..."

"Mama?"

Nataliya froze as Pasha stepped into the room, his eyes locking helplessly with hers. Yulia turned and saw her nephew and cringed. His hair stood in tufts around his head, his deformed features registering confusion and pain. He did not look human, and Yulia knew that if she, his own flesh and blood, could hardly stand to look at him, then the world would become an increasingly unsafe place. She just wanted her sister to quit fooling herself that she could find Kolya, convince him to come home, and somehow create a life of normalcy for her child.

"Pasha," Yulia said, reaching for his hand. Peter pushed his hands into his pockets and looked at his mother.

"I'm not feeling well," he said softly. "I think I should just stay home and not go to the circus."

Nataliya blinked back tears and tossed a glare at her sister. "Nonsense!" she said. In a few short steps, she crossed the room and put her hands on her son's shoulders. The way that his back curved made one shoulder a little higher than the other.

"We have been looking forward to this all week. We'll go together, you and me, and we will have a wonderful time. Okay?"

Peter forced his mouth into a crooked smile and nodded his head slowly. He would do this to please his mama, but he knew that he would not see the magic anymore.

"I'll go change my dress and we'll leave, yes?" Nataliya said, smoothing his hair back out of his eyes and tipping his head back so she could look him fully in the face. "Today is for you," she whispered. Yulia sighed in the corner.

Nataliya stepped past Peter, and with a glare at her sister, she disappeared into the bedroom to change. Peter stood uncomfortably, unable to look at his aunt. He tried to process the words he had just heard, running them slowly through his head.

"But, my dear, he is more terrifying to look at with each passing year. And you know how those deformities turned out for Kolya—how they drove him to make the choice he made."

They were talking about his father, and they were talking about *him*. Suddenly Peter felt sick to his stomach.

He walked to the table, the lilt in his steps a further reminder of all the ways that he would never be the same as everyone else. He picked up the story he had been writing and cringed at the opening line.

"*Once, there lived a boy named Peter the Great. He ruled a magnificent land atop a glorious mountain where the sun shined brightly every day. He was a good and kind ruler, loved by all who lived in his kingdom. Handsome and confident, Peter the Great was the kind of man everyone wanted to know...*"

His cheeks flushed, Peter glanced over his shoulder at his aunt who stole quick looks at him through fluttering lashes. Peter sighed and folded the thin paper into a small square, sticking it in his pocket. He would drop it in the gutter on the way to the circus later.

Peter turned to find his aunt now looking at him without attempting to hide her gaze. Her eyes were soft around the edges, her lips pressed into a thin line. Yulia was prettier than her younger sister. She had a rounder figure and fuller features. Where Nataliya stood stooped and thin, Yulia held her head high, and despite the lack of food, she held more weight, which gave her a more pleasant appearance. Her hair was blonde, and she painstakingly set it in elaborate curls atop her head every morning.

Despite her beauty, however, Yulia had never married. Peter heard his mother talking to their neighbor about it once, years ago when his mother thought he wasn't paying attention.

"She's a difficult woman, my sister. Very loyal to those she loves but intimidating to everyone else. I'm not sure any man could ever have kept up with her."

Yulia stared at him for a long moment, then opened her mouth to speak but was interrupted by the bedroom door swinging open. Nataliya swept into the room, her thin frame wrapped in a dress that engulfed her. Her cheeks were wet, but her mouth was set in as sincere a smile as she could muster.

"Now then, my boy," she said, reaching for Peter's hand. "Shall we go have an adventure?"

Peter nodded, wishing desperately that he had not overheard his aunt's words minutes before, longing to recapture the hope and joy he'd felt when he woke up that morning. But one look at his small, ugly hands wrapped inside his mother's delicate grasp and Peter knew he'd never get that back. All innocence had fled the moment he heard his aunt speak out loud what he'd known all along.

Abandoned by his father, Peter was a freak.

They made their way down the street, Peter's eyes down as he walked close to his mother's side. He kept his face turned toward her, hoping to conceal his features from passersby. Nataliya blinked continuously, forcing back the tears that threatened to spill to her cheeks. She was determined to redeem the broken pieces of this day.

They rounded the corner, stepping off the cobbled street and into the dusty field, and then they stopped. For the first time since they'd left their small flat, Peter moved from his mother's side, his mouth agape as he took in the sight of the bright white tent stretching high into the crystal blue sky. His heartbeat quickened as a glimmer of anticipation returned.

"Oh my," Nataliya breathed next to her son. She had been to the circus once as a child, many years ago in her native Russia. It was December 1877, and she had just turned eleven years old. Her father had bounded home that afternoon, bellowing for her and Yulia to put on their finest dresses.

"We are going to a show like nothing you have ever seen my girls!" he'd said with a grin, dancing inside the foyer of their fine home while her mother looked on through narrowed eyes from her rocking chair in front of the fire. Nataliya had joined her father's dance, but Yulia, ever loyal to mama, had held back, trying to determine if she should put up a fight to please her mother or join in the dance to please her father.

Dancing over to her mother's chair, Nataliya's father had grabbed her hands and pulled her up, ignoring her protests and glares and dragging her across the floor.

"I have a ticket for you as well, my darling, if you feel up to it," he said, a tender smile splitting wide his face. Nataliya's mother had lost a child three months earlier. She had carried the baby nearly to term when the movements inside her womb grew still. A piece of her soul was buried the day they laid Nataliya's tiny baby brother to rest under the tree behind their home. Since then, a quiet heartache had settled over the house. But this day had been the spark to bring them all back to life.

An Italian horseman by the name of Gaetano Ciniselli had brought in fabulous acts from around the world, setting up a brilliant building right there in St. Petersburg where performers and animals stunned onlookers with their skill and bravery. Her father had explained to them all that he had seen and heard of the St. Petersburg Circus, and when he finished, both Nataliya and Yulia looked at their mother, hope flooding their eyes as they waited for her response. She looked down for a long moment, then turned her bright eyes upward and offered a thin, but genuine, smile.

"It sounds very nice," she said, her voice barely a whisper. "I suppose it would be good for me to join you."

And that had been the night where healing had begun. For the first time since her heart tore in half, Nataliya's mother smiled again, and with her smile came a flood of joy that worked like a salve to the wound in each of their hearts.

That was also the night that Nataliya fell in love with the circus. The lights and the feats of wonder, the smells and the sounds—all these things worked together to form a sort of obsession in her. Nataliya spent hours upon hours of her life envisioning what it must be like to be part of the show. She longed for a skill, some sort of talent, that would allow her to run off and join the circus.

But her father insisted on schooling and learning, waving off any fanciful notions of acrobatics or showmanship.

"That's all lovely to watch on the occasional night out, my dear," he would say, "but the circus is reserved for those who don't know enough to strive for a better life. The circus is for freaks and half-wits. My daughters will not fall to the level of the circus."

And so, it had remained nothing more than a passing fantasy that filled her head in between the long hours of studying and reading. Of course, the irony of it all was that her education had meant nothing when they disembarked the ship in America. No one cared that she could speak French, Russian, and German fluently. No one cared that she was a master at Russian grammar, and that she could solve complex equations in minutes. Despite all her painful efforts at studying, Nataliya found herself working in the factory like everyone else, and when the dust of the move settled, she found she no longer had the free time to learn and study the language of the land in which she now lived.

Nataliya pulled herself back to the present and looked down at her son, taking in the way that the sunlight glinted off his dark eyes, hidden beneath the hair that grew thick around his drooping lids, and she felt that same glimmer of hope from so many years ago begin to sparkle. There was magic in the circus; she had seen it.

Nataliya and Peter walked across the field, Peter forgetting all about hiding behind her sleeve, and they stood in line outside the tent. A little girl in front of them turned when she felt Peter and Nataliya step up behind her. She took in the sight of Peter and gasped. She grabbed her mother's hand, who looked first at Nataliya, then down at Peter. She turned a disgusted face back to Nataliya.

"Come, Rachel," the woman said, her voice cold and hard. "Stay close to me now."

Peter slipped back behind his mother's shadow to conceal himself. Nataliya shifted her gaze down to him, her heartbeat quickening against the anger she felt at the woman's ignorance and the pain she felt at her son's shame. She shook her head slowly.

"It doesn't matter what that woman says, you know," Nataliya murmured, her native Russian slipping from barely parted lips. "She has no idea what she's missing not knowing you." Nataliya forced the corners of her mouth into the faintest attempt of a smile. "She is actually quite blind. If she could truly see, then she'd be able to look right into your beautiful heart." Peter could feel the little girl in front of them peeking around the folds of her mother's skirt.

"Ignore the stares, Pasha," Nataliya continued. "You look right through them. Those people, and what they may think of you, mean nothing."

Peter nodded his head because he suspected that was the response she needed to see. But he could sense the fear and the doubt in her eyes, and he knew she didn't believe her own words any more than he did.

The line began to move as the outside gate opened and the ticket master shouted that tickets were now for sale. Nataliya stood and smoothed out her skirt, while Peter drew in long gulps of air. He peeked up to see the little girl staring at him, but her eyes no longer registered shock or fear. She looked curious, and perhaps even a little apologetic. A fine layer of freckles dotted her nose, and her hair hung in long, red waves around her face. She turned her mouth up in a soft smile, taking Peter entirely by surprise. Before he could think to smile in return, she had turned back around and was moving forward with her mother, each step leading them closer to the tent up front.

Slowly they approached the main gate where a bald man sat in a ticket booth calmly taking people's money and handing them tickets in return. When it was their turn, Peter ducked his head and pressed into his mother's side, afraid that if anyone associated with the circus saw him, they'd forbid him from entering. Nataliya, fingers trembling, dropped her coins into the man's hand, and he gave her two tickets with a gruff "Enjoy the show." Nataliya reached down and squeezed her boy's hand.

"Today will be a good day, Pasha," she whispered. Her eyes flitted from his face and moved around the grounds outside the tent, sweeping the area quickly. Peter followed her gaze, wondering what they were meant to be looking for.

Peter pulled away from his mother's side and took in the sights around him. While many people were heading for the main tent like he was, some had broken off and headed for the smaller, adjacent tents on the circus lot. Children strolled the grounds clutching brightly colored balloons while their parents bit into large hot dogs. Others held sticky caramel apples or plates piled high with gooey pie, and Peter watched with envy as they indulged in the sugary treats. He knew his mother didn't have the money for such things, so Peter said nothing, pulling his eyes away and focusing instead on where they were headed.

Together, Nataliya and Peter approached a man standing at the flap of the tent holding a wooden box where they dropped their tickets. Peter couldn't help but gape, trying to determine if he was real or made of wood. He was a handsome man, with dark hair and eyes, his red coat closed tight with golden buttons. It hung in pointed tails in the back, and stretched down his long, stick-like legs, which were wrapped in tight, black pants. The man's eyes shifted to Peter, and a strange smile tilted his mouth upward. Peter yelped and leapt back toward his mother.

"Enjoy the show," the man said, breaking his stiff stance and nodding at Peter, who tightened his grasp on his mother's hand and nodded in return.

They stepped into the tent and waited a moment, allowing their eyes to adjust to the darkness inside. Immediately, Peter was overwhelmed with an unfamiliar smell. It was buttery and salty, and his stomach immediately growled. A man with a cart stood between them and the stands, and in his hand he held out a thin bag filled to overflowing with fluffy, white puffs, glinting beneath slick butter.

"Popcorn?" the man asked.

Peter gazed at him quizzically, then looked up at his mother whose mouth had pressed into a thin line. She turned to Peter. "Tell him we are sorry, but we can't pay for that today."

His face turning a deep red, Peter relayed the message to the man who smiled and held out his hand more forcefully.

"Everyone who walks through these tents gets popcorn," he said with a wink. "Whether they can pay for it or not."

Peter took the bag reluctantly, then looked at his mother and told her what the man said. She began to protest, and the man raised his hands and shook his head.

"Please tell your mother I insist," the man said. He turned and filled another bag, offering it to the next family who walked through the door.

"Interesting," Nataliya murmured. Peter stared into the bag in his hands.

"Popcorn," he whispered. He pinched a single kernel between his fingertips, then placed it on his tongue. His eyes widened as the unfamiliar taste filled his mouth. He looked up at Nataliya with raised eyebrows.

"He called it popcorn," he said. He held the bag up. Nataliya smiled and nodded.

"Yes," she said. She took a piece and popped it in her mouth. "I've had it before."

Peter grabbed another piece and put it in his mouth, delighted at the sensation it spurred inside.

Nataliya smiled. She raised her eyes and scanned the long rows of stands surrounding the center ring. "Come, *sinok*, let's find a place to sit before it gets too crowded."

"Mama let's not sit too close to the front, please," Peter pleaded, feeling panic well up in his chest as he took in the sights of all the people filing into the tent through the various open flaps around the arena.

Nataliya grabbed Peter's webbed hand and began walking him around the ring to the seats that were still open. They climbed to the top row, and Peter leaned back, hoping his face was hidden enough in the shadows to stay inconspicuous. Nataliya's heart constricted at her son's fear of being seen. She reached her hand into the bag of popcorn in his lap and popped a few more kernels into her mouth. Closing her eyes, she chewed slowly. When she opened them back up, Peter was looking at her curiously.

"This is delicious," she said with a wink. "Nothing bad could possibly happen when you're eating something that tastes as good as this."

Peter plunged his hand into the bag and quickly took another bite of popcorn. He chewed carefully, letting the buttery kernels crunch between his small teeth. He tried to identify the taste, to compare it to something he had experienced before, but he found himself so overwhelmed that he couldn't speak. He closed his eyes like his mother had done and simply let himself experience it. After a few moments, he opened his eyes to find his mother staring at him, her delicate features alight with tenderness and a twinkle of humor.

"Well now," she said with a wink. "I'd say that treat alone was magic enough for the day, would you agree?"

Peter smiled in return, a genuine smile that made his head feel light. The knot in his stomach unwound a little bit as he took another bite.

"Why haven't we eaten this before?" he asked, his mouth full.

Nataliya reached over and dug out another small handful of popcorn, cradling it in her hand and delicately placing one kernel on her tongue. After she'd chewed and swallowed, she shrugged her shoulders.

"I don't know," she replied. "Except that I think some things are better experienced at a certain moment in time. I don't know if this would have ever tasted so good coming from the corner market, the smell all mixed together with the fish and meat and sweaty men."

Peter smiled and shoved more popcorn in his mouth.

"No," Nataliya said thoughtfully. "I think you needed to taste this for the first time today." She leaned close so that her mouth was against his ear.

"Remember today as a good day, my boy," she said quietly. Peter turned and stared into her eyes. "Promise?" He nodded slowly.

They sat quietly after that, watching as the tent filled with people until finally it seemed it would burst at the seams. Eventually, the seats around Nataliya and Peter began to fill. A large man who smelled of factory smoke slid onto the bench next to Peter. Their hips touched, and he glanced over, his mouth open to apologize when he froze, staring at the form of a little boy who looked as grotesque and deformed as anyone he'd ever seen. Peter turned his face away, but then realized that the man would just be staring at the bald patches on the back of his head, and his cheeks grew hot.

The man turned to the big woman sitting beside him. On her lap she held a chubby little boy who clutched two fistfuls of popcorn, moving his hands back and forth to his mouth one at a time until the popcorn had left him with nothing but greasy fingers and a lap full of crumbs.

"Look at the freak sitting beside me," the man whispered, his low voice just loud enough for Peter to hear. Nataliya looked toward the center ring, lost in thought and oblivious to the words that were burning their way into her son's tender heart.

"Oh, my heavens," the woman exclaimed. She pulled her fat son tighter to her chest as he plunged his hand back into the bag of popcorn.

"Don't stare at him, Clive," the woman whispered.

"I can't help it," the man hissed back. "I ain't never seen nothin' like it. I wonder if he's a part of the show. I hear they got all kinds of freaks at this circus. Unique freaks—not like that Barnum fellow who makes up his weirdos."

"Hush, Clive."

Peter kept his face turned, forcing himself to remain expressionless, but he could feel the couple staring at him.

"He can probably hear you talkin' about him, poor little thing," the woman said with a cluck of her tongue. The man shifted next to Peter so that the two of them weren't touching anymore.

"I'm keepin' an eye on this one during the show," the man murmured out of the corner of his mouth.

Just then, the tent went dark. The woman gasped, and Peter reached over to clutch his mother's hand, swallowing hard over the lump that had formed in his throat.

When light exploded into the tent and the performers began their acts, Peter briefly forgot the conversation he'd overheard. He was, instead, transported into the world below. He watched in awe as the trapeze artists, *The Fabulous Flying Fernandez'*, flipped and spun through the air like birds, suspended without fear above the world. Their costumes were so breathtaking that Peter found himself leaning forward, willing his eyes to focus in for a closer look. Señora Fernandez's leotard matched her husband's shirt and pants, both made of bright blue, red, and green sequins, which caught the lights and made them look like human torches from where Peter sat. Señor Fernandez let go of his wife's hands and she flew gracefully above the stands, a collective gasp drawing the air from the room. She landed lightly on a small platform and lifted her arms triumphantly as her husband swung away. The tent exploded in applause.

Peter barely had a moment to catch his breath when the light shifted to the right and a man in a long, black cape stood with shoulders pushed back, his white beard glinting in the spotlight.

"And now, ladies and gentleman," a voice boomed from thin air, "Prepare yourself to be amazed by…" A dramatic pause filled the air as the sound of drumbeats drew the audience to the edge of their seats. "*Mortimer the Magnificent, Master of Magic!*"

Peter gasped as the man in the black cape threw up his arms, tossing a bouquet of white flowers into the air. The flowers promptly turned into birds which flapped frantically in a line around the width of the tent as children shrieked with delight. Mortimer the Magician continued to amaze, pulling a rabbit out of a hat, cutting a squirming woman in half, and then finally disappearing into thin air.

Peter clapped his conjoined fingers together in great delight when the elephants came lumbering into the tent, swinging their trunks in rhythm while the band played a raucous tune. When their trainer, a tall, lanky man wearing a top hat and long coat, whistled loudly through his fingers, the elephants all sat down together, their back legs splayed outward to make space for their large backsides. The audience roared at the sight, and the elephants seemed entirely smitten with the attention, their heads held high and large smiles pasted across their faces. Peter laughed, but as he did so, he blinked back tears because he'd never seen anything so beautiful in all his life.

For her part, Nataliya spent most of the hour watching her son. She soaked in the delight that spread across his face like sunshine splashed across a spring day. She fought the urge to reach out to him, to pull him into her side and hug him tightly because she didn't want to interrupt the magic of the experience. For that brief moment in time, she allowed herself to imagine that she had a normal child—a child who looked like the others instead of bearing the same features as his father, a man whom she loved with her whole heart, but whom she had never really been allowed to share with the world.

The first time Nataliya met Kolya, she had gasped out loud, much the same way most people now reacted to her boy. Kolya had been so different from anyone she had ever seen before, and she'd been quite taken aback by his monster-like features.

They were children back then, barely fourteen when their paths crossed in the schoolyard. Kolya was a student at her school, but he'd been sequestered to a small room where he learned mostly on his own, a teacher coming in at intervals to check his progress and administer exams. He mostly came and went in secret, though there had always been rumors of the freak that was hidden in the corner closet.

The day Nataliya met Kolya, she had stayed at school later than usual. Her marks on her last test had not been to her father's approval, and so he had set up regular tutoring sessions with her teacher until she fully understand chemistry and its use and function in the world.

"Some may find it foolish to educate girls, but I am not one of those people. I will not raise stupid young ladies given only to fashion and finding a husband. You will learn everything you can learn so that you can hold your head high, do you understand?"

It was the same speech he always gave when one of the girls came home with marks that were less than perfect. Nataliya's father expected more of his daughters, and he had one daughter who met his high standards every time.

And then he had Nataliya.

When she ran into Kolya in the dark hallways of the school, she drew back in shock. His face had been illuminated by a single light, highlighting his crooked nose and bulging eyes. Hair grew in patches on his head, and down his forehead, giving him the look of a rabid, mangy dog.

"Forgive me," he said to her when she drew back in disgust. "I didn't know anyone was here."

The teacher rushed from the room then and grabbed Nataliya's arm, hustling her down the hallway to the door exiting outside.

"You didn't see anything," she hissed as she pushed Nataliya out the door into the icy winter air. Nataliya nodded and turned to respond, but the teacher pulled the door shut with a definitive clink, and Nataliya was left quiet and dumbfounded.

It took her another month before she could find him again. In that time, she could not stop thinking about the boy hidden in the shadows, his face seared into her mind. But it had been the look in his eyes that made her long to see him again. It was a sad sort of look, but also one of curiosity. One glance told her that he craved interaction, and for reasons she could never identify, she felt an odd sort of fascination with finding the boy in the shadows.

Because he was meant to be invisible, Nataliya had to hide in order to meet him. She huddled, shivering, behind a tree late one afternoon, watching the door and waiting for it to open. Finally, when the street outside was quiet and the sky quickly darkening, the shadow of a boy slipped outside the building. He turned, and she watched him talk briefly to the teacher, but she couldn't make out their words. He nodded and turned to walk down the street. His head was wrapped in a hat and scarf so that there only opened a slit where his eyes would be. He walked quickly, head down, and Nataliya pushed forward until she was steps behind him. He whirled around to face her and froze.

"*Privyet*," she said, her voice weak. He nodded his head but didn't speak. Nataliya took another step forward, and the boy backed up.

"What is your name?" she asked.

"K-Kolya Pavlovich," he replied. She smiled. His voice was soft and gentle, not at all what she expected coming from his crooked mouth.

"I'm Nataliya Andreevna," she said. She reached out her hand and after a brief pause, he reached out and grasped it weakly. And that had been the beginning. That innocuous, uneventful beginning led to more walks, always hidden in the shadows, where Nataliya learned what it meant to truly love someone for who they were on the inside. It didn't make sense then, and wouldn't make sense later, but as Nataliya looked down at her son and felt her heart swell beyond what she could comprehend, she found herself once again thankful for the brief and good love she had with an unexpected man so many years ago. She refused to dwell on how it all ended—about the pain surrounding their last days together, or the way that Kolya looked at her when he said goodbye.

"Mama?"

Nataliya shook her head and focused on her son's face. He was pulled back slightly, trying to obscure himself in whatever shadow might be available. All around them people stood up, stretching and laughing, talking loudly about their favorite parts of the show. The large man next to Peter stood, his eyes trained on the top of Peter's head. Nataliya felt her heart sink as the man shook his head in obvious disgust, and she resolved once again to try harder to master the English language so that she could speak directly to such people when necessary.

"The circus is over now. Can we go?"

"LADIES AND GENTLEMEN!"

Both Nataliya and Peter snapped their heads up to see the ringmaster down below in the center of the ring. His feet were surrounded by sawdust and bits of hay, evidence of the acts that had only just preceded him.

"The main event may be over, but there is still plenty left to see on this fine afternoon! For just two pennies, you may enter our fabulous, fantastical sideshow where you will see some of the most amazing, the most terrifying, the most unbelievable freaks of mankind ever to walk the planet. This goes beyond anything in your wildest imagination, folks! From the world's tallest man who will mesmerize you with his skill on the harmonica, to the most beautiful girl in the world with the voice of an angel, and every kind of unique talent in between—this part of the show is a once in a lifetime experience! Continue your experience right through that doorway!" He gestured dramatically to an open flap in the tent, and Peter watched as a crowd of people funneled into a line to get through.

The ringmaster waited a short beat, then threw his hands up and spun around in a circle, the flaps of his coat fanning outward and swinging around his body. Peter watched him go, his eyes drawn to the man as though there were magnets on his back.

"What did he say, *sinok*?" Nataliya asked. She had caught only snippets of the man's announcement, his words eventually blurring together to leave her confused and unsure.

"He said there is a…um…a sideshow in the next tent. But it costs two pennies to get in, so we should just leave."

Nataliya looked down at the stream of people walking out of the tent toward the sideshow tent, and she felt her heartbeat quicken. This was truly why she'd come, what she hoped to find. And suddenly her sister's voice echoed in her head.

"*A fool's errand…*"

Nataliya swallowed hard, at war with herself as she stared at the flap that led to the adjoining tent. "Yes," she replied softly. "Let's go home."

They stood and walked down the stands until they reached the bottom. Peter reached over and touched the rim of the circular ring. He thought of the acts he had just seen, magical displays of talent and awe, all of which had been confined to this small circle. But they had seemed so much more vibrant earlier. It was as though the memory was already dulled in his mind.

"Come, Pasha," Nataliya said gently, a hint of sadness clinging to her words. She reached out her hand, and Peter grabbed it. Just as they turned to go, they found themselves facing the ringmaster himself. He stood smiling, his hands clasped in front of his large, round belly. Nataliya jumped in surprise.

"Pardon me," the man said, bowing slightly. Nataliya nodded and offered him an embarrassed smile. Peter tried to pull behind his mother. The man looked around and smiled at him. Peter shrank back, attempting to hide his face as much as possible.

"Hello there," he said. "I am Monsieur Beaumont, and this is my show." He raised his arm and swung it out over the empty tent.

His voice was gentle, though it wasn't necessarily kind. There was an edge to his words, as though they were being carefully clipped, one at a time. Peter heard the rounded sounds of the man's vowels and knew immediately that this was a Frenchman.

"How did you and your son enjoy the show?" he asked Nataliya. She cocked her head to the side, trying to decipher what he said. She squeezed Peter's hand, a signal that she expected him to be a part of this conversation.

"He wants to know how we enjoyed the show. He's French," Peter whispered, his eyes down. He could feel the man staring, trying to get a good look at his ugly face.

Nataliya smiled and gave a small nod of her head. "Very good," she replied in stilted English. She could have answered him in French and the three of them carried on a conversation in that language, but something told her to hold her cards close to her chest with this man. Monsieur Beaumont drew himself up, a smile spreading across his face.

"That is wonderful," he said. "Just wonderful." He turned his gaze back to Peter and bent over at the waist.

"Tell me, young man," he said. "Why are you hiding from me?"

Peter shrugged his shoulders, his face burning hot as the man looked at him with eyebrows raised.

The man knelt down so that he was eye level with Peter. He raised his finger, beckoning Peter to step away from his mother's side. Nataliya watched the exchange curiously. Peter slowly pushed away from her enough to face the man full on.

"Do you not want to see our fabulous freaks?" the man asked. Peter's eyes drifted to where the last of the patrons were now exiting toward the second show. He shook his head.

"Too many people in there," he said, his voice just above a whisper. "And it costs too much." As soon as he said that last part he wished he could take back his words. His mama wouldn't want him sharing such personal information. He looked up at her, prepared to apologize when the man interrupted.

"You know," he said, straightening back up. "I think I would like to escort you to the next show personally. You will be my guests, and I'll take you to the special backstage area where you can watch the acts in the shadows without anyone seeing you."

Peter's eyes widened. The man smiled at him, then jutted his chin toward Nataliya. "You'd better tell your mother what I said and see what she thinks," he said.

Peter translated the man's words quickly. Nataliya studied her son's face, then turned to the man with the jet-black hair and mustache. "Why does he want to do that for us?" she asked. "He doesn't know us, and we don't know him."

"She wants to know why you would do that," Peter said, looking up at the ringmaster.

"Tell her that I don't think anyone should have to miss out on a life-changing experience. Not at my show. Also," he paused, his fingers fiddling with the point of his mustache, "I think you might be surprised, my boy, at what you will see in that tent."

Peter translated the man's words the best he could, though he wasn't sure he could interpret the meaning behind them for his mother. Nataliya drew in a long, slow breath, chiding herself for being so foolish to bring her son here and possibly expose him to the greatest shock of his life without any warning. Her hands trembled as her heartbeat quickened.

"Do you want to go?" she asked Peter. He nodded. Nataliya gave his hand another squeeze. "Okay then," she said, her voice quavering. "I suppose it would be rude to turn down this generous offer."

She turned to Monsieur Beaumont and nodded her head with one, sharp movement. Her breathing came out in short gasps as her stomach twisted in knots. What would they find behind the flap of that tent? *Who* might they find?

Monsieur Beaumont clapped his pudgy hands. "Delightful!" he said. "Please, do follow me." He swung around, the tails of his coat swinging behind him like a welcome parade, drawing Peter and Nataliya forward. Peter gripped his mother's hand, nervous and unsure about the man in front of them, but otherwise entirely intrigued by what lay in wait on the other side of the tent.

"Don't let him know that you speak French," Nataliya whispered.

Peter squeezed his mother's hand. They approached the tent's edge, and Monsieur Beaumont spun back around, his chin held high as he looked down at Peter over his prominent nose. His mustache twitched as his mouth spread into a wide smile. Peter caught sight of a few greys inside the man's perfectly combed facial hair. They glinted in the faint overhead light. It was unsettling, as though he were peeling back a layer of the genteel ringmaster and seeing something he ought not see.

"Behind this curtain are wonders to make you gasp," Monsieur Beaumont said, eyebrows raised and voice hushed. He leaned forward so that his eyes were more level with Peter's. "I think, my dear boy," he said, "that you will be entirely amazed. Perhaps more so than anyone else who will enter today."

Peter swallowed hard and nodded. Monsieur Beaumont stood and with a mighty flourish of his hand, he swept the curtain aside to reveal a room bustling and teeming with people. Their backs were to Nataliya, Peter, and the ringmaster, and for that Peter was thankful. He was able to absorb the scene without the shame that so often accompanied him in a crowded room.

In front of the preoccupied group were several stages, crudely built from rough-looking wood. Some of the stages even had bars erected as walls in order to keep their inhabitants in. Peter gasped as the sea of people parted momentarily and one of the cages came into view.

Inside stood a man in chains, his matted hair hanging down to the back of his knees. His body was covered in spiked rods, all of which pierced through his skin at odd angles. He had nails through his earlobes and spikes lacing through the skin from his wrists to his shoulders. His muscles bulged, arms so strong that it looked as though melons had been stuffed inside. A giant hoop hung from his lower lips, and his bare chest was pierced with two long spikes driven straight through his nipples.

The man tugged and pulled at his chains, his mouth foaming as guttural growls dug from his throat and filled the space above the people's heads. Small children hid their faces in their mother's skirts, and proper women clucked their tongues, turning their faces away in shame from the spectacle. Men, young and old, all watched, some with a great deal of humor and others with an air of indifference, as though the spiked man were not an anomaly but rather an everyday vision of which they were quite familiar.

"*Bozhe Moi,*" Nataliya breathed next to Peter, and she pulled him closer to her side. "What is this?" she gestured at the man and shot a hard look at Monsieur Beaumont, who looked back at her with a knowing smile.

"Tell your mother that I know it can be a bit of a shock. He is our very own Goliath."

Nataliya narrowed her eyes as Peter quietly translated. He pulled his gaze away from the snarling man and turned his head. On the next stage over sat a man without legs or arms. He was merely a torso, strapped to a chair. He wore a fitted tuxedo, the suit tucked tight up underneath him, and a top hat stood awkwardly on top of his long head. He was saying something as he swiveled his head from side to side, looking directly in the eyes of all who stopped to gawk. Peter strained to hear his words.

"The full-orbed moon with unchanged ray
Mounts up the eastern sky,
Not doomed to these short nights for aye,
But shining steadily."

Peter pulled back and looked up at Monsieur Beaumont curiously. The man stared back at him with a half-smile, which lifted up just one side of his mouth making his moustache look as if it had been drawn crookedly onto his face.

"That's James Adams, our limbless man and resident poet. He's always got his face in books. I believe today he is quoting Henry David Thoreau."

Monsieur Beaumont waved his hand and directed them to follow him. Nataliya looked warily around the room. They walked along the tent's edge, careful to stay behind the crowd, until they could tuck behind the stages. There were fewer people here, all of them employed by Monsieur Beaumont, and each too preoccupied with the people on the stage to notice Peter and his mother gaping at them in shock.

"Follow me," Monsieur Beaumont said, and they walked through the shadows behind him until they came to the next stage. They stood to the side, out of sight of the watching patrons, but in full view of the woman who sat upon the wooden platform, her face turned upward with an air of haughty pride. She was a large woman, the largest Peter had ever seen, and she sat primly on a very small couch. Her hair hung in ringlets around her wide face, and rolls of flesh hung from the folds of her dress. She sat still, her eyes pinned to the back of the room. Peter could see beads of sweat trickling down her neck and dripping into the soft flesh of her cleavage, which was pushed out of the top of her dress so that it seemed her head just rested on it. Her eyes shifted down just as the three of them came into view, and she locked gazes with Monsieur Beaumont. Peter glanced at him and took in the way his eyes flashed. He looked back at the fat lady and saw her jaw clench. Then a forced smile pushed back her ample cheeks, and she turned her face back to the audience and began speaking in a high-pitched voice.

"Romeo! Oh Romeo!
Wherefore art thou, Romeo?"

The words of Shakespeare came out warbled, as though the woman were fighting back tears. She looked away from the ringmaster and continued the famous soliloquy. Monsieur Beaumont looked back at Peter and Nataliya, drawing in a deep breath.

"That is Miss Clarabelle, our resident fat lady. She's quite the actress, that one." He threw her a sharp look once more. "She once commanded the center stage of her hometown in Mississippi. That was, of course, long ago when she looked much different." He looked down at Peter and offered a quick wink. "She's found a place here, though. A place where she can be who she was meant to be despite how she looks."

Nataliya pulled Peter close to her side and tossed a wary look at Monsieur Beaumont. She scanned the room with a measured combination of hope and dread, but her search came up empty. She hadn't found who she was looking for after all, and perhaps that was a blessing. She squeezed Peter's shoulder gently.

"I think it's time for us to leave, *sinok*," she said. "Please tell him I said thank you for the lovely day."

Peter nodded, pulling his eyes away from Miss Clarabelle and her sad monologue. He opened his mouth the relay the message when he was stopped by a song drifting over the room. The melody was haunting and lilting, like the gentle trill of a waking bird.

"Beautiful girl
Most lovely in
All of the world
White-gold hair
Milky-white skin
So fair
Beautiful girl."

Peter craned his neck, looking for the source of the voice, his heart tapping wildly against his small chest. Taking a step away from his mother and dropping her hand, Peter pushed to the side and came into view of a small platform. He stared, mouth slightly open, and took in the sight. He could only see her from the side, and he suddenly wished he was out in the crowd looking at her straight on.

"Now that, my boy, is my most special act and prized possession. You're looking at my Emmaline, The Most Beautiful Girl in the World." The ringmaster's voice tore through Peter, and he jumped at the sound. He glanced at the man who had a knowing smile plastered across his face. It was a smile that made Peter feel uncomfortable. He looked back at the stage.

In the middle of the platform stood the girl. She was young, perhaps not much older than he was. Her long, golden hair hung down in thick curls around slender shoulders. Her pale skin glowed under the lights, and her cheeks were flushed from all the stares. She grasped her hands primly in front of her slender waist. Her blue dress was cinched tight with a satin bow. Peter thought she looked like an angel.

"What a lovely girl," Nataliya breathed from behind Peter. He felt his face flush, and he stepped back to his mother's side. Monsieur Beaumont watched him closely.

"She is the beauty of the Big Top," he said. The melody of her song continued to play over them, her voice innocent and pure and entirely captivating. The audience all stood in rapt attention as she finished, the final note echoing through the tent and drowning out all other sounds. When she was done, a round of applause burst forth. Peter wanted to clap, but he found that he could not draw his eyes away from her profile.

The girl smiled politely and curtsied before resuming her position with hands clasped, her chin held high. She didn't make eye contact with anyone. She stood regal as a princess above them all.

"Emmaline has been with us since she was a baby. Poor child. An orphan." Monsieur Beaumont *tsk'ed* his tongue and shook his head. "It is her great benefit that we found her when we did. We have given her a better education than any schoolhouse could have ever provided. And she is seeing the country! What opportunity for a child." He leaned down until he was eye level with Peter.

"We can offer the best in the world to anyone with a unique look or talent. They simply have to join us."

Peter looked into the man's eyes, momentarily mesmerized. Nataliya watched the exchange uneasily, wishing she could better understand the words passing between her son and this man.

"Do you understand what I'm saying?" the ringmaster asked. Peter hesitated, then shook his head no. But a strange sensation grew inside his stomach. Whether it was hope or dread, he could not tell.

"I'm saying that I think you are about as unique as they come. Out in the real world," Beaumont gestured his hand, "I imagine no one really appreciates who you are. But here," he stood, his arms stretching out wide and a smile splitting his face, "here we know the value of a young man. We know that he is worth more than his outward appearance, and we allow him to shine for who he truly is. Here, we show the world that freaks and anomalies have purpose."

Monsieur Beaumont stopped and drew in a deep breath. He glanced at Nataliya, who watched him warily, clearly conflicted as she grasped her son's hand. Leaning back down, Monsieur Beaumont got eye to eye with Peter.

"My boy, we could make you famous. You could travel with us and show the world that you are more than simply what's on the outside. I mean, look at Miss Clarabelle!"

Peter turned to look again at the fat woman who had stood up, her monologue approaching its dramatic end. She panted under the strain of her performance, and she was now sweating profusely. The audience watching her seemed both in awe of her passion and disgusted by her appearance. Peter didn't know quite what to think.

"Miss Clarabelle was a nobody when I met her. She was a broken woman who had once tasted fame, but then lost it, and the loss left her in the state you find now." Monsieur Beaumont stood up and hooked his thumbs in his jacket, rocking back on his heels slightly. "We gave her purpose once again, despite her grotesque appearance. And we can give you a purpose as well."

He looked at Peter who stared back, wide-eyed. "You...you want me to join the circus?" Peter asked. Monsieur Beaumont nodded once, then looked at Nataliya.

"I have a feeling it will be hard to convince your mother, though," he said with a thin-lipped smile. He bowed slightly to Nataliya and gestured for the two of them to follow him out of the room. With one last glance back, Peter took in the sight of the girl. Just as he looked her way, she turned her head and glanced down, and their eyes met. She did not flinch or react at all to his appearance, and Peter felt as if his legs would fall out from beneath him. She looked away, and he turned to leave, his heart beating rapidly.

The three of them made their way back into the dimly-lit main tent and stopped. Monsieur Beaumont turned and looked down at Peter.

"We will leave tomorrow morning at sunrise," he said. "We're headed south this time. Our first stop will be in Virginia—a beautiful state this time of year." He drew in a long breath, then let it out slowly. "If you would like to join us, be at the train station, platform 13, by 6:00."

Peter blinked, trying to fully grasp the man's invitation. "Can my mother come with me?" he asked.

Monsieur Beaumont narrowed his eyes and rocked back on his heels again. He contemplated the ramifications of extending the offer to the boy's mother. It meant one more mouth to feed, which meant more money out of his pocket. But then he considered how he could boast of not only having the most beautiful girl in the world, but also the ugliest boy in the world, and he decided to take a chance.

"Of course she can," he said, pasting a smile on his face. "I would expect nothing less." He looked at Nataliya, who glanced between the two of them with growing annoyance.

"I'm certain I could find a job for your mother," Monsieur Beaumont continued. "The two of you could travel the country together." He gestured his hand toward the exit of the tent, where sunlight streamed into the darkness. "Tell your mother what I said and do your best to convince her to join you. But listen to me."

Monsieur Beaumont leaned down, his hands on his knees as he searched Peter's ugly little face. "If she refuses, then I want you to consider coming on your own. You won't ever find another opportunity like this, my boy. I can change your life. You will simply need the courage to get on that train."

"Come, Pasha," Nataliya said, interrupting the conversation. She tugged his hand, and he followed her reluctantly toward the tent exit. "Stop looking at him and tell me what he said this minute." She squeezed his hand.

"Tell me, son," she said again. They stepped out into the sunlight and squinted, letting their eyes adjust for a moment before retracing their steps toward home. "What did he want from you?" she demanded.

Peter stopped and looked up at his mother, astonishment, hope, and confusion all swimming in his eyes.

"He...wanted me to join the circus," he said.

Nataliya wiped her eyes and sat up, moonlight streaming through the window above her bed. Her eyes drifted to her boy, sound asleep on the small cot next to her. His hands were curled around his face, and his hair fell over his eyes. His mouth was slack and his breathing even, and for the briefest moment Nataliya imagined him to be a normal child. But the sight of his fingers, webbed together in an awkward fashion, tugged her back into reality. She slowly lowered back onto her thin pillow and remembered the night Peter was born.

It had been one of those unusually warm autumn nights - *Baba Leto*, as it was known in her native country. It was the rare event when impending winter winds were pushed out with one last blast of warm air, and the city came alive for a few days in late October.

Nataliya had been seventeen years old and was the shame of her father's life. Her mother had tried to be understanding of the circumstances, tried to figure out where they had gone so wrong that her youngest daughter had a secret affair with an unnamed boy and wound up pregnant. Her parents both flitted around her, avoiding long conversations for different reasons—her father because he was so angry with her foolishness, and her mother because she simply didn't know how to respond.

Only Yulia had been sympathetic, and in a rare act of allegiance, she had not revealed Nataliya's secret. Yulia had not told her parents of Kolya, and in so protecting Nataliya she had earned a position of confidante over the few months leading to the baby's birth.

On that late October day, Nataliya had ventured outside for a few brief moments to enjoy the weather. Her father wouldn't let her stray far, too ashamed and unwilling for her to be seen in her "shameful" condition. So, she would slip into the trees behind their flat and wander in and out of the trunks, her feet crunching in the leaves already fallen to the ground, their cycle in life completed. It was here that Kolya found her that last day. He'd stepped out from behind a tree, and Nataliya had screamed in surprise.

"I'm sorry! *Prostiye menye!*" He cried, holding up his hands. His fingers were webbed together in the middle, and his hair had grown all the way down over his eyes and onto his cheeks. He looked like a wolf come to life, but when he pushed the hair from his face and Nataliya could see the center of his eyes, her heartbeat slowed. She stepped forward and looked intently at him, her stomach twisting into a knot. She rushed to him and fell in his arms, a sob escaping her throat.

"I didn't think I'd ever see you again," she'd whispered. Kolya stood still, his arms hanging stiffly by his side. She tilted her face up to his.

"After today I don't think you will," he replied. His eyes were hard, almost completely devoid of emotion, so unlike him. It had been his gentleness that had drawn her to him, the softness in his gaze and tenderness of his words that had made his outward appearance melt away and allowed her to fall in love with the real man inside.

"What do you mean?" she asked. He pushed away from her and took a step back. His eyes drifted to her protruding stomach and then back to her face.

"I'm sorry," he said, his words stilted and uncomfortable. It was as though his mouth were full of hot coals, burning away the edges of his voice so that everything came out heated and hard. Nataliya's hand settled uncomfortably on her stomach.

"I didn't mean to put you in that position," he gestured awkwardly to her midsection. "I never thought anyone would give themselves to me the way that you did." His words came out like a tremor, as though he was just barely keeping the emotion behind the surface. "You were the only person who ever looked at me like a real person, and I let that carry both of us to a place that wasn't safe. I shouldn't have done that."

"Kolya, no," Nataliya said. She reached her hand out toward him, but he took another step back, his face hardening into a fixed stare.

"I probably shouldn't have come here," he continued. "I should have just disappeared to save you the trouble."

Nataliya dropped her hand and shook her head slowly. "I...I don't understand," she stammered.

"I'm leaving tomorrow."

"Leaving?" She furrowed her brow.

"I'm going to America. A man from an American circus found me. He's offered me a job there." Kolya tossed her a wary glance. "I will be one of his freaks."

"But...why? Why would you do this? You already work for the circus here. You're a good worker for them. Why would you leave?"

Kolya had been employed by the St. Petersburg circus to help as a stagehand. He stayed hidden high in the rafters, above the crowds, and he made sure that everything from curtains to lights to confetti all ran on time. He'd long been told that he could make a better name for himself as one of the freaks, but he'd staunchly refused, claiming he had too much dignity to stoop to such a level.

"Why are you doing this, Kolya?" Nataliya asked, grimacing at the tightening in her abdomen.

"To get away from you," he replied. Nataliya's blood ran cold in that moment, and she struggled to draw in a breath. This man whom she'd given herself to looked lost now, small and angry and torn. It had been months since they'd seen one another. Once Nataliya's father had discovered her secret, he had forbidden her to leave. Her only hope of communicating with Kolya had been through her sister. Yulia had taken several notes to him, but he'd never written back. Yulia said it was because he didn't want to cause any more trouble for them, but now Nataliya began to question the truth of that.

Kolya's face was dark that day, but Nataliya had seen the conflict slicing through his eyes.

"I don't believe you," she'd whispered through trembling lips.

"I have to get away," Kolya said with a frustrated sigh. "I can't stay here. I can't do it. I won't."

"Then wait for me," Nataliya interjected. Kolya froze, his lips parted. "Wait for me, please," she begged, reaching her arms out to touch him. "I'll have the baby, and as soon as it is safe, you and I can run away together. We can make a life as a family."

Kolya pushed her arms away and shook his head, his hair flopping around his face. "No," he replied. "It would never work."

"Why not?"

"Look at me, Nataliya!" he'd growled, leaning over her. His eyes grew red, tears springing to the corners. "I *am* a freak! What kind of life can I give you? The only place I belong is with other freaks like myself. I cannot jeopardize your life anymore. I just won't."

He stepped back again, this time out of her grasp. "I didn't come to talk about this," he said. "I came to tell you goodbye." He turned to leave, and Nataliya cried out after him.

"Please, Kolya! Please don't do this! Please!" She'd watched his slumped shoulders move quickly in and out of the trees until he finally disappeared over the crest of a hill, and she slid to her knees, sobbing. Finally, spent and sore, she'd pushed to her feet only to discover that her skirt was soaked and her stomach taut. Three hours later, throat raw and body spent, she'd pushed one final time and her son had been released from her womb. No longer tethered in safety to her inside, he was forced into a cruel world.

Nataliya shifted in her bed and looked down at her child once more. It had been twelve years since that day—the day when her dreams were shattered and realized all at once. The day when her mother gasped in horror at her only grandson, and her father shook his head in disgust, mumbling about how she'd birthed a cursed child because of her deception and deceit. That was the day that Nataliya had realized her purpose on this earth—it was to give her son more than his father had been given. She would not hide Peter away the way that Kolya's parents had hidden him. She would not leave him without options in the world. She would fight for him, and she had. She had fought with her parents until they were finally able to see beyond Pasha's outward appearance and fall in love with the smart little boy on the inside. She had fought to ensure that a cruel and judgmental world really looked at him, not allowing people the opportunity to continue their days in ignorance, as if those who looked just like them were the only people worthy of daylight and public spaces. Nataliya had spent more than a decade fighting for her boy, and now there was a new fight.

She'd told Yulia of their offer to join the circus after dinner and had been met with predictable scoffs.

"Of course, you won't do that," Yulia had said with a wave of her hand. Peter had gotten up from the table and grabbed his cat, whisking him out of the room so that they could speak in private. Nataliya hadn't answered her sister, but rather sat back in her chair, picking at the skin around her nails.

"You're not considering it. Surely!" Yulia exclaimed.

Nataliya shrugged. "I don't know."

Yulia slammed her hands against the table and leaned forward, fire dancing in her eyes. "That is the wrong answer, sister!" she hissed. "You will not consider this. You will not run away with the circus. You won't make that boy a spectacle to be jeered and laughed at. He is better than that. You *know* he is better than that."

"Of course, I know that!" Nataliya snapped. "I know that better than anyone else in this world. But perhaps, *sister*," she paused and searched Yulia's face. "Perhaps *this* is the way that we prove that."

The conversation had spiraled from there, ending with Yulia storming from the room in tears. And Nataliya had gone to bed, but not to sleep. There would be no sleep this night.

She blinked her eyes and stared hard at her boy. "What do we do?" she whispered. As if he'd heard her, Peter opened his eyes. He blinked several times, then pushed up on his elbow and stared intently at his mother.

"Hi, Mama," he whispered.

"Hi," she replied.

"You can't sleep tonight?"

Nataliya reached out and ruffled his hair gently. "Perhaps I will soon," she said. "I'm just...thinking."

"You're thinking about if we should go?"

Nataliya nodded, her eyes filling with tears. "I don't know what to do, my darling," she said. "What do you want?"

Peter blinked several times. "I want to go," he said. "But I do not want to leave *Tyotye* Yulia alone."

"Yes," Nataliya said. "That's a terrible choice to have to make."

"Do you think she would go with us?" he asked, his eyes lighting up with hope.

Nataliya looked at him gently and shook her head. "No, my dear. She would not be able to come with us. We would have to say goodbye to her."

Peter slumped back onto his bed, his arm flopping over his forehead as he stared at the ceiling above him.

"We shouldn't go then," he whispered. As he said this, tears pricked at the corners of his eyes. Nataliya reached down and stroked his cheek.

"I believe you're right, my darling," she said. "This decision is bigger than you or I alone." As she said it, Nataliya felt a knot settle in her stomach. Perhaps it was the fleeting hope that if they went, she might still find Kolya. She sighed and laid her head down.

Both Nataliya and Peter jumped when their bedroom door opened. Yulia appeared in the doorway, her frame filling the small space, moonlight giving soft illumination to her face. Her cheeks glimmered, and her chin trembled.

"If you must go," she said, her voice quaking. "You have my blessing."

Nataliya sat up and shook her head. "No, *sistrenka*," she answered. "We've decided that we won't go. We won't leave you."

"Well, that is just the thing," Yulia replied. "It is I who am leaving you." She stepped into the room and stood tall, pushing her shoulders back as she looked down at them through tear-filled eyes. Nataliya stood to her feet and crossed her arms.

"I don't understand," she said, her brow furrowed as she studied her sister in the dim light.

"I was going to wait to tell you, but this seems to be the most appropriate time. I have had a marriage proposal, and I've decided to accept."

Nataliya snorted. "A marriage proposal?! From whom?"

Peter looked back and forth between his mother and aunt, trying to keep up with the conversation.

Yulia sniffed. "From Jack Adams." Her words came out loud, as if she had to push hard to get them past her tongue.

"Jack Adams?" Nataliya cried. "Jack Adams, the man who sells newspapers on the street corner?"

Yulia nodded, shifting her eyes away from her sister's. Nataliya shook her head slowly.

"*Nyet*," she said. "I don't believe you. You're just saying that because you think it will make me want to leave."

Yulia sighed, her shoulders slumping slightly. "It is true that he asked me, Nataliya," she says quietly. "He asked me several months ago, and he has been persistent in his asking. I've only just decided to say yes."

"But...but why?" Natliya asked, her eyes wide. "You always said you would never marry unless it was a man worthy of your love. Is this man worthy of it? Of you?"

Yulia wrapped her robe tighter around her waist, crossing her arms to stave off a chill. "Perhaps he is," she said quietly. "He's a man of simple means, but then I am a woman of simple means as well. And he hasn't stopped asking, which makes me believe that he really does want to marry me."

"Yes, but do you really want to marry him?" Nataliya asked.

"I want to find some freedom, and I want you to find it as well." Her eyes teared up again as she glanced at Peter, then back at her sister. "I'll learn to love him," she said with a slight shrug of the shoulders.

Nataliya's arms fell to her sides. Peter stood up and walked slowly to his aunt, wrapping his arms around her waist. He buried his face in the soft flesh of her midsection, feeling the tremor of her arms as she returned the embrace.

"I love you," he whispered, tears wetting the fabric of her night robe.

Yulia grabbed his face and tilted it up toward hers. She pushed his hair back so that she could look into his eyes, drinking in the sight of his deformed face.

"You have been the greatest surprise of my life, Pasha," she whispered, blinking hard to keep the tears at bay. "You are much more than this outer shell. Remember that when they put you on stage in front of people who don't know anything about you. Remember when they stare that they are only seeing a little piece of who you are. The best parts of you are hidden."

Peter nodded and fell into her again. He felt his mother step up behind him, and the three of them were suddenly wrapped tight, intertwined as they bid their goodbyes. Finally, Yulia pushed back.

"You will write me, of course," she said. "You'll tell me about all of your adventures and the places you see in this great, big land." She gave Peter a little wink. "And I expect fantastic stories from you, young man. Entertain me with all the things you see. Make me feel as though I'm there with you."

Peter smiled and nodded his head, wiping his eyes with a shaking hand. "I promise," he said. "I'll write you in three languages!"

Yulia chuckled, the sound coming from her parted lips a mixture of sadness and joy. "I expect it," she said.

Turning to Nataliya, she reached out and put her hands on her younger sister's shoulders. "I hope you find what you're looking for, *sistrenka*."

Nataliya lowered her head and wept quietly. "I'm sorry," she whispered.

Yulia pulled her chin up and looked tenderly at her. "I love you," she said. They stood still under the weight of the moment before Yulia pushed herself back up.

"*Nu tak*," she said, looking around the room. "You need to pack quickly, and you need to try to get a little sleep. Tomorrow will be a long day for you both."

Nataliya nodded. She grabbed her sister's hand and gave it a squeeze. Yulia turned and left the room, slowly closing the door behind her.

Peter turned to his mother and swallowed, afraid to speak, unsure if any sound would actually escape his lips.

"Well then," Nataliya said, swiping her hand across her cheek. "Let's pack a bag, *sinok*. We have an adventure waiting."

ACT TWO

TWO

Peter stepped off the train and blinked in the morning haze. A fog left the air around the open ground thick and moist, and Peter shivered as it nipped at his bare arms. Despite the fog, the roustabouts were already pulling out the long poles and fabric, carefully carrying it all above their heads in a long line so the tent wouldn't hit the ground and get dirty. Within a few hours, Peter knew the tents would be up and the parade would begin in town. Monsieur Beaumont had told him that he could observe a few more shows, and then he would be expected to perform.

"I didn't bring you on to watch," the Frenchman had said. "I brought you here to work."

Peter felt a flutter in his stomach when he thought of standing on his own stage to be gawked and stared at by strangers.

"Mornin', Pete."

Peter turned and craned his neck upward to look at the towering man who ducked out of the opening in their train car and unfolded to his full height, his head so high in the fog that his face looked fuzzy. Peter nodded and offered a half-hearted smile.

"Morning," he answered.

This man, the one they called the tallest in the world, was the first one to greet Peter weeks ago when he stepped onto the train, eyes wide and heart thumping. Beaumont had immediately separated him from his mother, telling them that performers were required to bunk with performers. Since Nataliya had been assigned as a kitchen hand, she slept on a separate train and helped to set up the mess hall before the performer's tent arrived in each location.

Fighting back tears, Peter had followed Monsieur Beaumont to the drafty train car that he was to share with his fellow sideshow performers. When they entered, two of the smallest men Peter had ever seen scrambled to their feet and glared at him. The smaller of the two, Manny, who stood only as tall as Peter's waist, shook his head adamantly.

"Sorry, Boss Man," he said. "Ain't no room in here for one more." His sidekick, Jessop, crossed his arms and pressed his mouth together in a tight scowl so that his face looked a little like a squished grape. Beaumont had calmly looked down at the two men, his singing little-person duo, and clucked his tongue.

"Now, gentlemen," he tsked. "That's no way to treat my new, prize act. You'll find space for him. Perhaps you," he jutted his chin toward Manny, "can slide on over to your brother there and share his bed."

"He ain't my brother!" Manny exclaimed. "I told you that a hundred times! Just cause we're both small don't mean we're related. I don't claim this stinkin' sack of—"

"I'll get him set up, Boss Man," a voice had rumbled from the corner. Peter had shifted his gaze to see the silhouette of a man who looked to be folded in half sitting on a hay bail in the darkest corner of the train car, his knees up by his chin and long arms crossed over what appeared to be even longer legs. Beaumont had given a nod of his head, then turned to look down at Peter. He tossed a glance of annoyance at Manny and Jessop, who had begun shoving one another, Jessop's feet slipping from beneath him and sending him crashing to the dirty floor. Manny chortled as Beaumont rolled his eyes.

"*Imbeciles*," he muttered, turning on his heel and marching out of the train car, leaving Peter behind with his new roommates. Manny and Jessop had retreated to their corners, both cutting their eyes at Peter.

"What's your name, kid?" the man in the corner finally asked. His voice was lower than Peter anticipated. It rolled out of him like the early thunder of an approaching storm.

"Peter."

The man nodded then. He'd stood up, his body unfolding like an accordion, and walked across the room to Peter, who stared up in fascination. He looked like a giant, his body stooped, and his head bent forward so he didn't hit it on the top of the car. He'd stepped in front of Peter and looked down at him, then thrust his hand forward.

"Robert James," he said. "But everyone calls me Tiny."

They'd pushed crates around after that and tossed Peter a pillow and blanket. He'd made his bed on the floor in the only empty corner of the train car, sitting down and pulling his knees to his chest. Manny and Jessop grumbled bitterly as they moved their own beds closer together.

"Keep your swamp breath away from my side of the bed," Manny had growled, as Jessop leaned over and shifted his blankets around. Jessop responded by letting loose a loud fart right in Manny's face. The two tumbled to the ground in a heap of swear words, elbows and knees flailing. Peter had watched, eyes wide, then shifted his gaze to Tiny, who looked back at him with amusement.

"Welcome to the circus, kid," Tiny said that night.

Now, two weeks later, Peter had grown to depend on Tiny. Standing beside him, Tiny stretched his arms out and opened his mouth in a wide yawn. "How'd ya sleep, Pete?" he asked.

"Better," Peter answered. He was still unused to the clanking of the train wheels beneath his head. And the sound of Manny and Jessop snoring rivaled that of the train.

Tiny nodded. "Well, that's good then," he said. He leaned against the side of the train car and stuck a cigarette in his mouth, the smoke stick looking oddly small between his giant lips, which were tucked beneath a bulbous nose. Tiny was neither deformed, nor was he handsome. He was just...big.

"Tiny?" Peter asked, looking up at him. "How'd you end up in Boss Man's circus?"

Peter had figured several things out through observation these first two weeks of traveling in Monsieur Beaumont's circus. First, no one called Beaumont by his name—they all referred to him as 'Boss Man.' And Beaumont didn't appear to have the respect, nor the fear, of his employees. People more regarded him with a weary disdain.

Tiny looked wistfully off in the distance as a tendril of smoke floated from his cigarette and up around his face. "Well," he began, "it wasn't too different from the way you ended up here, Pete," he said. "Guess you could say I was discovered." He offered Peter a little wink. Peter sat silently staring up at him, waiting for more information, so Tiny drew in a deep breath and let it out slowly as he sank to sit down.

"Been about ten or twelve years since I joined up with old Boss Man, I reckon," Tiny began. "He found me a lot like he found you... while I was watching his very own show. It was smaller back then, but still mighty magical."

"So, the circus came to town and you went to see it?" Peter asked.

"Somethin' like that," Tiny nodded. "I didn't want to go, but my sisters—I had two of 'em—they heard about it, and they had a way of makin' me do things I didn't want to do." Tiny chuckled.

"*You gotta take us, Tiny!*" they whined, tugging on my arms and blinking up at me with their big eyes. I gave in 'cause I loved those girls as much as I loved anyone in all my life." Tiny shifted his gaze up at the morning sky.

"Your sisters called you Tiny?"

"Sure did. Everybody called me that from the time I was a schoolboy and grew like a weed in a rainstorm one year. Had a schoolteacher who looked up at me after a few weeks when I'd clean passed her height and said 'Well, no one can ever call you tiny now, can they?'" He smiled. "The rest of the kids in class thought that was so funny, they all started to call me Tiny. The name stuck."

Peter smiled. "It's funny," he conceded.

"I'm told it's called irony," Tiny said with a laugh.

"So, you watched the circus with your sisters and Boss Man found you, then?"

"Right as rain, Pete. It was a morning a long time ago, one of them sunshiney days that makes you squint just to see what's in front of you." Tiny screwed up his face and squinted, narrowing his eyes to slits and wrinkling his nose. Peter grinned.

"I squinted into the morning sunshine as the calliope whistled out its happy little song, and before I knew it I was staring straight in the eyes of a real lion! I ain't never seen nothin' like that before. Then the girls ridin' on horses came by, and some of them were standin' up while they rode." Tiny looked down at Peter. "You been to the parade yet?" he asked.

Peter shook his head. "Boss Man says he doesn't want me to go. Wants to save me for the show." Peter's cheeks grew hot.

Tiny pressed his lips together and narrowed his eyes, pausing for a brief moment. "Well," he finally continued, "even though my sisters had to drag me to that circus, I gotta say I was pretty amazed. I was real caught up in it all as the acrobats came tumbling by. It was a different troupe then. They weren't nearly as good as the Amazing Freemans, but it was the first time I'd seen anything like that!

But the real kicker for me was when the clowns came 'round the bend. I tell you what, Pete, they were the funniest sight I ever did see. They tripped and tumbled all over one another, and even though I'd told my sisters I wouldn't enjoy myself, I had to laugh right out loud at them." Tiny leaned forward and put his elbows on his knees.

"It was while I was watching the clowns that everything changed. I was wipin' the happy tears from my eyes when I felt a polite tap on my elbow. I looked down at a man standing by my side. He had jet-black hair, and a black mustache that looked almost like it had been pasted on his face. He stared up at me with a big, ol' smile.

"*'Excuse me,'*" he said, and his words sounded real strange, like they were tight in his throat or somethin'.

'*If you don't mind my asking,*" he said, "*how tall are you?*'"

Peter laughed at the way Tiny did a near perfect imitation of Boss Man's accent.

"I answered him real quick and turned back to watch the clowns tumble around the corner. And that man tapped my elbow again. I looked down at him, and he was holdin' his hand out to shake my hand, so I took it and he held on tight."

"*'My name is Monsieur Beaumont,*" he said. *'I own this circus. I think you would be a wonderful addition to our show.*'" Tiny leaned back and clasped his hands in his lap. It was quiet for a beat before Peter spoke up.

"And what did you say?" he asked.

Tiny threw his head back and let out a hearty laugh that sounded almost like the bleat of a sheep. "Well, whatd'ya think I said?" he cried out. His arms swung out to the sides. "Here I am, Pete. Same as you."

He dropped his hands and the smile quickly faded from his face. "Old Boss Man can be real persuasive when he wants somethin'," Tiny said quietly.

"So, you left your sisters?" Peter asked.

Tiny nodded. "And my mama, too," he replied. "My daddy died when I was fourteen, and I'd been doin' my best to scrape some money by to help mama and the girls. And all of the sudden, there stood that funny little man with his strange voice and a promise to help me care for my mama and sisters using nothin' but the height the good Lord had seen fit to give me!" Tiny sighed.

"I left the next mornin'. Wiped the tears off my sisters' faces and told them not to worry. 'Bout tore the heart right outta my chest, but my Mama made sure I knew she loved and supported me."

They were quiet for several minutes before Peter spoke up. "Mama and me had to leave my Aunt Yulia behind," he finally said. "I miss her." He blinked back tears and turned his face away, embarrassed to be crying in front of Tiny.

"Well, it ain't an easy thing to do, Pete," Tiny said. "Nobody likes to say goodbye to the people they love."

Peter swiped a hand over his eyes and nodded, swallowing hard. Tiny clapped his hands on his knees and pushed to a stand. The cigarette in his mouth was now a stub. He pulled it out and flicked it beneath the train car.

"I'm gonna stretch my legs a bit before things get crazy 'round here. They're gonna be movin' the train into the train yard in town in just a little bit."

Peter nodded, craning his neck to look up at Tiny.

"Wanna come walk with me?" Tiny asked. Peter shook his head.

"I think I'd like to stay here and watch, if that's alright," he answered.

Tiny smiled. "I s'pose that's no problem. Just stay close to the train, hear? Don't go wanderin' around while they're settin' up. You're liable to get stepped on." Tiny winked at Peter, and the boy smiled back at him.

"Okay, Tiny," he answered. Tiny clapped a hand on his shoulder and walked away, his long strides taking him straight into the fog until it swallowed him up.

Peter kicked a rock with his shoe and turned to walk down the length of the train.

"Pst! Hey, kid! Pete!"

Peter turned to the voice calling to him from between the train cars. At first he couldn't see anyone, but then he saw Manny's head peek out. Jessop poked his head out beneath Manny's.

"Wanna have a little fun?" Manny asked, eyebrows raising up and down. The two men were constantly pushing and shoving and causing a scene, unless they were on stage where they were dressed in pristine suits and sang in such perfect harmony that grown women sometimes wept listening to them. They were known as the Sensational Singing Duo from Saskatchewan, though in reality Peter believed them both to be from somewhere in Ohio.

"What kind of fun?" Peter asked.

"You ever ridden an elephant?" Manny asked. His mouth split into a wide grin, revealing yellow-stained teeth. Peter shook his head slowly.

"Well, then today's your lucky day, little man!" Jessop laughed. Manny beamed next to Jessop.

"Boss Man likes us to give the elephants proper exercise every once in a while. It's good for their health to run and stretch their legs, especially after long stretches on the train. So today is elephant race day!"

Manny and Jessop glanced at one another sideways. Jessop snickered.

"I don't...know," Peter said. "Tiny told me to stay close to the train."

"Aw, that's cause Tiny is afraid of elephants. Won't go near 'em. Plus, he just don't want you wanderin' around by yourself. But you'll be with us, so it's fine," Manny said.

"Yeah, come on, Pete! You gotta get the full circus experience if this is gonna be your life from now on. You can't keep sittin' in the background watchin'. You gotta live a little!"

Peter swallowed hard and looked from Manny to Jessop. "Well..." he hesitated. "Alright, I guess."

"Atta boy, Pete!" Manny said, laughing out loud. "C'mon, let's go get the beasts out before it's too late to run them."

"Stay close to us now, kid," Jessop said, his eyes darting left and right. "We gotta get to the elephants without ol' Hank catchin' us.

That old coot is mean as a snake, and he takes his job as elephant man seriously."

"Doesn't he know about the Boss Man telling you to run the elephants?" Peter asked. "Why can't he see us?"

Manny glared at Jessop and jabbed at his ribs. Jessop jabbed back at Manny and the two scuffled for a brief moment. "Naw, kid," Manny finally said. "It ain't that he can't see us. He knows Boss Man's orders. He just don't like 'em, so we try to avoid him on race days."

Peter nodded slowly. He felt a funny roll in his stomach.

Staying close the train, the three hustled down the track until they reached the last car. Manny and Jessop darted into the fog, and Peter followed as quickly as his uneven gate would allow. The giant animals were staked in the ground about ten yards from the end of the train, and the area around them was empty.

"They'll be around here soon to set up the feeding tents. Now's our chance," Manny whispered. Jessop nodded. He grabbed Peter's arm and pulled him to the first elephant, the smallest one of the group.

"Pete, this here's gonna be your girl. This is little Maisie. She's the sweetest thing you ever did lay eyes on."

Peter leaned back and looked up at Maisie. She stared back at him with indifference, then flicked her ear and turned away, raising her chin almost as though she was disgusted by the humans before her. Jessop chortled.

"And I," Manny said, "am gonna ride Miss Bella here." He patted the knee of the largest elephant in the group. Bella chewed slowly on some hay as she glanced down at Manny.

"Hold on now!" Jessop protested. "Why you?"

Manny turned to Jessop and sneered. "Because I'm better on the back of an elephant than you are, and you know it."

"The hell you are!" Jessop cried. He swung out a short arm and cracked it across Manny's jaw. Manny shoved back and in a moment, they were both rolling on the ground as Peter and the elephants looked on.

"Uh...excuse me?" Peter interrupted. "Why can't we all ride?" he asked. "There are seven elephants here. Don't they all need the exercise?"

Manny and Jessop scuffled and pushed until they were both back up on their feet. "Oh, uh...no. That ain't the way it works. Boss Man only likes us to take them out two at a time so's we don't overwork them. It's Bella and Maisie's turn."

"Oh," Peter said. "Well, then you two ride. I'll watch."

"Naw, Pete," Manny said, shaking the dirt from his hair. "You gotta ride! You gotta experience this thrill. Everyone does it at least once. That's how to really become one of us!"

"I s'pose I could let y'all two ride," Jessop grumbled. "Someone's gotta get the beasts movin' from the ground, 'specially since Pete don't know how."

Manny smiled haughtily and nodded his head. "Very right," he said, tapping his finger on the tip of Jessop's nose. Jessop lunged at him, and Manny scuttled away. He grabbed the long, wooden ladder that lay in the grass at the elephants' feet and laid it up against Maisie's side.

"Alright then, Pete!" Manny said, gesturing toward the ladder. "Up you go!"

Peter looked up at Maisie again and swallowed hard. "What do I do when I get up there?" he asked. "What do I hold on to?"

"Just tuck your hands up under her ears and grab hold of the flap of skin. Then squeeze real tight with your legs."

Taking in a deep breath, Peter nodded. He quickly climbed the ladder and threw his leg over Maisie's back, shuffling his way forward until he sat just behind her head. He reached under her ears and felt a soft flap of skin. Maisie's ears flicked at his touch, but she didn't seem to mind him being there. Peter grinned and looked down at Manny and Jessop who seemed miles away below him.

"I can't believe I'm sitting on an elephant," he said.

"It's somethin', ain't it, Pete?" Manny called up. He grabbed the ladder and shuffled with it over to Bella. Within moments, Manny was nestled on top of her, and Jessop had removed the ropes from both animals' legs.

"Alright, so here's what we'll do," Manny said. "When Jessop yells go, we're gonna let these animals take off. Jessop will give them a little prod from behind."

Peter looked down, and his eyes widened as Jessop stood below them with a large bull hook in his hand.

"Don't worry, Pete!" Jessop grinned up at him. "It don't really hurt 'em. Just gives them a little poke is all."

"Right," Manny answered. "Then we're gonna let them run straight that way where the field is empty. When you get to the middle, just give a little tug on the ear like so." Manny pulled at Bella's ear and the elephant grunted and turned her head. "That'll turn Maisie around, and we'll run back here. Got it?"

Peter swallowed hard and nodded his head.

"Alright then. Ready Jessop?"

"Ready!" Jessop replied. "On your mark."

Peter tightened his grip on the skin beneath Maisie's ears and squeezed his legs tight.

"Get set!"

His heartbeat quickened, and Peter leaned forward.

"Go!" Jessop jabbed the bull hook into the back end of each elephant. Maisie let out a small cry and stomped at the ground. Bella took off running as Manny began laughing maniacally.

"Go, you stupid animal!" Jessop cried, and he stabbed at Maisie's backside again. This time, she took off, her legs lumbering against the fog-moist ground as she chased after Bella. Peter held on as tightly as he could, suddenly acutely aware of just how high up off the ground he was.

Maisie was fast, and she quickly caught up to Manny and Bella. "Yeow!" Manny yelled with a laugh as Peter and Maisie ran past him. "Slow down, Pete!" He called. "You gotta stay in control!"

Peter tried to tug on the back of Maisie's ears, but that only seem to agitate the animal and make her run faster. His legs burned as he bounced around on her back. They reached the middle of the field, and Peter pulled on Maisie's ear, but nothing happened. Maisie kept on running straight.

"Turn around, Pete!" Manny called from behind him.

"Hey! What the blazes? What are you doing?" Old Hank jumped out of the side of his train car and ran after Peter and Maisie, a towel slung over his shoulders and water dripping from his chin. "Stop that animal now, you hear me?" he cried.

"I don't know how!" Peter cried out. Maisie continued lumbering forward. She shifted her head slightly, and they turned. Peter looked up and saw the Big Top looming ahead of them, having been set up early that morning in preparation for the day's shows. He leaned down and hugged his arms around the giant's neck, squeezing hard.

"Please stop, Maisie," he called out. "Please stop right now!"

The Big Top came at them faster and faster until, without warning, Maisie skidded to a stop. Peter felt himself begin to slip, and he held on for dear life, managing to stop himself from falling. Maisie panted underneath him and swayed from side to side. A minute later, Old Hank was by them, shooting daggers at Peter with his eyes.

"Son, you better have a damn good story for why you're on the back of my elephant this morning," he seethed. He tossed a rope up and over Maisie's neck and tied it beneath her chin, then gave her a tug. He puckered his lips and kissed at the air. Maisie turned and obediently followed.

"I'm sorry," Peter trembled. "Manny and Jessop told me Boss Man has them run the elephants every once in a while to get exercise. They said it was good for them."

Hank looked up at Peter and shook his head, muttering in disgust. "Stupid kid," he said. "Don't listen to a word that comes outta the mouths of those two. They don't know their backside from their upside, and they ain't ever up to no good."

Hank tugged Maisie back to the stakes. Bella was already back in her spot, her trunk swaying as she stomped in agitation at the ground. Manny and Jessop were nowhere to be seen. Hank leaned the ladder against Maisie's back and Peter climbed down, his legs shaking the whole way. He got to the ground and held himself steady on the ladder for a moment.

"You coulda got yourself killed, kid," Hank said with a shake of the head. "And you coulda killed my girl here. Not to mention the damage you coulda done to the tents."

"I'm sorry," Peter replied, his voice shaking.

Hank waved a hand at him. "Go on," he muttered. "Get outta here. And don't listen to those two nimrods again, you hear?"

Peter nodded and turned to walk away, weak-kneed and teary-eyed.

"Hey kid!" Hank called out behind him. Peter turned back around. "That was some pretty good ridin' for your first time." He gave Peter a quick wink, then turned back to the elephants.

Peter hurried back down the train line toward his car. When he approached the entrance, he heard Manny and Jessop howling inside.

"Did you see his face?" Jessop cackled. "I can't believe you didn't tell him how to stop!"

Manny hooted. "Ol' Hank didn't even see it comin', the ugly kid racin' his elephants through the field! Best day of my life!" Peter heard Manny slap his knee, and he turned, quickly walking away. He kicked his shoes on the ground as he walked the length of the train, trying to swallow his embarrassment. He finally glanced up and found himself face to face with Emmaline. She stared back at him through the window of her own train car and offered a shy smile and wave. Peter's face and neck grew hot, and he lowered his head and walked on.

Turning, he made his way toward the cookhouse. He knew he wasn't supposed to interrupt his mother this early, as they would be making breakfast preparations, but he needed her. Peter walked quickly, blinking hard with each step. He reached the cookhouse and looked around for his mother. He couldn't find her, but he did see the head cook glaring at him from behind the fire pit.

"What do you want, kid?" he called out.

Peter didn't reply. He just turned and walked away as quickly as he could. He rounded the corner and ran smack into Tiny.

"What're you doin' here, Pete? I told you to stay close to the train."

Peter looked up at Tiny and blinked hard, his chest heaving in and out. Tiny leaned down and looked at the kid's flushed face. "You alright, little man?" he asked.

Peter shook his head, and the tears spilled down his cheeks. "I didn't listen to you," he sobbed. "I raced the elephants, and Manny didn't tell me how to stop, and Hank was so angry. And I couldn't find my mama." Peter sniffled and swiped the tears from his cheeks. "Sorry I didn't listen," he mumbled.

Tiny clapped a large hand over Peter's shoulder and guided the boy away from the cookhouse and back toward the train yard. "Well, Pete," he said, his voice soft as the two trudged alongside one another. "I s'pose you had to learn your lesson, didn't you?"

Peter nodded, shame washing over him.

"Ain't nothin' wrong with that," Tiny said. "Sometimes the best lessons are the ones learned the hard way. The wise ones learn from those hard lessons. The fools don't."

Tiny stopped and leaned down, his hands on his knees so that he could look directly in Peter's eyes. "Now tell me, which one do you think better describes Manny and Jessop? Wise? Or foolish?"

"Foolish?" Peter replied, his voice small. Tiny nodded.

"Them two's about the dumbest people on the face of this planet, and they show no signs of ever changin'. But you ain't dumb, Pete. No sir. You're smart as they come. Smarts won't carry you far, though. You gotta be *wise*. You gotta make good decisions. You can't be foolish like those two idiots. You hear?" Tiny looked hard at Peter.

"I do, Tiny," Peter answered. Tiny smiled and ruffled Peter's wiry hair.

"Atta boy," he said. Peter smiled back. "Now, come with me," Tiny said. "I'm 'bout to go rip those two a new one."

"Stand up straight, Emmaline! Stop slouching."

Emmaline straightened her shoulders and lifted her chin, wincing as Beatrice jabbed her once again with the needle. Beatrice sighed in frustration as she pulled needle and thread through the material, securing the hem in a straight line at her unwilling mannequin's ankles.

"Child don't need more fancy clothes," she muttered under her breath. Emmaline heard her and scowled. She didn't ask for another new dress, and she was tired of standing still for the fittings. Monsieur Beaumont insisted that Beatrice make this new costume fit her to perfection.

"Nothing but the finest for my beauty!" he'd thundered when he laid the fabric on the table in the compartment she shared with Bea. Pierre had followed his father into the car and stared at her with that smile that made Emmaline feel uncomfortable, but she wasn't sure why. He always looked at her like he was hungry.

"My father ordered that material all the way from Paris," he'd said. He'd smiled to reveal a line of crooked teeth that marred the naturally handsome features of the ringmaster's son. Emmaline found that she much preferred Pierre when he wasn't smiling.

Emmaline sighed, and her shoulders slumped again. She was glad that Beaumont and Pierre weren't here right now. She watched out the window at the foggy grounds below. She no longer felt awe when looking out the window. She had seen the mountains and the ocean many times over in her young life. At twelve years old, Emmaline was jaded to the beauty of the world.

"Now don't go gettin' all down in the mouth, child," Beatrice said as she knotted her final stitch and cut the string. She pushed to her feet slowly, groaning at the ache in her knees. "Most girls would be right happy to have a dress as fine as this one."

Emmaline looked down at the dress that Monsieur Beaumont had ordered to be made for her. It was the lightest shade of mauve, and tiny flowers dotted the full skirt that reached to her ankles. Beatrice had pulled the pleats at the waist until they cinched tight against her body, making it difficult for Emmaline to draw in a deep breath.

"Don't know why a circus child needs a dress made of silk," Bea muttered. She shook her head and took in the sight of Emmaline standing so forlorn and uncomfortable before her. The sash and belt of the dress were made of taffeta silk, the cream-colored ribbon standing in contrast to the crepon silk of the skirt and bodice. The sleeves puffed out wide in the fashion that was common and expected among the upper class of Paris, but which looked odd and out of sorts on the backdrop of the Big Top. Emmaline reached up and tugged uncomfortably at the neck of her dress. The collar was made of *mousseline de soie*, a fabric Beatrice loved running her hand over, but found herself terrified of touching with a needle. This was the finest dress Bea had ever made, and she admired her own work as she took in how perfectly the dress fit young Emmaline.

"Alright then," Beatrice said, stepping behind Emmaline and beginning to undo the buttons on the back bodice. "This is only for performances. Go on and get into the day dress."

Emmaline felt a rush of relief as the final buttons were undone and she stepped out of the prison of her newest gown. She shook out her arms and legs, her thin, white undergarments feeling loose and free. Bea gently slipped a hanger into the dress and reset the buttons. She tied the sash carefully around the waist and smoothed out the silky fabric before hanging it in the armoire that had been bolted to the floor in the corner. She glanced over her shoulder.

"Well don't just stand there, child!" she barked. "Git on yer dress before you catch yer death of cold."

Emmaline complied, pulling her soft day dress over her head and turning so that Bea could fasten the buttons and tie the sash. She wasn't cold, like Beatrice feared. Most of the time, she was so constricted by her clothing that she felt she might suffocate. She much preferred the feeling of the air kissing her bare skin.

The train lurched and Emmaline grabbed the table in front of her to keep from falling over. Bea took hold of Emmaline's shoulders as her feet skittered out from beneath her.

"Don't git no warning when they decide to move," Bea muttered. "Be nice if they let out a whistle or somethin' so we knew to hang on." Emmaline stared out the window at the unfamiliar territory. Today would be another day of waiting for the next performance—another day of staring out the window, wondering what it would be like to take off running through one of the grassy meadows that waited just on the other side of the circus grounds. Emmaline sighed, a long, deep sound that rushed from her chest.

"Now don't you go gettin' all mopey," Beatrice said as she straightened Emmaline's skirts. She smoothed the girl's hair back off her face and turned Emmaline to face her.

Beatrice had a face that Emmaline imagined was once quite pretty. Her eyes were spread apart nicely, and they stared back at Emmaline, dark brown and revealing much more kindness than generally escaped her parted lips. Bea's dark face was long and thin, worn like she'd lived more lives than just this one. She was a spinster in her 40's who had stumbled upon this job as Emmaline's caretaker and seamstress when she had visited the circus many years before with her ailing mother. Not wanting her daughter to be left alone when she passed, Bea's mother had approached Beaumont at the end of the show and hailed her daughter as a brilliant seamstress in need of work. Beatrice said goodbye to her mama that night, boarded the train, and never went back to her old life.

Emmaline thought of Bea's life story again, and she felt sad. She had never known freedom in her lifetime, and this joined the girl and her caretaker in ways that young Emmaline did not yet fully understand.

Beatrice ran a hand over Emmaline's cheek and paused, just for a moment. "You hungry?" she asked. Her voice was rough, but her touch was gentle. Emmaline nodded, and Beatrice dropped her hand.

"Yeah, I s'pose you would be. I'll go get yer breakfast while you rest."

"Okay," Emmaline replied, her voice soft and impassive.

Bea ducked down and checked her appearance in the small mirror that hung on the wall. She licked her hands and smoothed out a few fly away hairs, then stood up and ran her hands down her worn skirt.

"Alright, child," she said. "Go on and sit down. I'll go tell Butch you and me's gonna eat in our car this mornin'. Seems you don't feel up to eatin' in the tent with everyone else."

Emmaline gave Bea a grateful smile. Somehow, though true tenderness never really passed between them, Bea always seemed to understand how Emmaline was feeling.

The train sputtered and shook as it groaned forward. Most of the cars had been unloaded, and the fields were already transformed into a city of tents. The fog would burn off later, and people would start to show up, waiting in line to enter the world of astonishment that Monsieur Beaumont had so carefully crafted. The process of setting up the Big Top was a bit like a summer storm, fast and furious for a short time until suddenly they were all settled, as if they had been there all along. Once the living quarters were established, the train would be sent to a nearby station to wait until they were ready to move to the next town. The train slowed to a stop again as more men jumped off and began pacing out the final markers for the performer's tents. Bea grabbed her shawl and quickly made her exit in case the train decided to move again.

Emmaline sat down by the window and watched as men unloaded crates and canvas. Tent poles were pulled from the holding cars. She was always amazed by this process. It almost seemed magical, the way the tents appeared. It was as though the cars housing the tents must be controlled by some kind of spell as the tent poles stretched out in never ending succession.

Down a bit further, Emmaline stared as the clowns stumbled from the train, clutching glass bottles that held their own secret recipe of hooch. The raucous group pitched into the earth, swaying back and forth, their drunken laughter floating across the landscape like a welcome call. Without their makeup, the clowns looked like ordinary men. Two of them were bald, and the third had long, wavy hair that touched his shoulders. He was the younger one—the one responsible for the hooch, Emmaline heard. The older men, James and Isaac, were twin brothers, both in their fifties and neither one married, though Emmaline heard that Isaac had a child somewhere in Kentucky. But people only talked about that behind his back, and they usually did so with sad eyes and pitying shakes of the head.

Clarice followed the boys, her slender hands shielding her eyes from the bright sun. Clarice was the female clown, though when she was in costume no one knew she was a woman. Emmaline loved watching her perform. Clarice threw herself into the work, almost as though she was fit to prove everyone wrong that a woman couldn't do the job as well as a man.

"Don't take no scientist to act a fool in make-up," Clarice would mutter whenever someone told her they were surprised at her choice to be a clown.

Clarice was no fool. She was the one who got the crowd roaring with laughter most shows. She tripped the men relentlessly, pushing them this way and that to the sheer delight of the spectators. Emmaline thought that Clarice was a hero.

Clarice stepped around her fellow clowns with a look of disgust on her face. She marched away, shaking her head as the men all tried to get their bearings amidst their drunken stupors.

Emmaline knew the secrets of just about everyone on this train. She made it her habit to listen, to observe and watch and take in all the information she could gather. And for their part, the others did not mind the pretty little girl with big eyes and a quiet demeanor. In fact, they all felt quite protective of Emmaline and she, in turn, felt safe when she was with them. For better or worse, Emmaline knew this was her family.

Two figures rounded the bend and walked toward the train. Emmaline observed as Tiny strode along the dusty ground, his long, thin legs stretching wide with each step. Beside him was the new boy. He was young, her age, and he struggled to keep up with Tiny's long strides. He blinked and kicked the ground, a look of sadness etched on his distorted features. The first time Emmaline had seen him in the mess hall, she had to fight the urge to recoil in horror. His face looked as though perhaps one of the hooch-infused clowns had drawn him into existence after a night of too much drink. His eyes were not in line with one another, and his mouth drew down in a crooked line.

His back was curved, which made one shoulder pull higher than the other, and his hips didn't fully line up, so he walked with an uneven gait. He compensated for this deformity, Emmaline observed, by measuring his steps in a sort of rhythm. She suspected that if needed, he could walk quickly.

He had yet to actually perform, but Emmaline knew that this

weekend would be his first show. She heard Monsieur Beaumont discussing it with Pierre the day before.

"The ugly one will have his stage right next to Emmaline," he'd said as he gulped down a cup of coffee that morning. "The Ugliest Boy in the World standing next to The Most Beautiful Girl? Oh, it will be a sight!" His voice was laced with laughter, making him sound like a child who could hardly wait to open a special gift.

Emmaline watched the boy, who she knew to be named Peter, and a sadness washed over her. She didn't know why, or where this feeling came from. It simply filled her chest and settled in a lump at the base of her neck. The boy looked up, and his eye caught hers through the window. Emmaline stared at him and lifted her hand in a small wave. He simply looked back at her, his mouth curving up into a shy smile.

Peter's face warmed as he dropped back behind Tiny, too tired to try to continue matching his tall roommate's steps. Tiny's head bobbed with each step, a small hat perched on top and touching the sky above.

"'Bout time to head to breakfast," Tiny said, turning back to look at Peter. A scuffle caused Peter to stop and turn around. Manny and Jessop waddled toward them, scowls pasted across their wide faces. Manny elbowed Jessop, who pushed back at him with a curse.

Peter watched as Manny and Jessop walked by, glaring up at Tiny as they passed him. He'd marched into the train car earlier and grabbed them each by the shirt, lifting them off the ground and carrying them out, plunking them on the ground in front of Peter and demanding an apology. They'd complied reluctantly, then scuttled away from Tiny, shooting daggers at him with their eyes.

Now, dust kicked up behind their small legs as they passed by. Tiny stopped and watched them go, staring down at them with a mixture of amusement and reproach. Peter tried to lift his chin and look brave, but he could still hear the sound of their laughter as he clung to poor Maisie's back, and his face burned with shame once again. How soon until everyone knew about the ugly boy who raced the elephant?

Peter glanced back over his shoulder again at Emmaline's train car. He paused, thinking about the wave they had shared earlier. Tiny stopped and turned around.

"Whatcha lookin' at, kid?" he asked.

"Nothin'," Peter answered quickly with a shrug of his shoulders. He rushed to catch up with Tiny, who stared back at Emmaline's train car behind them.

"You know, Pete," Tiny said. "Little Emmaline there is Boss Man's favorite. You ain't gonna want to go talkin' to her without permission. Boss Man is protective."

Peter blushed and nodded without response. He followed his roommates toward the cookhouse. Ducking beneath the flap of the tent, Peter blinked as his eyes adjusted to the dim light. Tables were still being dragged into place.

"You fellas are early," Butch called out, his white apron pulled tight over a protruding gut. Sweat already wet his underarms and collar. He wiped his brow and tossed a glare in their direction.

"Aw, we don't mean no trouble, Butch," Tiny called. "Just ready for some of those mighty fine eggs and biscuits of yours!"

Butch grunted and turned his back to them. "Be awhile. Sit and wait, and no fightin' inside the tent, you two!" he barked, glaring over his shoulder at Manny and Jessop who looked at one another and simultaneously shrugged their shoulders.

Peter looked around the room for a glimpse of his mother. He finally saw her as she ducked into the tent, a platter balanced in her arms. She saw him, and her face lit up. She set the platter down and rushed across the room, leaning forward to kiss his cheek.

"*Dobriy utra*, good morning, my dear," she said, her face close to his. "How did you sleep?"

Peter gripped at her neck, burying his face against her skin, which smelled like the earth. It wasn't a scent he was used to coming from his own mother. He shrugged his shoulders.

"Hey! We got stuff to do. Back to work!" Butch hollered across the room. Nataliya straightened up and tossed a wary glance over her shoulder.

"I must go," she whispered. "I will look for you this afternoon."

Peter blinked as she rushed out. Butch muttered something in her direction, and his mother stared at him in return. Peter wondered if her language was beginning to catch up yet.

"Yer mama's a pretty one," Manny said with a grin, stepping up beside him. Peter looked down in surprise.

"What?" he asked.

"That's yer mama, ain't it?"

Peter nodded.

"Well, she's a pretty thing. Better keep an eye out cause the pretty ones don't last long 'round these parts."

"What do you mean?" Peter asked.

Manny shrugged. "Boss don't like nobody to be prettier than his prize, Emmaline. Ain't you noticed that all the other ladies round here look like they got worked over by the ugly stick?"

Peter furrowed his brow, trying to think of the few women he'd seen around the circus. He shrugged his shoulders.

"How 'bout Miss Mabel?" he asked, thinking of the woman who rode on the backs of camels and elephants, her sequin leotard flashing in the lights of the Big Top.

Manny snorted. "Miss Mabel wears a wig and false teeth to perform. She's bald and toothless otherwise!"

Peter's eyes widened, which sent Manny and Jessop into a fit of laughter, both hooting and slapping their knees. Tiny looked on with mild amusement.

"Well Señora Fernandez is pretty," he said when they quit laughing. Jessop shrugged.

"Only if you like the hairy European type, which Boss don't, so she's safe."

"What about Jenna?" Peter asked, thinking of the acrobat that tumbled through the Big Top with her brothers. Jessop shook his head.

"Nope. Not pretty enough to be a threat. Plus, she ain't the boss's type. Too strong. It's the dainty little ones that gotta watch out."

Peter looked back as his mother returned to the tent, two pitchers clutched in her delicate hands. Her hair was pulled back off her face, and her apron tied tight around her thin waist. He'd never thought of his mother as pretty before. She had seemed very plain to him, especially next to his aunt who always outshined her smaller, more timid sister. But stand her in a group with the other women in the circus, and Peter knew she stood out. She looked young and fresh and, yes, she looked pretty.

"You might tell her to keep her face a little dirty," Tiny murmured.

"Yeah and stay in the shadows so's the boss don't really notice her," Manny quipped.

"What happens to the pretty ones?" Peter asked.

A knowing smile spread wide Manny's mouth. "They just disappear," he said. "No one really knows."

"'Member Paulette?" Jessop asked. "Now that was a pretty one. Worked the sideshow as a dancer. Brought in a lot of money for the boss but stole the show. People gawked at her more'n the girl, so one day just *Poof!*" Jessop laughed.

Peter felt a lump form in his throat, and he blinked hard. Tiny tossed a glare at Jessop, who snickered as he watched Peter's features melt into fear.

"Shut up, you two," Tiny growled. He looked back at Peter. "Don't worry, kid. Yer mama will be alright. She just needs to be careful is all. She's kitchen staff, so she ain't gonna be in front of nobody."

Peter nodded. Another woman ducked into the tent. Gerta was Butch's wife, and she matched him in girth. Her frizzy hair was also pulled back revealing a harsh, pock-marked face, sweat glistening on her ample brow. Her upper lip was dotted with black hairs, and her mouth drew down in a hard line. She and Butch glared at one another as they passed by, his face twisting into a sneer.

"Now that," Manny whispered, pushing up onto his tiptoes so his mouth was closer to Peter's ear. "That's the kinda woman who's safe 'round here. Ain't no way old Gerta will steal Emmaline's thunder."

"She can't even get her own husband to look at her," Jessop added, and the two let out whoops of laughter. Tiny rolled his eyes and settled onto a bench at the nearest table. Peter slid in next to him, dwarfed by the tall man's massive stature.

Breakfast passed without incident, and by mid-morning, Peter found himself sitting on a crate outside his train car and watching the activity. He could hear Manny and Jessop arguing in the car behind him, and Tiny barking at them to shut up, but he had no desire to step back in, though he knew it would be better than baking in the hot sun.

Men ran from one side to the other, carrying large poles and swaths of fabric as they put the final touches on the circus grounds. Somewhere in the distance, a hammer beat out a rhythm, and Peter heard the whinny of a horse.

A loud clanking noise drew his gaze, and he watched as the animals were unloaded from the back of the train. First, the camels were pulled down the ramp, the men tasked with guiding the bored-looking animals cursing as they tugged them across the dusty earth toward the menagerie tent.

Next, the alpacas meandered down the slatted wood. There were ten of them, with the newest arrival only a few months old. He pranced down the steps, head swiveling from side to side as the mangy animals blinked in the afternoon sun. Peter smiled at the baby alpaca, his white-grey fur matted and mussed from days spent in a cramped train car. While his adult counterparts looked bored and confused by their march toward the menagerie, the little one seemed completely delighted. Peter almost thought he saw a smile spread across the creature's lips.

His gaze shifted to a large, burly man standing next to the train cars, watching as the march of animals moved past him. Sal ran the menagerie. He was the circus veterinarian, though based on late night chatter between his roommates, Peter knew he had never been trained as such. Sal was also the lion tamer and the overseer of all the horse acts. Sal was the man behind most of the menagerie magic, watching, correcting, giving orders, and making sure the animal acts went off without a hitch in every show. Peter had even seen Sal working with Boss Man, the two of them training the horses together. It turned out that Monsieur Beaumont had been a master horseman back in France in his earlier days.

Peter thought Sal must be the real magician behind Monsieur Beaumont's show. Sal rarely raised his voice, and he only used the whip as a tool for signaling the animals their next trick. He never harmed the animals, and from what Peter could see, no one else did either.

A lit cigarette dangled between Sal's lips as he stepped to the next train car and kept watch over the horses. Six beautifully groomed mares stepped gingerly down the planks, gentle plumes of dirt rising in puffs beneath their hooves as they were led toward the menagerie.

"Wait!" Sal called. He inhaled deeply on his cigarette, then flicked it beneath the train as he walked toward the horse at the end of the line. She skittered as Sal approached her, then calmed down to the gentle "Sssshhhhhh..." that came from his parted lips. Cigarette smoke wafted into the sky above man and beast as Sal patted the horse's neck gently, then ran his hand down the animal's side. He finally smoothed out the hair on the horse's back leg until he was able to grab the hoof and bend it up to inspect the bottom of the foot. He let out a curse.

"Did you see this?" he asked the man holding the lead rope.

"See what?"

"This," Sal replied, his voice tight. The man followed Sal's gaze down to the horse's hoof himself.

He let out a curse to match Sal's, and Peter shifted forward, straining to hear their quiet conversation, words flying in heated whispers as the horse sighed and tutted. Sal finally lowered his hoof to the ground, the horse lightly resting it there but refusing to put full weight on it.

"Take her back inside," Sal said. "I'll talk to the boss about it later."

Sal looked up and caught Peter's eye as the man turned the injured horse back toward the train car. He gave a brief nod of the chin, then turned his back and walked to the next car to see the progress they were making on guiding the show dogs to the menagerie.

"*Privyet.*"

Peter turned to find his mother standing before him, squinting and smiling in the morning sunlight.

"Mama!" he cried, jumping up and tumbling into her arms. Nataliya leaned down and planted a kiss firmly on the back of his head.

"Take a walk with me?" she asked. Her eyes shifted left and right nervously.

Peter grabbed her hand, and the two walked between the cars to the back side of the train where the noise of the circus faded significantly.

"I thought you couldn't get away until later," Peter said, still gripping his mother's sweaty palm.

"Butch didn't need me anymore this morning. He told me to come back in an hour to set up for the lunch crew."

Peter nodded. "Is your English improving?" he asked her. Nataliya shrugged.

"I suppose it is a little," she answered. "I understand more, but I still can't seem to wrap my mouth around the words." She glanced down at him and offered a tender smile. "I don't think you understand how special it is that you can pick up languages so easily, *dorogoy*."

"I've been listening to Señora Fernandez at night around the fire,"

Peter replied. "I think I could learn Spanish, too." He raised his chin, a look of pride sweeping across his features.

"I believe that you could," Nataliya murmured. She stopped and turned to face Peter.

"So," she began. "Tonight, you perform for the first time, *da?*"

Peter nodded in return, swallowing against the fear that pushed against the back of his throat.

"Do you feel prepared?" Nataliya asked.

Peter shrugged. "I don't think it will be that hard," he mumbled. "They just want me to growl and snarl and pretend to be a wild child." Peter could feel his cheeks burning at the thought of standing before a group of people and growling against chains on his wrists and ankles.

Nataliya nodded as she looked at her son. She narrowed her eyes and pursed her lips, thinking for a moment before speaking.

"Pasha," she began. "You and I both know that you are most likely the smartest person in this entire group." She swept her hand out, gesturing toward the train cars. Peter shrugged his shoulders.

"It's true, *sinok*," she said. "And you know that it's true." Peter remained still and quiet, looking up and searching his mother's eyes.

"So now they are asking something of you that feels humiliating, but so what?" Nataliya grabbed his hands and squeezed them between hers. "You have an opportunity to show them what you can do."

"By growling and pretending to be crazy?" Peter asked, confused.

"Yes!" Nataliya responded. "Show them that whatever you do, whether it is acting like a crazy person, or walking with those idiots you share a train car with—show them that you do everything excellently. Leave them in awe of your talent, my boy. Because deep down, you know that you're not crazy, and I know that you are *not* crazy. And the others around here…they will know it, too."

"How can you be sure?" Peter asked.

"Because I see the way they look at you, my darling. You fascinate people."

Peter shook his head. "No, they look at me like they're scared of me. They think I'm a monster," he said. His voice quavered.

Nataliya grabbed Peter's chin and tilted it up so that he was looking in her eyes. "You are not a monster," she said.

Peter nodded and tried to offer his mother a smile. She smiled in return. "You are quite an amazing young man," she said. "You believe *that* when you're up on that stage. Make those people watching believe what they want to believe—what they paid to believe. But don't forget who you really are—who your mama knows you to be."

The train whistle blew, and both Nataliya and Peter jumped at the sound. Nataliya looked up at the sun and let out a long sigh.

"I should head back and be available if Butch needs me," she said. Peter grabbed her hands and squeezed them.

"Mama," he began. "Tiny and Manny and Jessop all told me that you need to make sure you don't look too pretty because Monsieur Beaumont doesn't like women to be pretty and draw attention away from...her." Peter's cheeks flushed.

"Her?" Nataliya asked.

"Emmaline," he mumbled in reply. "The pretty girl."

Nataliya looked at him tenderly. "Don't worry, my darling," she said with a laugh, pulling him into an embrace. He wrapped his arms around her waist and melted into her hug. "I don't think I am a threat to outshine Emmaline."

Peter turned his head and pressed his ear into his mother's stomach. He could hear it growling.

"Are you hungry?" he asked, pulling back.

Nataliya shrugged. "I'm fine," she said with a wave of her hand. She grabbed Peter's hand and tugged him along behind her.

"Come, my dear," she said. "I must get back to work, and you need to prepare for tonight." They circled back around the train, and Nataliya left Peter standing next to his train car. It was quiet inside now. Peter assumed Manny and Jessop finally quit scuffling and fell asleep. Tiny stood in the doorway, shuffling a deck of cards from one hand to the next. Nataliya looked up at him and offered a brief nod.

"Miss Nataliya," he said with a nod in return.

"Don't forget, my darling," Nataliya breathed, leaning in to Peter so that her lips grazed his ear.

Peter watched as his mother hurried off toward the mess hall. He shoved his hands into his pockets and stood for a long time, letting her words work their way into his heart.

"Yer Mama seems real nice, Pete," Tiny said behind him. Peter turned to look up at the towering man with the gentle eyes.

"She is," he answered. He didn't know why he felt like crying.

Tiny looked down at him for a moment with narrowed eyes, then turned and disappeared into the train car. He emerged a minute later carrying in his hand a small hatchet. He tossed it in the air so that it flipped once before he caught the wooden handle again.

"C'mon, Pete," he said. "I got somethin' to show you."

Peter watched for a beat before following Tiny around the train car to the other side, where a row of trees stood a few yards back. Tiny flipped the hatchet again, then looked down at Peter.

"You ever thrown one of these?" he asked.

Peter shook his head.

"Well," Tiny said. He turned and looked at the trees up ahead. "The thing about throwin' a hatchet is it can be real soothing. It's just you and that tree up there, and you gotta calm your mind right down and focus in tight." Tiny bent forward at the waist, then honed in on the trees up ahead. In one swift move he pulled his hand over his shoulder and flung it forward, releasing the hatchet. Peter watched as it flipped through the air, then buried itself in the center of the tree's trunk. Tiny laughed and smacked his leg on his knee.

"See there, Pete?" he asked. "That there is might satisfying, and it's a pretty fine release on the days when all of this," he gestured toward the circus springing up behind them, "gets to be too much."

"Can I try?" Peter asked.

"Sure thing, little man." Tiny strode forward and p et from the tree. He motioned for Peter to come close him the small axe. "Alright," he said, leaning down so closer to Peter's ear. "What you gotta do is focus real tignt on the tree there. Don't think of nothin' else. Don't think of yer mama, or yer life before the circus, or those idiots we share a room with. Let all that fade away and just concentrate on the tree."

Peter took a deep breath and tried to push all other thoughts out of his mind.

"Now, when yer ready, pull the hatchet up and swing it forward, letting go just as yer arm reaches its full extension."

Peter closed his eyes, drew in another deep breath, then pulled his arm back and swung it forward, releasing the hatchet and watching it sail through the air. It landed with a dull thump in the grass at the base of the tree, blade side down.

"Whoooeeee!" Tiny exclaimed dancing a little jig next to Peter. His knees and elbows jutted out to the sides as he flapped like a gigantic, oversized chicken. Peter laughed out loud at the sight. "That was a fine first try, Pete!"

Peter grinned, his cheeks flushed. "I liked that," he said. "Can I do it again?"

"Pete," Tiny replied, turning and walking to the hatchet. He pulled it up out of the ground and flipped it in his hand. "You can try any ol' time you want. This here is the best thing for gettin' yer mind off the world. So anytime yer feelin' worried, you grab this hatchet and throw it til yer worries fade away, okay?"

Peter nodded. He smiled up at Tiny, his new friend, then took the axe, closed his eyes, and let the world fade away once more.

The afternoon melted quickly to evening, and before Peter knew it, he stood at the base of his small stage drawing in long, deep breaths. He closed his eyes and listened to the show in the next tent over. He let his mind drift back to the day he and Mama watched the show together, the colors, sounds, and smells all working their way into his heart and settling there permanently.

The drums were rolling now, a low, rumbling sound that would begin rising slowly. Señora Fernandez was standing on the high wire, making her way across the highest point of the Big Top. Peter could feel the tension even as he stood on the other side of the tent. Would she make it, or would she plummet to the ground below, where a group of men stood silently at the ready to catch her in case the unimaginable happened?

The drum roll grew louder. She must be getting closer to the other side. Peter could feel his heart begin to trill alongside the increasing beat of the percussion. He glanced to his right and saw Emmaline step up to her little stage. Miss Bea stood behind her, tying the ribbon that cinched Emmaline's dress tight. Emmaline tugged at the lacy neck of her dress and grimaced. Peter glanced down at his costume, which had been given to him after dinner.

"Boss Man wants you to wear this for your performance," Tiny had murmured as he handed Peter a crumpled pile of what looked to be rags. The clothes were filthy, and they smelled as if they'd been cut from a dead man. The pants hung loose on his thin frame, and the shirt, which had once likely been white but was now soiled and stained, wouldn't stay on his shoulders. Peter adjusted it once more, then looked back at Emmaline and found her staring at him in return. He lowered his eyes quickly, swallowing hard and pulling the shirt back up on his slender shoulders.

A moment later, Peter felt a tug on the back of his shirt, and he turned in surprise to find Miss Bea standing behind him, a needle and thread in her mouth. She looked at him with a grimace, then her eyes shifted to the tent opening.

"Don't go starin' now," she murmured. "I ain't got much time to make sense of this mess they're makin' you wear." She grabbed his shoulders and turned him around, tugging the shirt up and pinching it tight in front of his chest. Peter blushed as her fingers began working needle and thread through the thin fabric, and she muttered to the beat of her own hands.

"Don't make no sense why they can't give you a real costume. Throw you in these dirty rags like you some kind of trash. 'Spect people to git on up there on them stages and act the fool."

On and on she muttered as she closed the gaps in the shirt, folding and tucking the material in and sewing it together until she reached the bottom of the shirt. She knotted her thread and bit it, tearing it off with her teeth, then standing back and checking her work.

"Well, I suppose it'll do," she muttered. "Won't go fallin' off yer shoulders now at least. Tuck that shirt in, boy."

Peter reached down, his hands trembling, and he grabbed the waist of his shirt, tucking it into the worn pants, which only stayed on his hips thanks to a necktie that Tiny had given him to use as a belt. The woman shook her head and pinched the bridge of her nose.

"After the show, you come see me and I'll fix them pants for you," she said.

A burst of applause wound its way from the next tent over into theirs as the band struck up its merry, finishing song. She glanced nervously at the tent flap, then looked back at him, her dark eyes studying his features.

"Listen here," she said, her eyes running over his face and down his crooked body. "You make sure you don't look right at the people who comin' to watch you, now, hear? And don't pay no mind to the things they say when they walk in this tent. People has a way of sayin' things they don't mean when they think someone ain't able to understand or hear." She leaned a little closer. "You just do yer job out there. That makes you better than them. They ain't doin' nothin' but watchin'. You the one doin' the work. So, you do yer job, and you don't pay those people no mind, hear?"

Peter nodded, wide-eyed. He heard the tuba playing its final up-down beat, and the applause fading in the tent. Then, the ringmaster's voice cut through the space. Peter watched as the sideshow acts began climbing their stages and settling into place. Tiny crouched into the small chair in the center of his stage, which was built smaller to accentuate his height.

Manny and Jessop, in their matching suits and top hats, strutted onto their stage, pushing and shoving each other into place on opposite ends. Their hair, usually greasy and hanging in their eyes, was now slicked back, Manny's parted straight down the middle, and Jessop's combed to the side with a small curl pasted to his forehead in front. The small men looked dignified and classy, a far cry from the pair who, an hour earlier, had been striking matches and trying to light one another's farts on fire outside the sleeping quarters. They'd succeeded, but in so doing had lit Jessop's pants on fire. While everyone was standing around bent over laughing, Jessop howled and rolled across the ground to try and scuff out the flame on his backside. And now, in just a few short minutes, the two of them would start their vaudeville act, crooning out humorous songs between comedic acts filled with raucous jokes and pratfalls, and they would be completely charming.

Miss Clarabelle huffed and panted as she lumbered up her steps and sank onto her couch, sweat beading around her temples and upper lip. She shook her head, shiny ringlet curls bouncing around her fleshy skin. She looked over at Peter, and he tried to smile, but he wasn't sure he managed it. Her gaze hardened, and she shifted away, turning slightly so that her back was to Peter.

Albert the tattooed man punched at the air, and when he looked at Peter, his mouth opened in a wide grin revealing blackened teeth. Peter shuddered. When the show began, Albert would perform acrobatic skills that left the onlookers slack-jawed. With each flex of a muscle, the tattoos on his body would seemingly transform into entirely new pictures, and when he turned upside down, the image on his back morphed from that of an elephant with a dangling trunk and floppy ears, into a swan with wings spread regally. This final trick would elicit gasps and applause.

Peter didn't like Albert. He was strange and unpredictable. He muttered nonsensically throughout the days, and if you got too close, he liked to grab your arm and pull you in to tell you stories about his many tattoos and where they came from, his foul breath immediately eliciting a gag reflex from those listening. Peter learned early on not to get too close to Albert.

Peter slowly stepped up onto his stage, heart beating rapidly. He leaned down and grabbed the chains that were rolled in a pile in the middle of his performance area. He pulled them up and slipped his wrists into the rings at the end, making sure to tuck his thumbs into the holes in the side of the rings so that they'd stay on his hands. He stepped over the pile and spun around a few times, pulling the chains up around his ankles, then shrugging them onto his shoulders until he was sufficiently tangled and tied down. He closed his eyes and thought back to the instruction Monsieur Beaumont had given him earlier that day before the show started.

"You will growl and snarl and foam at the mouth, boy," the ringmaster had said, his voice low. It was almost as though he were holding back hysterical laughter. "Your performance should be over the top. Give the paying customers their money's worth, understand?"

Peter had nodded his head, but now that he stood on the stage, he wasn't so sure. The thought of what he was being asked to do sent fits of humiliation down his spine. His cheeks burned as he waited for the tent flap to open and people to come streaming into the sideshow tent.

"Psst. Hey, Pete!"

Peter looked over at Tiny who looked comical sitting on his little chair, his knees folded up around his chin. The pants he wore were three inches too short, as was his shirt, and he had a tiny little hat pinned to his head.

"Pay no mind what people say when they walk in."

Peter thought of Beatrice's advice just a few moments earlier, so similar to Tiny's. They all seemed to know something he didn't, which made him more nervous. He nodded at Tiny, then glanced over at Emmaline as she positioned herself in the middle of the stage, her chin held high. She looked back at him, and as their eyes met Peter's knees went weak, nearly collapsing him in his pile of chains. Emmaline said nothing. She just looked at him with sad eyes, then turned away.

The sound of approaching voices pulled Peter's gaze toward the tent flap. Moments later, it burst open, and a stream of people filed into the performance tent, their faces immediately changing from jubilant to horrified to amused. Men, women and children streamed in and stopped in front of the different stages, gazing up at the freak show acts, most of them so different in this circus than in others because these freaks were performers.

Tiny began playing a foot-stomping tune on the harmonica, mesmerizing his watchers with the way his giant feet moved to the rhythm of his music.

Miss Clarabelle quoted Shakespeare in a voice that sounded both bored and indifferent. Those who watched her muttered in disgust, shaking their heads back and forth.

Peter watched it all light up in a moment, the room now filled with noise. There was laughter from some and jeers from others as patrons wandered slowly from stage to stage. A man and a young boy walked up to Peter's stage and stopped. The man read the sign at the base of Peter's area slowly.

UGLIEST BOY IN THE WORLD

The man snorted and the boy sneered up at Peter. Backstage, he could hear Beatrice hissing at him.

"Do somethin', boy! You gotta do somethin'!"

Peter blinked as he stared at the boy who was laughing and pointing while his dad stood to the side.

"That kid is clearly as dumb as he is ugly!" the man exclaimed.

"Yeah," the boy parroted. "Dumb and ugly. He's like an idiot freak!" The boy hooted and slapped his knee, and something snapped inside Peter. Something he didn't know was there unleashed, cutting loose and spilling out of him. Peter crouched low and strained against the chains around his knees. He let out a snarl, then a deep scream that pulled from his throat with such forced that it felt like claws scraping against the inside of his neck. The boy below gasped and stumbled backward into his father with a yelp. The older man grabbed his trembling son's shoulders and pulled him away from Peter, who continued to writhe and snarl at the two as they scuttled away.

Peter stood up again, panting as his eyes fanned across the room. He caught a glimpse of Tiny, who had paused his playing for a moment to take in the sight. Tiny looked back at him, laughter dancing in his eyes. He gave Peter a nod, then he stuck the harmonica back in his mouth and continued playing.

Next to Peter, Emmaline stood tall, hands folded in front of her waist and chin held high.

"Beautiful girl
Most lovely in
All of the world
White-gold hair
Milky-white skin,
So fair."

Her song was haunting, and those who stood before her stage were transfixed at the angelic child with the voice that sounded refreshing and gentle as a spring rain. Peter paused for a moment, struck by her song, until the jarring sound of a kid below him cut through her harmony.

"Look at this ugly kid!" the boy yelled, pointing up at Peter. A small crowd stepped up behind him, and Peter crouched low, growling and snarling and pulling against the chains. Meanwhile, Emmaline continued singing next to him. A woman stood in the back of the crowd watching carefully, a young girl standing next to her. The woman gripped the girl's hand, her eyes shifting from Peter to Emmaline and back. Meanwhile, the boys in the front of the crowd growled and snarled back at Peter between fits of laughter.

"Now that's a real freak!" one of them exclaimed. After a few moments, they grew tired of watching and taunting, and they drifted away, but the woman stayed where she was, with her daughter standing silently by her. The daughter's face moved from side to side toward each sound. Peter watched her hollow gaze, the way her eyes never seemed to register anything.

The woman led her daughter forward, closer to Peter's stage. "What's there, Mama?" the girl asked. "Describe it to me."

"It is the ugliest child I have ever seen," the woman replied. "And he's acting like a wild child, but something tells me he isn't as wild as he'd like us to believe." She cocked her head to the side and stared at

Peter. He remembered Beatrice's admonishment to not make eye contact with the audience, and he shifted his gaze away from hers, but her stare had already pierced him.

"I do believe this boy is a fraud," the woman said, disgust lacing its way through her words and worming into his heart.

A fraud.

Peter wasn't sure he fully understood what she meant, but the way that she said it made his cheeks warm. He breathed a sigh of relief as she led her daughter away from his stage and the two stopped in front of Emmaline, who now stood silent.

"Now what do you see, Mama?" the girl asked.

"Well, this here is the most beautiful girl in the world," the woman replied.

"Oh," the girl said, her face lighting up in a grin. She squinted in the direction of Emmaline as though willing herself to see the sight. "Describe her to me!"

"Well, she has golden hair that looks almost as though it's made of silk. And her skin is exquisite. She likely has not spent much time outdoors—skin is too pale to have seen the sun." The older woman squinted, studying Emmaline who shifted from one foot to the next. "Her eyes are set apart nicely, though perhaps they are a bit wide. They are a very pretty blue, though. Yes," the woman nodded her head as though giving approval. "I suppose she is quite a pretty girl. Of course, she isn't the most beautiful girl in the world," the woman continued. "That's absurd. That title is reserved for you, my dear."

Peter took in the blind girl's appearance, then looked back at Emmaline and bit his lip. The woman looked back at him for a brief moment.

"Very clever, having the two of them next to one another," she said. She turned and led her daughter on to the tattooed man's stage where he was currently flexing the muscles in his back, which caused the tattooed birds on his shoulder blade to look as though they were flapping their wings. The crowd below him laughed and cheered.

The sideshow only ran for one hour, but it felt like an eternity to Peter. By the time it was over, and the final patron had wandered from the room, his throat was raw from growling. He untangled himself from the chains and stumbled down the steps where Tiny waited for him with a wide grin plastered on his face.

"Well son of a…" Tiny shook his head, staring down at Peter. "You did alright out there, Pete," he said. Peter smiled in return, warming under the prideful gaze of the tall man. "You had me believing you were crazy the whole time."

Tiny clapped Peter on the shoulder, and the two turned to leave the room out the back flap of the tent, which would empty them out into the field behind the circus where paying customers couldn't see the ragtag band of misfits stumbling toward a waiting fire and post-show rabblerousing.

"Good job."

Peter's heart skipped a beat at the sound of her voice. He turned to see Emmaline standing at the base of her stage. Beatrice fluttered around her, untying the ribbon around her waist and wiping Emmaline's brow with a handkerchief.

"Thanks," Peter whispered.

Emmaline shifted her gaze away and walked quickly by with Beatrice, whose steps kicked at the dusty earth as she hustled her charge back toward a waiting train car.

"I'll pick up those clothes in the mornin', boy!" Beatrice called to Peter over her shoulder. "Can't have yer pants fallin' down around yer ankles mid-show!"

Peter's cheeks burned as Tiny let out a hearty laugh. Peter cleared his throat.

"Where are they going?" he asked, nodding toward Emmaline and Bea's retreating figures.

"Back to their train car." Tiny looked down at Peter and watched the way his eyes followed Emmaline's every movement. "She won't be joining our post-show party," Tiny said. Peter looked up at him in surprise.

"Why not?" he asked. "How come she never joins the rest of the group?"

Tiny shrugged. "The rules are different for Emmaline," he said. The way the words rolled off his tongue made Peter sad. He found himself aching for the girl whose world seemed controlled and pinned down.

"C'mon, Pete," Tiny said with a sigh. "Time to unwind."

Peter balanced his plate in his hands as he settled down next to Tiny in front of the fire. All around them, performers and circus hands mingled and talked, a raucous noise rising from their small camp. The sky above them was fading into the kind of black that you only find way outside the city. Peter looked up and knew that soon it would be lit up with stars. The thought made him smile. He had never noticed the stars when he lived in New York, but they were his favorite part of circus life.

Thinking of his home in the city melted the smile from Peter's face. He wondered how Yulia was doing. Had she married the newspaper man yet? Was she still living alone in their tiny flat? Peter decided that he would write her a letter before bed.

Craning his neck, Peter looked around the group for his mother. His shoulders slumped when he realized she wasn't there. He grabbed the small roll from his plate and took a bite, chewing slowly and swallowing against his disappointment.

Tiny glanced at Peter, then took a bite of the roll on his own plate. "Yer mama ain't comin', kid," he said. "Ol' Butch runs a tight ship in the cookhouse. All these mouths to feed means he keeps his workers busy into the night."

Peter's shoulders slumped over his plate. He pushed the chicken and vegetables around with a long, sad sigh. In front of him, the fire crackled, its steady pops filling in the cracks of sound that surrounded them. The post-show amusement was joyful and fun. All the performers came together like a big family, laughing and singing, eating and drinking. In the background, Peter could hear the scuffle of hooves and bleats and cursing as the menagerie was bedded down for the night in their own special tent. Peter took it all in, every movement and sound thrumming against the disappointment of not seeing his mother.

Tiny watched the boy next to him with some amusement. "There are a lot of things moving through yer mind, aren't there?" Tiny asked.

Peter looked up at him. "I guess," he said with a shrug.

Tiny smiled and shoveled a piece of greasy chicken into his mouth. Peter took another bite of his roll, his eyes scanning the crowd again for his mother.

"Why'd you tell me to pay no mind to what people say when I perform?" Peter asked. Tiny looked down at him, one eyebrow raised. "Beatrice said the same thing when she was fixing my shirt," Peter continued. "I don't understand what that means."

Tiny took another bite of chicken and chewed slowly, then he slid down off the log that he shared with Peter and stretched his legs toward the fire. He set his plate aside and leaned back, gazing up at the stars.

"Look up there at that sky, Pete," Tiny said. He stretched out a long arm and pointed toward the sky where the stars were beginning to twinkle above their heads. Peter gazed at the sight and waited.

"What do you think is up there in that big, ol' sky?" Tiny asked.

Peter swallowed, unsure exactly how he was supposed to answer this question. "Um, well. The stars, I guess," he replied. "And the moon. And..." Peter hesitated before going on. "I read in a book once that there are different galaxies out there. Just...lots of stars and planets floating in space." He glanced at Tiny. "But I don't know if that's true or not."

"Well, if you read it in a book then it may well be the truth," Tiny said. He folded his hands back behind his head and turned to look at Peter. "But there's more out there, Pete," he said. Peter squinted up at the sky in confusion.

"There is?" he asked.

"Beyond the stars, there are the heavens," Tiny said with a sweep of the arm. "And in the heavens are entire worlds waiting for us."

Peter swallowed hard. He slid from his seat to the ground beside Tiny and leaned back so that his head rested on the log and he could look right into the vast expanse of the sky above.

"You ever heard of the Creator?" Tiny asked. Peter shook his head.

"Well," Tiny said. "Up there, beyond the stars and in the heavens, there's this Creator, see. And this Creator is the one who set this whole world in motion. He's the one who fixed the sun in the day and the moon in the night. And He's the One who lit those stars up so that they burned holes in the sky."

Peter soaked in Tiny's words, the way they flowed from his mouth almost like a stream of water on a hot day. He blinked slowly as the fire crackled at his feet and his fellow circus performers hooted and hollered in the background.

"Now this Creator didn't stop when He made the world, of course," Tiny said. "He had to fill this big ol' world so it'd be nice to look at. So, he made the mountains and the oceans, and all the plants and animals." Tiny chuckled. "Can you imagine the creativity it took to come up with something as wild as the elephant."

Peter smiled.

"Then this Creator got his grandest idea—the thing that would be his greatest, most prized creation of all." Tiny shifted so that he looked right into Peter's eyes. "He finished His work by making man and woman. He created people so they could fill the world with more people."

Behind them, Manny and Jessop walked up, both clutching bottles of hootch in their hands. Jessop's pants hung low on his waist exposing the crack of his buttocks, which didn't seem to bother him in the slightest. They stumbled over to Tiny and Peter and stared down at them.

"How you two doin'?" Manny asked. Jessop let out a loud belch.

"We're just fine," Tiny murmured.

"Tiny tellin' you stories, kid?" Jessop asked. Peter nodded.

"Yeah, I knew he would be," Jessop jeered. "Ol' Tiny here loves his fairy tales. He talkin' 'bout the Creator who made the world yet? That's his favorite."

Peter nodded again, wide-eyed. Jessop snorted, and Manny stumbled off toward the sound of Clarice singing on the other side of the fire, her golden gown shimmering in the sinking sunlight. Absent her clown makeup, Clarice looked almost pretty. Jessop followed Manny, his short legs scuffling against the dusty earth. Tiny was quiet for a moment before he continued.

"See the thing about this Creator, Pete," he said, his voice so soft that Peter had to lean in to better hear him. "The thing is He knows all about His creation. He knows all the deep-down stuff about the people He created. He knows who they are way down in here." Tiny tapped his chest. "Only problem is, His creation don't always know who they are."

Peter looked steadily at Tiny, trying hard to understand the meaning behind his words. Tiny sighed and turned so that he leaned on his elbow.

"See Pete, those people who come watch our show—they ain't the Creator. They ain't got the power to see beyond the outside. They only see what they want to see, or what they're told to see. This is why we're able to make them believe things. Understand?"

Peter nodded slowly, then paused. "No, I guess I don't," he replied sheepishly. Tiny looked through the fire at the group on the other side.

"Look over there and tell me what you see," he said with a nod of his chin. Peter looked and studied the group for a moment.

"I see Miss Clarabelle looking sad," he said. "And Manny and Jessop look a mess."

Tiny chuckled.

"I see Miss Clarice singing. Her voice is nice. And I see…" Peter squinted through the hazy smoke that danced toward the sky. "I see Mortimer the Magician and his rabbit." Peter smiled at the sight of the magician stroking the back of the rabbit's head. He still wore his black cape from the show, but he had removed the mask that hid his eyes when he performed.

"Well Mortimer's real name is Cletis," Tiny said, laughter lacing through his words. "He's from South Carolina, and there is nothing magic about him. It's all slight of hand and smoke bombs to trick the mind."

Peter gaped at the magician.

"Manny and Jessop are as stupid as they seem," Tiny continued. "There's no hidin' there. And Miss Clarabelle eats her way through each day in an attempt to push away the sadness that overwhelms her. She had a son, you know," Tiny said softly. "He died in a farming accident when he was two. Fell off the plow his Pa was drivin'. Miss Clarabelle's husband couldn't handle his guilt and put a shotgun in his mouth. Miss Clarabelle ain't lazy like people would have you believe. She's just as sad as they come."

Peter blinked. He turned to face Tiny. "But…I still don't understand," he said, his confession laced with an apology.

Tiny sighed. "What I'm trying to tell you, Pete," he said, "is that people only see what they're told to see. They can only see the outside because they ain't the Creator. Take Miss Bea, for example." Tiny nodded as Beatrice walked past the group, two plates in her hands.

She hustled toward the train car where Emmaline sat, her back to the window, golden hair brushing the glass and causing Peter's heart to skip a beat.

"Miss Bea is one of the kindest ladies you will ever meet in your life," Tiny continued. "And she's talented to boot! Can sew just about any piece of clothing there is."

Peter nodded, glancing down at his patched-up shirt.

"But ain't nobody gonna pay her no mind 'cause of the color of her skin. People see her brown face, and they immediately form an opinion without getting to know the woman beneath the skin." Tiny shook his head. "It's a damn shame," he said.

"Now," he leaned over so that his face was closer to Peter's. "Look at that little girl in the train car over there—the one who makes your face go all funny every time you see her."

Peter blushed, glancing over at Emmaline's train car.

"That poor girl can't hardly dress herself in the mornin'. She can't read or write or tie her own shoes 'cause no one's ever taught her to do so. But she's right pretty, and she's got that milky white skin, so everyone who walks into that tent assumes she's smart and educated. They don't know beyond what they can see." Tiny paused briefly before continuing. "And then there's you, Pete."

Peter swallowed hard. He self-consciously ran his hand over his head, smoothing back his wiry hair.

"People are gonna make assumptions 'bout you as well. You're the ugly wild child, wrapped in chains and dressed in rags. The ugliest boy in the world standing next to the most beautiful girl in the world. They're only going to believe what they can see, and they will talk about what they believe. They won't know that you speak more than one language." Tiny gave Peter a sideways glance. "How many languages do you speak anyway?" he asked.

"Three," Peter confessed quietly. "I want to learn Spanish, too, so I can communicate with Señor and Señora Fernandez."

Tiny chuckled and shook his head.

"See what I mean, Pete?" he continued. He reached behind him and pulled a piece of hay from a nearby bale, sticking it in his teeth and rolling it around slowly. "Those people who wander into our tent won't know how smart you are because they ain't the Creator. They can't see the inside. This is why *you* gotta know who you are—who the Creator made you to be. And you gotta believe it hard. Because if you start listening to what those people say about you—the ones who are stuck only seein' the outside—you might start to believe them. And when you start to believe people who can only see the outside, you're in for a world of hurt." Tiny leaned back with a sigh. "You understand now?"

Peter swallowed hard. He leaned back and looked up at the sky. "Yeah, I understand," he said quietly. Tiny nodded.

"Good," he said.

They were silent for a moment before Peter spoke again, his voice cutting through the sounds that surrounded them.

"Tiny?"

"Hmm..." Tiny replied, eyes focused on the stars above their heads.

"If you're not the Creator, then how come you can see past the outside better than others?"

Tiny's mouth tilted upward. "Well," he said, offering Peter a sideways glance. "See there's something real interesting that happens to those of us who are born different. We have eyes that see deeper than the surface 'cause our outsides aren't like everyone else's. I think that's a gift the Creator gives us misfits. We get special vision that no one else gets." Tiny fell silent for a long minute.

"Problem is," he finally continued, his voice lowering to a hum, "we gotta remember to use those special eyes. Otherwise we ain't really no different from the rest of them."

With that, the unlikely pair both fell silent, each one staring up at the stars. The two lay next to one another for a long time that night, the ugliest boy and the tallest man, surrounded by laughter and noise and circus freaks.

THREE

1900

Nataliya wiped her hands on her apron and let out a long sigh. She rolled her head side to side, stretching out the muscles that had tied themselves up after a long day spent bent over the kitchen fires. She had finally finished cleaning up the dinner meal and prepping the post-show food for performers when she snuck out to see if she could find her son. She paused for a brief moment in the cool night air and drew in a deep breath, letting it out slowly.

It had been four years since they'd left to join Beaumont's circus. Time had somehow both slowed down and sped up, and Nataliya felt like she'd aged one hundred years since then. They'd fallen into a rhythm, she and Peter, each one making the most of this life they'd chosen for themselves. Nataliya knew that Peter got tired of acting like the wild child, especially lately. He was no longer a little boy enamored with the circus but was now a young man who was simply there to do a job. He still reserved a little affection for her, though, and for that she was grateful.

Nataliya was making her way through the maze of tents when she heard a conversation that stopped her in her tracks.

"There's another show behind us," the voice hissed from the shadows. "A sideshow act. You're going to check it out for me." Nataliya had recognized Monsieur Beaumont's clipped French immediately. She halted and hid behind a tent to listen.

"Who cares?"

The other voice belonged to Pierre, Beaumont's sniveling excuse for a son. Nataliya shivered at the thought of the handsome boy with a mean streak that followed his father around like a puppy dog, hanging on his every word, and terrorizing the rest of the performers in his father's absence.

"They're just a group of freaks. They don't have the *l'energie* we do." Pierre whined.

"I care! I want to know what talent they've got in that group of freaks. I heard whispers in town that they also have a deformed performer in their show—some crazy looking freak they've billed as the world's ugliest man. I want to know about him, and about any other acts they have up their sleeves. Nobody is going to accuse me of being a copycat."

"So, what? You want me to go into town and see what I can find out?" Pierre sniffed. "Why can't you do it?"

"That would be too obvious, boy!" Beaumont snarled. "They would recognize me. You need to go and see what you can find. Maybe we can lure a few of their people to our company."

Pierre sighed the long sigh of a spoiled child who wasn't getting his way. "How am I supposed to find out that information?" he whined. "Where do I find these people?"

"The local saloon," Beaumont replied. "There are bound to be people there who will talk, and the later it gets, the looser their tongues will be. Here's some money. Go find a table to sit and just observe. Find the loneliest person you can, then sit next to him. Ask questions and listen. Find me answers."

The voices faded as father and son retreated, but Nataliya was left shaking in the shadow of the tent. *"I heard that they also have a de-*

formed performer in their show—some crazy looking freak they've billed as the world's ugliest man."

Nataliya drew in a deep, shaking breath. She glanced toward the Big Top. In the distance, she could hear the faint sounds of the postshow party kicking up, the trill of a harmonica floating across the night breeze. She looked back over her shoulder at the cookhouse tent. Butch had lightened up a little over the years. By working hard and keeping her head down, Nataliya had gained enough of his respect that he didn't mind her occasionally hurrying over to say hello to Peter. But he would expect her back shortly, and he would have work for her to do.

She shifted her gaze in the other direction, toward the nearby town that blossomed at the other end of the train yard. It was dark, the sliver of a moon providing very little light. But Nataliya knew the way to the town center because she'd walked there with Butch when they first arrived to gather supplies. Whenever they arrived in a new city, crates of food supplies waited for them, gathered ahead of time by a team who was always one step in front of Monsieur Beaumont's traveling circus.

There were baked goods from the locals, many of whom were thrilled to be offering some assistance to the mighty circus. There were choice cuts of meats from nearby butchers, crates full of fruits and vegetables from local farmers, and so many loaves of bread that they often had leftovers to feed to the animals. Nataliya drew in a deep breath. If she hurried, she could get into town before Pierre. She could simply tell Butch that she'd taken ill and laid down for some rest and lost track of time. He'd be angry, and he'd probably make her pay by working her extra hard the next few days, but…

Ducking into the shadows, Nataliya made her way through the tents and hustled out the back side, quickly finding the path that led into town. She didn't know what she expected to find when she got there. She was a woman alone after dark, a circus worker with a moderate grasp of the English language. She had no plan but was driven solely by a desire to know if it could possibly be true. Could Kolya be this close?

It took her fifteen minutes to pick her way down the darkened path. When she finally arrived, she found the vibrant town alive with action. Nataliya blinked several times, surprised at how many people were still on the streets. Many had only just left the final circus performance, still high on the awe and astonishment they'd felt beneath the tent.

Horses lined the sides of each building, and the raucous sound of laughter drifted out onto the cobblestone street. This was one of the larger towns they had visited. Over the last five years, it seemed that the country had expanded and grown, particularly in the bigger cities in the south. They were in Tennessee this month, making their way from city to city before the winter forced them to set up camp at their Oklahoma base for a few months. The winter was when Beaumont liked to train new hires and to prepare new acts for the spring show.

Nataliya stepped into the noisy street and quickly made her way to the walkway on the side, getting as close to the nearby building as she could. At the end of the street she turned a corner and saw the local saloon tucked in the back alley. Her heart hammered as she took timid steps toward the building. Piano music danced from the swinging doors, and the sound of men laughing and clinking glasses turned her stomach. Nataliya stopped and shook her head. She couldn't go in that place alone. She turned to leave, and that's when she saw him. He was walking across the street, eyes down, with a bowler hat atop his head. He was dressed in a dark suit, and he had his hands shoved in his pockets. He was far away, but he'd paused beneath a streetlamp and glanced up briefly, long enough for Nataliya to recognize him.

"Kolya," she whispered.

He continued walking, unaware of her presence. He was clearly trying to move quickly and to remain unseen. Nataliya recognized that posture—it was the same way her son walked when he felt ashamed and afraid.

Rushing back toward the main street, Nataliya turned and followed Kolya from a distance, her eyes pinned to his retreating back. One of his shoulders sloped lower than the other, and he walked unevenly. Nataliya took it all in with a racing heart, unable to believe she had really found him after all these years. She was so intent on keeping up with Kolya that she didn't see Pierre on the other side of the street watching her with narrowed eyes.

Kolya turned at last, ducking into a small building. Nataliya stopped outside and stared up at the sign.

JOHNSON'S HOTEL

She glanced up and saw a light flicker on in a room one floor above the lobby. Drawing in a deep breath, Nataliya pushed into the dimly lit hotel. A woman sat behind the desk, her head in her hand as she wrote on a small piece of paper. She looked up when the bell above the door jingled and eyed Nataliya suspiciously.

"Can I help you?" she asked. Her hair was pulled in a tight, severe bun on top of her head. A few pieces had been spared the bun and were curled into ringlets around her pudgy face. Her nose was large, and it sat nestled beneath small eyes, giving her a striking resemblance to an otter. Her plump bosom spilled over the top of a tight corset, and her shabby dress made her look much wider than she really was. In all, she was an unsightly woman, and Nataliya immediately pitied her for it.

"I..." Nataliya hesitated, formulating the words in her mind before speaking them slowly. "I am looking for my friend. He is here." Nataliya pointed at the ceiling, hoping that the gesture would help her communicate who she hoped to see. The woman behind the desk narrowed her eyes.

"I don't know of no one expectin' no visitors," she said. Nataliya cocked her head to the side quizzically, trying to decipher the woman's words.

"Please," Nataliya asked. "I must to see my friend. He is here."

The women pursed her lips and shook her head. "Listen, we are a respectable place, miss," she said, folding her fat arms over her breast. "We don't want your kind in here hopin' to...*entertain* our guests." Her eyes flicked up and down a few times, taking in the sight of Nataliya's small, thin frame with unmasked disdain.

Nataliya blinked a few times and, realizing that she would not get past this woman, slowly retreated, her arms hanging limply by her side as she stepped back onto the cool street. Fall was pushing its way quickly into the hills of Tennessee. It would turn cold soon. Nataliya crossed her arms to stave off the chill and turned to look up at the window where the light glowed. She gasped when she saw Kolya's face peering back down at her. His eyes were wide, a look of both shock and horror washing over his distorted features. Nataliya raised her hand toward him, and he quickly backed away from the window. She waited, watching the glass above to see if he would reappear. She was still looking a minute later when he suddenly appeared before her.

"Nataliya?" he asked. His voice was laced with shock. "Is it you?"

Nataliya's eyes filled with tears. She nodded her head slowly. "*Da, eta ya*," she replied. *It's me. It's really me*, her heart cried.

"I...I don't...understand," Kolya stammered. "How are you here? Where did you come from?" He reached for her, then stopped and pulled his arm back. He looked around the busy street and ducked his head, suddenly aware that they could be seen.

"Can we go inside?" Nataliya asked, her shoulders quaking. Kolya nodded and together they turned and walked back inside where the chubby girl gaped at the two of them.

"Excuse me," she said, "but I already turned this woman away. I don't want her kind in here. We are a respectable place of business."

"She's my sister," Kolya said. His English was perfect, flawless and without accent. Nataliya stared at him in surprise. She followed him up the wooden staircase, not daring to look back at the woman behind the desk.

She followed Kolya into his room, a simple space with a small bed, a dresser, a mirror, and a bowl and pitcher for washing up. It was cold in his room, but warmer than the outdoors. Kolya stepped to the other side of the bed and turned to face her, blinking hard.

"I can't believe it," he said. "What are you doing here?"

Nataliya wrung her hands in front of her waist, suddenly shaky and off balance. "I..." she paused and looked at him, taking in the sight of the man before her. He was no longer the boy she remembered, his features having filled out some with age. His hair was unruly, growing thickly around his eyes and down the side of his face, and hanging to his shoulders. He had it pulled into a loose ponytail at the nape of his neck.

The area around his eyes was wrinkled, and his skin had the weathered appearance of a man who had spent too many hours in the sun. She stared into those eyes, searching for the boy she had fallen in love with all those years ago. He was so different now. Changed.

"I don't know what I'm doing here," she finally answered, her voice no more than a whisper. Kolya stared at her for a long moment, then looked away. "What are *you* doing here?" Nataliya asked.

"My job," he answered. His words were clipped and weak. He sat shakily on the bed and ran a hand over his face. "It's been a long time, Nataliya," he said.

"*Da*," she replied. "Too long."

She sat down on the other side of the bed, careful not to sit too closely to him. "Are you still traveling with the circus?" she asked. Kolya nodded tentatively.

"Yes, in some way," he answered. "I'm part of a small, traveling sideshow now. The big show was too much for me. There were too many people, and the expectations were much too high. I had to get out. Now I'm just with a smaller group of people who come through and perform day shows." He offered her a wry smile, his mouth just barely turning upward.

"You know," he said, bitterness tainting his speech. "We let the people gawk and stare and marvel at the freaks for a few pennies at a time so they can feel better about themselves at the end of the day."

Nataliya swallowed hard at the heat in his words.

Kolya drew in another long breath and looked away from her probing stare. "We're preparing to set up a show tomorrow, but I often try to get away on my own beforehand, so here I am." He turned to look at her again. "And here *you* are. I can't believe I'm seeing you." His eyes were full of questions.

Nataliya drew in a deep breath. "I'm traveling with a circus, now, too," she said quietly. Kolya's eyes widened.

"The one that just set up outside of town?" he asked. "The big one?"

Nataliya nodded.

"But...but how?" he stuttered. "The last time I saw you, you were having a...baby." He stopped, his eyes growing wide. "You were having our child in St. Petersburg, Russia. You were half a world away, and now you're here." He pushed to his feet, a look of horror sweeping across his features.

"Where is the child?" he asked.

Nataliya stood up slowly and met his eyes. She raised her chin, hoping to portray more courage than she actually felt.

"He is with me. He works in the sideshow."

Kolya slumped against the wall, his eyes glazing over. "So, it was a boy?" he asked.

Nataliya nodded. "*Da*," she answered. "His name is Pavel Konstaninovich. Pasha. But the Americans call him Peter."

Kolya shook his head slowly, back and forth. "And...he is part of the sideshow act. So that means he..." Kolya's eyes glassed over, and his head dropped. "He looks like me."

Nataliya took a tentative step toward him. "Yes," she said. "He looks like you—his papa. And he is magnificent, Kolya. He is smart—so, so smart. He speaks four languages now. Four! He taught himself Spanish just in these last few years. He can read any book you put in front of him. He's kind and gentle, and you would be so proud of him if you knew him--"

"I'm not going to know him," Kolya interjected. He looked at Nataliya through heavy lids, his hands clenched into fists by his side. "I don't want him to see me—to know that I'm the freak who made him the way that he is. I was weak when I met you. We were young and impetuous and foolish." He glared at her. "I let myself think for a moment that with you I could be normal. I won't fool myself again."

Nataliya stared at Kolya in surprise, tears pricking at the corners of her eyelids. "Kolya," she whispered.

"*NYET!*" he roared. "I don't want to know more." His face was red, and he shook from head to toe. Nataliya blinked several times.

"Our son is so much more than what he looks like on the outside," she finally said quietly. "Just like you."

"And yet you've allowed him to become the freak in a sideshow, stared at and ridiculed *because* of what he looks like on the outside," Kolya seethed. "How do you explain that, Nataliya?"

Her eyes filled with tears. "You don't understand what it was like for us," she answered. "Joining the circus was Pasha's idea. It was what he *wanted,* and we needed to do *something*. People were making fun of him and ridiculing him anyway." Nataliya swiped a tear off her cheek and shrugged her shoulders. "At least this way he is in control of what they say."

Kolya shook his head in disgust. "He'll never be in control," he growled. "Parading him out in front of people will only kill his soul. It will happen slowly over time, and he'll never get that part of himself back."

Silence engulfed the room as the two stared at one another, Kolya shaking with anger and Nataliya clasping her hands together to try to warm herself against the fear that had settled in her chest.

"You could meet him, you know," she finally said. "We could meet, the three of us. We could find some place to go, away from the crowds and the staring eyes. We could be a family, and you could help him learn to be a man."

Kolya laughed, a mirthless sound that leeched from his throat and cut through the air.

"And where would we go, Nataliya?" he asked. "Two freaks, and the foolish woman who claims to love them both? Where would we go and what would we do?"

Nataliya stared at him, not moving, barely breathing.

Kolya shook his head. "I don't want to meet him," he said. The anger and hatred had left him. His arms dropped limply to his side, and his eyes glazed over.

Kolya turned his back to Nataliya and lowered himself slowly onto the bed.

"You should go," he murmured. "Pretend we never met. And don't mention me to the boy."

Nataliya reached out tentatively, her fingertips grazing the top of his hunched back. Kolya pulled away as though he'd been burned and swung around to face her.

"LEAVE ME!" he bellowed.

Nataliya spun on her heel and ran from the room, tripping down the stairs and past the ugly desk keeper who watched with disdain in her eyes.

Nataliya stumbled into the street and gulped in the frigid air, tears streaming down her cheeks. The steady hum of voices and horse's hooves mixed with the faint strains of piano music beating from the saloon. She wiped her face with shaking hands and turned to look back up at Kolya's room. He stared down at her through the glass of the window, his eyes narrowed, face contorted with pain and anger. He turned away, drew the curtain, and left her alone in the cold air.

Emmaline woke early, stretching her arms out above her head and groaning as she forced open her eyes. The room was still dark, the early morning sunshine not having peeked its way high enough over the horizon to chase out the night sky. She blinked a few times, then yelped and pulled the covers to her chin at the sight of a shadow sitting in the corner.

The shadow jumped up, moving toward the door like a ghost floating on air. It was familiar, the way this shadow moved. Emmaline gulped in a few long, shaking breaths as she watched it duck through the open rail car and slip out the doorway, disappearing into the hazy morning fog. She pulled the covers over her head and fought off panic.

On the other side of the room, behind a small partition, Emmaline could hear Beatrice's heavy breathing, the long, rasping sounds drawing up and into the still air that surrounded them. Emmaline huddled under her sheet, heart pounding, and listened to the woman who cared for her day and night. She was Beatrice's charge, this she knew, but Emmaline was never quite sure if Bea was completely on her side. She knew for certain she could never wake Beatrice in the night and tell her about bad dreams. Nor could she wake her now and tell her about the moving shadow that fled their room. Emmaline often wondered if Beatrice would come to her aid if real danger arose. She wasn't sure.

Slowly, Emmaline's breathing steadied, and she gathered the courage to peek up over the top of the bed sheet. It was a little brighter in the room now, and the shadows seemed less defined. Had she really seen someone sitting in the corner, or had it just been her mind playing tricks?

Outside her window, Emmaline heard the sounds of a new day dawning. Train car doors slid open, and the *thwap, thwap, thwap* of the many groundsmen as they jumped from their cars to the ground beat a morning hello. Somewhere in the distance, a rooster crowed. Emmaline closed her eyes, and for a brief moment, the flash of a memory crossed her mind. At least she thought it was a memory.

There was a rooster crowing in this vision, too. Emmaline was tucked into a soft bed, and next to her lay an older woman with soft brown hair and a kind face. Emmaline stared at her in this vision, and the woman opened her eyes and smiled back. She reached over and smoothed the hair off Emmaline's face, then opened her mouth as though she might speak, but no words came out. Her face simply shimmered, then disappeared.

Emmaline's eyes flew open, and she sat up quickly, rubbing her face. She had this vision often, and it always seemed so real. She felt as if she knew that woman in her dream, but she couldn't figure out who she was or the place where she came from.

Pushing to her feet, Emmaline wrapped a blanket around her shoulders and padded to the window seat. Her curly hair stood in unruly waves around her face, but she didn't care. She was tired of people caring about her hair and her clothes, sick of having to paint her face or wear bands around her teeth to keep them lined up straight. Sitting down, Emmaline leaned toward the glass and watched as the day dawned around them.

It would be a full morning for the groundsmen as they cleaned up after last night's show and prepared for tonight's. Monsieur Beaumont ran his show differently than most circuses. Rather than packing up immediately after every show and moving to the next town, he decided to stay and do two shows in the same place.

"Saves money, and maximizes our earning potential in each town," he declared when asked why he did this. No one argued with him, either, because it allowed them time to better rest and settle into their shows in each town.

Emmaline knew that this morning, the groundsmen would spend hours picking up trash and sweeping broken bits of popcorn from the night before into waiting crates, which would then be hauled into nearby trees and dumped, left behind for the local townspeople to deal with.

At some point, the men would check the rigging for Señor and Señora Fernandez's act, and they would rake the hay in the center ring so that it lay flat and neat again. As she watched, Emmaline saw a group of teenage boys making their way toward the Big Top, hands clutching rags and pails of sudsy water. They were the ones tasked with scrubbing the tents, making sure they shined and gleamed in the sunshine. It was something she knew people admired when they visited this circus.

Emmaline wondered what other circuses were like. Did they pay this much attention to detail, or was Monsieur Beaumont really as difficult as many claimed him to be? Emmaline heard whispers from the others. She heard the way people talked about the ringmaster when he left the room. Nobody seemed to like him at all, not that Emmaline could blame them. Monsieur Beaumont was a difficult man to please.

A movement caught Emmaline's eye, and she shifted her gaze to see what it was. Darting out from between the train cars, Pierre ran down the line. He still wore his outfit from the night before, the back of his long coat wrinkled as though he'd been sitting on it for a long time. He turned slightly and caught sight of Emmaline watching him.

His mouth twisted into a smile, but his smile wasn't kind. Instead, it made Emmaline shiver and pull away from the window, away from his hungry eyes. When she slowly peeked back out the window a moment later, Pierre was gone, but not before it registered that his run was familiar. She had seen that movement in the shadow that fled her room earlier, the way the elbows kicked out at an angle and the head tilted to the left. Emmaline felt a knot form in the pit of her stomach. It had been Pierre sitting in her room, watching while she slept. Emmaline shuddered.

"What are you doin' up, child?" Beatrice's voice broke through the stillness. It was low and raspy and laced with annoyance.

"Couldn't sleep," Emmaline mumbled with a shrug.

"Well, go git back in yer bed and try to rest some more," Beatrice mumbled, shifting in her bed and turning to her side. "Can't have you gettin' no bags under yer eyes. Boss won't like that. His prize needs her beauty sleep."

The way Beatrice said "prize" made Emmaline's stomach turn. She pushed to her feet and trudged back to her bed, laying down on the soft mattress and staring quietly at the ceiling. She wouldn't sleep anymore this morning; she knew it. But there was no sense fighting Bea. Instead, she lay blinking quietly at the ceiling as the sounds of life rose just outside her wall—the sounds of a freedom that Emmaline simply did not understand.

Peter hopped from the train car and steadied himself. His mouth stretched into a wide yawn, and he blinked against the water that gathered in the corners of his eyes. His neck and shoulders were stiff from another late night lying on the ground beneath the stars. When he and Tiny finally stumbled back to their train car, it had been well past midnight. His sleep had been fitful after that. Even after four years, he wasn't sure if he would ever get used to the sounds and smells of this place, especially after dark. There was no aroma of popcorn behind the scenes to quell the true scent of the circus. Hay and animal manure mingled with the gag-inducing odors of Manny and Jessop's sweaty bodies, causing Peter to have to sleep with an old rag tied around his nose in order to stifle the smell.

Peter's dream had been filled with visions of his mother, and Yulia, and his grandparents. He woke up with an ache in his chest—a longing for his family that was so thick he felt as though he were being pressed on. Glancing from left to right, Peter took in the sights of the morning. The sun was just beginning to light the sky, painting streaks of pastel colors above the tree line. A faint orange tinged the lower horizon, which faded into pink, and from there into light blue, then the darker blue of the night sky, which seemed to be fighting a losing battle with the impending day. The air felt cool and fresh outside the train car, and Peter gulped in long, deep breaths.

He turned and began quickly making his way toward the cookhouse tent, hoping to catch his mother before the morning breakfast had to be served. Peter passed a group of teenage boys who looked to be about his age. They were scrubbing and cleaning the outside of the sideshow tent. Peter knew they would move on to the Big Top next. Their entire day would be spent wiping the dirt away from last night's show.

The boys didn't speak as he walked by, but Peter could feel their stares, and he heard the snickers as he loped past them, his uneven gait drawing their attention. He raised his chin higher, refusing to look in the boys' direction, but inside his stomach tied all up in knots, and his cheeks burned with shame.

Peter rounded the corner and stopped short at the sight of her. He tucked into the shadow and watched as his mother walked through the awakening tent village. Her head was down, and she kicked nervously at the ground in front of her. Something about her posture made Peter uncomfortable. He wanted to cry out to her, to rush over to greet her, but he hesitated, choosing instead to pull back and simply observe. He took in the sight of her rumpled shirt and the muddy bottom of her long skirt. Her hair was a mess, the bun at the nape of her neck having come unraveled so that loose tendrils flew around her face in the breeze. Peter had never seen his mother in such a state. His hands shook as he watched her go.

Moments later, after Nataliya had disappeared around the bend, Peter pushed himself back out into the morning sunshine and slowly followed his mother's path. He looked up in surprise as Monsieur Beaumont stepped up beside him, a smug smile plastered on his round face. His jet-black hair was slicked back, and the skin around his eyes crinkled in that way that makes men look dignified rather than old. Today was Tuesday, which meant that yesterday had been the day he dyed his hair and mustache. He dyed them every Monday night after the show. There was much speculation among the performers as to what color his hair really was beneath all that black dye.

"White as a fresh snow," was the general consensus whispered among the group, though a small percentage maintained that his hair may actually be something even more unsightly, like a dull blonde the color of dirty water after laundry day.

Boss Man's clothes were freshly pressed this morning, though he didn't yet wear his performance costume, but rather had on dark trousers and a crisp, white shirt, which was tucked neatly into his waist. Suspenders stretched taut over his protruding stomach, and his shirtsleeves were rolled to just below his elbows. He looked like any other workingman, and for the first time Peter realized that Monsieur Beaumont had grown quite short.

"Good morning, boy," Boss Man said quietly. Peter nodded back at him.

"Morning," he murmured.

"Where are you off to so early?" the ringmaster asked. He slowed to a stop, and Peter reluctantly stopped with him.

"Um, just on a walk," Peter stammered.

Monsieur Beaumont narrowed his eyes. "Just a walk?" he asked. He shook his head. "I don't believe you," he said. "I think you're going to see your mother this morning. Am I right?"

Peter swallowed hard and nodded his head, keeping his eyes down.

"You don't have to lie, boy," the ringmaster said. His voice wasn't kind or gentle. It was mocking, as though he found Peter to be the punchline of a grand joke. "You've never been forbidden from seeing your mother, just as long as you don't distract her from her work."

Peter looked at him. The ringmaster stared back, an indiscernible look plastered on his face.

"Go on, now," he said to Peter, tucking his thumbs inside his suspenders and gesturing toward the cookhouse tent with his head. "Go to see your mother."

Peter turned slowly, bewildered by the conversation.

"Oh, and boy?"

Peter stopped and turned back to face Monsieur Beaumont.

"Be sure to tell your mother that I know where she went last night. Tell her if she does it again, I will leave her behind, and she'll never see you again."

Peter's heartbeat slowed, and his vision swirled for a moment. He blinked as Monsieur Beaumont turned with a laugh and began walking back toward his tent.

"Where did she go?" Peter called out. His voice sounded hollow and far away. Beaumont turned and tossed him a withering stare.

"Ask your mother that question. Not me," he hissed.

Peter swallowed hard and waited as Beaumont rounded the corner and disappeared from sight. He took a deep breath and turned toward the cookhouse tent. It was quiet this early. Breakfast wouldn't be ready for the performers for another hour, so the empty tent loomed before him, large and still. It was as long as a football field, and inside were rows and rows of tables lined up, one after the other. The circus staff would come in waves to eat, with the performers being first. They got the best pick of each meal—the warmest food, the freshest fruits and vegetables. By the time the laborers came along, much of the meals would be picked over, but they wouldn't complain, because for most of them it was more food than they'd see anywhere else.

Peter very slowly drew back the flap of the tent and peeked inside. He blinked in the dim light, willing his eyes to adjust quickly. The sound of sniffling drew Peter's gaze to the front of the open space. He saw his mother slouched over the table, head in her hands, and his heart sank. Pulling back, Peter let the flap drop closed. He turned on his heel and walked away as quickly as he could, his heart racing and a lump in his throat. He rounded the corner and ran smack into Tiny, both of them stumbling over one another.

"Hells bells, Pete!" Tiny exclaimed. "Where you runnin' off to like that?"

Peter shook his head. "Sorry," he mumbled.

Tiny grabbed his hat off the ground and brushed the dirt from it. "S'alright, I s'pose," he said. He perched his hat back on top of his head, his unruly hair sticking out in a thousand different angles beneath it. He studied Peter for a brief moment.

"You alright, kid?" he asked.

Peter shrugged.

Tiny squinted up at the rising sun. "Well I was headin' over to the cookhouse to see if I couldn't sweet talk old Butch into givin' me a piece of bread before breakfast. Gotta feed the beast." Tiny rubbed his stomach with a smile. His body was long and lean, and he was always hungry.

"No, I'm going to go lay down," Peter answered. He sniffed and pushed his hair back out of his eyes with shaking hands.

"Did somethin' happen, Pete?" Tiny asked.

Peter paused and took in a deep breath. "Dunno," he finally said.

He looked up at Tiny. "You'd have to ask my mama that question, I think."

Peter spun on his heel and raced away. Tiny watched him go, concern swimming through his eyes. His stomach growled, and he sighed, turning back toward the cookhouse. A few minutes later, Tiny pushed through the tent and into the dim light. His eyes adjusted quickly. He saw Nataliya sitting at the front table, her head in her hands, and he approached her slowly.

"Mornin', miss," he said gently. Nataliya gasped and sat up.

"Good morning," she replied, wiping the tears off her face and pushing to a stand.

"No need to get up," Tiny said. He held up his hand. Nataliya froze and tilted her face up to stare at the man who stood nearly half a body length above her. After a moment, she slowly lowered herself back into the chair. Tiny sat down beside her.

"You alright, Miss Nataliya?" Tiny asked.

Nataliya sighed and shrugged her shoulders. Tiny smiled gently as the gesture was so similar to the one her son had just made outside the tent

"I do not know if I am alright," Nataliya said in stilted English. Her language was much better after years of working with Butch and Gerta, but while she understood everything that people said to her, she still felt nervous speaking.

"Well," Tiny began, "when I was a kid, my mama always told me that a problem seemed smaller if you talked about it with someone else. Maybe I could be an ear to listen."

Nataliya looked at him with a sad smile. "Maybe," she said. "But this problem of mine is very...uh, big. Is a big problem," she repeated.

Tiny leaned back and folded his hands in his lap. "Well, lucky for you I am a big man," he answered.

Nataliya drew in a deep breath then let it out slowly. She stared at her hands in her lap, glanced up at Tiny, then looked back down.

"I see him last night," she said, her voice just above a whisper. Tiny leaned in to better hear her.

"Saw who? Pete?" he asked.

Nataliya shook her head and blinked back tears. She looked up and met Tiny's eyes. "I see Pasha's…uh, Pete's…father," she replied.

Tiny leaned back, his eyes widening. "Pete's daddy? You saw him? Here?"

Nataliya nodded.

"Pete told me he ain't never met his daddy. Said he thought he must still be back in Russia somewhere. How in tarnation'd you run into him here in Tennessee?"

Nataliya sighed. "I never tell Pasha too much about his father," she answered. "He was not in Russia. He leave Russia before us and go to America to work…with the circus."

Understanding registered on Tiny's face. "Pete's daddy looks like Pete, don't he?" Tiny asked. Nataliya nodded.

"He wanted to get away…to protect me. He…uh…*leave* before Pasha is born."

"And you saw him last night? How?" Tiny asked.

Nataliya's hands shook as she sat before Tiny. She thought of the night before and blinked back fresh tears.

"I tell you," she said slowly. "But you cannot tell Pasha…Pete. You cannot tell him because he does not know. Please, Mr. Tiny. Please not to tell Pasha." She looked up at him with pleading eyes. Tiny reached forward and placed his large hand over hers.

"I promise I won't say nothin'," he said. "Ain't my place to tell Pete about any of this. I'll leave that to you."

Nataliya nodded gratefully.

"Well," she cleared her throat and launched into the events from the night before, stumbling over her words as she tried to convey it all to Tiny.

Nataliya stared at her hands as she spoke, fingers clasping and unclasping. When she finally finished, she kept her eyes down, afraid to look up at Tiny.

"So that is what happened," she said, blinking back fresh tears.

Tiny drew in a long, deep breath and let it out slowly. "That's really somethin'," he said quietly. "I'm real sorry that happened, Miss Nataliya."

Nataliya nodded. "I am sorry, too," she replied.

Tiny leaned forward and looked closely at Nataliya. She raised her eyes to meet his gaze.

"Miss Nataliya," he began, "somethin' happens to a man when he loses control of his life. It's real dangerous for us to feel useless. We gotta know that we're worth somethin' to others. If we lose that worth... well, it's just real hard to get it back." Tiny rubbed his hands over his eyes and let his words linger in the air for a moment.

"It's hard for a man to hold onto his worth when he's an act in the sideshow," Tiny finally finished. His words were quiet and heavy.

"Have you held on…to worth?" Nataliya asked.

Tiny leaned back and stared at the wall behind her head as he thought about his answer.

"I was losin' it for a while," he finally answered. "I got to feelin' real hopeless a few years back, but then somethin' happened." Tiny paused and looked at Nataliya. "I met your boy. Pete is somethin' special, Miss Nataliya. And bein' his friend has given me back my worth as a man."

Nataliya blinked as fresh tears flooded her eyes. "Pasha is very special boy," she nodded. "But will he lose worth?"

Tiny shook his head and paused before answering. "I'm real sorry that Pete's daddy wouldn't listen to you, Miss Nataliya," Tiny finally answered. His voice was soft and warm. "Maybe he's just too far gone. Maybe he's felt worthless for too long to overcome it. But I know one thing for sure—Pete is better than his daddy. He's growin' up into a fine young man. You be proud of him, and you trust him. Pete's gonna be alright."

"Thank you," Nataliya said through trembling lips.

"Yes, ma'am," Tiny replied.

"You do not have to call me ma'am," she said, sitting straighter and wiping her face.

Tiny grinned. "Old habits. My mama didn't let me speak to any lady without callin' her ma'am. But I'll try with you."

Both of them turned as Butch pushed into the tent, his round stomach entering first and the rest of him following. He glared at Tiny and Nataliya.

"Work don't do itself, girl," he growled. Nataliya stood quickly and gave Tiny a sad smile before turning and rushing from the tent. Butch watched her go, then turned and snarled at Tiny.

"Why're you here. Don't serve breakfast for another forty minutes."

"Aw, c'mon now, Butch," Tiny replied. He pushed to a stand, his long, lanky frame stretching up high above the tables. "Have a little mercy. I gotta get food in this body in order to operate." Tiny rubbed his hand up and down his stomach.

"You wait with the rest of 'em," Butch muttered. He plopped a large bowl onto the table at the front. Inside, rolls of bread piled high. Tiny stared at the bread, then looked back to Butch.

"Can't spare even one roll for a hungry man?" Tiny asked, eyebrows raised.

Butch let out a frustrated sigh and grabbed a roll, tossing it through the air at Tiny, who caught it with a wide grin.

"You sir," Tiny said. He took a bite of the roll and worked the bread into his cheek. "You are a god among mortals."

"Get outta my tent!" Butch bellowed.

Tiny chuckled, then turned and strode swiftly from the cookhouse. Before his feet hit the sunshine, the bread was gone.

Tiny made his way back to the train car where he found Peter sitting on the stoop, his eyes closed, and head leaned back against the cool metal of the train. Tiny thought of Nataliya's story, and he felt a wave of compassion for the boy and his mother.

"Heya, Pete," he said stepping between the boy and the sun so that Peter could look up and meet his gaze.

"Did you see my mama?" Peter asked.

"Yeah, I saw her."

"Did she tell you what happened?" Peter pushed himself up and stared expectantly at Tiny.

"Well, Pete," Tiny began. He thought of Nataliya's plea and chose his words carefully. "Sometimes mamas gotta do what they think is best for their kids. Sometimes they make choices that don't make no sense in order to protect their babies."

"I'm not a baby," Peter mumbled.

"No, you ain't a baby," Tiny responded. "That's not what I meant. I just mean that your mama has some secrets that she ain't ready for you to know yet, and you just have to be okay with that. When she's ready, she'll tell you."

"Did she tell you?" Peter asked.

"A little. Not all," Tiny admitted. "And I promised her I wouldn't tell you, and I'll keep that promise, Pete."

Peter flopped back and let out a frustrated sigh. Tiny reached down and put his hand on Peter's shoulder.

"Your mama ain't done nothin' wrong," he said. "She's just workin' through some things on her own right now. You need to give her space."

"Yeah, well whatever it is she did, Boss Man knows about it." Peter told Tiny about his conversation with Beaumont that morning. "So, if my mama isn't going to tell me whatever it is that's going on, then she better at least know to be careful because Beaumont is watching." Peter looked up at Tiny. "Will you tell her that, Tiny? Will you tell her to be careful?"

Tiny leaned forward and nodded his head. "I got yer back, kid." He narrowed his eyes and stared in the direction of Boss Man's tent.

Peter nodded. He shifted over on the stoop to allow Tiny space to sit down. Together they passed the time until the breakfast bell rang in the distance.

"Come in."

Emmaline stood outside the Boss Man's tent, hands shaking. There was only a flap of fabric separating her from him, but she felt exposed already. There were a couple of hours left in the afternoon before the final show would begin. She clasped and unclasped her hands nervously, wondering why Monsieur had summoned her.

"Emmaline!" he barked from the other side of the tent. "Come in here this minute!" She hated when he yelled. His accent came out thicker, making his words seem warbled and uneven.

With a deep breath, she pushed the flap open and stepped inside. She blinked several times as her eyes adjusted to the dim light. Monsieur Beaumont sat behind his desk and watched her through narrowed eyes. On the other side of the desk sat Pierre, his sniveling face twisted as he looked her up and down. His eyes moved slowly over her frame.

The lanterns in the tent cast shadows across the wall, illuminating the room with an orange glow that was so different from the vibrant sunshine of the outside world. Monsieur Beaumont hated sunshine. He liked to comment to anyone who would listen that he much preferred the night.

"That guy has to be a vampire," one of the grounds workers had told Emmaline earlier that day. "Just watch the way that he moves." The boy jutted his chin toward the ringmaster, who stood in the shaded pathway just outside his personal tent. Emmaline was standing to the side, waiting for Beatrice to finish stitching up a hole in Señora Fernandez's costume when the boy approached her.

"He has to be a bloodsucker." He had grinned at Emmaline then. It was the enamored sort of grin that she was used to receiving from boys. Emmaline had shifted to face him, unsure of how to respond. Usually people ignored her, but this boy had stopped and was leaning on his shovel, grinning at her like the two of them were old friends.

It was a stupid thing for the boy to do, smiling and staring at her like that right out in the open. Most people knew it, keeping their distance and limiting their conversation with Beaumont's beauty to polite hellos and nods. But this boy was new and hadn't yet learned the ropes or the hierarchy of performers.

"You there!" Monsieur Beaumont had roared from across the dusty lot. The boy turned to see what the commotion was about and found Beaumont walking toward him, his portly body waddling with great effort through the dirt. He stopped in front of the boy as Emmaline took several steps back.

"What is your name, boy?" Beaumont asked. The boy looked around nervously, as most people tended to do when faced with the Frenchman.

"Uh...Jacob, sir," he replied. "Jacob Thomas."

Beaumont nodded once, a terse movement of the head. "And what is it that you're doing here Jacob Thomas?" he asked.

"I'm one of the hands, sir," Jacob replied.

Beaumont laughed, a mirthless sound that made Emmaline take another step back. "That's impossible," Beaumont said. "You can't possibly be one of the hands because you are not employed with my circus. I do not give work to slovenly little worms who insist on flirting with the talent. You're dismissed. Leave the premises now and don't return."

Jacob stood stunned. "B...But, sir?" he pleaded. "I...don't understand."

Beaumont had stepped up to him then, nose to nose with the boy who, despite being the same height, looked much smaller next to the great ringmaster.

"You are dismissed," he repeated. "Fired. No longer needed. How must I say it, boy, for you to understand?"

Shoulders slumping, Jacob slowly turned and trudged away through the maze of tents spread out across a backfield beyond the tree line. Emmaline had watched the boy go, and she felt sad. Monsieur Beaumont turned to her and sighed, pinching the bridge of his nose.

"I must go to a meeting right now," he said, annoyance simmering beneath each clipped word. "I want you to come to my tent in one hour so we can talk about this incident."

Now Emmaline stood in the tent and waited for him to speak. Monsieur Beaumont sat behind a small, wooden table, his feet resting on top of it as he leaned back in his special made chair. The back of the chair was wound together from thick wood, its intricate pattern and design given to him as a gift by the royal woodworker of France, whom Beaumont claimed to be a dear friend. But Emmaline had heard the others whisper, and she knew that Monsieur Beaumont didn't actually know anyone from France's royal line.

"Gets his stuff second hand - *used*," they hissed after he marched by them with his nose stuck imperiously in the air. "He ain't got no connections with nobody big."

Monsieur Beaumont lowered his feet to the ground and leaned forward, pressing his fleshy elbows against the table. He wore his less formal jacket right now, saving the red one for the coming show. The black coat was unbuttoned, revealing his ruffled white shirt underneath, which was tucked into pants that were always buttoned just a little too tightly. Beaumont's jet-black hair was slicked back off his forehead, and his mustache twitched as he stared at her with beady, black eyes.

Emmaline smoothed the front of her dress. She wore the green frock today, the fabric soft against her milky skin. This was the dress that Beaumont most liked to compliment. It had grown tighter in the chest, and Bea said she couldn't let the fabric out any more, so she insisted Emmaline wear corsets to pull in her waist and a wrap to flatten her chest. Every morning, Emmaline dutifully bound herself to preserve her girlish figure because that's what sold tickets, according to Monsieur Beaumont.

Standing still before his piercing eyes, Emmaline avoided Beaumont's gaze, forcing herself to draw in long breaths. It was stifling hot inside the tent.

"That was an unfortunate incident that occurred today, my darling," Beaumont began. Emmaline didn't respond, but she did raise her eyes to meet his because she knew that was expected of her.

"How many times do I have to tell you that you are not to converse with the help? At all. Outside of that insidious woman who handles your clothing, you may not have conversations with anyone not directly related to the performances. What about this instruction do you not understand, my beauty?"

Emmaline blinked several times. "Nothin'," she replied quietly. "I'm sorry."

Beaumont sighed and leaned back in his chair again. He studied her for a moment, taking in the sadness that always seems to sit right at the surface of her gaze.

"Please, sit, my love," he said, gesturing her to sit in the chair next to Pierre. She hesitated, then timidly stepped forward and lowered herself into the stiff wooden chair. She heard Pierre draw in a long, rasping breath beside her, but she didn't dare glance his way. She felt him lean closer to her, his sour breath tainting the air. She fought off a gag.

"You must be more careful, my darling," Beaumont said, leaning forward on his elbows and staring hard at her. "You will be seen as a girl who is out for the affection of slovenly boys if you continue to give them attention like that. You don't want anyone getting wrong ideas about you now, do you?"

Emmaline shook her head no.

"And don't forget," Pierre piped up, his voice so close to Emmaline that she jumped at the sound. "You belong to us. You don't have the freedom to give yourself to anyone else." He inhaled deeply, the scent of lavender from her hair sending a shudder through his body.

Emmaline stiffened at his words. Monsieur Beaumont leaned back again in his chair, crossing his arms over his chest and nodding at his son. Emmaline fixed her eyes on the coat hanger in the corner of the room. Monsieur Beaumont's hat stood proudly atop the rack, the lantern light gleaming off the shiny material so that the hat nearly twinkled.

"Sir, may I come in?"

Pierre leaned away from Emmaline's chair and let out a sigh of disgust at the sound of Sal's voice outside the tent. Emmaline shrank into her chair, trying to make herself small.

"What is it?" Beaumont barked.

Sal stepped in and paused, blinking several times to adjust to the dim room. His eyes drifted to Emmaline hovering in her chair, then slid to Pierre sitting beside her, and his face darkened. He cleared his throat.

"There's a tear in the side of performance tent A. I'm told that we have two women working to fix it now."

Beaumont nodded dispassionately. "Is that all you came to tell me?" he asked, his voice cold and distant.

"No, sir," the man replied, clearing his throat. "We need new poles for the round top. The center poles are weakening, and I fear they could snap, which is obviously an accident we would want to avoid."

Beaumont let out a long, frustrated sigh. "And how do we replace the main support poles for the round top?" he asked. His accent always grew thicker when he was angry.

"We wire New York and order them, then have them shipped to our next location in Oklahoma."

Beaumont shook his head in disgust. He pushed to a stand and walked around the table. The small tent suddenly felt like it was caving in on them.

"I do not like these expenditures, Sal," Beaumont said.

"I understand, sir," Sal replied. "But sometimes they're necessary for the overall operation."

He glanced at Emmaline and offered a quick wink as Monsieur Beaumont turned away. She turned her mouth up in return. Sal was the real magic maker of the circus, and everyone knew it. He was the man responsible for most of the animals, but he also acted as the boss canvas man, overseeing the erection of the tents and their maintenance. He was so good at his many roles that people often wondered if he really was a magician. He had the process perfected, from where to drive the stakes, to how to lay out the canvas so that it stayed looking pristine and white. The purity of the tents was one of the things that visitors to this particular circus marveled about the most. That all led back to Sal. Everyone liked and admired him. He was a hard worker and demanded hard work from his team, but he was the kind of man people liked to work for—the kind that people could respect and appreciate, and so they wanted to please him. Sal was the one who held Beaumont's circus together.

"Very well," Beaumont said at last, looking back to Sal. "Send the wire and tell them where we'll be next. I will write the check and give it to you when I see the order receipt."

"Yessir." The two men stared at one another for a moment longer.

"Well, is there something else you need, Sal?" he asked. Sal cleared his throat and shook his head.

"I'll head back to work now," he said. He hesitated for a minute then spoke again. "I heard Miss Beatrice say that she needed the girl for a fitting and rehearsal for tonight's show. Want me to deliver her for you?"

Beaumont glanced at Emmaline, his eyes only briefly flicking to Pierre's face before he looked back at Sal and shrugged.

"Yes, yes, of course," he said with a dismissed wave of the hand. Sal jutted his chin, and Emmaline pushed herself to a stand and scuttled toward him. She followed Sal back into the sunshine, squinting as the world around her exploded in that blinding white light of the midafternoon sun.

"Keep walkin', kid," Sal said, and Emmaline followed close behind him. They rounded the corner and stepped behind the ticket building. Sal stopped and pulled his hat off his head, wiping the sweat from his brow. Emmaline watched him, the way his strong forearm raked across his weathered face, leathery from years of baking in the sunshine. Emmaline liked to think of Sal as one of the breakfast rolls that Miss Bea insisted on making her eat every morning. They were dry and crusty on the outside, but the inside was usually soft and a little sweet.

Sal perched his hat back on the top of his balding head and squinted down at Emmaline.

"You okay?" he asked. She nodded. Sal sighed and shook his head. "Look kiddo," he began. "You gotta be real careful with those two men in there, ya hear me?"

Emmaline nodded again, slowly this time.

"It's just..." Sal paused. "Well, they ain't really lookin' out for your best interest. Which means you gotta be on guard whenever one of them comes near, especially that snake, Pierre. Try not to git yourself in situations like that one today where you're alone with them, and never be alone with Pierre, 'kay?"

"But Monsieur Beaumont told me to come see him in his tent," Emmaline responded.

Sal nodded. "Yeah, I know. And if that happens again, you make sure me or Miss Bea knows so we can be standin' nearby keepin' an eye on things. You understand?"

Emmaline nodded slowly.

Sal paused for a brief moment. "The thing is, Boss Man is fairly harmless," he said. "But that kid of his? He ain't no good, so don't you get stuck with him." His voice was quiet, and his eyes darted around as he spoke the words out loud.

Emmaline nodded. She thought of the shadow that had been in her room when she woke up that morning, and of the way Pierre had grinned when he saw her looking at him through the window. A knot tied in her stomach. She opened her mouth to tell Sal about it, but the words wouldn't release from her tongue, so she closed her mouth again and glanced down at the ground.

Sal crossed his arms and stared down at Emmaline.

"I ever tell you about my daughter?" he asked. Emmaline shook her head.

"Well, you remind me of her quite a lot," he said, his eyes going misty and sad. "An awful lot."

"Where is your daughter?" Emmaline asked. Sal cleared his throat.

"Well, that's a story with a sad ending, I'm afraid," he replied. "She died when she was thirteen. Got scarlet fever, and it just ate her right up."

The silence between them made Emmaline uncomfortable. She stared up at Sal, a man so strong he could practically hoist the Big Top straight into the sky with his bare hands but who suddenly looked sad and small.

"I'm sorry," she said, blinking her bright eyes up at him. Sal smiled back at her, trying to reassure her that it was alright, but his eyes didn't match with his mouth and that made his smile the saddest thing she had ever seen.

"S'alright, darlin'," he said. "It was a long time ago. But you just listen to what I said and watch yourself, okay?"

Emmaline nodded.

"Alright then," he continued, jutting his chin toward the spread of tents behind him. "Miss Bea really is lookin' for ya. Best git on and find her now, y'hear?"

Emmaline turned and walked toward the tent where she knew Beatrice would be fussing over one of her dresses or spit shining a pair of her shoes. She turned to look back at Sal again, but he was gone, disappeared in the land of tents that she called home.

Peter sat on the step and watched her walk across the dusty earth. He clutched the book between his hands, its worn pages pressed tightly together as he tried to keep himself from trembling. He'd found the book on the side of the train track the day before and had been thrilled at the feel of paper between his fingers again. They hadn't had many books delivered to them over the years. It was a rare treat for Peter to hold a story in his hands. He ran his fingertips over the cover of the book, letting them rest on the embossed words: *Uncle Tom's Cabin*.

The book was enlightening for Peter. He had never given much thought to slavery other than to nod his head in agreement when Tiny *tsk'ed* his tongue at the topic. He didn't truly understand the depth of the issue, but this book had filled his head with questions.

Peter studied Emmaline silently. Her head was down as she moved silently toward her train car. She slept at the front of the train, a space reserved only for the more important members of their traveling group. Peter stared at her, the way her hair swung down below her shoulders in perfect waves. Her thin arms were crossed over her chest, and she kicked at a rock before her. She glanced up, and their eyes met. Peter's heart thumped in his chest, and he tried to keep his face still and calm as he lifted his hand in an awkward wave.

Emmaline looked sadly back at him. She glanced around briefly, then veered in his direction. Peter's mouth went dry as she approached. He didn't stand up for fear that his legs wouldn't hold him steady.

"Hi, Peter," she said quietly. There was always a haunting lilt in her voice—a sadness that seemed to simmer just beneath the surface of every word she spoke.

"Uh...hi," he stammered.

Emmaline sighed, glancing over her shoulder again. She looked nervous. Peter wanted to ask her if she was okay, if she needed help, but the words wouldn't come together on his tongue.

"Whatcha readin'?" she asked, jutting her chin toward his book.

Peter held it up so she could see the front. The book was dirty and worn, fraying at the spine, but the title was clear enough. Emmaline squinted at the letters, then shifted her gaze away, her cheeks flushing.

"Oh," she said. "That must be a good book." She swallowed over the lump in her throat.

"It's really good," Peter blurted out. "I bet you would enjoy it, Emmaline."

She shrugged. "Doubt it," she mumbled. "I can't read." She blinked furiously as the confession spilled from parted lips. Peter, feeling suddenly emboldened and steady, pushed to his feet.

"I can teach you to read," he said.

Emmaline looked back at him. She was quiet for a moment as she studied his face. Peter's palms grew moist as he stood shakily in front of her. He felt strange when she was around, like he wanted to reach out and pull her close and protect her from the world around him, but also nervous and jumpy at her nearness.

"I don't know," Emmaline finally replied. "I think I'm too old. Plus, how would we find time to meet?" She tossed a furtive glance over her shoulder once more. Peter knew she was looking for Boss Man.

"Let's do it in the early morning," he said with a shrug, though his heartbeat quickened even more at the thought of secretly meeting with the most beautiful girl in the world.

A quizzical look washed across Emmaline's face, and Peter fought the urge to clutch his chest, fearful that the sound of his heartbeat would give him away.

"Bea sleeps like the dead. I think I could get out without her hearin'," she said. "But…" she hesitated then shook her head. "It ain't a good idea. Monsieur wouldn't like it."

Peter shrugged. "So, we'll be careful not to get caught," he said.

"I don't know," she replied. She thought of the grounds man, Jacob, who had been so quickly dismissed earlier. "It ain't safe."

Peter's chest puffed out with much more courage than he actually felt on the inside. "I'm not worried about it," he said, hoping she didn't notice the tremor in his voice.

Emmaline bit her lip, then looked down at the book in his hand. The thought of learning to read gave her a sense of freedom she had never felt before. It would be her idea, and her power.

"Okay," she said. "But we gotta be real careful not to get caught."

Peter grinned. "Okay, then," he said. "Tomorrow mornin' at sunrise. Meet me on the other side of the train cars."

Emmaline looked at Peter with a genuine smile. He clutched the book to his chest and stared at her like a loopy puppy dog longing to be scratched behind the ears.

"Emmaline!"

Both of them jumped at the sound of Miss Bea's voice. She marched toward the two teenagers, her long skirts gathered in one hand. Emmaline dropped back a few paces, the smile fading as quickly as it appeared.

"What're you doin' out here, girl?" Miss Bea said, taking Emmaline by the elbow. She glanced at Peter and pursed her lips, nodding once as she turned Emmaline around and gave her a tug.

"Now you know you can't be standin' in the sunshine like that. Yer face will get all red and leathery, and Boss Man will have my hide for that. Not yers, we know that's right. Can't be standin' out in the open talkin' to no boys, neither. That will not work, no ma'am."

"It's just Peter, Bea," Emmaline muttered. Peter's heart dropped, and a lump pressed the back of his throat. He watched the two of them until they disappeared inside the train car, then he slowly lowered himself back onto his step.

"Better be careful, Pete."

Tiny's voice cut through the air. Peter looked back to find his friend standing inside their own train car, his head stooped to avoid hitting the ceiling. Tiny held a hand-rolled cigarette between his long, slender fingers, the smoke drifting lazily upward in tiny tendrils.

"You're messin' with fire with that one," he said.

Peter shrugged. "I'll be alright," he mumbled.

Tiny put the cigarette to his lips and inhaled deeply, then let the smoke out slow. "Maybe," he said finally. "But don't forget who that girl belongs to. She ain't yers to mess around with."

Peter looked down at the book in his hand, then looked back to where Emmaline's figure had retreated. There was more than one kind of slavery, he realized. People are always going to be slaves to something. But the thought of forced slavery, of belonging to someone else and forever doing their bidding settled on his chest like a weight. It made him sad.

He waited until Tiny ducked back inside the train car before swiping a hand over his eyes, erasing the tears that had gathered in the corners.

Peter woke long before the sun the next morning. The train rocked and lurched beneath him as they hammered on toward their next destination. They had only one more month before they settled for the winter. Everyone was tired and ready for the break. The exhilaration of performing had long since worn off. It was time to rest.

With a screech, the train began to slow. Peter sat up and stretched, yawning wide. Manny and Jessop lay curled on their beds on the other side of the car, both snoring so loudly that they nearly drowned out the sound of the clanking wheels below.

Tiny was curled up against the far wall. His blanket covered only the top half of his body, so he slept with his pants and socks on for added warmth. Peter pushed to his feet and steadied himself as the train continued to slow. They would stop soon, and shortly after that, the sun would begin to rise. The groundsmen would already be at the site for today's shows. By mid-morning, much of the empty field would have been transformed into a maze of wonder that would soon be filled with novelties most people had never even dreamed of seeing. Townspeople would start gathering on the outskirts of the field to see the performers descend their trains and the animals unloaded. Children would watch, eyes saucer-wide, as the elephants were guided down the planks. Their mouths would fall open at the sight of kangaroos jumping around in a makeshift pen and camels strolling lazily through the grass, chewing a slow rhythm as they stared back at the children.

Peter knew that he was a part of something special. Despite the many flaws in their operation, he recognized that his being a part of the circus was a gift. He remembered that morning so many years ago when he woke up with a stomach full of excited butterflies, knowing that he would be seeing his first circus. He remembered his first taste of popcorn, and the way the colors and acts dazzled. He still felt a sense of awe at this thing that he was a part of. Somehow, it made the indignities of his particular job feel so much smaller.

Standing on his toes, Peter peered through the small window at the top of their train car. It was too dark out to see much, but a faint glow at the farthest point of the horizon gave way the impending sunrise. The train lurched once more. Peter craned his neck, and he could make out the faint glow of lanterns and firelight that signaled they were nearly to the train yard. The performers would be granted a few more hours of sleep before they had to get up and ready themselves for the town parade, which would serve as the final call for the townspeople to make their way to one of the two shows that day.

The calliope would lead the way as they paraded through town. Peter usually skipped the parade. Monsieur Beaumont liked for Peter and Emmaline to remain hidden until the big show, not wanting to give away his favorite surprise for free in the parade. Peter smiled as he lowered himself back onto his bunk. He reached under his pillow and pulled out the small notepad that he had secured a few months back when they passed through a town with a large drugstore. Using some of his money, Peter had quietly ducked into the store and bought the notepad and pencils so that he could write down the stories and sonnets that so often flitted through his head. He wrote these in Russian to ensure that no one in his close circle could read his thoughts if they happened upon his journal.

Last night, before he'd drifted off to sleep, he had written out the alphabet. His first lesson with Emmaline today would be simply learning the letters. Peter ran his fingers over the neatly written block letters and his stomach did a flip. Soon, they would meet.

Peter slid the notebook into his breast pocket and stood up. He tucked in his shirt, then licked his hands and tried to smooth out his unruly hair. His breath smelled sour, and he cringed. He reached into his small bag and pulled out a sprig of mint that he'd found next to the stream at the last stop. He chewed the mint for a moment, then spit it out, satisfied at his forethought.

Taking a deep breath, Peter gripped the handle of the door and turned it as slowly as possible. He only needed to slide the door open far enough to slip out. He cringed at the squeak of the metal and glanced over his shoulder. Manny and Jessop hadn't moved, nor had their snoring abated. Their racket helped cover him.

His eyes shifted to Tiny, and he startled when he saw the tall man staring back at him. Wincing, Tiny pushed to his elbow, a yawn splitting wide his long face. His brown hair stood in tufts atop his head making him look a bit like one of the show's clowns. Peter bit his lip.

"Don't get caught, kid," Tiny said. His voice was barely a murmur. Peter nodded once, slid the door open, and slipped out.

He jumped to the ground below, then stood and stretched, goosebumps rising on his flesh. Rubbing his hands together and blowing into them, he followed the track to a break between train cars and stepped between them, walking around the backside of the train and heading toward the front where Emmaline slept. He slowly crept up to her car, the gravel beneath his feet crunching loudly in the quiet morning chill. He stopped and looked at the side of her carriage. THE BEAUTY was painted in bold, block letters on the side of the dark wooden train car, second in line. This was where Emmaline slept - where she ate and spent most of her waking hours between shows. This was where she was trapped, in the train car right behind Monsieur Beaumont and Pierre.

Peter felt a pang of sadness grip his chest as he thought of the way Emmaline's every movement was managed. He felt a surge of anger and indignation on her behalf. Teaching her to read suddenly felt like more than just an excuse to spend time alone with her. This would give her power.

Peter's heart jolted at the sound of footsteps on gravel coming around the train car. He shrank into the shadows, pressing against the cold wood and wishing that he could make himself invisible. Dropping to his knees, Peter shimmied beneath the car, hiding on the tracks below. He watched as booted feet stumbled by, then stopped and turned back around. Peter held his breath, watching as the person slowly raised to his toes. He was trying to look inside Emmaline's window. The man stumbled, his ankles twisting and collapsing, causing him to fall to the side. He landed on his knees and let out a string of curse words in French, all of them slurred together to make one long, ridiculous phrase.

Pierre.

Peter narrowed his eyes and waited as Pierre pushed back to his feet and stumbled away. His heart thrummed in his chest. Several moments later, when he was certain Pierre was gone, he pushed himself out from under the train car and stood up, brushing off his clothes. The night was quickly fading now, the sky a hazy blue above his head. Peter stared in the direction that Pierre had stumbled off, wondering what on earth the boss's son had been doing lurking around Emmaline's window before dawn.

"Hi."

Peter gasped and whirled around. She stood before him with a small smile on her face. Her eyes danced with amusement.

"Sorry," she said with a giggle. "Didn't mean to scare you."

Peter forced a nervous smile. "I didn't hear you coming."

She nodded, then looked around. "Well, I don't got much time before I should be back in bed. Where should we go?"

Peter waved his arm. "Follow me," he murmured. He turned and walked down the path, then veered to the right into the trees. The canopy above would make it a little darker and more difficult to see, but at least they would be hidden. Peter walked forward until he found a small clearing with a few tree stumps gathered together.

"This should work," he said, his voice a little louder this time. Emmaline nodded. They sat down and Peter reached into his pocket, pulling out the small notebook.

"Okay, um…" he cleared his throat and looked at her. In the dim light, she looked even more beautiful than usual. Her hair was pulled back in a loose ponytail at the nape of her neck. She blinked, dark lashes framing her blue eyes. Peter's hands shook.

"I thought that today we could just start with the alphabet and learn the sounds of the letters."

Emmaline drew in a deep breath and blinked hard. She reached for the notebook as Peter held it out, and she leaned forward, squinting at the writing on the page. "I know a lot of the letters," she said. "But when they're put together, I always forget the sounds they're supposed to make, and the words don't make sense."

Peter nodded and swallowed hard. "That's okay," he said. "Let's just start slowly." Emmaline nodded, then looked back at the paper.

"What letters do you know?" Peter asked.

"That's 'A'," she answered. "And 'B'. 'C', 'D', 'E'...um..." she faltered and look hard at the paper. "That one is 'M', and I know that's 'S'. Is that a 'T'?"

Peter smiled and nodded.

Emmaline lowered her hands to her lap and turned to face him, her eyes sad. "I don't know the rest of 'em."

"It's alright," Peter answered. "Really. That's a great start. Now we can build on what you already know."

Emmaline tried to smile, her cheeks growing warm. "It's embarrassing," she admitted.

Peter shrugged. "It's not so bad," he said. "You're going to learn quickly." He settled in a little closer and pointed to the letters one by one, naming them out loud and making their sounds. The feel of her close to his shoulder sent a shock of warmth down Peter's spine.

Time passed quickly, and before they knew it the sun was higher in the sky, and Emmaline could successfully remember nearly all of the letters and their different sounds. They stood up and glanced back toward the train yard.

"We should get back," Emmaline said. "Bea will be wakin' up soon, and she will not be happy if I'm missin'."

Peter nodded. Emmaline held the notebook out to him.

"No," Peter said, pushing it back to her. "You should keep it. You can practice whenever you have a few moments."

"I don't have no time to myself," Emmaline answered. "I'm never alone."

Peter reached over and took the book from her without answering. They turned and walked back toward the train. As they approached the tree line, both slowed and peered out through the opening.

"You go first," Peter whispered. "I'll wait until you're in your car before I go."

Emmaline glanced at him and smiled. "Thanks, Peter," she said, and Peter felt his cheeks grow hot. Emmaline quickly stepped out from beneath the canopy of trees and walked around the front of her train car, disappearing from his sight. A moment later, her face appeared at the window. She held up a hand in a quick wave, then turned and vanished.

Peter stood for several long moments watching her train car for another sight of her. Finally, drawing in a deep breath, he pushed from the trees and walked back to his own train car. He cut through the still train and saw Tiny sitting on the crate beneath the car's cracked doorway. Tiny had a cigarette in his hand and drew in a long, deep breath, slowly pushing the smoke from his lungs so that it created a haze about his head. Peter approached quietly.

"Hey kid," Tiny said.

"Hey," Peter replied.

"How'd it go?"

Peter shrugged. "Good," he murmured.

Tiny squinted at Peter and took in another long drag on his cigarette, which was now a stub between his long fingers.

"Well, I s'pose that's good then," he answered.

Peter sank down on the ground next to Tiny and sighed. The sun had ascended all the way above the tree line, and the tented field was now wrapped in the lazy blue of an autumn morning. The two sat in silence, Peter thinking about Emmaline, and Tiny thinking about the boy who knew so much and so little all at the same time.

THE FABULOUS FREAKS OF MONSIEUR BEAUMONT

Nataliya sat up slowly, rubbing her dry eyes as a yawn overtook her. She let her feet settle on the ground beneath her small cot. She'd been up since 3:00am helping prepare the cookhouse for the rush of performers who would swing through hungry and cranky in just a few hours. It was always hardest right near the winter break when everyone was tired from months of performing. Attitudes were short, and demands were high.

Pushing to a stand, Nataliya stretched and rolled her shoulders. She reached for her apron, which she'd laid over the chair beside her cot. Several of the other kitchen hands were also resting before they had to head back to work. Nataliya glanced around the room at the group of people she worked with every day. She knew them all, but none of them really knew her. They all worked cordially with one another, but Nataliya kept her distance, always awkward and unsure of herself in a group of people.

She reached into her pocket and pulled out the latest letter she had written to Yulia. Her hands shook as she thought about the confession written on the pages inside the envelope.

"I found him, Yulia. And you were right. He didn't want to be found.

He didn't want to be near me, and he wanted nothing to do with Pasha. You were right, my dear sister. I'm sorry I didn't listen."

Nataliya blinked back fresh tears and slid the envelope back into her pocket. She longed to see her sister again, yearning for Yulia's calming presence and motherly wisdom. She rarely got an update from Yulia, as they were so often on the move. She wondered how Yulia's children were doing. The twins must be three by now. Nataliya thought of the last letter she had received from her sister many months ago.

"I can finally say that I am happy. Jack is good to me, and he loves the girls so fiercely that I sometimes wonder if he might burst. He's started his own publishing company. Did I tell you that? It is a struggle financially, but he's a smart man. I've no doubt he will find success. We may have very little, but when we're together it always seems as though we have all that we need."

Nataliya sighed and stepped through the flap of the tent, squinting in the morning sunshine. It was time to prepare for the morning rush. The performers would be making their way to the cookhouse for breakfast soon before heading off for the morning parade. Nataliya could hear shouts from the roustabouts as they put the finishing touches on the circus grounds. Large sledgehammers beat a rhythm as poles were nailed into the hardening earth. In the distance, she heard the whinny of horses and bleating of goats.

Nataliya thought of her sister and found herself longing for the simplicity of Yulia's life—the quiet peace of raising a family and keeping a home. How different Nataliya's world was, and now even her hope of reunion with Kolya had been snatched away.

She didn't hear him approach, she was so deep in thought. She stood just behind the cookhouse tent, her mind wandering, eyes focused on nothing when he stepped up beside her.

"It is a fine morning, yes?"

Nataliya jumped and turned to face Monsieur Beaumont. She licked her lips and squeezed her hands together in front of her waist.

"Yes," she answered. The single word came out weak.

"Tell me," Monsieur Beaumont said, turning so that he faced her squarely. He stretched himself to full height so that he could look directly into her eyes. "Are you happy working for me?"

"Am I happy?" Nataliya asked.

"Yes," he replied, his voice measured and cold. "Are you happy here?"

"Yes, of course," she stammered.

Monsieur Beaumont nodded, then put his hands in his pockets and narrowed his eyes as he studied her face. Her eyes were wide and shiny, lined by dark circles over a thin, drawn face, which gave her the appearance of being much older than her thirty-four years. Her mousy brown hair had been pulled into a loose bun at the nape of her neck. Her dress needed to be cleaned, and it hung awkwardly on her thin frame. Monsieur Beaumont had once thought her to be a pretty enough girl, but now he found her haggard and ugly.

Nataliya drew in a long breath and waited for him to speak again. She fought the urge to fidget with her hands as the Boss Man's eyes ran over her, drinking in her appearance without even trying to mask his disdain.

"So, you *do* claim to be happy working here in my circus?" he asked again. Nataliya nodded.

"If that is the case, then why would you sneak off to town and meet with the act of another show and not tell me about it? Are you looking to leave?"

Nataliya's eyes widened, and her heart hammered in her chest. She searched her mind for the right response in the language that still felt so foreign to her. "No, sir," she whispered.

"Then what were you doing the other night with that freak?" he demanded. His brow furrowed over dark eyes. He took in the look of surprise that washed over her face and let out a cold laugh.

"I know where you went, and I know who you saw," he said. "You can't get anything past me." He clasped his hands behind his back and leaned back on his heels. "So, who was he?"

"I...I was...seeing a friend. Old friend," she replied. "I know him when we are children in Russia."

Monsieur Beaumont narrowed his eyes. "You're telling me you just happened to meet a man that you knew as a child in Russia here in Tennessee?"

Nataliya swallowed hard and nodded her head.

"I don't believe you," Monsieur Beaumont hissed. "Who was that man?"

Nataliya blinked and pressed her lips together, returning his gaze as steadily as she could.

Monsieur Beaumont let out a sigh of disgust and turned his head, squinting into the sunlight for a brief moment.

"Rotten whore," he muttered in French. Nataliya felt her cheeks grow hot, and a surge of anger spiked in her chest. Monsieur Beaumont turned back to her with a glare.

"You're not to leave the circus grounds again for any reason without permission from me first. Are we clear?"

Nataliya blinked hard and nodded.

"You're lucky I don't leave you behind altogether," he hissed, taking a step toward her. "I don't tolerate people talking with other shows for any reason."

Nataliya fought for composure, taking in short, slow breaths. Monsieur Beaumont glared at her.

"The only reason I'm keeping you here," he continued, "is because your dog of a son is important to my show, and I can't risk him losing his will to perform. You're lucky I am a man of mercy. You can thank me now."

"Yes. Thank you, Monsieur Beaumont," Nataliya murmured, blinking back tears.

"Very good," Monsieur Beaumont said, taking a step back and

glaring at her. "That is all." Spinning on his heel, Monsieur Beaumont stormed off, ducking beneath the shade of the tented walkway and into his own tent. Nataliya watched him go, her fear quickly melting into anger. She pushed her hair back off her face and drew in a long, shuddering breath.

"Time to go, girl!" Butch barked from the cookhouse. Nataliya pressed her trembling lips together and hurried forward. Performers were starting to arrive, making their way to their assigned seats beneath the tent. Rows and rows of tables were lined up in a long line. Nataliya took her place toward the front, prepared to refill serving bowls and help out the waiters who attended to the tables. Soon the tent would fill with the anticipatory din of acrobats and clowns, of trapeze artists, and animal tamers, and musicians. The sound of all their voices was always overwhelming, but today Nataliya found herself dreading it. Her heart raced and hands shook as people began to trickle in for breakfast.

She'd heard once that the Ringling Brothers tent was twice the size of their own. "As long as two football fields," some of the others whispered as they cleaned up after a meal. "Can you imagine?"

Nataliya could not imagine having to prepare food for, and serve, 1,300 people on a daily basis. That they were responsible for nourishing seven hundred people three times a day was almost difficult for her to comprehend. She still had never been to a Ringling circus, The Big One, as Butch like to call it, and supposed she never would.

"*Dobriy utra*, Mama."

Nataliya blinked and shifted her gaze to her son. Peter stood before her with a strange look on his face. It was a mixture of apprehension and elation, and were it not for the fear ringing through her ears, she would be intrigued to know what it was that caused him to look this way. His hair was wet, and he had slicked it to the side, pushing it back off his forehead as much as he could. She knew that as soon as it dried, his hair would stand back up in wild tufts around his head, but when it was brushed like that, he almost looked a little handsome. His cheeks were still painfully thin, which naturally matched the rest of his skinny frame. His shoulders were hunched, and his teeth now jutted out from his lips at odd angles. He was the oddest-looking child she had ever seen, but looking at him now, she realized he was no longer a child. He was a young man, sixteen years old, growing up before her eyes. Her heart swelled with love for him.

"*Dobriy utra*, Pasha," she replied, running the back of her hand down his cheek. A lump pressed against the back of her throat as she considered Beaumont's reprimand.

"You okay?" Peter asked, cocking his head to the side and studying his mother.

"Yes, yes, of course," she answered, swallowing hard. "You look tired today, my dear," she continued, shifting her gaze to survey the room briefly before turning back to him.

"I got up early," he said. A smile crept over his face.

"What is this smile?" Nataliya asked.

Peter opened his mouth the tell his mother about the secret meeting with Emmaline, but then shut it quickly, unsure of how she might react.

"Nothing," he said with a shrug. "Just feeling excited about today."

Nataliya studied him. "Well," she said finally. "You should sit before those two eat the food off your plate." She jutted her chin toward Manny and Jessop, who scuffled next to one another in their seats. Peter smiled. He leaned over and gave his mother a quick peck on the cheek.

"Love you, Mama," he said, before turning and walking down the row to his table, settling into his chair next to Tiny, who looked at Nataliya and nodded his head in greeting. On the other side of Peter sat Manny and Jessop, Albert with all his tattoos, and the newest act acquired for their show, a small woman who could be no more than three feet tall. They called her Little Sue. Her stage would be placed next to Tiny's.

"The little girl next to the tall man. The ugly boy next to the beautiful girl. The fat lady next to the skinniest man. Ol' Boss Man do like to keep things even, don't he?" Butch's wife Gerda had mumbled when she heard of the new act. Nataliya watched as Peter sat down at his table. Little Sue looked sad and lost as she tucked back into her chair. No one really knew how old she was. Her stature made her seem so young, yet her face was weathered and aged. Nataliya watched as Peter leaned over to her and said something, which caused a smile to split her small, thin face.

Manny and Jessop were still fidgeting in their seats next to one another. Tiny leaned back in his chair, his long legs stretching all the way beneath the table and sticking out the other side. His arms were crossed over his chest, and his eyes closed as though he were trying to block out the din surrounding him.

Emmaline pushed through the side of the tent and made her way to the head table where she sat down next to Beatrice. Nataliya knew that soon Monsieur Beaumont and Pierre would join the two of them. She watched as Emmaline looked up and made eye contact with Peter. The two smiled shyly at one another, then lowered their heads again. A small well of fear knotted Nataliya's stomach.

Swallowing hard, Nataliya turned and grabbed a serving spoon to hand to one of the waiters. She thought of Kolya and the way he'd looked at her before, the stolen smiles they had shared when they thought no one was looking. Her gaze shifted back to her son, and she knew in an instant he had fallen in love.

Peter leaned back on his cot and closed his eyes. In the distance, he could hear the calliope whistling the tune that would serve as the final cry to the locals to come check out today's shows. The first show would kick off as soon as the parade returned, and the second at 5:00 that evening. Peter had one hour to rest before they all got back, and a flurry of activity would begin. A grin spread across his face as he thought again about his meeting with Emmaline earlier. He could still smell the scent of the trees that surrounded them as he sat next to her, and he let his mind linger on her bright smile and blue eyes. With a contented sigh, he stood to his feet and stepped outside the open flap of his rest tent.

Men and women buzzed frantically back and forth through the maze of walkways and tents, each one intent on some issue that would help ensure today's show was a success. Sal walked slowly around the perimeter of the Big Top, examining each section carefully. Every once in a while, he'd stop and jot down a note in a small notebook before he continued his inspection.

The tent looked extra white today. Boss Man had ordered it bleached after the last show, and Peter heard that a team of men and women stayed up all night carefully washing each layer of canvas until it sparkled.

"Every show should look brand new!" Monsieur Beaumont would shout at their weekly performer's meetings. He would use these times to offer criticism and encouragement to the stars of his show. When he was feeling happy and pleased, the meetings felt like a giant party. But when something had gone wrong, the meetings could be torturous.

Peter thought about the meeting two nights ago when Boss Man had Miss Clarabelle come to the front and stand by him. He'd made them all watch as she labored pitifully to his side, her body having grown so large that even walking was an exhausting effort. She'd stopped beside him and turned, her hair caked with sweat, stains darkening the underarms of her wide dress. Her eyes were slits beneath the fleshy folds of her face.

"Miss Clarabelle," Monsieur Beaumont had begun. "Tell the group why you are attempting to sabotage my show."

She didn't respond, and the room had gone painfully quiet.

"I asked you a question," he repeated.

"I ain't tryin' to sabotage no show," she murmured.

Beaumont nodded. "Is that so?" he asked. "Then tell me why you refused to do anything in tonight's show but sit on your stage and cry like a child?"

She remained mute.

"ANSWER ME NOW!" he'd screamed as the rest of them cast their eyes downward. Boss Man's face was inches from hers, but she never met his gaze. She kept her eyes down, her mouth a tight line.

Drawing in a deep breath, Beaumont glanced around at his cast of performers. He'd raised his chin high and pasted a fake smile on his face.

"I expect 100% from you all at every show!" he began. "I know you're tired, and a break is coming. But don't..." he had paused then, looking back at Clarabelle. "Don't give me anything less than your best from now until our final show for the season, or I will leave you behind."

His voice had been measured and cold. Even now, days later, Peter felt a shiver work its way up his spine. He couldn't imagine being left behind when the show moved on. The thought of it tied his stomach into a knot.

He glanced to his right and saw Miss Clarabelle lumber out of her own tent. Her hair had been curled in tight ringlets around her face. She walked toward him, eyes trained on the ground before her, almost as though she expected the earth to reach up and snatch her straight into its belly.

"Morning, Miss Clarabelle," Peter said when she walked slowly past. She paused and turned to him, her sad eyes taking a moment to focus.

"Mornin', Peter," she answered.

"Are you doing alright today?" Peter asked. He never did forget the story Tiny had told him of Miss Clarabelle's family, and his heart ached for her.

"Jus' fine," she answered. She stared off in the distance.

"You look nice," Peter offered.

Miss Clarabelle turned back to him. "You don't have to say that," she said. "But thank you." She drew in a deep breath. "Have a good show today, kid," she said.

Peter nodded and watched her slowly walk away, wondering where she was going. She rarely left her tent before show time. He waited a few minutes, watching as she trudged down the tented lane. When she turned the corner, Peter pushed forward and followed her, an odd feeling churning in his stomach.

He kept a safe distance, watching as she walked out of the tented village and into the open field behind the Big Top. Keeping his distance, he continued to follow her as she waddled through the tall grass, under a canopy of trees, and down a dusty, graveled path. After ten minutes of walking, Peter drew up behind the trunk of a tree and observed as Miss Clarabelle walked tentatively onto a bridge that hung high over what looked to be a shallow creek below. Peter imagined this creek swelled in the rainy season, but now it was no more than ankle deep.

Peter watched as Miss Clarabelle looked over the side of the bridge. Her thick hands reached up to wipe sweat and tears from her cheeks, then she gripped the side of the bridge and put one foot up on the first railing.

"Wait!" Peter cried, rushing out to her. Miss Clarabelle turned to look at him and sighed, tears streaming down her cheeks.

"You shouldn't have come here," she said, her words almost a moan. "You shouldn't have come."

Peter shook his head. "Miss Clarabelle, what are you doing?" he asked.

She looked at him for a long time. "I've got nothing worth living for," she said." I can't go on pretending that this thing that I do is okay. I can't keep being the burden holding people back or the butt of people's jokes." She looked down at the stream of water below.

"I'm done with it all Peter," she said, so quietly Peter had to strain to hear her. "You shouldn't have come here."

Panic rose in Peter's chest. His raised his hands up in front of him. "Miss Clarabelle," he said. His voice caught in his throat. "Please, wait. Please."

She looked at him sadly. "You're a sweet kid," she said. "You're so much smarter and better than most people give you credit for. Your outsides are just a shell. Inside, you're something special." She closed her eyes and turned her face up to the sun. "Go on, now," she continued. "You shouldn't be here."

"But so are you!" Peter cried out. "You're much more than your outsides, too. You're…" Peter's words faltered. He suddenly thought of Tiny and wished his friend was here. Tiny would know what to say.

"Miss Clarabelle, I'm going to run get something that I think will help you. Will you wait for me to come back? Please?"

Miss Clarabelle looked at Peter, his eyebrows raised over his crooked features. She sighed.

"I'm making no promises," she answered quietly.

Peter turned on his heel and began running as quickly as his uneven legs would allow. "I'll be right back!" he yelled over his shoulder. "Please wait!"

Tearing back through the tents, Peter weaved through stagehands and performers, all of whom were frantically preparing for the show.

"Watch it, kid!" one of the roustabouts yelled, as he tripped trying to move out of Peter's way.

"Sorry!" Peter called out. His lungs were burning from the exertion, and his hips hurt from running. He raced around the corner to the sideshow's break tent and pushed open the flaps. Scanning the room, his heart dropped.

"Where's Tiny?" he asked Jessop. "Have you seen Tiny?"

Jessop shrugged. "He was just here," he said impassively.

Peter put his hand on his head and turned, running back out of the tent and scanning the area. "He probably went for a smoke break," Peter said out loud. He ran around the corner and sighed with relief as he caught sight of Tiny standing in the corner, smoking with Billy, the littlest clown.

"Tiny!" Peter raced up to him, his chest heaving. "You have to come with me right now," he gasped. "It's Miss Clarabelle!"

Tiny dropped his cigarette in the dirt and stepped on it. "Lead the way, Pete," he said. Billy stepped up beside Tiny.

"What can I do?" he asked.

"Make sure Boss Man doesn't know she's missing," Peter begged.

Billy nodded. "You got it, kid," he replied. Peter nodded gratefully. He turned and began running as fast as he could toward the back of the tent. Tiny jogged by his side.

"What's going on, Pete?" he asked.

Peter shook his head. "I just…hope…we aren't…too late," he gasped. Tiny's lips pressed together to form a tense line across his wide face.

They raced through the field behind the circus and under the canopy of trees. Finally, Peter led Tiny around the corner to the bridge where Miss Clarabelle now balanced unsteadily on the second rung of the railing. She had only to pitch herself forward and it would all be over. Peter and Tiny skidded to a stop. Peter leaned forward and put his hands on his knees, drawing in deep breaths. Tiny walked slowly to the edge of the bridge.

"Mornin', Miss Clarabelle," he said. His voice was steady and smooth, as though he hadn't run at all.

"You shouldn't have come, Tiny," she replied. Her hair was now matted with sweat to the side of her face. Her makeup had smeared down her cheeks, and her whole body trembled.

"Naw, that ain't true. Pete here told me you needed some help, so here I am." Tiny took a very small step forward.

"Clarabelle," he said. "Please look at me."

Slowly, Miss Clarabelle turned her face toward Tiny. "I can't do it no more," she whimpered. "I can't live like this."

Tiny nodded. "I don't blame you," he said. "It's no way to live, and life hasn't done you right."

Miss Clarabelle shut her eyes. "Life hasn't done me right at all," she whispered.

"Clarabelle, I don't believe you ever told me about your husband and little boy," Tiny said. He leaned his elbow against the railing of the bridge, almost as though he were talking to a dear old friend over afternoon tea. "Could you tell me about them now?"

Miss Clarabelle opened her eyes and looked at him. "I know what you're doing, Tiny," she said. "You're not stopping me."

"I ain't tryin' to stop nothin'," Tiny replied. "I'm only tryin' to talk to my friend, Clarabelle."

"You think we're friends?" she asked.

"Sure," Tiny said with a nod. "We gotta stick together." Tiny glanced back at Peter whose heart had finally quit hammering in his chest. Peter raised his eyebrows as Tiny nodded for him to walk closer.

"See, old Pete here came runnin' as fast as he could because he knew you were in trouble. His friend was having a hard time, and he wanted to help her. That's what friends do, Miss Clarabelle. They care. Maybe we haven't cared enough about you these past few years. I'm real sorry about that."

"I'd really like to hear about your husband and son, too, Miss Clarabelle," Peter said.

Clarabelle was quiet for a long time. Peter's hands shook as he waited for her to speak and prayed that she didn't lunge over the edge.

"William," she finally said quietly. "My husband's name was William, and my boy was named Timothy. Little Timmy."

"Timmy," Tiny said. "That's a nice name. What was he like?"

"He was smart," she replied. "So smart. Only two years old and he spoke in sentences. He would come with me to the theater and watch rehearsals. Sometimes he could quote entire passages of the plays I was working on."

"I bet that was somethin'," Tiny said. "What did Timmy look like?" Tiny took a small step forward toward Miss Clarabelle. Peter followed suit.

"He was a big boy, like his Pa. And he had the most beautiful red hair, also like his Pa. I think he would have been a freckled boy given time." She blinked. "But he didn't have time," she whispered. A soft moan escaped her lips. Peter blinked back tears.

"Clarabelle," Tiny said softly. She turned to look at him. "I'm so sorry about your boy. I'm so sorry that Timmy didn't have time."

She nodded her head. "Me too." Miss Clarabelle leaned forward a little.

"Wait!" Peter cried. "What about your husband? What about William? You didn't tell us about him."

Miss Clarabelle sighed. "You two are wastin' time," she said. "You're makin' this too hard. Please leave me be!"

Tiny took another step forward. He was close enough to touch her now but kept his hands in his pockets.

"Tell us about William, Clarabelle," he said.

"My Will," she finally replied. "He had been my sweetheart since we were kids. He was quiet. He didn't talk too much, but when he did talk, people wanted to listen. A little bit like you, Tiny." Miss Clarabelle glanced at Tiny briefly before turning away again. "My Will was the kind of man who didn't sit around waiting for life to pass him by. He fought to enjoy every moment of every day."

She looked down at her pudgy hands, clinging white-knuckled to the railing. "What would he think if he saw me now?" she whispered.

"What do you think he would say to you?" Peter asked.

Miss Clarabelle looked at Peter. "I don't know. I'd be terrified for him to see me like this. I'm nothing like the woman I was back then. This shell I'm living in is a disgrace. "

"Well, I don't know, Miss Clarabelle," Tiny said. "I believe I'm seein' somethin' different than what you're seein'."

Clarabelle sighed. "How so, Tiny?" she asked.

"Well, remember years ago, when little Miss Emmaline first came to us?"

Peter's head whipped to the side at Tiny's mention of Emmaline.

"'Member how that poor child cried and sobbed?"

Clarabelle nodded. "I remember," she said. "Just awful."

"Well, what I remember, Miss Clarabelle, is the way you scooped that little girl up and hugged her so tight she stopped cryin'. You whispered somethin' into her ear that made her smile for the first time since she joined us. And she never fell to those pitiful sobs again after that."

"Yeah, and Beaumont snatched her from my hands and told me not to poison her mind with lies and stories," Miss Clarabelle replied.

Tiny nodded. "Yes, he did do that," he replied. "But what did you say to her that day, Clarabelle? What did you tell her that calmed her straight down?"

Miss Clarabelle closed her eyes as if reliving the moment. "I told her she was heading on a grand adventure and to keep looking up with a smile on her face, because smiles chase away fear."

They all stood in silence for a long moment.

"That's pretty good advice, Clarabelle," Tiny finally said.

"Miss Clarabelle?" Peter asked. She turned to face him. The tears had stopped flowing, and her body had gone still. "Please don't do this. Please stay with us. I don't think I could stand getting up on my stage without you nearby reciting your monologues."

Clarabelle shook her head. "Why would y'all want me to stay here? What good am I? You heard Boss Man the other day. I'm sabotaging the show." She sighed and shook her head. "I ain't worth nothin'. Nobody needs me at all."

"Now, Miss Clarabelle," Tiny said gently. "Don't you know that everybody's got worth?"

Peter nodded. "You matter to me, Miss Clarabelle," he said.

Clarabelle turned and looked at both of them, first at Tiny, then at Peter. With a small sigh, she slid her foot down off the railing and stepped away from the edge. In the distance, they could hear the raucous sound of the circus band starting up.

"Will you come back with us?" Tiny asked, reaching his hand out to hers.

Clarabelle shook her head in frustration, her lips pursed together.

"I'm not making promises that I'll stay long," she said. "But I promise to stay today at least, if only so y'all two will leave me alone."

Tiny smiled at her and tipped his hat. "I'm real glad to hear that, Miss Clarabelle," he said.

Peter grabbed her other hand and turned back toward the circus, which loomed before them just across the big stretch of golden field. The tall man, the fat lady, and the ugly boy walked together back to the broken world that waited for them—the world they called home.

FOUR

Peter stood at the base of his stage and stared at the four uneven steps that led to the small platform above. The chains waited for him like they had every night before for the last four years. He arms hung leaden by his side as he blinked several times, trying to will himself to play the part of the wild child yet again.

"Five minutes! Up on your platforms!"

Pierre's voice cut through the noise of the sideshow tent as one by one they each made their way up onto their small stages. Tiny bypassed the stairs altogether and settled himself on the small chair in the center of his platform. He lifted the harmonica to his lips and blew a few notes into it, then turned his head side to side and moved his shoulders around to loosen up.

Manny and Jessop were on their stage, fighting with one another as usual. Peter turned to look at them just as Jessop cuffed Manny on the back of the head. Manny turned around and socked Jessop in the stomach, causing him to double over briefly. He then straightened up and reached his short arm out, grabbing Manny's nose and twisting it as hard as he could as Manny cried out in pain.

"Knock it off, you two!" Someone, Peter couldn't see who, barked from across the tent. Manny and Jessop pushed away from one another, grumbling and straightening out their suits.

"Psst…"

Peter turned at the sound of the whisper. He saw Emmaline standing at the base of her own stage as well.

"This is it. We get a break soon." She gave him a quick smile, then turned and walked daintily up the stairs and to the center of her stage where she tossed her long, golden hair behind her shoulders and stared out at the soon-to-be-filled expanse of the tent.

Tonight was their final show of the season. They were headed back to Oklahoma for the winter break. They'd finally have a few months off to rest, to perfect new routines, and to recharge. Peter's heart ignited with the thrill of knowing they'd be stationary for a time. Secret meetings with Emmaline would be easier once they were all set in the cluster of cabins beneath a canopy of trees in the southern Oklahoma hills that Beaumont had purchased in a shrewd business deal years before. The large plot of land had space for the animals to roam, enough housing for everyone to keep a roof over their heads, and ample storage for a lot of their equipment. Best of all, Peter knew there were a handful of quiet places away from all the bustle that he and Emmaline could meet to continue working on her reading skills.

Peter drew in a deep breath, energized by the thought of the impending break, then quickly climbed up the stairs, pulled the chains over his shoulders, and wrapped them on his wrists. He didn't notice Pierre from across the tent, observing him with narrowed eyes. The music from the final number of the main show picked up its pace, the steady pounding of the drum a signal that there were only moments left. Soon, people would pour into the sideshow tent with the promise to be both awed and horrified by Monsieur Beaumont's Fabulous Freaks.

The final beat sounded, and Peter could hear the mounting applause and cheers. He rolled his head around and closed his eyes, willing himself to get to the place he needed to be to convince the coming onlookers that he was unhinged. The World's Ugliest Boy, a foaming, growling mess. Untamed and wild.

Tired.

The flap of the tent opened, and a crowd jostled through, talking and laughing, though several people fell silent as they took in the sight of the stages arranged in a semi-circle around the tent. Tiny played a merry tune on his harmonica, stomping his big foot up and down as the small hat pinned to his head jiggled in time.

Manny and Jessop, hands clasped primly in front of their waists, closed their eyes and began singing in perfect harmony.

Miss Clarabelle sat on her couch, staring into the crowd. She had changed since the event at the bridge earlier in the week—no longer sad, but somehow quietly confident and contemplative.

Emmaline smiled serenely at the crowd, waiting for a few moments before beginning her song. Peter stood in a bit of a daze, taking it all in.

"Do something, you idiot," a voice hissed from behind him. He looked back to see Pierre glaring up at him. Turning around, he drew in a deep breath, then crouched and pulled against the chains, twisting his face in such a way that he knew made him look tormented and angry. A cluster of five boys stepped up to his stage. They all looked to be around his age, with dirty white shirts tucked into wool pants held up by suspenders. They regarded him with a measure of boredom before one of them elbowed his friend and pointed at Emmaline's stage.

"Check it out," he said, and the group moved on to Emmaline, stepping right up to the base of her platform and staring up at her. One of them let out a low whistle.

"Hey there, darlin'," he called up.

Emmaline, accustomed to being shown extra attention from the younger boys at these shows, kept her head up and eyes trained forward. The boys snickered and jostled around one another. The first boy reached out his hand and grabbed ahold of the hem of Emmaline's skirt, giving it a tug.

"What's a pretty little thang doin' all stuck up on that stage alone?" he crooned. "C'mon down here with us. We can show you a real good time."

The boys around him laughed. One of them slapped Emmaline's stage with the palm of his hand. She jumped and pulled back just enough to release her dress from the grasp of the boy's hand.

Peter stopped straining against the chains and stood up a little straighter as he watched the boys lean into Emmaline's space. The ringleader reached for her again, and Emmaline took another step back. One of the boys let out a howl like a dog.

"Now, darlin'," the head boy sang. "I'm just here to make your dreams come true. Don't be mean." He reached for her once again. Emmaline kicked at his hand. Without even a thought, Peter threw down his chains and in one swift moment leapt off his stage and landed next to the boys. He let out what sounded almost like a roar, and he lunged at the group who all stumbled back away from Emmaline.

"What the…" the boy who'd been grabbing for her cried. Peter lunged at him, snarling, his hands balled into fists. The boys stepped back further.

"That kid's crazy," one of them yelped as Peter lunged forward again. Just then, Tiny stepped up beside him, stretched to his full height. At this point, the entire tent stood frozen as they watched the scene play out.

"I'm gonna ask you fellas to leave," Tiny said, his voice low but firm. Peter stepped toward the group again, but he stopped when Tiny's hand clamped down on his shoulder. The fight went out of him, and his arms dropped to his sides.

"We ain't leavin'," the head boy said, pushing his shoulders back. "We paid extra to come in here."

Tiny nodded. "I understand, and I'm sure a refund can be provided. But there is no touching the talent, so I'm afraid you'll have to be goin'."

"C'mon, Dusty," one of the other boys said. "Let's just git. This ain't that interestin' anyway."

The boy looked from Tiny to Peter, then back again. "Y'all are a bunch of frauds," he said with a sneer before turning on his heel. The group of boys moved quickly to the exit and walked out just as Boss Man walked in. He took in the sight of Tiny and Peter standing ground level, and the patrons all still.

"C'mon, Pete," Tiny said softly. "Back to work."

Peter climbed back up on his stage, keenly aware of the eyes that watched him. He stood among his chains and stared back out at the crowd. His fight was gone.

Tiny sat in his little chair and picked up his harmonica. He looked out at the crowd. "Well, now, folks. How'd you like our little show?" he called out. A murmur swept over the crowd, and a few people even clapped their hands. Tiny pulled the harmonica to his lips and blew out a foot-stomping tune, and immediately the tent jumped back to life. Albert, the tattooed man let out a warrior's cry, causing a few women to yelp and jump, then he turned and flexed, the tattoos on his back dancing to the audience's delight.

Clarabelle pushed to her feet and cried out, "Romeo! Oh, Romeo! Wherefore art thou Romeo?"

Manny and Jessop resumed their song, and Emmaline, though still clearly shaken, stepped back to the center of her stage and folded her hands in front of her. She opened her mouth and begin to sing her shaky tune.

Beautiful Girl
Most lovely in
All of the world.

Peter watched it all unfold, then slowly stepped back into his chains, wrapping them around his wrists and shrugging them onto his shoulders. No one seemed to be paying him any attention anymore, and for that he was grateful. He looked toward the back of the tent and watched as Pierre walked up to his father and whispered in his ear. Monsieur Beaumont's eyes narrowed. He pointed at Peter, then quickly pointed at himself, and Peter knew that he was meant to see Boss Man after the show. A pit settled in his stomach.

The hour dragged on and finally ended. Peter trudged down the steps of his stage, stepping into the shadows and gulping in long, deep breaths.

"Boy, ain't you in for it," Manny sneered as he and Jessop waddled by.

"Ain't supposed to leave yer stage," Jessop piped in.

Peter hung his head and closed his eyes.

"Thank you."

Peter looked up to see Emmaline standing a few paces away. She glanced over her shoulder, then looked back at him.

"Meet me outside my room tonight," she whispered.

Peter nodded, then pulled back as Beatrice stepped up to Emmaline. "Come on," Beatrice said, grabbing Emmaline by the elbow and turning her away. Bea turned and glanced back at Peter, a mixture of admonition and sympathy stretched across her face.

"Well, now, Pete." Tiny stepped up to Peter, drawing his gaze away from Emmaline. He looked up at Tiny, then looked away again.

"Yeah, I know," he muttered. "What do you think Boss Man will do to me?"

Tiny shrugged. "Best go find out together," he said.

The two quickly exited the back of the tent and wove their way through the maze of walkways and constructed paths toward Beaumont's tent, which stood in the back corner of the circus lot. Already, the groundsmen were beginning the tear down process. There was an extra pep in everyone's movements as they anticipated the upcoming winter break.

Tiny stepped up to the entrance of Beaumont's tent and coughed. "Boss Man?" he called. "You in there?"

There was a brief beat of silence before Beaumont's voice called back.

"*Entrez!*"

Tiny ducked into the tent first with Peter following him reluctantly. Beaumont stood in front of his desk, hands clasped firmly back his back as he looked up at Tiny sternly.

"I had to give those boys their money back," he said, anger coursing through each word making his accent more pronounced.

"I understand, Boss Man. Feel free to dock that from my pay this week."

"Oh, I absolutely plan to," Beaumont seethed. He turned to Peter. "And I'll be withholding your pay as well."

Peter nodded, unable to formulate any words.

"Hey, Boss Man," Tiny began. Beaumont held up his hand, cutting Tiny off. Stepping toward Peter, Beaumont narrowed his eyes.

"I would rather hear what happened from you," he said.

Peter swallowed hard, his mouth dry. "Well," he began. "Those boys were harassing Emmaline. They were grabbing her skirt and pulling at her. I just…I didn't think it was right." Peter's words didn't come out as confidently as he wanted them to, but he pushed his shoulders back and raised his chin in an effort to show more boldness than he felt.

Beaumont nodded once, then took another step toward Peter. "And why is it that you feel so protective of my Emmaline?" he asked. His words were soft, but there was an undercurrent of danger that coursed through them.

"It's the right thing to do, to protect her," Peter answered, his words steadier this time.

"He was just tryin' to make sure yer girl wasn't bein' harassed, Boss Man. No harm done."

Beaumont stepped back. He glared up at Tiny, then shifted his gaze back to Peter. "You're lucky this was the final show of the season," he began. "When we arrive in Oklahoma, you will provide extra work for me around the grounds to make up for this humiliation. And you are to stay away from Emmaline, do you hear me?"

Peter looked up at Beaumont, alarmed. Tiny stepped in quickly.

"Now, Boss Man," he crooned. "Pete here don't ever go around Emmaline. He was just lookin' out for her tonight."

Beaumont waved his hand, dismissing Tiny's words. "You are never to interact with the audience again," he said. "If you do, I will leave your mother behind, and I will make sure you never see her again. Are we understood?"

Peter nodded slowly.

"Leave my tent," Beaumont said, turning abruptly. Tiny grabbed Peter's shoulder and pulled him out of the tent. Peter let out a long sigh. He looked up at Tiny, his friend's head framed by the full moon above.

"Thanks, Tiny," he said, his voice meek.

Tiny was quiet for a long minute. "You gotta be careful, Pete," he said. "This thing that's goin' on…" he ducked his head and glanced back at Beaumont's tent. "It's gonna catch up to you."

Hours later, Peter lay on his cot, the rocking and clanking of the train beneath him muddling his mind. Thoughts of his mother and Emmaline and Tiny all rolled together as he fought sleep. He glanced over to where Tiny slept. Tiny's legs were folded up as tightly as possible, his long arms hugging them to his chest. Across from Tiny, Manny and Jessop both shared a cot, their heads on opposite ends of the bed. Jessop's dirty feet were tucked up under Manny's chin, and Manny had his arms wrapped around Jessop's legs.

Slowly and quietly, Peter pushed himself up and slid from his cot.

He pulled on his shoes and his coat, shoved his hands in a pair of mittens, and pulled a hat down over his ears. The train car rocked, and Peter grabbed the wall, steadying himself before he fell over.

"Where'd ya think you're goin'?" Tiny whispered, pushing to his elbow and peering at Peter through sleep-crusted eyes. Tufts of hair stood in a halo around his head, and his bulbous nose seemed to glow in the lantern light.

"Just stretching my legs," Peter replied.

"No, you ain't," Tiny said. He sat up, his legs unfolding beneath him, and he rubbed his eyes. "Yer goin' to see Emmaline."

Peter said nothing.

Tiny looked up at Peter, eyebrows raised. "It's one thing to be sneakin' out and meetin' her in the trees, but yer takin' a whole new risk tryin' to meet up with her on the train while it's still movin'. And after what happened tonight."

Peter sighed. "I told her I'd meet her, Tiny," he said. "I can't let her down." Tiny shook his head.

"Pete, listen to me. I know you're sixteen now, and that means you think you know all there is to know 'bout the world. And I know you think yer invincible. But you got plenty still to learn, and Boss Man does not make empty threats." Tiny paused, staring into Peter's eyes before speaking again.

"I know you love her, Pete," he said softly. "But yer messin' with fire."

"I do not love her!" Peter protested. "I'm just helping her learn to read."

Tiny shook his head. "Naw, that ain't what yer doin'," he said. "You love her. It's okay to admit it. You ain't foolin' nobody."

Peter's face grew hot, and he shifted from foot to foot as the train continued to rock beneath him.

"I'm not trying to fool anybody," Peter finally said, his voice shaking. "I'm just trying to help my friend."

"That's right, Pete. She is your friend. That's what you are to her, and it's what she's got to be to you. Emmaline ain't yours to fall in love with."

"She's not property, Tiny," Peter shot back. "She has a mind of her own and can fall in love if she wants."

"Not she can't, Pete," Tiny answered sadly. "And she knows that as well as I do. You're the only one who don't seem to know it." Tiny sighed. "Miss Emmaline can never be yours."

Peter opened his mouth to protest, but stopped when Tiny raised his hand, his long, spider-like fingers stretching out between them.

"It ain't right—don't hear me sayin' that. I hate this for her, and I hate it for you. But it's the fact. And you tryin' to mess with that fact is gonna get you and her in a heap of trouble."

Peter yanked his hat down over his ears a little tighter and jutted his chin out in defiance. "I'm just goin' on a walk, Tiny," he said, his words laced with frustration.

"Alright then, Pete," Tiny replied. "Don't do nothin' foolish. Think about yer mama."

Peter paused, his stomach doing an uneasy flip. He could feel Tiny staring at him, and he kept his face turned away.

"I'll be right back," he said, then he pushed open the small door at the end of their car and stepped delicately into the next, blocking out the sound of Tiny's worried sigh. He slowly made his way forward through the train cars, past all the sleeping and snoring performers. He held tightly to the rails between cars, the cold air nipping at his cheeks and the tracks clacking beneath his feet. With unsteady hops, he crossed from car to car as the train barreled onward through the night sky, the sliver of a moon offering little light to the world around them.

His heart hammering in his chest, Peter finally made it to the second train car. He knew that Emmaline slept on the other side with Miss Bea, and in the car beyond them slept Boss Man and Pierre. Tiny's warning clanged in his head as he drew in a deep breath and shrank into the corner of the hallway, hidden in the shadows. He convinced himself that this was the right thing to do—that he was simply here to check on his friend.

"I'll be quick about it," he whispered into the quiet expanse.

Peter knew Tiny was right. This was dangerous, but he could see Emmaline's gaze every time he blinked, the way her eyes lit up when she asked him to meet her.

One minute stretched into five, and then Peter lost track of time altogether. He stayed pressed against the wall, eyes shifting back and forth as his ears strained to hear any sound other than that of the rocking train. He was about to give up the wait when her door clicked softly and shifted, pulling open. Emmaline slid through the opening and slowly, silently, pulled it shut behind her. She turned and gasped when she saw Peter standing in the corner. He put his finger to his lips.

"You scared me!" she whispered. Then she smiled, and Peter's heart melted. He smiled back at her, running his hand self-consciously over his head. He was thankful for the shadows and their willingness to let him forget, just briefly, what he looked like.

"Sorry I'm late," she said. She stepped toward him. "It took Bea forever to fall asleep tonight, and then I fell asleep. I only just woke up!"

Peter licked his lips and shrugged his shoulders. "It's fine," he murmured, suddenly tongue-tied and shy.

Emmaline looked around, then shivered. "This is kind of foolish, isn't it?" she asked.

Peter shrugged. "I don't think it's foolish," he lied. "We can just sit here as long as we're quiet." His hands shook by his side. Emmaline nodded and stepped to him. She leaned her back against the wall and slid down to the floor, tucking her feet up beneath her nightdress and robe. Peter sat next to her.

"Thank you for what you did tonight," Emmaline began. She

looked intently toward Peter, his features hard to decipher in the dim light. They sat in awkward silence for a long minute.

Peter nodded. Emmaline sighed and shook her head.

"Did you get in terrible trouble?" she asked.

Peter shrugged. "Tiny took the brunt of it. Boss Man docked our pay and made a couple of threats, but I'm not worried." He hoped he sounded convincing.

"I'm sorry you went through all that on my account," she finally answered.

"I'd do it again," Peter replied.

They were silent for a long time, the rocking of the train pushing their shoulders closer together.

"What are you thinking about?" Peter finally asked.

Emmaline sighed. "Just about tonight. I couldn't get away from Bea at all this evening. And when she finally did step out of the room for five minutes, Pierre and Monsieur came in." Emmaline shuddered. "I hate Pierre," she said.

"Why?" he asked, though he could assume why on his own.

"He stares at me. It's like he's hungry, and I'm his supper." Emmaline glanced at Peter then looked back down at her hands. "I'm scared of him," she admitted.

"I'm sorry," Peter murmured.

Emmaline shrugged. "Ain't nothin' we can do about it, I guess." She turned to face him. "What's your story, Peter?" she asked.

"What...what do you mean?" Peter stammered.

"I mean, everybody on this train knows my story. I'm the little girl who was abandoned and taken in by Monsieur, all out of the goodness of his heart." She covered her forehead dramatically with the back of her hand.

Peter smiled.

"But no one really knows your story," she continued. "You and your mama just showed up one day. How'd you get here?"

"Mama and I saw the show in New York. I guess I stood out in the crowd, because Boss Man noticed and pulled me aside."

"*You* stood out in a *crowd?*" Emmaline gasped, then giggled. Peter stared at her for a moment before grinning back.

"I know," he said. "Imagine that."

Emmaline put her hand over her mouth to suppress her laugh.

"Anyway, Boss Man took me back to see the sideshow, and he told me he could give me work. We needed money, so mama and I agreed." Peter looked away from Emmaline's penetrating stare.

"Just like that? You just agreed?" she asked.

"Well…" Peter hesitated.

"Well…what?" Emmaline urged. He glanced back at her.

"I agreed because of you," he admitted, his voice so soft that it seemed to get caught in the clanking wheels of the train. Emmaline held his gaze.

"Oh," she said.

"I saw you singing that day, and I just wanted to be where you were." Peter's face grew hot, and his hands trembled in his lap at the admission.

"But it took you so long to notice me after you got here," Emmaline finally said after a long pause.

Peter shook his head. "No," he said. "I noticed you right away. It's just that…you're so beautiful, and I'm so…" his voice trailed off. "I didn't know how to even begin talking to you," he finished.

Emmaline reached over and grabbed his hand, pulling it into her lap. "I'm glad you finally did," she said quietly. Peter looked at her and blinked hard. He shifted his gaze away, embarrassed and unsure of himself.

"And Peter?" Emmaline whispered. He turned back to meet her gaze. Her face was barely a shadow, yet she still looked beautiful. He wondered what he looked like to her in return. "I…" she hesitated, her thumb sliding over his deformed hand. "I think you're wonderful."

Peter shook his head. "I'm a freak," he whispered. Emmaline pursed her lips and narrowed her eyes.

"Not to me," she answered. She leaned forward and kissed him, gently and swiftly. Their lips met for the briefest moment, then parted. She swallowed hard and dropped Peter's hand.

"I should go back to bed before Bea wakes up and sees that I'm gone," she said.

Peter cleared his throat. "Yes," he whispered. "Yes, of course."

They both stood up and braced themselves against the wall as the train rocked.

"Night, Emmaline," Peter said.

"G'night, Peter," she replied. Her mouth turned up in the faintest smile. Peter's whole body trembled as he watched her push open the door to her train car and slip back inside, closing it silently behind her.

Turning, Peter put his hands to his face and lingered for a short minute, the touch of her lips against his still fresh. He smiled in the moonlight, then silently pushed open the car door in front of him and began making the walk back to his own sleeping quarters. He didn't know that outside the door of Emmaline's train car, clinging to the side railing that surrounded the narrow platform, Pierre had peeked through the window and seen them. Peter trembled with delight, not knowing that the secret was out, and Tiny had been right all along.

The first days in Oklahoma were a blur of activity as train cars were unloaded and everyone settled into their winter quarters. The cabins were big enough to house up to twenty people, though many more often packed into them, sleeping in sacks on the floor and in dark corners of every room.

In previous winters, Peter had always stayed with his mother and the other servers in the cookhouse cabin, but this year he decided he wanted to stay with the performers.

"You won't stay with me?" Nataliya asked in surprise.

"Well, Mama," he began. "It's just, I want to be with the others, so I don't miss out on the fun. This is the time of year when everyone really enjoys themselves!"

"Very well," Nataliya had sniffed. She tried to make a joke out of it. "You will leave your mama to grow another year older all alone."

"Aw, don't say that." Peter looked at his mother with big eyes. He was taller than her now, though his back hunched over more than it did when he was a child. His hair still grew in patches around his head, thick and wiry. Peter tried keeping it longer to cover the bald spots. His distorted features had grown more pronounced with age, but maturity had somehow given him a confidence despite his appearance. Nataliya felt that her son was no longer ugly so much as simply odd-looking.

"It's okay, *dorogoy*," she said gently, patting his hand. "I will be fine. But don't forget about your old mama, okay? Come around and see me every once in a while so I don't get lonely."

Peter leaned over and kissed his mother's cheek. "I will, Mama," he said, with a lopsided grin. He turned and loped off toward the performers' cabins. Nataliya watched him go, swallowing over a lump in her throat.

She leaned against the railing of the cabin that she would share with the other cookhouse hands. The air was crisp and cool. Oklahoma winters were known for their unpredictability, sometimes quite cold and other times unseasonably warm. Today was somewhere in between. Nataliya crossed her arms and stared at the line of trees that stood behind their camp, her mind drifting over the last six years.

"You look mighty far away."

Nataliya blinked and shifted her eyes to meet Tiny's. He stepped forward, standing before her, his hat in his hands and a grin on his face. She smiled in return.

"Yes, I guess that I was thinking," she answered.

"Penny for yer thoughts?" Tiny asked.

Nataliya cocked her head to the side and looked at him quizzically. "What does it mean? *Penny for your thoughts*?" she asked.

Tiny chuckled. "It's a phrase we use when we'd love to hear about what yer thinkin'."

"Is an interesting phrase," she murmured. "I am thinking about all the things we have seen since we leave New York. I did not really understand the big decision when we made it."

Tiny nodded. He leaned his shoulder against the porch railing and looked out over the horizon as well. "Yeah," he answered. "This circus life is a strange one. A person can't really understand it at all if they don't live it."

"This is true," Nataliya said.

"Has it been all bad for you?"

"No," she answered. "I do not think it has all been bad. I saw the circus first time when I was little girl. In Russia." She glanced at Tiny, who stared back at her with wide, interested eyes. "My papa," Nataliya sighed. "He did not wish circus life for me. He wished for me to be scholar, to teach and be…how do you say in English…" She pushed back her shoulders and raised her chin with an air of authority.

"Respectable?" Tiny asked.

"Yes, this," Nataliya answered. "But circus was inside me all along. And when Pasha is born looking so much like…" She looked back down the path where Peter disappeared. "He is different these days—my Pasha. Happy. I do not think circus life has been terrible for him. I am pleased with that."

Tiny nodded. "Yeah, ol' Pete is growing up," he agreed. "He's becoming a young man, but he's also still a boy who has some learnin' to do."

"What does this mean?" Nataliya asked, turning to look at Tiny. He stood on the ground below the porch, his full height reaching up so that he was eye-level with her. She searched his broad face, his large eyes set evenly above a wide nose. He wasn't a handsome man in appearance, but the kindness in his gaze drew her in, and she blinked several times at the tenderness that met her. Tiny stared back for a beat of silence before clearing his throat.

"Just means he ain't done learnin' things yet. That boy is the smartest kid I ever met—knows a great many things about the world. But he don't know everything there is to know about life." Tiny put his hat on his head and gave her a smile. "S'okay, though. He'll figure it out same as the rest of us—by livin'."

Nataliya nodded. "Yes." She paused, formulating her next sentence, translating her thoughts from Russian to English. "Thank you for teaching him, Mr. Tiny," she said.

Tiny gave a little shrug. "Not sure I taught him much," he replied.

"You did," Nataliya said. "My Pasha," she paused. "My Pasha needs someone to teach him to be good man. He did not have that until we came to circus and he meet you." She gazed at Tiny. "Thank you," she said again.

Tiny swallowed hard and offered a nod. "You're welcome, Miss Nataliya," he said with the tip of his hat.

"Hey you! Girl!"

Nataliya turned to see Butch hollering at her from the bottom of the hill.

"Boss Man wants to see you. Now!"

Nataliya's throat tightened, and she froze, staring back at him.

"Didn't you hear me?" Butch yelled. "He said now!"

Nataliya glanced at Tiny. He raised his eyebrows and gave a shrug of his shoulders. She moved to the stairs and descended quickly, then headed down the hill toward the main cabin where Beaumont stayed with his son. Within minutes she stood on his front porch, hands shaking as she reached up and knocked on the door.

"*Entrez!*" barked the command from the other side of the door.

Nataliya pushed open the front door and walked into the cabin. It was warm, a fire crackling in the nearby fireplace. Beaumont sat behind his desk in the front room, glasses perched on the end of his nose and a stack of papers before him. He glanced up at her.

"Ah, yes. I'm glad you came so quickly," he said. There was an odd shape to his words, almost as though they had been braided with glee.

"You want to see me?" Nataliya asked.

"Yes, yes. Come in, please." He gestured her closer.

Nataliya tentatively stepped into the room.

"Yes, Nataliya," Beaumont began, clapping his hands together in front of his waist. "I decided to do a little more investigating into your late-night meeting. It was very curious to me that you would happen to run into a friend from Russia in the middle of Tennessee. So, I looked into the situation, and I was very fascinated with what I found."

Nataliya's breathing grew shallow as she focused on Beaumont's words.

"I followed up with the sideshow act that's been trailing us for some time, and I found the man that you met with," Beaumont continued. "Imagine my surprise when I discovered that he looked an awful lot like your son."

A mirthful smile stretched across Beaumont's face.

"*Pourquoi ferais-vous ça?*" She didn't mean to speak French. The words simply slipped out. Beaumont's eyes narrowed.

"*Tu parle français?*" he hissed, the words snaking their way from his lips.

"*Oui,*" she whispered.

"All these years, you have spoken French? Like a SPY?" Beaumont blustered in his native tongue, pushing to a stand and leaning his hands against his desk.

Nataliya just stood still, staring back at him.

"Well, then," he continued in French. Nataliya closed her eyes for a brief moment before opening them back and staring at him. "I will continue in a language that's easier for us both."

"I would like for you to meet my newest side show act." He gestured to the side and Nataliya's gaze shifted. She gasped at the sight of Kolya brooding in a chair in the corner, his legs crossed, hands folded in his lap. He stared at her beneath a furrowed brow.

"What?" She turned to Beaumont. "*Je ne comprends pas.* I don't understand." She turned back to Kolya. "What are you doing here?" she asked, this time in Russian.

"Oh, this is all getting very confusing," Beaumont said, switching back to English and waving his arms. He rolled his eyes and shuffled from behind his desk. "I brought him on board as a favor to you. And to the boy, of course."

"What does it mean? As a favor?" Nataliya asked, again speaking French. She pulled her eyes from Kolya's face, too stung by the anger in his stare.

"Well," Beaumont answered in English, a delicious smile spreading across his face, "I simply told him that you were in danger of losing your place here in my circus, and that would also endanger young Peter's future. I appealed to his manhood and offered him the chance to protect the two of you by joining our show."

"You blackmailed me," Kolya growled. "He told me he'd kick you both out if I didn't join. He put that on *me*." Kolya glared at Nataliya. "And so did you, by coming to me that night."

Nataliya blinked slowly. "*Ya eta ne hotyela*," she said quietly in Russian. "I didn't want this."

Beaumont laughed, crossing his arms over his chest. "Oh, this is going to be fun," he said, looking back and forth between the two. After a lingering moment of silence, he drew in a deep breath and clapped his hands.

"Well, then," he said. "I suppose that is all I need from the two of you. You may go back to your cabins now. Unless, of course, you'd like for me to make arrangements for the two of you to share a room?" He looked at Nataliya, then Kolya. "No?" He burst out in hearty laughter, then finished it off with a facetious sigh. "So sad when young love doesn't work out." He turned to Kolya. "I'll have someone come and escort you to your living quarters. I believe you'll be staying in the house with the other freaks. You should enjoy that—you'll be with your son."

Nataliya gasped. Beaumont turned to her. "I guess, *ma chere*, you may want to go ahead and tell the boy that his long-lost papa has finally come home."

Nataliya spun on her heel and tore from the room, flinging open the front door and racing up the hill. She crested and turned the corner. Tiny sat on the porch steps of the cabin, harmonica in his hands as he played a joyful tune. He caught sight of her and pushed to his feet.

"What's wrong?" he asked.

"He...he's horrible. He's horrible person," Nataliya choked out. "I must to find Pasha. I need to tell Pasha."

"Whoa, whoa. What's goin' on?" Tiny asked, grabbing her elbow.

"He's here," she gasped, craning her neck to look up at him. "Kolya is here. Pasha's father is here!"

"*What?*"

Nataliya froze, closing her eyes. Peter stood at the top of the stairs staring at his mother and Tiny.

"What did you say?" he asked. He slowly walked down the porch steps and approached his mother.

"Mama." Nataliya took a deep breath and shifted her gaze to Peter. Tiny dropped her arm and took a step backward.

"Pasha," she began. "Your papa..." She paused, not really sure where to begin. "Your papa is also circus performer. He left Russia before you were born to join American circus. I did not know I would ever see him again, but then...I did. And now...now he is here."

Peter blinked slowly. "My father is...here?" he asked. "But, how? He's also in the circus? What does he do?"

"He is sideshow act. Like you, my darling," Nataliya reached up and smoothed Peter's hair back off his face.

Peter took a step back. "So, it's true, then. I look like my father."

Nataliya's eyes welled up with tears, and she nodded. "Yes, is true. But you are not *like* him. You're different."

The sound of footsteps crunching on the trail behind them made Nataliya's hands start to shake. "Just trust me, Pasha," she whispered, switching to Russian. "You are not like him. And the man you're about to meet is not the man I loved many years ago. He's changed."

Peter's gaze shifted as a man stepped around the corner. He came face to face with a version of himself that he suspected was waiting in his future. Their eyes met, and Kolya's face darkened.

He walked forward and stopped next to Nataliya. "So, this is the boy?"

Nataliya straightened and nodded. She put her arm around Peter's shoulders and turned him to face his father. "*Da*," she replied, jaw set tight. "Meet your son. Pavel Konstantinovich...Pasha."

Peter stared into the eyes of the man before him. He saw the same drooped eyelids, the same offset mouth. Wiry hair framed his face, tied into a ponytail at the base of his neck. His back was less hunched than Peter's, but he clenched together the same webbed hands. This was the man responsible for it all.

"Well, do you speak or not?" Kolya growled. His English was perfect, without accent. Peter nodded his head.

"I speak," he said, his voice hoarse. "And I go by Peter. Only Mama is allowed to call me Pasha."

Kolya drew in a deep breath and let it out slowly. "Okay, then," he said. He grasped his small carpetbag and stepped to the side. "I'll go in and settle into my new home." His voice hummed with anger, his eyes cutting at Nataliya. He brushed past them and stormed up the steps. A small crowd had gathered around to watch the scene, and murmurs trailed behind Kolya as he stomped into the cabin. Peter turned to his mother.

"You saw him a few weeks ago, didn't you? The night you snuck into town alone?" he asked. "And you didn't tell me?"

"Pasha."

Peter spun on his heel and walked away, the up-down motion of his uneven gait drawing snickers from Manny and Jessop on the porch behind them. Tiny's head whipped around.

"Y'all two shut up," he barked. Manny lifted his arms in surrender and turned back toward the cabin with Jessop on his heels.

Nataliya looked up at Tiny with tears in her eyes. "I just," she began. "I do not believe this is happening."

Tiny ran the back of his hand over his forehead and glanced down at Nataliya, her thin frame trembling from head to toe. "Let's give Pete a few minutes to cool off. Then I'll go find him and talk with him," he said. "You need to sit down for a little while."

She nodded. She grabbed his hand and squeezed it tightly. "Tell him I am sorry?" she whispered. "Tell him I was weak and scared, and that I am very sorry."

Spontaneously, Tiny bent down and kissed the top of her head. "Maybe you were scared," he said. "But ain't no way I'm lettin' you claim yerself as weak." She covered her face with her hands. "Go lay down, Miss Nataliya," Tiny said. "I'll work this out."

Nataliya nodded and turned away, walking slowly back toward her cabin. Tiny sighed and pushed his hat back on his head, eyeing the path where Peter had fled.

Peter stood beneath her window and stared up. He grabbed a small pebble and tossed it, missing her window altogether and hitting the side of the cabin. He sighed in frustration and picked up another pebble, tossing it higher this time. It hit the glass with a ding, and he ducked behind the tree and waited. When her face appeared in the window, Peter stepped out and raised his arm. The sun was setting, and the light was fading fast. He needed her to see him.

Emmaline looked down, and her eyebrows raised in surprise. Peter gestured wildly for her to come down. She looked over her shoulder, then looked back at him. He put his hands together in a silent plea. She held up one finger and disappeared from the window.

Peter ducked back behind the tree and shoved his hands in his pockets. The warmth of the sun was waning, leaving the impending night air cold and moist. His shoulders began to quake as he thought of the look on his father's face when they met. Even his own father, who looked just like him, was ashamed and disgusted by what he saw.

"My father is alive," he whispered. "My father is here." His shoulders shook harder.

"Hey!"

Peter jumped as Emmaline skidded around the corner, wrapped in a fur coat, her hands stuck inside a muff.

"You scared me!" he gasped.

"Sorry," she breathed.

"How'd you get out?" Peter asked, glancing around the tree.

"I'm sneaky and quiet," Emmaline replied. "Bea was takin' her bath, and Monsieur and Pierre were arguing about who knows what. I just crept out real soft." She glanced around. "I can't stay long, though," she said. "What is it?" She stepped back and really studied him. "Peter what's wrong?" she asked.

"My father is here," he said, his voice breaking.

"Your father!" Emmaline stared at him. "Your father who you've never met?"

"Yes," Peter replied. "My father who left Russia before I was born to join the American circus as one of their freaks."

"Oh. Oh my…" Emmaline's voice trailed off. "I heard Monsieur talkin' about his new act at breakfast this mornin'. He was goin' on and on about how it was going to be his best act yet. I never heard him so happy 'bout anything." She took a step toward Peter, pulling one hand from of her muff and grabbing his. "Peter, I don't know what to say."

"He hates me," Peter mumbled, holding tightly to her hand, his heart beating rapidly. "My father hates me, and I don't understand why. He looked at me like I was a monster."

Peter froze and stared up at her face. "He looks just like me," he said. Tears pricked the corners of his eyes.

"Oh, Peter, I…"

"Emmaline! Emmaline!"

Bea's voice caused both of them to freeze.

"Girl, I know yer out there. You best git on back in here right now 'fore we both git in trouble."

Emmaline locked eyes with Peter. "I gotta go," she whispered. He nodded. She leaned forward and kissed his cheek.

"There's a clearing in the woods behind this cabin. About a hundred yards in," Peter whispered. "I'll be there early tomorrow morning. If you can get away, do it. Dress warm."

She nodded, then dropped his hand and stepped out from behind the tree.

"Land's sake, child!" Bea hissed. "What you doin' down there? You done lost yer mind!"

"I just wanted to see the moon rise, Bea," Emmaline said, stepping delicately up the hill toward the back door.

"Mm-hmmm..." Bea replied. "And I don't suppose there's someone hidin' behind that tree watchin' the moon rise with you?"

"What are you talkin' about?" Emmaline said, the pitch of her voice raising. She laughed nervously.

"You just git on in here without bein' seen. We'll talk about this later," Bea hissed. She slammed the window and disappeared from view. Peter peeked at Emmaline from behind the tree.

"I'll be fine," she whispered, motioning for him to stay back. He ducked and waited several minutes before pushing away and sneaking back under the canopy of the trees and the fading night sky toward his cabin. Then he froze, suddenly realizing that when he got to the cabin, he would have to see his father again. Peter leaned against a tree and set his head back, closing his eyes.

"Been a day, hasn't it?"

Tiny's voice broke the silence, and Peter gasped.

"Sorry, kid," Tiny said with a chuckle.

"Don't know why everyone thinks it's so funny to scare a guy around here," Peter muttered.

"So…didya see yer girl?" Tiny asked.

"Emmaline isn't my girl," Peter answered with a sigh.

"Well, you got that much right, Pete. But…didya see her?"

"Yeah."

Tiny drew in a long breath and let it out slowly. "Yer gettin' reckless, Pete. It's gonna come back to bite you."

"I didn't ask for advice, Tiny, okay?" Peter pushed off the tree and stomped away. With just three long strides, Tiny caught up to him.

"Naw, you sure didn't, Pete, but yer gonna get some anyway. Now listen, this thing with yer pa comin'—this is hard, and it's no good. It's no good for you or yer mama, and don't seem to be good for yer pa, either. But you won't be doin' Miss Emmaline any favors draggin' her into this messy business, hear?"

Peter looked away from Tiny.

"Aw, Pete," Tiny continued. "This ain't easy. It's plain confusin', am I right? You gotta talk to me." Tiny stopped walking. He put his hands in his pockets and rocked back on his heels.

"Why is he here?" Peter asked, spinning around to face Tiny. "Why? And why is he so angry? And why did my mama spend my whole life saying nothing about him? How did she find him, and why didn't she tell me?"

A light flickered in Peter's eyes and they widened. "That's what she told you that day, isn't it?" he asked. "That's what she was so upset about, and she told you and asked you not to tell me."

Tiny nodded his head.

"How could you not tell me, Tiny?" Peter cried. His voice quaked. "How could you do that?"

"Yer mama asked me not to, and I felt I needed to honor her," Tiny replied. "None of us coulda known it would come to this."

Peter shook his head and stepped back from Tiny. "No," he said, his face morphing from understanding to anger. "No, you should have told me! *She* should have told me. Now I have to go sleep in a room next to that man who looks like me and hates me for it."

"Yer pa don't hate you, Pete," Tiny replied, taking a step forward. "He hates himself. He's a sad man, an angry man, who don't know who he is or what he gave up when he walked away."

Peter shook his head and turned away from Tiny. "You should've told me," he said. He shoved his hands deep in his pockets and walked away from Tiny, the darkness quickly engulfing his retreating figure.

Tiny sighed and dug his toe into the ground. "Yeah," he said softly. "I s'pose I shoulda told you."

Peter woke early the next morning, long before the sun, and dressed quickly. He hadn't seen his father the night before when he returned, Kolya having taken a bed in another room.

Creeping out of the house, Peter shivered at the cold blast of air that greeted him. He burrowed deeper into his coat and shuffled down the path, using the moonlight to point him toward the tree line at the bottom of the hill.

When he reached Beaumont's house, he paused, looking up. The rooms were dark and still. He wondered if Emmaline would even be able to escape. This was different from the train. She would have less privacy and cover. Peter swallowed, thinking of Tiny's warning, then shook his head and pushed forward, making his way silently past the house and into the trees all the way in the back. It was dark beneath the branches and leaves, all of them interwoven and tangled together. Peter had to move slower and more carefully to stay upright. He suddenly felt foolish for suggesting they meet like this, in the dark and cold. He was about to stop when he heard the crunch of a stick behind him. Peter froze and waited.

Footsteps made their way delicately toward him. He shrank back behind the nearest tree and tried to make out any shadows in the dark.

Finally, a figure took shape. He squinted his eyes. The figure drew closer. When she pulled up next to his tree, Peter let out a sigh of relief and stepped out to face Emmaline.

"Ah!" she shrieked. She took a swing at him. Peter caught her arm.

"Sshh! Emmaline!" he whispered. "It's me. Peter."

She grabbed her heart and took a step back. "You scared the fire outta me!" she gasped.

He grinned. "I guess it is a little funny to scare someone," he replied with a snicker. She hit him playfully on the arm.

"Follow me." Peter grabbed her hand and led her forward. A minute later, they stepped into a clearing where the moonlight beat down, shining a soft, white circle around them.

Emmaline stepped into the light and turned around. "This almost feels like magic," she whispered, a smile on her face. Peter smiled back, totally taken by the sight of her. She stopped to face him.

"How're you doin'?" she asks. "Did you see your father anymore last night?"

Peter shook his head. "No," he answered, kicking at the ground. "Hopefully I can just avoid him all winter." He drew his shoulders up in a shrug.

"So sorry about it again, Peter," Emmaline said, her eyes swimming with compassion. She took a step toward.

"It's fine," he answered. "Let's just get to your reading, okay?"

"Oh." She stopped. "Okay."

Peter stepped up next to her and pulled a reading primer out of his pocket. He'd purchased it at the last town they visited and tucked it under his bed on the train. Of course, Manny had snooped around his corner of the train car, likely looking for money to steal, and he'd found the book.

"Goin' back to basics there, Pete?" he'd snickered when Peter caught him. "Circus life has a way of dumbin' a fellow down, don't it?"

Peter shook his head as he thought about the way Tiny had cuffed

Manny on the back of the head and snatched the book back while Manny yowled in frustration.

Peter handed Emmaline the primer. "I got you a new book," he said. "You're ready for more challenging sentences."

Emmaline smiled. It was a different sort of smile, proud and confident. Peter's cheeks warmed watching her. He leaned forward and pointed. "Start here," he said, pointing to the first sentence.

"S-ah-m. Sahm. Sam!" She looked up at him triumphantly. Peter smiled back with a nod.

"Keep going."

"Sam p-e-t-s...pets! Sam pets...h-i-ss...um, hiss...his! Sam pets his... dog! I know that word. I know 'dog' without soundin' it out." Emmaline grinned up at him with pride.

"That's great, Emmaline! You've been practicing."

She gave him a triumphant nod of her head. "I write the letters on my pillow at night and say the sounds over and over." She looked back down at the book.

"Sam pets his dog," she repeated. "S...ah...Sam is...h...ah...peh... peh...yeh?" She glanced up at him for help.

"Remember," Peter reached his hand across her and pointed to the word. "The 'Y' at the end of the word makes the "EE" sound."

Emmaline stared back at the word for a long time, her lips moving silently as she put together the sounds. "Happy!" she finally cried out.

"Yes!" Peter nodded, hopping up and down with excitement.

Emmaline sighed. "Does this get easier at some point?" she asked.

"Sure, it does!" Peter said. "You just read two whole sentences by yourself! You couldn't do that a month ago."

Emmaline smiled at him, the moonlight highlighting her rosy cheeks and soft lips. She shivered and leaned in closer to him.

"Thanks, Peter," she said. "I think you might be the only person who's ever believed in me."

Peter put his arms around her and pulled her in tighter. His stomach flipped as she leaned her head against his shoulder. Feeling bold, Peter planted a kiss on top of her head. Emmaline turned and looked up at him. She leaned her face toward him, her lips grazing his lightly.

"What. Is. This?"

Peter and Emmaline gasped, pulling apart and turning to face the voice that had spoken. Stepping out of the shadows, Kolya took in the site of the two teenagers bathed in moonlight. His gaze shifted from Peter to Emmaline, then back to Peter.

"What do you think you're doing?" he hissed.

Peter didn't respond. He simply reached his hand over and grasped Emmaline's hand.

"C'mon, Emmaline," he said. "I'll walk you back."

The two made their way toward the path. They approached Kolya and stepped to the side to walk around him. As they moved past, Kolya grabbed Peter's arm and yanked him to the side.

"You're messing with something you can't control," Kolya hissed, his Russian words seeping through clenched teeth. "Boys like you and me don't get to have girls like that. It never works."

Peter yanked his arm free and stepped back, glaring at Kolya.

"You don't know me, and you don't know her," he replied. Turning on his heel, Peter grabbed Emmaline's elbow and led her to the still-dark path, breathing heavily as he strained his ears to make sure Kolya wasn't following them. When they reached the top of the hill, Emmaline stopped.

"What did he say to you?"

"Doesn't matter," Peter replied. "He has no right to say anything to me at all."

Emmaline paused, staring at Peter through the glow of the moon trickling through the canopy of trees. "He is your father, Peter," she said, her voice quiet.

"He's not at all my father," Peter shot back. "I've known him less than a day. Tiny has been more of a father to me than that guy!"

Peter thought of Tiny's admonition about his meetings with Emmaline and fought off a cringe. He shook his head. Emmaline grabbed his hand and squeezed.

"Still," she said. "You have actual parents who are alive, and who are tryin' to look out for you. That's more than I got." She dropped his hand and looked away, blinking hard.

The two turned and slowly made their way out of the clearing of trees. Emmaline's entire body shook with cold and adrenaline. Peter stopped and turned to her awkwardly.

"I'm sorry about this," he mumbled.

"S'okay," she replied. "But maybe we ought not meet for a few days just to be safe."

"No, Emmaline," Peter shook his head. "We can't let him tell us what we can and can't do. He's a coward who ran from his life. He has no right to talk to you or to me about anything."

Emmaline sighed. "It's just..." she turned to Peter. "If Monsieur or Pierre found out what we were doing it could be real bad. Especially for you."

"I'm not scared of them," Peter bluffed, straightening his shoulders defiantly.

"You should be," Emmaline answered.

"Emmaline!" Peter whispered. She turned back to face him. "I'll be here tomorrow." Emmaline sighed and tried to look away. Peter grasped her hand and pulled her back just slightly. She skimmed over his misshapen face. He tilted his head so that they locked eyes.

"Knowing I'll get to see you is the joy of my days," he whispered. "Please."

"I'll think about it," she said. She turned and disappeared into the shadows.

Peter dropped his hands, listening until her footsteps had faded into the darkened morning. He then turned his ear toward the path, his heartrate quickening as he listened to make sure Kolya wasn't coming up behind him. Moving steadily through the shadows, Peter made his way back toward his own cabin. He no longer felt the cold, nor did he feel the silent stare of the man lurking in the shadows of the trees.

Peter spent the day avoiding Kolya. He blinked back fatigue from his early morning meeting in the woods, and he pushed through the day's activities, his head constantly swiveling from side to side as he checked to see if his father was nearby.

Beaumont liked to fill their days with activities to "freshen the mind" and "sharpen the body" on their down time. Nobody really liked these exercises. They ranged from gardening and weeding, tending the earth around the compound, to long stretches of calisthenics, half of which Peter could not accomplish. Beaumont took special delight in watching them struggle, often sitting on a chair beneath an umbrella and barking out orders for them to run in place, lift their knees higher, pump their arms harder, and all the while he'd laugh unapologetically as they faltered.

Peter hated the exercises. After very little sleep, the morning calisthenic routine felt especially cumbersome. His joints ached, and he longed to simply stretch out flat and close his eyes. As he raised his arms above his head, then swooped them downward in an attempt to touch his toes, he bit his lip in anger.

The only thing that made the morning routine bearable was watching Tiny try to keep up. His long arms and legs seemed to move beats behind everyone else's, and he made exaggerated grunts and groans through each movement, inciting snickers from the group. When Tiny leaned forward to try and touch his toes, he let out a loud fart, which sent the rest of the group into fits of hysteria, Manny and Jessop collapsing on the ground and howling with laughter.

Tiny, his arms dangling over the hardening ground like two limp noodles, just shrugged his shoulders. "Can't ask a feller to bend in half and not expect some wind to escape," he murmured, which only made Manny and Jessop laugh harder.

Beaumont glared at them from his chair, less amused when it appeared everyone was having fun than he was when he saw them suffering.

Miss Clarabelle stood in the back of the group, arms crossed over her wide chest. Sweat matted her hair to her head. She looked around at the group of performers and shook her head. She was different lately, changed since that day on the bridge. She cried less, and somehow seemed more alive and determined than Peter had ever seen her. Fire flashed in her eyes instead of sadness, and Peter liked the look of it. Little Sue had taken a liking to Miss Clarabelle, and she stood close to her at every opportunity. After several days of these humiliating group exercises, Miss Clarabelle now stood defiant, her buxom chest heaving as sweat dripped down her round cheeks. She shook her head, muttered something under her breath, then turned to look at Boss Man.

"I'm done," she said, her voice barely carrying over the din of everyone else. Little Sue stopped and looked up at her, head cocked to the side. Little Sue, simple-minded and sweet, didn't really understand much of what people said, but she read tone better than most anyone else, and she watched Miss Clarabelle keenly in that moment, somehow processing the gravity in her words before the rest of the group.

"Get back to work, Clarabelle," Beaumont said lazily from his chair. "Heaven knows you need it more than anyone else here." He snorted with laughter. Pierre, who walked slowly back and forth in front of their group with his hands folded behind his back like some kind of army sergeant, followed suit.

"No," Clarabelle said. This time her voice was louder and stronger. Everyone froze and turned to face her. Tiny, who was standing in the back, cupped his hand over his eyebrows and squinted through the morning sun at Clarabelle. The glare of the sunshine framed her from behind, making her seem an apparition, a spirit come down to set the world right.

"I'm sorry. What did you say?" Beaumont pushed to a stand and walked toward Clarabelle. Pierre stepped up beside his father.

"I believe she said 'no'. The fat cow," he sneered.

Clarabelle raised her chin and straightened her shoulders. Beaumont and Pierre glared at her.

"Say it again, and you're done," Beaumont threatened. "You will leave, and you will never return."

Clarabelle clutched her hands at her side, then pursed her lips and shook her head. She leaned forward so that her face was closer to Beaumont's. She could smell the sardines on his breath and see the flecks of grey that he tried so hard to cover up at the roots of his head.

"No," she said quietly. She glared as Beaumont's mouth twisted into a snarl.

"Leave," he hissed. "Take nothing with you. Everything you have is mine. Turn around, follow this path, and walk your fat backside to the nearest town. See what they can do with a talentless slob like yourself."

Clarabelle straightened up, nodded her head once, then turned and lumbered past the group who stared at her with wide, horrified expressions. Little Sue whimpered and tried to follow Clarabelle, but Beaumont grabbed her hand and held on to her.

"No, you belong to me," he said, tightening his grip on her wrist. Clarabelle turned and shot her a look of tenderness, which calmed Little Sue down.

Tiny stepped out of the group and faced Beaumont. "Boss," he began, but Beaumont rose his hand.

"I don't want to hear anything from you, Tiny," he growled.

Tiny turned as Clarabelle waddled past him.

"Clarabelle, you don't have to do this," he murmured. "You don't have to go."

"Yes, I do, Tiny," she replied. She glanced at Beaumont, then back at Tiny. "Everybody has worth, right?" she asked.

Tiny nodded, his mouth turning upward in the faintest smile.

"I won't go far," Clarabelle continued, her voice dropping to a whisper. "I'm gonna be fine. But, promise me something, Tiny?" She peered up at him.

"What are you two whispering about?" Beaumont shouted. He thrust Little Sue at Pierre and marched toward Tiny and Clarabelle.

"Promise me you'll look after Little Sue?"

"You stop that whispering right now! This instant!" Beaumont stepped between Tiny and Clarabelle, his face red. His moustache quaked as his upper lip trembled with anger. Tiny took a step back and nodded at Clarabelle. He offered a wink, and she returned the gesture with a tilt of her chin. Shifting her eyes to Beaumont, she gave a cursory nod of the head, then pushed past him, knocking her shoulder into his and throwing him off balance. He stumbled to the side, quickly recovering and letting out a frustrated growl.

Stomping to the front of the group, he grabbed his megaphone and pressed it to his lips. Pierre shoved Little Sue away from him and rushed to join his father. Tiny moved over to Little Sue and squatted down so that she could look in his eyes.

"It's going to be okay," he said. Tears streamed silently down her face.

"Listen here!" Beaumont barked into the megaphone. "Insubordination of any kind will be swiftly dealt with. Anyone who so much as looks in a direction that I deem unnecessary will be sent packing. *Do you understand?*" He screamed the last question, and everyone winced as his voice pierced the air around them.

Peter stood on the fringe of the group. He ran his eyes over the crowd. Everyone was there, from the clowns to the acrobats, all of the sideshow acts, and the performers—everyone stood riveted in spot, watching Beaumont melt down before them. Peter's eyes fell on Kolya, who stood in the back corner, hands shoved in his pockets. His dark brows were furrowed and chin down as he glared over droopy lids at the ringmaster. He shifted toward Peter, and for a brief moment the two held one another's gaze.

Peter turned away and looked to his right, down the path and away from Kolya. Emmaline was there, walking next to Bea. She clutched a parasol in her hand, and her long dress swayed with each step. Emmaline was exempt from the group exercises. Instead, she and Bea walked the paths around the cabins, Bea mumbling about her latest frustrations, and Emmaline longing for something she couldn't quite verbalize. It was a need to belong somewhere and to someone. She looked up at Peter at that moment and blinked as he stared back at her.

She lowered her eyes and turned abruptly back toward the house at the bottom of the hill.

"I want to go back and lie down," she said as Bea turned alongside her.

"What's wrong?"

Emmaline shrugged. "Must've been somethin' I ate," she answered. "Not feelin' so good."

Bea sighed. She looked over her shoulder at Peter, whose gazed still lingered on Emmaline.

"Well," Bea said, leaning in close to her charge. "Maybe if you wasn't meetin' that boy in the wee hours of the night, you might not be feelin' so bad."

Emmaline looked at Bea, eyebrows raised.

"Oh, don't look so surprised," Bea said. She turned and began walking down the path, pressing her hand into the small of Emmaline's back and guiding her steps. "I wasn't born yesterday, child."

"But, if you knew, then why'd you let me go?" Emmaline asked.

Bea sighed. "I s'pose I's feelin' soft toward ya," she replied. "Girl's gotta have some freedom to make her own choices."

Emmaline was quiet for several long beats. "Thanks Bea," she finally replied.

Bea shook her head. "Don't you go thankin' me. Plumb foolish what yer up to, meetin' that boy. Learnin' to read."

Emmaline stopped. "You knew I was learnin' to read?"

Bea laughed. "Girl, I just told you I wasn't born yesterday. 'Sides, there ain't nothing you got that you can hide from me. I seen those books you been shovin' under yer pillow. I hear you practicing at night when you think I'm sleepin'."

Emmaline's mouth fell open as Bea chuckled. "S'alright, honey," she said. "Yer secret's safe with me. I ain't never thought it was right the way Boss Man treated you, like you was some kind of delicate prize. Ain't nobody the sum of what they look like on the outside. We all made up of much more on the inside."

Emmaline's eyes filled with tears. She grabbed Bea's hand and gave it a squeeze. Bea squeezed back, then dropped her hand.

"Now, that's enough a' that," she said. "Won't do us no good to start blubbering like a couple a' little school girls."

Emmaline nodded. They approached their cabin and trudged up the steps. As they reached the front door, Bea stopped. She turned and stared at Emmaline, her dark brown eyes searching the girl's crystal blue gaze.

"You listen to me, child," Bea said. "You gotta end that thing with the boy. It ain't safe, for you or for him."

Emmaline looked at her for a long moment, silently formulating a response.

"I know it ain't fair," Bea continued, "and I know it don't make no sense, but you gotta trust Old Bea on this one."

Emmaline nodded. "I know," she sighed. "It's just…" she paused. "Peter is the first person who ever made me think I could be more than just," she waved her hand up and down over her face, "this."

Bea nodded. "Well, he ain't wrong about that. You a smart little thing in a lot of ways. But you ain't ready for love because you don't know what that is."

"Do you know what it is?" Emmaline asked.

Bea's face clouded over, her eyes turning glassy as she slipped into a memory that Emmaline couldn't see. She blinked a few times, focusing back on Emmaline.

"Never mind you what I know," she finally said. "Just promise me you'll stop this thing with the boy."

Emmaline sighed. "I promise," she finally answered. She looked up at Bea. "Can I meet him tonight and tell him?"

Bea sighed. "I s'pose one last meetin' won't harm nobody. But this will be the end, you hear me?"

Emmaline nodded. Bea pushed open the door to the cabin and stepped inside. "Land's sake," she said, running her hands up and down her arms. "It's gettin' colder 'round here. Gonna need to start keepin' that fire goin' through the day." She went about stoking the embers of the fire as Emmaline shut the door and walked to the nearby chair by the window. Sitting down, Emmaline looked out into the morning sun and ran through what she would say to Peter later that night.

Nataliya hustled across the dirt path toward the performer's cabins. The morning meal had been served and cleaned, the lunchtime prep was finished, and she had a short bit of downtime before Butch would expect her back to the mess hall.

She breathed in deeply, relishing the clean air in her lungs. The animals had been moved to their own offsite facility, tended by the keepers and trainers who kept them in top condition for the winter months and prepared them for the grueling spring schedule. Absent the hay and dung, the air smelled fresh and invigorating. Nataliya hurried up the path and around the corner, slowing down as she took in the sight of Tiny sitting on the stoop of his cabin with Little Sue by his side.

Little Sue looked so small next to Tiny, like a little fragile doll. As Nataliya approached, she noticed the tears shimmering on Little Sue's face. The girl was crying, the sound so pitiful it reminded Nataliya of a wounded puppy.

"What happened?" Nataliya asked. Tiny looked up as Little Sue pushed tighter into his leg, her wide eyes set far apart on her small head.

Tiny patted Little Sue's shoulder reassuringly, his giant hand covering the span of her back. "Well, it was a rough mornin'," he said.

"I'm sorry about Miss Clarabelle," Nataliya murmured. Little Sue sniffed. Nataliya leaned forward and grabbed the girl's hands, squeezing them between her own.

"Little Miss here is right sad 'bout losin' her friend," Tiny said. "And I s'pose I'm a little sad myself."

Nataliya nodded. "I'm so sorry," she repeated.

Tiny nodded. "We're just gonna sit here a while and feel our sadness. Sometimes, that's all a person can do 'fore he can move on. Just feel the sadness for a little bit."

Nataliya nodded. "Yes, I suppose this is true," she answered. She straightened up and looked at the open doorway of the cabin behind Tiny. "Is Pasha here?"

Tiny shook his head. "Left a bit ago to take a walk. Said he needed to think through some things and clear his head."

"Maybe he is also feeling the sadness," Nataliya said, blinking back tears. Tiny nodded.

"You might be right."

Behind him, inside the cabin, the sound of a fiddle rang out, the merry tune quickly accompanied by feet stomping in rhythm. A pocket of laughter cut through the air and floated over the three of them, almost as though it meant to punctuate Tiny's words. Tiny smiled. He looked down at Little Sue and nudged her.

"There's always a little joy to be found, though, you know?" he asked. He looked back up at Nataliya with a lopsided grin.

"You are very interesting person, Mr. Tiny," Nataliya said. She smiled at him, her eyes fluttering shyly down to her feet then back to his face.

"Yer only sayin' that cause I'm so tall and awkward," Tiny replied. Nataliya cocked her head to the side.

"What does it mean? 'Awkward'?"

"Means I'm a little strange, is all."

Nataliya furrowed her brow. "Everyone is strange here," she said.

Tiny chuckled. "Well, ain't that the God's-honest truth?"

Nataliya wrapped her arms around her waist and peered up at the sky. Wisps of clouds trailed across the bright blue, framing the treetops above them. "If you see Pasha, tell him I look for him?" she asked.

Tiny nodded. "You got it." He glanced down at Little Sue. "Whatcha say, Little Miss? Want to head inside and see what all the fuss is about?"

Little Sue looked up at him curiously. Tiny grabbed her hand and gave her a gentle tug, pulling her to her feet, then stretching himself to a stand. When they each stood up to their full height, Little Sue stood just above Tiny's knee. Nataliya smiled at the sight of them together.

Tiny tipped his hat, then turned and walked up the steps of the front porch, Little Sue trailing behind him. Nataliya watched them go, Tiny's words running through her head.

There's always a little joy to be found, though.

Joy.

Nataliya shook her head. "What does it mean?" she murmured. "Joy."

Peter walked alongside the creek bed, kicking at rocks with his toe. His arms hung by his side and dangling from his right hand was the small hatchet that Tiny kept tucked in his carpet bag. Peter pulled to a stop and stared at a tree several yards ahead. With a frustrated cry, he threw his arm back, then flung it forward, releasing the hatchet and watching it fly through the air and bury itself in the center of the trunk. Thrusting his hands in his pockets, he stomped forward and yanked the hatchet out of the tree, then went back and threw it again. Over and over, he threw the hatchet, burying its blade repeatedly in the trunk, which was starting to look like it'd been mauled by a bobcat.

Finally, panting and dripping with sweat despite the cool air, he stopped and turned to look at the meandering creek. He dropped the hatchet to the ground with a thud and mulled over Miss Clarabelle's exit earlier. He wondered what she would do next. He wondered what it would be like to just walk away. The thought terrified him. Where would he go looking the way that he did? Were it not for the sideshow tent, he didn't know who he would be.

"Hi."

The voice came from behind Peter, startling him. He whirled around to find Kolya leaning against a tree, watching him with a brooding gaze. Peter froze and stared back at his father, a face that so mirrored his own it left him nearly speechless. Kolya stared back for a long moment, then pushed away from the tree and walked toward the creek bed. He stopped a few feet from Peter and stared down at the trickle of water at their feet.

"Hi," Peter said. He turned away and looked down at the rocks, smooth and dark from months spent beneath the moving water. Tension hung between them in the silence. Peter glanced sideways at Kolya again. His father's shoulders were stooped, his hands shoved deep in the pockets of his worn pants. Peter ran his hand self-consciously over his head.

"Where'd you learn to throw like that?" Kolya asked. There was a tinge of admiration in his voice. Or at least Peter imagined that he heard it.

"Tiny taught me," Peter replied.

Kolya raised his eyebrows. "The tall guy?"

Peter nodded.

"Can't believe they call him Tiny," Kolya muttered. "Not even trying to be ironic."

Peter furrowed his brow but didn't turn to look at his father. The two stood in an awkward silence for several long minutes.

"So, I hear people talking around here," Kolya began, finally breaking the tension. The edge in his voice wasn't nearly as pronounced as it had been earlier that morning. "They say you're pretty smart."

Peter blinked a few times, unsure of how to respond. Finally, he shrugged his shoulders.

"I guess," he replied.

"They say you can learn any language you want to learn, and that you read every book you can get your hands on," Kolya continued. Peter nodded.

Kolya sighed. He squatted down, sifting through the rocks in the creek bed until he found a dark one, buried beneath a pile of lighter rocks. He picked it up and turned it over in his hand, running a calloused finger over the smooth surface.

"You and me are like this black rock here," he said. His voice was quiet, all the fight and anger siphoned away. He sounded tired. Defeated. He stood and turned to face Peter.

"We're different. We aren't like all the other rocks." He gestured to the ground beneath them where white and grey rocks stretched down the length of the creek's path. There were a smattering of brown rocks mingled in, but Peter noticed that within their line of sight, there wasn't another black rock to be seen.

"We're always going to be covered and buried by the more acceptable people of this world, just like this rock was buried under that pile of clean, white rocks." Kolya dropped the black stone and kicked it.

"Nature isn't so different from the human world, kid," he said. "There's an order, and the ones who deviate from that order have no place."

Peter stared down at the black rock for a long time, then shifted his gaze upward. It was midday now, the sun high overhead. He drew in a deep breath, letting the fresh air settle in his lungs before pushing it out in a long sigh.

"Mama said you were smart, too," Peter finally said. "She always told me that you were the smartest person she had ever met, and that I got my intellect from you." Kolya turned and met the gaze of his son.

"I don't think she's right, though," Peter continued. Kolya raised an eyebrow.

"And why is that?" he asked.

"'Cause you weren't around," Peter replied with a shrug. "You weren't the one who sat beside me while I learned to read. You weren't there pushing me to write sentences over and over. You weren't around to make me do arithmetic by the moonlight after a long day of working."

Kolya nodded, shifting from one foot to the other. He lowered his head and kicked at the ground.

"Mama did all of that," Peter said, his voice lower. "Everything I learned is because of her pushing me. She never once made me feel incapable, and she didn't let me settle for mediocrity just because of the way I look." Peter shook his head and took a step back. "I got my intellect from my mother," he said quietly. "I got everything I have because of her."

"Yes," Kolya said with a single nod of his head. "You did. So, tell me, why are you risking everything your mama has worked for to meet that girl in the middle of the night? Why are you putting yourself in danger, and your mama? If you're so smart, boy, then explain that to me?"

Peter took another step back, a lump forming in his throat. He blinked and let out a frustrated sigh. Kolya took a step forward.

"I'm no father," he said. "I know that. But your mama..." he paused. "Well, your mama clearly raised you better than I could have. Maybe you ought to think about her before you go sneaking off into the trees in the middle of the night. Take it from someone who knows the inevitable outcome of sneaking around." Kolya's eyes flicked down Peter's thin body and back up, and all at once Peter understood and knew what he was in the eyes of his father. He was a mistake, a regret even.

Peter opened his mouth to respond, but Kolya raised his hand and shook his head.

"I'm done, kid," he said. "I'm not going to pretend to be a father. I know I haven't earned that right." He leaned down and picked up the hatchet, flipping it once in his hand. "But if there's one thing I do know it's that it isn't easy being the black rock in a world that likes conformity," he said. In one swift motion, he threw the hatchet forward, hitting the center of the tree trunk in the same spot Peter had hit on his very first throw.

Peter stared for a moment at the hatchet, then turned and glanced down at the stones. A smile turned up his lips at the way the black stood out against the backdrop of the white. He remembered that night so long ago under the stars when Tiny told him he needed to know who he was on the inside because the world would try to tell him he was broken. Peter looked up Kolya, his eyes dancing. "But the world is much more interesting with the black rocks sprinkled in."

Kolya squinted and gave a brief nod of his head.

"You're right about one thing, though," Peter continued. "You haven't earned the right to be my father. Seems the only thing you gave was...this." Peter gestured toward his body.

Kolya's jaw tightened. He turned and quickly made his way up the path and out of sight. Peter walked slowly to the tree, tugging hard to release the hatchet from the wood. Overhead, a breeze rustled the branches of the trees, whispering through the sky as birds chirped their noonday song. Peter's stomach growled, reminding him that lunch would soon be served. He tried to busy his mind with any thought but the obvious one—that he had to stop meeting with Emmaline.

Peter picked his way silently through the brush, the light of the moon cutting through the holes in the trees to illuminate the path ahead just enough for him to stay on it. He finally came to the cluster of trees down the hill from Emmaline's cabin. A chill ran the length of his spine as he settled behind the thick trunk of a tree just off the narrow path. He should have worn his coat, but it was hanging in the closet, and there was no way to pull it out without waking anyone up, so he left it behind. But it wasn't the cold that quaked his shoulders. It was the war raging inside. He knew what he should do.

"I don't want to do it," he whispered into the night air. Behind him an owl hooted, the sound mournful and dark. Peter glanced around him, trying to make out the shadows that swayed and danced in the night. Trees looked like people and, despite the chill, a trickle of sweat snaked its way down the back of his neck and under his shirt.

The sound of a stick cracking pulled his head around. He glanced at the cabin where Emmaline slept. There was no movement—no sign that anyone stirred. Peter strained his eyes and watched as a shape picked its way down the path. Blinking hard, Peter stared, relief washing over him when he finally recognized Emmaline's delicate figure. A small smile involuntarily tilted his mouth upward. He pursed his lips and let out a low, short whistle. He watched as Emmaline stopped, then started back up again a little more quickly.

"Peter?" she whispered when she entered the canopy of trees. Peter stepped out from behind the trunk that hid him and held up his hands as Emmaline gasped.

"It's me," he said. Emmaline let out a long sigh. Peter reached out his hand.

"Come on," he whispered. "Let's go."

Emmaline hesitated for a beat, then placed her small hand in his, and Peter's stomach flipped. Together they walked as quickly and quietly as they could deeper into the trees, out of sight from the cabin where Boss Man slept. Peter could hear Emmaline's breathing grow more labored as they walked, but he kept pushing forward. They needed to be far away from it all.

Finally, he stopped and turned around. They stood in a small, round clearing, moonlight bathing them from above. Emmaline looked like a shimmering vision. Peter blinked several times as he took in the sight of her milky white skin glowing in the blue moonlight. Her eyes were wide, and her blonde curls circled her face like a halo.

"You're beautiful," Peter murmured, then immediately blushed and looked down. Emmaline, still catching her breath, dropped Peter's hand and took a step back.

"We have to stop this," she said. "It ain't safe."

Peter stared at her, knowing that she was right but unable to agree.

"I can't keep puttin' you in the way of harm like this," Emmaline continued. Tears pricked the corners of her eyes.

"We could run away," Peter blurted out. Emmaline looked up and locked eyes with him.

"What?"

"We could run away," he said again, this time more confidently. It suddenly was the only option that made sense. Peter knew he couldn't continue to live and work in Monsieur Beaumont's circus with Emmaline on a stage next to his and never be with her.

"Peter, we…"

"Just listen, Emmaline," he interrupted. "There's nothing here for you and me. As long as we're property of Beaumont, we're trapped. But out there…" He gestured beyond them. Emmaline glanced toward the expanse of trees that separated her from the only life she'd ever known.

"Out there, we can be free. You can learn all the things you want to learn with no one telling you no. I'll help you. We'll learn it all together."

Peter grabbed Emmaline's hands and pulled her closer. She drew in a sharp breath and tried to avoid Peter's gaze. Finally, she looked up. It dawned on her that Peter's face no longer looked misshapen and deformed to her. She held his gaze, and all the words he had just spoken suddenly made perfect sense.

"We could leave," she whispered. Peter nodded.

"Right now. You and me," he said. "We could go. We could be long gone before they even realize it."

Emmaline pulled back and stared hard at Peter. "What about your mother?" she asked. "And your father? What about Tiny?"

Peter's eyes darkened. A lump formed in his throat as he thought about leaving his mother behind with no word of where he'd gone.

"I don't care about my father," he said. "But my mother and Tiny…" He paused and swallowed hard. "Well, my mother somehow managed to find my father seventeen years after he left Russia." Peter blinked hard. "She'll find me. She and Tiny both. They'll come looking, and they will find us. And then they'll be free, too. We'll all be free together to live as we please."

"This is crazy." Emmaline shook her head. "If they catch us…"

"They won't catch us if we leave now." Peter leaned forward and rested his forehead against Emmaline's. "I love you," he whispered.

The tears trickled from Emmaline's eyes down onto her cheeks.

She closed her eyes and leaned into Peter, kissing him gently at first, and then more passionately. A few moments later, they pulled apart and Emmaline looked up at him. She blinked several times, catching her breath, then nodded.

"Let's go," she said.

Peter stared hard at her for a long moment. He leaned in and kissed her forehead. Grabbing her hand, he turned toward the trees and took a step forward, then recoiled as a shadow stepped out and joined them in the clearing.

"Well, what have we here?"

Pierre looked from Peter to Emmaline and back again. A sneer twisted his features, changing his face into something monstrous and sinister beneath the moon's glare.

"You think you can just leave?" he hissed, stepping toward them. Peter pushed Emmaline behind him and raised his chin.

"Leave us alone," he said, his words coming out stronger and braver than he actually felt. Pierre laughed, a snakelike sound that danced between them and sent chills down Emmaline's spine.

"You're a fool, kid," Pierre answered, switching to French. Peter furrowed his brow.

"Yeah, your mother let us in on your little secret," he continued. "I know you speak French, and I know you've been spying on my father and me all this time. And now you're trying to steal what doesn't belong to you." He paused and stared hard at Peter. "You're a stupid freak who has no real idea how this world works."

He took another step toward them.

"Do you really think you could just leave and go make a life in the real world? You? Looking like...*that*?"

Another step.

"You're an idiot," he jeered switching back to English. "It doesn't matter how many languages you speak or books you can read. You can't change the fact that you're nothing more than a *freak*."

"Stop it, Pierre," Emmaline said, stepping to the side. She held tightly to Peter's hand to keep her body from quaking.

"And you," Pierre said. He let out a chuckle. "You're dumber than he is. Can't read or write. Can't spell her own name. A pretty face, yes, but you have nothing to contribute to the world other than those eyes and that..." His eyes ran down her body. Emmaline shrank back against Peter.

Pierre stepped forward again. Peter and Emmaline took a step back.

"You're promised to me, you know," Pierre said with a twisted smile. "I've been waiting until you were old enough, but Papa and I made the arrangement long ago. You belong to me, and since you're clearly old enough now to experience the..." He paused, a disgusted look sweeping across his face as he glanced at Peter, "*physicality* of a relationship, I'd say it's time you and I made things official."

"Too bad that won't be happening," Peter said, his voice low and thick. "You'll have to kill me first."

"Peter," Emmaline gasped.

Pierre laughed. "Is that all it will take?" He reached into his belt and pulled out a long, sharp knife. "Well, then that should be easy."

"No!"

Emmaline stepped between them and held up her hands. "No, Pierre," she begged. "Please don't do this."

"Emmaline," Peter said, placing his hand on her shoulder. She shrugged him off.

"I'll go with you," she said to Pierre, her words catching in her throat. "Just leave him be. Let him go, and you can have me."

"Emmaline, no," Peter cried. He turned her toward him. "He's not going to kill me."

"I wouldn't be so sure about that," Pierre cut in. Peter turned back to him just as Pierre moved forward, his face twisted in a snarl. Peter pushed Emmaline behind him and raised his hands up.

"Pierre," he began. He switched to French. "*Vous ne voulez pas faire ça.*"

"Oh, you have no idea how wrong you are, freak," Pierre answered. "I've wanted to do this for a long time." He swung the knife, slashing through the air between himself and Peter, who jumped back, knocking into Emmaline.

"Stop it!" Emmaline screamed. "Please, Pierre. Please stop!"

"Shut up, Emmaline," Pierre snapped. He jabbed the knife toward Peter again, the tip of it snagging Peter's shirt and tearing the fabric. Emmaline stepped in front of Peter and held up her hands.

"I said I'd go with you, Pierre! I'll go now. Just please don't hurt him," she begged. Peter grabbed her shoulders and pulled her back from Pierre's maniacal gaze.

"No, Emmaline," he said. "I won't let you do it."

Emmaline turned. "Peter, please," she said, eyes shining. "Please, I can't watch you die."

"You won't...NO!" Peter shoved Emmaline out of the way as Pierre leapt toward them both, the knife held above his head and an animal-like growl escaping his lips. Peter held up both arms over his face and cringed.

In the same moment, a cry rang out from the trees. Peter looked up to see a hatchet flying into the clearing, burying itself in the back of Pierre's skull. He dropped his arms in stunned silence as Pierre stumbled for a single step, then fell to the ground with a sickening thud.

Emmaline covered her face with her hands and wailed as Peter dragged her away from Pierre's body.

The air around them went still. Peter clung to Emmaline as her whole body trembled and quaked. He scanned the tree line, his heart hammering.

"We need to get out of here," he said, his voice shaking as he pulled her back.

"Stop!" The voice came from the darkness on the other side of the clearing. Emmaline and Peter whirled around.

"Who's there?" Peter called.

Two shapes floated into view, one tall and slim, the other short and disproportioned. Tiny stepped into the light first. His eyes settled on Pierre's body, then shifted to Peter.

"What happened?" he asked.

The second shadow materialized. Kolya came into the clearing several feet to Tiny's right. He stepped forward and took in the sight of Pierre on the ground, then looked up at Peter and Emmaline huddled together.

"Fool," Kolya muttered, his gaze resting on Peter. "I told you this was dangerous."

"I…I don't know…who…" Peter stammered. He looked from Tiny to Kolya, then back to Tiny, trying to wrap his mind around what had just happened. "What do we do?" he finally asked. He glanced down at Pierre's body, a stream of blood pouring from the wound in his head. The hatchet gleamed in the moonlight.

"Y'all two're gonna have to git," Tiny answered. "You're gonna have to run, right now. Go to the nearest town quick as you can. Here, take this money."

Tiny stepped around Pierre's body and handed Peter a roll of cash. "Git yourself a place to stay and hide until I come find you. Understand?"

Peter nodded. Emmaline stared at Pierre's body in horror. She looked up at Tiny, then at Kolya, then back down at Pierre.

"What about Mama?" Peter asked Tiny.

"Don't you worry about your mama. I'll take care of everything. You just git yourself hidden." Tiny glanced at Kolya. "You and me will take care of this situation," he said, jutting his chin toward Pierre's body. Kolya nodded. He stared at Peter.

"Do what he says," he commanded. "Hide and don't come out."

Peter nodded. He opened his mouth to speak.

"Just go," Kolya growled. "Get out of here now."

Peter nodded. He put the roll of money in his pocket and gently turned Emmaline away from Pierre's body. He glanced back over his shoulder and looked at the two men standing in the clearing.

"Thank you," he said, his voice meek, full of shame and gratitude all mixed up together. He gripped Emmaline's shoulders and pulled her into the shadows, away from the body of the man who almost killed him.

"What're we gonna do now, Peter?" Emmaline whispered. Her voice was hollow, her eyes glassy.

"Ssshhh…" Peter squeezed her shoulders. "We're going to survive. We're going to do what they said and survive."

Their breath came out in frantic puffs of air that danced in front of their faces in the chilled night. They moved as quickly as they could through the thick trees in the direction that Tiny had told them to go. Finally, after what felt like a lifetime, Peter and Emmaline broke through a clearing and saw the faint outline of a row of buildings, lit by the moon, off in the distance.

"Must be the town," Peter said, his chest heaving. Emmaline trembled beside him, her eyes still wide with shock.

"I never saw a man die before," she said, her voice soft. Peter put his arm around her shoulders and pulled her closer to him. She stiffened at his touch.

"Me neither."

In the distance, the sound of piano music floated out into the night sky. The whinny of a horse chased the music.

"The saloon," Peter murmured. "Must still be open." He turned to Emmaline. "We'll need to be careful." She nodded. Peter reached out to take her hand. Emmaline looked down at his webbed fingers and hesitated. It all seemed so foolish now.

Reluctantly, she placed her hand in Peter's, trying to keep the inward grimace from pushing outward, but Peter noticed, and his heart sank.

"Let's go," he said.

Together they walked quickly across the open field, anxious to get out from under the glare of the moon. When they reached the edge of town, they pulled up behind the nearest building and stood in the shadows, catching their breath as the music from the saloon swept over them. They could hear chatter in the street, the drunken sounds of men talking mixed with a lady's cackle coming from inside the building with the music.

Peter leaned around the corner of the building. They were next to the saloon. He watched two men stumble out, dust kicking up in small clouds as their sharp-toed boots tried to find steady footing.

Peter pulled back and glanced at Emmaline. She was pressed against the wooden planks, eyes closed, chest heaving. The moonlight bathed her in a ghostly glow, and Peter instantly knew he had lost her. She would never be his now.

She opened her eyes and met his gaze. Peter tried to smile, but his mouth wouldn't cooperate. Every vision he'd had of them running away and establishing a life together was gone, and he suddenly felt very tired and overwhelmed.

"We need to find the hotel," he said. "It must be close."

"Why would it be close?"

"Aren't they always near the saloons?" Peter asked.

Emmaline shrugged. "I ain't never actually been into a town. Monsieur didn't let me leave the train."

Peter looked back at her with sad eyes. He blinked a couple of times, then motioned for her to follow him. "Let's go see what we find," he whispered.

They crept around the side of the building into the dark alley. Next to them in the saloon, another song started pumping from the piano, the music cutting a dissonant rhythm against the clanking of glasses and chatter. They came to the end of the alley and poked their heads around the side of the building. The street was empty. Orange light spilled out from the saloon's open doorway, casting an eerie glow across the empty street. Peter looked up and noticed the sign across the road.

HOTEL

He tapped Emmaline's shoulder and nodded. Leaning in, he put his mouth close to her ear. She drew back with a shiver.

"You have to go in and ask them for a room," he whispered.

"What? Why me?"

"They won't give a room to me," he replied. "But they will give one to you."

Emmaline blinked, understanding washing over her face. "Of course," she murmured. She glanced at the building across the street.

"What do I do?" she asked.

Peter reached in his pocket and pulled out the cash. "You go in and tell them you need a room for the night. Then tell them your brother will be joining you and he will be along shortly after he boards the horses."

Emmaline looked at him skeptically. "Ain't no one gonna believe me sayin' all that stuff," she protested.

"They will if you hold your head up high and look them in the eye," Peter replied. "You'll have to be confident and sure of yourself. They'll believe anything you say looking like you do."

Emmaline blushed and looked away. She accepted the money from Peter and took a deep breath, letting it out slowly and watching it dance briefly in the cold air before disappearing.

"Wait, but how're you gonna get in?" she asked.

Peter looked toward the saloon. Outside the door, resting on a rickety rocking chair, was a dusty cowboy hat. He looked back at Emmaline.

"Don't worry about that. I'll work it out. You just get us that room."

Emmaline raised her chin and pushed her shoulders back, then tentatively stepped forward, her hands shaking as she took one step after another toward the hotel. She could see a small light through the glass door and the bent figure of someone sitting at the front desk. She glanced back over her shoulder, but Peter had tucked himself back into the alley, and she could no longer see him.

She made her way up to the front door, then gripped the handle and pulled it open. A bell clanged over her head. Emmaline jumped.

The person behind the desk looked up impassively. She was thin, her hair pulled back in a tight bun. She quickly pushed to her feet and stared at Emmaline in the dim light.

"H-Hello," Emmaline stammered. She remembered Peter's advice and pushed her chin higher, straightening her shoulders and forcing herself to look the woman in the eye. The woman stared at her with mouth slightly open. Emmaline wondered if it was unusual for people to come in this late.

"Um…I'd like a room please. For me and my brother. He'll be here after he boards the horses for the night." Emmaline shifted from one foot to the other. The woman behind the desk shook her head and rubbed her eyes, muttering something under her breath.

"You lost, child?" she asked.

"No, ma'am," Emmaline answered. "Just…um…travelin' through and need a place to rest."

The woman shook her head. "Busy day today," she said, motioning for Emmaline to step closer. "Don't usually get strangers wanderin' through town much, and today I've had you and…well…it's just been a busy day."

Emmaline looked at her curiously.

"Alright, well, I got a room for you and your brother. Two beds. Wash basin. Can't promise it will be quiet. The racket over there's bound to last through the night like usual." She jutted her chin toward the saloon across the street. Emmaline looked back over her shoulder, then turned to the woman who was studying her closely.

"I ever seen you around here before?" the woman asked.

"No, I don't think so," Emmaline answered. "I never been here before."

The woman shook her head. "You look just like...well, never mind. Here's your key. Room's at the top of the stairs, last door on the right at the end of the hallway."

Emmaline nodded. The bell over the door jangled, and she turned to see a figure crouch into the room. The man shoved his hands in his pockets. His dusty hat was pushed low on his head, covering his face.

"Hey sis," he mumbled as he sidled closer. "Get our room?"

Emmaline nodded. She glanced at the woman who was staring at the man who'd just walked in. "This your brother?" she asked Emmaline.

"Yes."

The woman narrowed her eyes, shifting her head to try and get a look under the cowboy hat.

Peter turned toward the stairs. "C'mon," he mumbled. "I'm tired." Emmaline fell into step next to him and together they made their way up the stairs, all the while aware that the woman behind the desk was watching them closely.

When they reached the top of the stairs, they turned down the narrow hallway and walked as quietly as they could past closed doors. They reached the final door on the right and slid the key inside. Just then the door next to theirs opened. Emmaline gasped and whirled around. Peter ducked his head, turning away to hide his face.

"Miss Clarabelle?" Emmaline whispered in surprise. Peter turned and found himself face to face with Miss Clarabelle. Her eyes were wide with shock.

"What're you two doing here?" she hissed. "That man didn't send you after me, did he? 'Cause I ain't goin' back."

Peter glanced down the hall. He pushed open the door to their room and motioned them all inside. Clarabelle sighed, gently shutting her door and following them.

"Miss Clarabelle, we didn't know you were here," Peter said when they were all safely inside the room. Outside the window, the saloon's noise gave them some cover for conversation.

"Well, what are y'all doin' here, then?" She looked from Peter to Emmaline and back to Peter.

"We're running away," Peter said.

Clarabelle raised her eyebrows. She looked at Emmaline. "You're runnin' away with her?" she asked. She looked back at Peter. "Boss Man'll kill you for that. Or he'll have his worthless son do it."

Peter swallowed hard. Beside him Emmaline squeezed her eyes shut. Clarabelle watched them both curiously.

"Pierre is dead," Peter said quietly. "Boss Man doesn't know yet."

"You..." Clarabelle took a step forward. "Did you...kill him?"

Peter shook his head. "Don't know who did it, but it wasn't me." He glanced at Emmaline. She had sunk down on the bed, her arms crossed tight over her chest. "We have to get her out of here," he said.

Clarabelle nodded. "Yes, you do," she murmured. "We're all gonna need to get away from here, and soon. This will be the first place they look tomorrow."

"Tiny is comin' to find us and help," Emmaline said, her voice small and scared.

"Now, that won't be much help. Lord knows we can't hide Tiny," Clarabelle sighed. She clasped her pudgy hands over her large belly and tapped her thumbs up and down. "Well," she said finally. "No sense in tryin' to figure it out right now. Best get some sleep. We'll decide what to do at first light."

"You don't have to help us, Miss Clarabelle," Peter said. "You have your own freedom to work out."

She looked at him with gentle eyes. "Pete, I owe more to you than

I know how to articulate," she said. "I'm not leavin' the two of you to work this out on your own."

Peter gave her a grateful nod.

"Y'all two get a little sleep. We'll make our plan soon." Clarabelle pulled open their door and peered out into the hallway. She looked back over her shoulder. "Don't open this door for nobody unless you know who it is first, you hear?"

Peter nodded.

Clarabelle slipped out and closed the door quietly behind her. Peter turned to Emmaline and a pained, awkward silence hung between them.

"Emmaline," he began. She turned and laid down on the bed, her back to him.

"I'm sorry, Peter," she said, her voice so quiet it nearly got lost in the outside din. "I'm so tired."

Peter blinked. He remained standing in the center of the room for a long time until her breathing grew steady and he knew she was sleeping. He backed up and sat on the bed across from hers, watching her sleep, thinking about how close he had come to living in a dream-come-true.

He slowly lowered himself onto the hard mattress and stared up at the ceiling. Just before his eyes drifted shut, a single thought coursed through him, tingling from the top of his head to the tip of his toes.

"Dreams don't come true for freaks," he mumbled before slipping into a fitful sleep.

Immediately, or maybe it was hours later, Peter was awakened by the sound of a soft tap on the door. The room was silent now, the noise from the street having finally tapered off. Outside the window, the sky was a hazy grey. Peter blinked several times, then shifted his gaze to Emmaline. She sat on the edge of the bed, eyes cast down at her feet.

The soft tap on the door sounded again, and Peter shot up. He and Emmaline locked eyes. He pushed himself from the bed, back and shoulders stiff, and walked to the door.

"Who's there?" he murmured.

"It's me, Pete."

Peter pulled open the door to find Tiny hunched down, arms hanging limp at his sides. His hands were caked in dirt. He'd slipped his muddy shoes off and set them beside the door.

"Might want to let me in, kid," Tiny said. "That lady downstairs is right suspicious of us at this point."

Peter pulled the door open wider. "Did you see Miss Clarabelle?" he whispered as Tiny ducked into the room.

"Clarabelle is here?" Tiny asked in surprise. Peter nodded.

"She's next door."

Tiny rubbed his eyes. "Well no wonder that woman looked at me like she done seen a ghost. She's had a stream of oddities come through her hotel in a few short hours. Best go get Clarabelle so we can all talk at once."

Peter nodded. He stepped to the next door and knocked softly. Moments later, he and Miss Clarabelle were tucked safely in the room.

"Hey, Tiny," she said with a sad smile. "Didn't expect to be seeing you again so soon."

He nodded, then turned to the teenagers.

"We bought you two a little time. Miss Bea is going to stall Boss Man, tell him she's lettin' you sleep 'cause you'd been up in the night with sickness. You know Boss Man don't like vomit, so I imagine he'll stay away for the day. Miss Bea's goin' to play it for as long as she can to give us time to get away. But it won't be too long before he'll realize Pierre is gone missin' along with the two of you."

"Bea is doin' that for me?" Emmaline asked. Her eyes lifted, haunted pools of crystal blue as she stared back at Tiny. "But she'll get in trouble when Monsieur finds out. He'll make her leave. What will she do?" Emmaline's voice grew shrill and panicked. Clarabelle waddled over to her bed and pulled her into a hug, Emmaline's face pressed into the soft flesh of Clarabelle's shoulder.

"Shh, child," Miss Clarabelle said, stroking Emmaline's curls.

"Now, you don't worry about Miss Bea," Tiny said. "That woman is one of the strongest and wisest women I ever did meet. She'll be just fine."

"Tiny," Peter interrupted. "Who…I mean. How did…Pierre." He couldn't bring himself to ask the question that plagued him.

"Details don't matter much now, do they, Pete?" Tiny asked, his eyes searching Peter's. *Don't ask because you don't want to know*, was the unspoken answer.

"One thing is certain," Miss Clarabelle spoke up, her hand still running down Emmaline's golden curls. "We can't stay here. The four of us together is trouble for sure."

Tiny nodded. "That poor girl down at the front desk 'bout fell outta her seat when I walked in," he said.

A knock on the door hushed them all. Peter raised his eyebrows at Tiny.

"Is anyone else coming?" he whispered.

Tiny shook his head. "See who's at the door, Pete," he said quietly.

Peter nodded. He stepped hesitantly to the door. Another rap caused him to jump. He turned the knob and pulled the door open just a crack. Standing in the hallway, a bonnet pulled down low over her dark eyes, stood Bea. Peter gasped and pulled the door open all the way. Bea immediately marched into the room, then motioned for Peter to close the door behind her.

"Bea!" Tiny exclaimed. She held up her hand.

"We got us a problem, Tiny," she said. "Ol' Boss Man didn't take too kindly to the notion that Emmaline was sick. He stormed into her room to find her empty bed. I had to pretend I didn't know where she coulda wandered off to. Told him she was likely hallucinatin' as her fever'd been real high. So, he sent for Pierre." She turned to Peter. "And he sent for you."

Peter swallowed hard, shifting his eyes to Tiny and back to Bea.

"We don't got much time, I'm afraid," she said. "He knows you're all three missin', and he's gonna come lookin' for ya."

Tiny sighed. He turned toward the window and looked out at the dirty buildings across the street. It was quiet this morning, the revelers from the night before having finally stumbled away to sleep off their cares. Bea stepped up to Tiny and motioned for him to lean down.

"We got to git Emmaline outta here straight away," she whispered. "That man will chain her up for the rest of her life if he catches her. And Pete…" her voice trailed off. Tiny turned and met her gaze.

"I know," he murmured. He straightened back up and turned to the others. Peter and Emmaline stared up at him with wide, frightened eyes.

"Well," he said. "We best get ourselves outta here now while it's still quiet."

"I'll go talk to the girl at the front desk," Clarabelle said, standing up. "See if I can get anything out of her on where we could go."

Tiny nodded. "We'll be down and ready to leave no matter what she tells you in a few minutes," he said.

Clarabelle left, and Bea took her place next to Emmaline on the bed. Emmaline sniffled and leaned her head onto Bea's shoulder.

"Shhh…don't you worry, now," Bea murmured. "Ol' Bea is here."

Emmaline closed her eyes and inhaled Bea's familiar scent. All the years she had been certain that Bea didn't really care for her fell away, and she melted into Bea's embrace. Bea had been the only mother she'd ever known.

Tiny grabbed Peter's elbow and pulled him to the other corner of the room. He leaned down so that he was looking into the boy's eyes. Peter's hair was wild after his night of fitful sleep, and he looked just like the wild child he was billed as on the side of the circus tent.

"Listen, Pete," Tiny said. "Boss Man knows this town well, so he'll be here quick, and he will be after you. But more," Tiny glanced over his shoulder. "He's gonna be after that little girl over there."

Peter looked at Emmaline, her eyes closed as she leaned against Bea. He shifted his gaze back to Tiny and his droopy eyelids narrowed. "He'll have to go through me," he blustered.

Tiny nodded and offered a sad sort of grin. "Well, I s'pose I expected you to say that," he said. "I know you love her, Pete."

"It's real, Tiny," Peter interrupted. "What I feel is real. Just because we're young doesn't mean our emotions are wrong."

Tiny held up his hand. "I ain't said that," he interjected. "I just said I know you love her, and I do believe you really love her. But if you love her, then you got to be willing to do what you need to do to protect her. And that might mean lettin' her go."

Peter swallowed. He glanced out the window, then shifted his eyes to his feet. "We should probably go meet Clarabelle now," he muttered.

Tiny straightened himself up, his head stretching nearly to the ceiling above. The four of them quickly left the room and shuffled down the narrow staircase to the lobby below where Clarabelle stood at the desk, her eyes trained on the girl behind the counter. The girl looked away from Clarabelle and up to the rest of the ragtag group, the tallest man, the ugliest boy, the most beautiful girl, and the dark-skinned woman who had raised her.

"Look," the girl began, "I don't want trouble. You all best get yourselves on outta here and quick."

"Yeah, that's the plan," Clarabelle huffed. "I already told you that. What we need to know is where we can go."

The girl sighed. She glanced up at Emmaline, her eyes narrowed, studying the girl as if trying to place her face against the backdrop of a memory. "So familiar," she murmured.

"What was that?" Tiny asked, taking a step toward her.

The girl shook her head and leaned back to gaze up at him.

"Nothin'," she said. "Look, there's a woman who lives not too far outside of town who might be able to help you. Or...well, she might be able to help her anyway." She jutted her finger at Emmaline.

"How so?" Tiny asked.

"They call her the Angel of Oklahoma. She takes in lost children, or children whose families can't take care of them no more. She just takes them right into her house and lets them stay until they either grow up or their families take them back. All the neighboring towns help her out. They built her a big house that can sleep a whole slew of kids. They bring her food and supplies." The girl looked at Emmaline. "She'd take you in and keep you safe."

Peter blinked back tears but remained silent. He watched as the girl leaned down and drew a map, writing out instructions on how to find the Angel of Oklahoma.

"If you walk fast, it might take you half a day to get there," she said. She leaned back. "That's the best I can do to help." She held her hands up in front of her.

Tiny nodded. "That's the deepest kindness you could offer," he said. He glanced around at the rest of them. "Alright then. It's time to move."

"I'm not goin', Tiny," Clarabelle spoke up. He looked down at her, opening his mouth to protest, but she held up her hand. "Now, you know I'll only slow y'all down," she said. "I'll be more use to you here. When Boss Man shows up, I can throw him off your trail. Besides, he ain't got no hold on me anymore thanks to you. And to Peter." She smiled at Peter.

Tiny reached out and clasped Clarabelle's hand. "It's been my highest honor knowin' you, Miss Clarabelle," he said. She squeezed his hand in return, blinking rapidly. Emmaline broke free from Bea and rushed into Clarabelle's arms. Clarabelle shushed her, pushing her back and looking in her eyes.

"Now you remember one thing, little one," Clarabelle said. "Keep a smile on your face, because a smile chases away fear."

Emmaline nodded, attempting a small smile. She stepped back, and they watched as Clarabelle lumbered up the steps and back toward her room. Bea stepped up and turned to the rest of them.

"Well, I s'pose now's as good a time as any to tell you I ain't goin', either," she said. The girl behind the desk swiveled her head, first to Bea, then to the rest to watch their reactions. Emmaline let out a gasp.

"No! Bea!" she cried.

"Now, listen. I got to get back to Boss Man and make sure he don't do nothin' crazy. That man is dumber than a rock. I'll be more useful to you all if I stick close to him."

"But," Peter protested. Bea held up her hand.

"My mind's made up. I'm goin' back." Emmaline grabbed Bea's hand and pulled it to her lips, kissing the back of it as tears streamed down her face. Bea pulled her into a tight hug, her own eyes shining. She looked at Peter over Emmaline's shoulder. "I'll watch over your mama and, if I can, I'll get her outta there and to this Angel lady y'all are goin' to find."

Peter nodded.

"So that's it, then?" Emmaline asked, pushing away from Bea and tossing a glare at Peter. "You're just gonna let her go so that you can protect your mama instead of me?"

Bea turned Emmaline's face to her own. "Now child," she crooned. "Don't you see that this is my way of protecting you?"

Emmaline blinked back tears. "But," she began, voice trembling. "What will I do without you?"

Bea leaned forward and planted a kiss on Emmaline's forehead. "You'll go right on livin' your life," she murmured. "And maybe I didn't say it when I should, but I'll say it now—I love you, child." She stepped back, then turned and nodded at Tiny, who nodded back. Her head held high, Bea walked quickly through the glass-plated door and out into the dusty street without a glance back.

Tiny turned to Peter and Emmaline who both stood in stunned silence. He looked back at the girl behind the desk and offered a final nod of thanks.

"C'mon, you two," he said, pushing his hat onto his head. Peter and Emmaline followed him out into the crisp morning sun. Tiny studied the directions that girl had drawn for a brief moment, then folded the paper and tucked it in his shirt pocket.

"Best get goin'," he said. "We got a long walk."

By mid-morning, they were all soaked in sweat. Despite the cooler temperature, the sun's intensity warmed them as they briskly walked up and over hills, through tree-lined paths, and along the edge of a wide river that meandered its way through the dusty terrain. Peter tried not to slow them down, but his uneven gate left his hips and knees burning after a couple of hours walking. He grimaced with each step, his breaths coming out in strained puffs. Finally, Tiny pulled up alongside the river and motioned for them to sit.

"Let's take a break," he said.

Emmaline nodded, her legs heavy and back sore. She quickly dropped down on a large rock and rolled out her ankles. Peter shook his head.

"We've got to keep moving," he huffed.

Tiny shook his head. "Naw, Pete. Y'all need a break. We need to drink some water. And when's the last time you ate somethin'?"

Peter shrugged. He couldn't remember his last meal.

Tiny sighed and pushed his hat up on his forehead. "I'm gonna duck into them trees and see if I can rummage up somethin' to nibble on," he said. "Y'all two stay here."

Peter nodded, then watched as Tiny ambled into the trees behind them. He wondered what on earth Tiny might be able to rummage up for them to eat.

When Tiny was out of sight, Peter turned to Emmaline. Her back was to him, and she stared sullenly at the water below her feet. He took a few tentative steps forward, lowering himself on the rock so that he sat behind her.

"I'm sorry."

Her words were so soft, Peter almost wondered if he'd really heard them. He turned, staring at the back of her head, her golden hair cascading over slumped shoulders.

"I think this is all my fault," she said. She shifted around to stare at Peter. "I got us into a real mess."

"What?" Peter cried. "You? If anyone is at fault here, it's me. Tiny warned me that this was a bad idea. Even my father warned me, but I didn't listen. I just pushed and pushed. And now…"

Emmaline turned back to stare at the water again. "Yeah," she sighed. "And now."

Peter sat silent. One day earlier, an entirely different future had seemed possible. His hands shook, and he looked down, taking in the sight of his webbed fingers. He ran his hand over his head, his wiry hair covering the bald spots now that it was longer. He closed his eyes and saw his own reflection in his mind, and then he saw Emmaline's, and he felt immense shame. How could he have ever thought that someone who looked like him could have a future with someone who looked like her?

"It was real for me too, you know."

Peter's eyes opened, and he turned to see Emmaline staring at him. "What?"

"I heard you talkin' to Tiny back there. I heard to say that what you felt was real. It was real for me, too." She sighed. "In a different world."

"Yeah," Peter said. He touched the back of her hand and smiled sadly at her.

The rhythmic thud started as a low rumble, but quickly built up speed. Peter and Emmaline pushed to their feet and turned toward the sound. In the distance, puffs of dust kicked up in the sunshine. Peter squinted at the far-off image, his eyes growing wide as it came into view.

"Emmaline, go!" he shouted.

"What?"

"Go! Run into the trees. Get out of sight!"

Emmaline turned to run, slipping on the rock and tumbling to her knees, crying out in pain. Peter looked down at her as she clasped her ankle. Behind him, Tiny came tearing out of the trees, a handful of berries falling to the ground as he lumbered toward Peter and Emmaline.

"It's Boss Man," Peter said, his chest tight. He pointed to the trio of horses galloping toward them. Monsieur Beaumont led the charge. Next to him was Sal, riding one of the larger horses. Behind Sal was a third horse. Peter could see his father on that one, another rider clinging tightly to his back.

"Mama," Peter whispered. Tiny stood up to his full height.

"Stay close to me, Pete," he said, his voice tight.

Boss Man and his fellow riders pulled up in front of Tiny, Peter, and Emmaline and skidded to a stop. Beaumont's eyes were wild as he stared at Tiny, who stood nearly eye to eye with him on his horse.

Peter looked at his father, then shifted his gaze to Nataliya, who stared back down at him, her mouth opened in silent horror.

"What is the meaning of this?" Beaumont snarled. The horse huffed and stomped at the ground as Beaumont pulled back on the reins.

"Hey, Boss Man," Tiny said with a tip of his hat.

"You," Beaumont seethed. "You will tell me what you are doing out here this instant." His words came out more heavily accented than usual, his voice humming with barely restrained anger. He shifted his gaze to Emmaline, who cowered next to Peter. "Where do you think you're going?" he snarled. He turned to Peter. "And where is my son?"

Tiny stepped to the side so that he was standing in front of Peter and Emmaline, then tilted his chin up. "You caught up to us faster than I thought you would," he said.

"That girl in the hotel had no problem telling me she'd had a group of freaks tramping through her building. And, of course, Clarabelle was there and tried to give me some story about where you had gone, but I suspected you'd be here." He sneered at Tiny. "You cannot fool me."

"Well, now," Tiny replied. "I don't suppose I thought we could."

"I want my prize performers back," Beaumont hissed. "And my son. Where. Is. He?"

"Well, now, I'm afraid we can't help you. These two are free to do as they please, and they're ready to leave."

Beaumont growled. Tiny held up his hand.

"As for your boy," he said, his voice even, "can't say I know where he's gone off to." Tiny's eyes flicked to Kolya and back.

Beaumont turned to stare at Kolya and Nataliya. He looked back and forth between them and Tiny. "You all know something," he said. "I want to know what it is."

"Look here, Boss Man," Tiny said. "It's time for these two kids to leave, and that's what we're gonna do." Tiny glanced over at Sal, who watched the scene play out in his usual quiet, brooding manner. He gave Tiny the slightest nod, a sign of solidarity.

Beaumont sidled up to Tiny, the horse stomping at the ground in protest. "I don't think so," he said, his voice low.

"Leave them alone now."

Nataliya's voice spoke up from the background soft, but firm. She spoke in French, the words steady as she glared at Beaumont.

"*Qu'est-ce que vous avez dit?*" he asked.

"I said leave them alone," she repeated.

She spoke the last words in English, her shoulders squaring back. Peter watched his mother with pride as she faced Beaumont.

Beaumont's head swiveled between them all. "YOU DO NOT GET TO MAKE THE DECISIONS!" he screamed, spittle spraying from his mouth.

"Hey, Boss Man," Sal piped up from the side. "Maybe we ought to let them be."

"You too, Sal?" Beaumont turned to stare at his boss canvas man. Sal shrugged.

"Just seems that this ain't worth the trouble," he said, his words long and drawn out.

Beaumont let out a frustrated growl and leaned forward, throwing his leg over the side of the horse and sliding down to the ground. He now stood in front of Tiny, his head barely clearing the man's rib cage. He leaned back and looked up at him.

"Give me back the girl," he seethed. "You can have that monster of a boy. But she is mine. She belongs to me."

"No."

Emmaline stepped out from behind Tiny. Her eyes were shining with tears and her hands shook at her side. "No, I don't belong to no one," she said with a shaky voice.

Beaumont stared at her, his chest heaving up and down. With a growl, he reached behind him and pulled out a pistol from the back of his pants.

"Whoa, whoa!" Tiny said, raising his hands and stepping in front of Beaumont. "Hold on now. We ain't goin' to be pullin' out guns here."

Kolya and Nataliya both slid off their horse. Nataliya ran to Peter and Emmaline, drawing them behind her small frame while Kolya stepped beside Tiny.

"Put the gun down," he said.

"Oh, shut up, freak!" Beaumont screamed. Sal stepped up beside him.

"Hey, Boss?" he said. "You don't want to do this."

"Don't speak to me, you traitor," Beaumont seethed. Sal sighed. He walked over and stood on the other side of Tiny, the three of them forming an unlikely wall between Beaumont and the teenagers.

Beaumont let out a growl. He stomped his foot on the ground in frustration. "You can't just take them away!" he yelled. "They're mine! I own them!"

"They're people," Tiny said calmly with a shake of his head. "There ain't a man or woman, boy or girl, who deserves to be owned by another. Just ain't right, and I can't let you go on thinkin' that it is."

Beaumont growled in frustration and mounted his horse. He turned in a circle, his eyes trained on Tiny.

"This isn't over," he said.

"I think it is," Tiny replied, his voice soft and calm. "And I'll thank you for the years you gave me in the show." He tipped his chin in a short nod.

Beaumont pulled the reins and turned the horse. They trotted forward a few paces before Beaumont let out a guttural yell and yanked the horse back around, pulling his gun out again and kicking the side of the animal. He galloped around the group and trained his gun at Nataliya.

"No!" Peter yelled. He pushed his mother aside and stepped forward just as a shot rang out. A second shot quickly followed. Emmaline screamed and covered her face.

The world around them grew still then, the sound of the horses' hard breathing filling the air. Emmaline opened her eyes to find Peter standing in front of her, his eyes wide. At his feet lay Kolya, a stain of red spreading out across his midsection. Behind him, Beaumont was splayed over the back of his horse, a single bullet hole in his forehead. Sal stood beside Tiny, his gun hanging by his side.

"Kolya? Kolya?" Nataliya dropped to her knees beside Kolya who looked up at her, his eyes glassy as he drew in long, labored breaths.

"Why did you do that?" she whispered. She grabbed his hand and bent over him, looking at the growing stain spreading across his shirt. Peter dropped down beside his mother, staring down at the man who had just saved his life.

Kolya shifted his eyes from Nataliya to Peter. "Your mama…" he gasped. "*Ona horosho spravilas.*" The Russian fell from his lips in a final, breath. Nataliya lowered her head and sobbed quietly.

Emmaline stood fixed in her spot, her eyes staring at Beaumont. "You killed him," she said, turning to Sal.

Sal nodded. "I'm real sorry I had to do that," he said.

Emmaline stepped forward and wrapped her arms around Sal's waist. "You saved me," she whispered.

He pulled her back and leaned forward so that they were eye-level. "Time you moved on to something better." He offered her a sad smile. "You take care of yourself, little one."

Emmaline nodded. "Thank you," she said. Sal straightened up and put a weathered hand on her head like a man passing on a secret blessing.

"Guess I'll have to disband it all," he murmured, turning to Tiny who nodded back in return.

"Get in touch with Ringling," Tiny said. "No doubt they'll be wantin' to snap up many of you." Sal nodded. He reached his hand out to Tiny, and the two men shook without a word.

Sal glanced at Beaumont's body hanging off the horse, then flicked his eyes to Kolya's still body on the ground, Nataliya and Peter sitting next to him in stunned silence.

"What're we gonna do about…" his voice trailed off.

Tiny sighed. "I'll take care of it," he said, his voice tired and sad. "Seems I've gotten rather good at this sort of thing."

Sal cocked his head to the side and stared at Tiny. "You know what happened to Pierre, don't you?"

Tiny didn't answer. He just stared at Sal who stared back.

"C'mon," Sal said. "I'll help you get him down."

The two worked quickly, sliding Beaumont's body off the horse and laying it gently on the ground. Sal stood and drew in a deep breath. He squinted at the horizon.

"It was nice knowin' ya, Tiny," he said after a long moment of silence. He walked a few paces over to where the horses now stood grazing and grabbed the reins of the largest one. He walked it back to Tiny and held out the straps.

"Take her for your journey," he said. Tiny accepted with a grateful nod.

Sal turned to the other two horses and in one swift move he mounted one and grabbed the reins of the other. He turned to look back at the group. With a tip of his hat and a click of his tongue, he was off, the rest of them watching him go.

Tiny turned and looked down at Nataliya, who sat crying silently on the ground, Kolya's head on her lap. Peter sat numbly next to her, and Emmaline stood back, her eyes trained on Beaumont's still body. Tiny put his arm around her shoulders and slowly turned her away from the sight.

Tiny squatted down next to Nataliya. "Miss Nataliya," he said. She looked up at him, her eyes swimming in tears. "I'm real sorry."

Nataliya blinked and nodded in response. She gently lowered Kolya's head to the ground, then stood, wiping her face. Tiny rose next to her. "So, I suppose we need to bury them," she said, her voice trembling. Tiny nodded.

"Pete and I can take care of that, if you'd like," Tiny said.

Nataliya shook her head. "No," she replied. "I will help." She pushed back her shoulders. "It is what I must do for Kolya."

Emmaline stepped up next to Nataliya. "I'll help, too," she said.

"Well, alright then," Tiny said. He looked down at Peter, who was staring at his father's lifeless body on the ground.

"C'mon," Tiny said. "We ain't got much time to clean this all up."

Four hours later, the ragtag group trudged forward, the shallow graves of the two men they'd buried far in the distance behind them. The sun was setting fast, tucking itself in for the night and, in the process, painting the sky a handful of colors from red to orange to yellow. Nataliya and Emmaline rode Beaumont's horse while Tiny walked ahead holding the reins.

Peter fell behind. His whole body ached after burying his father and Beaumont in the wooded area a mile back. They had all worked feverishly, covering both bodies with rocks until nothing was left but arched mounds, altars to two lives that intersected at the wrong time and in the wrong place. Peter thought of his father, of the brief and complicated time they'd had together. The complexities of everything that had transpired in the past week left him with a headache.

He looked up at his mother and Emmaline riding ahead of him, and he desperately wished it was all different. Peter came to a halt and drew in a deep breath. As he watched them amble further away from him, Emmaline's golden curls blowing in the light breeze, he suddenly understood his father completely. Knowing that the only thing that stood between him and the love of his life was his distorted appearance settled in his chest like a block of ice.

Tiny turned and looked back, noticing Peter behind them. Nataliya turned as well. She quickly swung her leg over the side of the horse and slid down, rushing back through the grass to her son who stood still, his eyes shining, fists clenched by his side. He was the spitting image of Kolya.

"Pasha," she breathed, slowing down as she approached him. Peter trained his eyes on his mother. "Come, son," she said gently.

Peter shook his head. "My father is dead," he said.

Nataliya blinked back fresh tears and nodded. "*Da.*"

"I understand it now," he continued. "I understand why he was so angry." He turned to look at his mother, his eyes flashing. "I'll never have her just like he could never have you."

Nataliya sighed. She reached over and grabbed Peter's hand. "I wanted so much more for you, son," she said. "You have grown into a better man than I ever could have imagined. But…"

Peter waited, his hand limp in hers.

"But the world isn't ready for you yet. I hoped it would be. I hoped this life we carved out among others who are different on the outside would offer you more than what I could on my own."

Peter pulled his hand back and dropped it to his side. He looked at Tiny, who stood next to Emmaline on the horse, talking softly to her. He watched as she offered him a small smile. Tiny looked over and caught Peter's eye.

Peter sighed and looked back at his mother. "I still think we made the right choice, Mama," he said. "We met Tiny."

Nataliya looked over her shoulder and smiled at the world's tallest man.

"I don't want to let her go," Peter continued, his voice soft.

"I know," Nataliya said. She put her arm around his shoulders, and they walked forward together toward Tiny and Emmaline. When they reached the horse, Peter looked up and met Emmaline's gaze. She reached down her hand, and he clasped it in his own.

"I believe that's the house we're looking for down there," Tiny said, pointing down the hill at a large home below. It looked like a long rectangle. Smoke curled from the chimney on top of the roof. Adjacent to the home was a large barn. A boy who looked to be about ten came out of the barn and glanced up the hill, catching sight of them. He froze as Tiny led Emmaline, Peter, and Nataliya down the slope. They stopped about fifteen feet from the boy, who watched with wide eyes.

"Evenin'," Tiny said.

The boy nodded. "Hi."

"Is this where the woman lives who they call the Angel of Oklahoma?"

The boy nodded again.

"Is she home?" Tiny asked.

The boy nodded once more. He and Tiny stared at one another for a long time before he spoke. "You're real tall, mister," he said, his voice full of awe.

Tiny chuckled. "Well, I've heard that before," he replied. "Now, can you go get the lady of the house for us? I got a favor to ask of her."

The boy shook his head. "Sure thing!" he exclaimed. He turned on his heel and ran into the house. They could hear him shouting behind the door. Emmaline leaned forward and slid down the side of the horse, landing on the ground with her back to the house. She stared at Peter who looked back at her with sad eyes.

"I'm scared," she whispered.

Peter leaned forward and pulled her into a tight hug. "You're going to be alright," he answered. "You'll be safe." He swallowed hard, then stepped back just as a woman came out of the house.

"Mercy, Timothy, what is all the squallin' for?" She stopped when she saw Tiny, her eyes going wide. "Well, I'll be," she said, her voice laced with surprise. "Can I help you?"

Tiny stepped forward. "Well, ma'am," he began, "I sure hope so." He stepped to the side so that Emmaline could come forward, and the woman gasped, clutching her hand to her chest and falling back against the doorway. Tears sprang to her eyes.

"Ma'am?" Tiny asked, furrowing his brow.

"It can't be," the woman whispered. A sob escaped as she faltered forward on shaky legs.

Emmaline took a step toward her and cocked her head to the side. She knew this woman. She felt it.

"Em...Emmaline?" the woman whispered, closing the gap between them. She looked into Emmaline's eyes, reached her hand up to touch Emmaline's face, then pulled it back to her mouth.

"I've seen you before," Emmaline whispered. "I know you."

Tiny stepped up beside Emmaline, and the woman pulled her gaze away to look up at him.

"May we ask your name, ma'am?" he asked.

She looked back at Emmaline, a single tear trailing down her cheek. "My name is Mary," she whispered. "Mary Landis."

ACT SIX

NEW YORK, 1946

The man meandered down the street, his hat pushed down tightly onto his head. It was misty that day, the crisp, fall air giving hints that winter was coming, and winter in the city was something he'd not quite gotten used to.

He hunched his shoulders forward and pushed his hands deeper into his pockets. He could feel the coins, and he brushed them together between his fingers.

Rounding the bend, the man paused and watched a group of little boys come racing by, waving sticks in the air, whooping and hollering in the way that only little boys can do. The war was over, and there had been a collective sigh of relief, maybe from the whole world, but certainly here in the concrete block of New York. Despite the fallout from those wretched years, the man noticed that everyone seemed to smile just a little bit easier. The camaraderie of survival made for gentler conversation.

The boy at the end of the pack skidded to a stop and looked up at the man. He offered a gap-toothed grin as he thrust his makeshift sword into the air. His mama had cut his hair into a buzz cut, and a cowlick right in front caused it to swirl and stand up. His nose was dotted with a smattering of freckles, and his clothes were dirty and dusty as usual. His other arm hung limply by his side, shorter and ending in a round nub where his hand should've been.

"Hiya, Mr. Tiny!" the boy called up.

Tiny offered a small bow. "Why, Mr. Ricky," he said. "It is a pleasure to see you today."

Ricky grinned up at him. "I'm playing swords with my friends," he said, his chest puffed out in pride. It had taken the other boys a little time to get used to the idea of little Ricky Samuels joining their pack, but when they saw him talking daily with his friend, the mysterious tall man who lived in the apartment on the top floor, they had more willingly pulled him in. Now the group stood on the sidewalk, looking back at the two.

"Hey Ricky, you comin'?" one of the boys yelled out. "Hey, Mr. Tiny!" he added.

Tiny turned and tipped his hat to the boys. "Best go join them," he said to Ricky with a wink. Ricky nodded and took off running after the group, his stick-sword swinging above his head. They all let out war cries and took off around the corner as Tiny chuckled in their wake.

Turning, Tiny made his way to the apartment building at the end of the street and entered the lobby.

"Afternoon, Ed," he said to the bored doorman who sat at a desk in the corner.

"Hey, Tiny," Ed replied. He held up the newspaper. "See the news today?"

Tiny shook his head. "Not if I can help it."

Ed nodded and lowered his paper back down. "Smart man."

Tiny continued down to the end of the hall and opened the door to the stairway. City-wide strikes had ground the local economy nearly to a halt, one of the fallouts being the loss of elevator operators. They'd walked right on out of their buildings after a dispute over something-or-other that Tiny hadn't really cared to follow. He paid it no mind, anyway. He didn't like to take the lift. He had to hunch down to avoid hitting his head on the top, and all the clanging and rocking made his stomach do little flip flops. He much preferred the stairs where his long legs could take three at a time and get him to the top, lickety split.

He reached the very top floor and headed to the end of the hall, pulling out his keys and shaking them in his hand. He slipped the key in the lock and turned it, then pushed into the room.

Books were stacked everywhere, in all the corners. A row of shelves lined one wall of the sitting room, and from top to bottom, it was filled with books. The table under the window, which looked out on the city in all its glory, was stacked so high with books that a man could sit on one side and not see the person on the other side.

Tiny tossed his keys in a little bowl on the sideboard table and shuffled into the spacious room. He drew in a deep breath and let it out slowly. City life hadn't ever really settled in his bones the way that country life had. He wasn't made for all these people and cramped spaces.

The sound of clicking from the next room pulled him out of his head, and a smile widened his mouth. He turned and passed the stacks of books on the table, pushing open the door to the little bedroom and watching for a moment as the man at the desk, his back to Tiny, tapped at a feverish pace on his typewriter.

This room was also filled with books, though they were a little more organized. They were lined up in order across the long, wooden shelf that stretched from one wall to the other. It was a single, solitary row of books, some thick, others thinner, their spines perfectly uncreased, for these books hadn't been read. But they had all been written by the same man, one P.K. Andrews of New York City.

"Whatcha workin' on?" Tiny asked in the brief moment of silence, as the man's hands settled. He whirled around in his chair, startled at the sound of his guest. It took his eyes a moment to focus and his brain another moment to settle back into reality before he could answer.

"The last one," he finally said.

Tiny stepped into the room and settled on the chair next to the desk. He often sat in here listening to the rhythm of the keyboard. There was something quite soothing about being in the presence of a new creation.

"The last one, eh?" he asked. "Well now, Pete. You've said that before."

Peter nodded, his mouth pressed into a thin line. "Yes, but this time I feel quite sure about it," he replied.

Tiny studied Peter's face, the lines of age having pulled his crooked features apart even more so that he hardly looked human these days. His health had been in steady decline for months now. The doctor said it was because of the way that Peter's torso had twisted over time, his ribs having pulled his shoulders off to the right while his pelvis pulled his hips off to the left. Watching Peter try to type was almost a marvel. In fact, though Tiny would never speak this aloud, it looked a bit like something that Boss Man would've delighted in putting in his sideshow. Sitting at the desk required Peter to turn his hips to the side, then reach his arms around to the keys. It resulted in severe neck and back pain, and he could only work for short increments these days.

"Well, you know how I feel about that," Tiny said. "Been time for you to give yourself a break. You done told all the stories there are to tell!" He gestured toward the shelf of books, all with Peter's pen name in bold black on the spine. P.K. Andrews—the name that Peter took when he came back to the city all those years ago after saying goodbye to the love of his life.

Tiny stood up and stretched his arms above his head, flattening his palms against the ceiling and giving out a long, low groan as muscles stretched and pulled. He didn't dare complain, though.

"Need anything, Pete?" he asked.

"A glass of water?" Peter asked. "I think I'm done for now. Come back in, though. I'd like to tell you something."

A few moments later, Tiny was back in the room, settled in his chair next to the bed where Peter had moved and now lay back against a stack of pillows. It was the only place he could get comfortable these days, and so he spent hours at a time propped against the pillows, staring out the window at the sky above the city. The two sat quiet for several long minutes, a comfortable kind of silence that can only settle between two people who know one another well enough to embrace it.

"I've been thinking about her more lately," Peter finally spoke.

"Who? Yer Mama?" Tiny asked. It had been a little over a year since Nataliya had passed away. The cancer took her fast, right after it took her sister, Yulia. The two were buried next to one another in the same cemetery as their parents. Tiny's thoughts now rested on the woman who'd brought him some of the sweetest years of his life.

They'd been married about a year after moving to New York City. Yulia's husband, Jack, had moved up the ranks from working as a newspaper man to running his own publishing company. He'd encouraged Peter to start writing, and the rest of the family had followed suit. The boy had stories to tell and a head full of knowledge to share. And once Peter got started, he couldn't stop. When his tenth book was published, Yulia was the first to shake her head in wonder.

"I told you," she'd said, as Jack handed Peter his newest volume of short stories, these ones following a merry band of troubadours who stumbled their way through pranks and hijinks. "I told you that the world would know that boy for his mind."

And indeed, that was the truth. Peter's stories were translated into thirty different languages and sold around the world. Peter did several of the translations himself, having perfected his fluency in four languages. The world was fascinated with the author P.K. Andrews, whose books made their way into the hands of the highest-ranking officials around the globe, and yet no one had actually ever seen the mysterious author. There were theories as to who he really was, entire columns in newspapers trying to answer the question, *"Where in the World is P.K. Andrews?"*

A couple of years back, a pair of little men who had worked in the Ringling Circus for a time claimed to believe P.K. Andrews was a boy they'd toured with in the sideshow of a circus run by a Frenchman who had mysteriously disappeared decades earlier. Their names were Manny and Jessop, and they'd told their story to a reporter in a small town in Tennessee, but no one had believed them.

P.K. ANDREWS A CIRCUS FREAK

The headlines tossed around the idea for a few days, but ultimately people couldn't believe that the great writer was the ugly, wild child of the circus. They much preferred to believe him a mysterious, handsome spy traveling the world and capturing the stories as he encountered them.

Tiny had originally planned to see Peter and Nataliya settle in New York, then he was going to make his way back home to Memphis, but something had happened that couldn't quite be explained between himself and Nataliya. His heart had finally found its home. The sweetest years of his life were spent with her as his wife.

Peter now stared at Tiny, both of them older and more like peers than father and son, though Peter had long claimed Tiny as the only father he had ever really known.

"No, not Mama," he answered. "Well...I mean, of course, Mama. I think about her every day." He shook his head, his thin, wiry grey hair standing up in a comical halo.

"Miss Emmaline?" Tiny asked.

Peter nodded. "Yeah," he answered, his voice wistful. "I'm finally telling her story—our story. It's the only one left to tell."

"Well, I suppose that makes sense," Tiny answered. "Seems to me you been leading up to telling this story for thirty years now."

Peter nodded. He reached over to the small table beside his bed and picked up an envelope. He looked over it, then held it out to Tiny.

"That arrived this morning," Peter confessed.

Tiny looked down and took in the name and address of the sender, then raised his eyes back to Peter's in surprise.

"She wrote?"

Peter nodded.

Years ago, Tiny had written to Miss Mary Landis to inquire about Emmaline on behalf of Peter. No one had asked him to do it. He just felt he'd needed to for Pete's sake. Miss Mary had written him back almost immediately.

Emmaline, she told them, had continued her studies after they left her. She had, indeed, learned to read. She'd also learned arithmetic. She had become the teacher of the small country school that she and Miss Mary started together near their home in Oklahoma. It was a school for the kids who were overlooked and underappreciated - a place where everyone believed themselves worthy of learning.

Emmaline had met another lost boy, like herself, and the two had fallen in love and married. They had two children of their own, a little girl named Grace and a little boy they had named Peter.

Miss Mary had periodically sent Tiny letters and updates over the years. Her final letter had arrived two years ago. In it, she had confessed that she'd been sick and feared she had little time left.

"*Emmaline and her husband Matthew will continue to run the home for lost children in my absence,*" Mary had written. "*I must tell you, though, Mr. Tiny. Emmaline has never stopped talking or thinking about you or about Peter. I've told her she needs to write you herself, but I believe she's afraid. She just doesn't know where to start or what to say.*"

That had been the last letter. Tiny wrote once more but received nothing back.

Tiny now stared at the envelope in his hand, at the sloping letters written across the front, addressed a *Mr. P.K. Andrews C/O Robert James.*

"May I?" Tiny asked. Peter nodded, leaning back and closing his eyes. Tiny stuck his finger under the flap of the envelope and pulled out the letter. He opened it and began to read aloud.

Dear Peter," he read. "*I've waited too long to write. I didn't know where to start or what to say. But it's far past time I told you all that needed to be told. More than anything, I want to somehow communicate to you that every happiness I have today is thanks to you. The fact that I can even write this letter is thanks to you.*

I think about you often, Peter. Maybe even every day. And I see you in the most unexpected ways. I see you in the children who come through our school. Did you know that I run a school? I opened it with my grandmother and my husband, Matthew, and I have continued to run it in her absence. Sometimes we have children come through who look so different on the outside, and when I see them I remember you. I'm able to teach them all the things that you taught me, Peter. I tell them how important they are, how valuable they are to this world, and how what we see on the outside does not define who we are on the inside. I teach them. The fact that I can even teach another human being anything at all is thanks to you!

This may sound crazy, but I even see you in my own son, who we named Peter after the boy who freed me. My Peter is grown now, but in his younger years he was so quiet and thoughtful, and I've only ever met one other boy who loved learning as much as my little boy did. In some odd way, he seemed so much like you, and I was grateful for that.

I've had a good life. Matthew is good to me, and we're happy. I will never take this freedom that I have for granted, and I've made sure that my family knows all about you and Tiny and your mother and Miss Clarabelle, and of course Bea. They know about my family.

And then there are your stories! Peter they are wonderful. Matthew and I have read them all. We save money every year so that at Christmastime we can buy one another a new P.K. Andrews book. Our little school has an entire library of stories by the great and prolific P.K. Andrews! Of course, I've never divulged my connection to you to anyone outside my own little family. It was too special.

Peter, I still love you. You will always hold a place in my heart. I'm sorry I didn't write before now. It took time to heal after all those years. I had to reconcile the life I could have had if Beaumont hadn't stolen me away when I was a little girl. I had to process the horrible events of that last day together. I needed to make a new life for myself away from the circus. But I suppose the circus never really left me. Does it leave any of us?

I hope you're well, dear Peter. Please do keep in touch. We are still young enough to enjoy a friendship, I hope. And give my love to Tiny.

All my love,
Emmaline

Tiny looked up, eyes shining and met Peter's gaze. Peter nodded in return, his eyes dry but face twisted in an indiscernible expression.

"Well," Tiny began, clearing his throat. "That was somethin' special, Pete."

"Yes, it was," Peter murmured. He leaned his head back on the pillows and gazed out the window, the evening sun casting a golden glow across his face. They sat quietly together for a long time, both of them contemplating and remembering the years that had defined and shaped them.

"Hey Pete?" Tiny finally asked, breaking the silence. Peter turned to look at him. "Does this new story—the last one...does it have a happy ending?"

Peter sighed, his gaze shifting to the ceiling above. He waited a beat before answering.

"It has the right ending," he said. "Which I suppose is as happy as an ending could hope to be."

Tiny nodded. The two sat together the remainder of the evening until the sun had long set in the sky and the memories had swept them into slumber.

ACKNOWLEDGEMENTS

I feel like every, single acknowledgement section I write should begin with the phrase *Dear Bethany*. My editor, and friend, Bethany Hockenbury is the real magic-maker of every book I write. She reads draft after draft carefully, and with meticulous detail helps me shape these stories into something magical. Without Bethany, my books would be filled with poorly crafted euphemisms and too many commas. And a whole bunch of other drivel as well, but we won't go there. So, my biggest thank you goes to Bethany for not letting me settle for anything less than my very best.

Thank you to my sweet writing friends from Her Novel Collective who have served as some of my biggest cheerleaders in the past year. I'm inspired by each of you and in awe of your talent. You make me want to grow in my craft, and I'm thankful for the challenge.

My family deserves my deepest debt of gratitude as they are the ones who are constantly offering grace as I yawn my way through each day due to too many late nights and early mornings spent with imaginary characters. Thanks for not only letting me do what I do, but for also supporting it so heartily. I couldn't do it without the constant support of my parents, Richard and Candy Martin, my husband, Lee, and my five children: Sloan, Tia, Landon, Annika, and Sawyer.

THE FABULOUS FREAKS OF MONSIEUR BEAUMONT

This book is dedicated to anyone who's ever felt different, like maybe they didn't quite fit the mold, whatever that means. We were, each of us, knit together by a Creator who has a very specific plan. There aren't any mistakes. May we all have the eyes to see the purpose not only in ourselves, but in one another. Imagine a world where differences weren't overlooked or covered up, but were, instead, celebrated. What a place that would be, yes?

More by Kelli Stuart

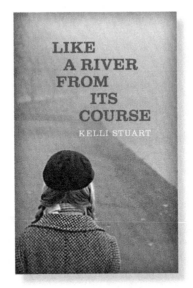

Like a River From Its Course

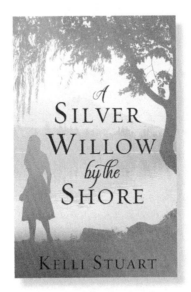

A Silver Willow by the Shore

Made in the USA
Middletown, DE
20 August 2024